MEDICINAL CHEMISTRY-III

For
B. Pharm., Semester - VII Students

As Per New Revised Syllabus w.e.f. from June 2016

K. G. BOTHARA

M. Pharm., Ph. D.

Principal and Professor
Sinhgad Institute of Pharmacy,
Narhe, Pune - 411 041.

NIRALI PRAKASHAN
ADVANCEMENT OF KNOWLEDGE

N1726

MEDICINAL CHEMISTRY-III (SEM-VII)   ISBN 978-93-86084-46-0

First Edition   :   **July 2016**

©   :   **Dr. K. G. Bothara**

Published By :   Polyplate

NIRALI PRAKASHAN

Abhyudaya Pragati, 1312, Shivaji Nagar,
Off J.M. Road, PUNE – 411005
Tel - (020) 25512336/37/39, Fax - (020) 25511379
Email : niralipune@pragationline.com

☞ DISTRIBUTION CENTRES

PUNE

Nirali Prakashan   :   119, Budhwar Peth, Jogeshwari Mandir Lane, Pune 411002, Maharashtra
Tel : (020) 2445 2044, 66022708, Fax : (020) 2445 1538
Email : bookorder@pragationline.com, niralilocal@pragationline.com

Nirali Prakashan   :   S. No. 28/27, Dhyari, Near Pari Company, Pune 411041
Tel : (020) 24690204 Fax : (020) 24690316
Email : dhyari@pragationline.com, bookorder@pragationline.com

MUMBAI

Nirali Prakashan   :   385, S.V.P. Road, Rasdhara Co-op. Hsg. Society Ltd.,
Girgaum, Mumbai 400004, Maharashtra
Tel : (022) 2385 6339 / 2386 9976, Fax : (022) 2386 9976
Email : niralimumbai@pragationline.com

☞ DISTRIBUTION BRANCHES

JALGAON

Nirali Prakashan   :   34, V. V. Golani Market, Navi Peth, Jalgaon 425001,
Maharashtra, Tel : (0257) 222 0395, Mob : 94234 91860

KOLHAPUR

Nirali Prakashan   :   New Mahadvar Road, Kedar Plaza, 1st Floor Opp. IDBI Bank
Kolhapur 416 012, Maharashtra. Mob : 9850046155

NAGPUR

Pratibha Book Distributors   :   Above Maratha Mandir, Shop No. 3, First Floor,
Rani Jhanshi Square, Sitabuldi, Nagpur 440012, Maharashtra
Tel : (0712) 254 7129

DELHI

Nirali Prakashan   :   4593/21, Basement, Aggarwal Lane 15, Ansari Road, Daryaganj
Near Times of India Building, New Delhi 110002. Mob : 08505972553

BENGALURU

Pragati Book House   :   House No. 1, Sanjeevappa Lane, Avenue Road Cross,
Opp. Rice Church, Bengaluru – 560002.
Tel : (080) 64513344, 64513355, Mob : 9880582331, 9845021552
Email:bharatsavla@yahoo.com

CHENNAI

Pragati Books   :   9/1, Montieth Road, Behind Taas Mahal, Egmore,
Chennai 600008 Tamil Nadu, Tel : (044) 6518 3535,
Mob : 94440 01782 / 98450 21552 / 98805 82331,
Email : bharatsavla@yahoo.com

niralipune@pragationline.com | www.pragationline.com

Also find us on 🅕 www.facebook.com/niralibooks

PREFACE

In the last two decades, the phases of ever-growing volume and ever-changing nature of the drug information are witnessed. This is mainly due to an increase in the rate of introduction of new drugs and an increase in the number and depth of published work on both, new as well as existing drugs. Above facts necessitated addition of all recent information wherever it deserves, while presenting the first edition of this book.

The book was appreciated in all corners of the profession. It has now attained the reputation as a class-room text book for undergraduate and post-graduate students of pharmacy. However, our aim remains the same as to present a review of basic principles of medicinal chemistry and to explain the effects of structural modifications of the lead nucleus on the selectivity of action, duration of action and on the intensity and frequency of adverse-effects.

Each chapter is revised thoroughly to meet the needs of future facts and fantacies. Since this book is written basically for degree students, a backbone understanding in basic disciplines is assumed.

I wish to place on record my sincere thanks to the publisher Mr. D. K. Furia for his kind cooperation. I am greatly indebted to my colleagues for their generous help and criticism. I also wish to acknowledge indebtedness to all who have assisted for the completion of the book.

Suggestions from all corners of the profession are welcome. I am responsible for any deficiencies or errors that might have remained and would be grateful if readers would call them to my attention.

Pune
July 2016   *Author*

SYLLABUS

History and general aspects of the design & development of drugs including classification, nomenclature, Structure Activity Relationship (SAR), mechanism of action, adverse effects, therapeutic uses, scheme of synthesis of drugs mentioned in bracket and recent developments of the following categories.

Section - I

1. **Narcotic Analgesics:** Opiods, receptor subtypes and opioid antagonists (Methadone, Propoxyphen, Dextromethorphan). **(07 Hrs.)**

2. NSAIDs, steroidal anti-inflammatory agents, analgesics & antipyretics (Ibuprofen, Diclofenac, Paracetamol, Piroxicam, Nambutone). **(10 Hrs.)**

3. **Autacoids** **(08 Hrs.)**

   3.1 **Antihistaminic agents:** Structural features of Histamine receptor and its Subtypes and their structural features, H1 blockers and H2 blockers.

   3.1 **Eicosanoids:** history and discovery, eicosanoids biosynthesis, drug action mediated by eicosanoids, eicosanoids approved for human clinical use.

   3.2 **Prostaglandin analogs** (Prolidine, Ranitidine, Diphenhydramine, Cetrizine, Chlorpheniramine, Promethazine)

Section - II

4. **Drugs Acting on Respiratory Tract** **(08 Hrs.)**

   4.1 Antiasthamatics

   4.2 Expectorants

   4.3 Antitussive agents

   4.4 Mucolytics

   4.5 Decongestants

   (Guaifensin)

5. **Drugs Acting on Gastrointestinal Tract** **(12 Hrs.)**

   (a) Antisecretory agents

   (b) Proton pump inhibitors

   (c) Antiemetics

   (d) Antidiarrheals

   (e) Laxatives

   (f) Prokinetics

   (g) Antispasmodics and drugs modifying intestinal motility

   (h) Drugs Used for Irritable Bowel Syndrome

   (Omeprazole)

❖❖❖

CONTENTS

1

NARCOTIC ANALGESICS

1.1 INTRODUCTION

Analgesia may be defined 'as a state of relative insensitivity to pain, where the capacity to tolerate pain is increased without the loss of consciousness'. The term "analgesic" is generally applied to the agents or actions required to produce analgesia.

Classification :

Analgesics are divided into two main classes :

(1) Narcotic analgesics (Centrally acting drugs)

(2) Non–narcotic analgesics (Peripherally acting drugs)

Narcotic analgesics :

Serturner, in 1805, isolated and discovered the potent analgesic activity of Morphine, an alkaloid isolated from the juice of unriped seed capsules of the poppy plant, *Papaver somniferum*. The word opium is derived from Greek word "opos" means juice.

The term opioid is used generally to designate collectively the drugs (natural or synthetic) which bind specifically to any of subspecies of receptors of morphine and produce, to varying degrees, morphine like actions. They are often known as the narcotic analgesics due to their ability to produce drug dependence. With the development of many analgesics which are morphine derivatives with little tendency to produce physical dependence, the term narcotic is no longer useful.

Other actions which are associated with narcotic analgesics are sedation, and constipation (useful in the control of diarrhoea). In therapeutic doses, morphine sometimes produces nausea or vomiting. The related compound, apomorphine is a powerful emetic agent.

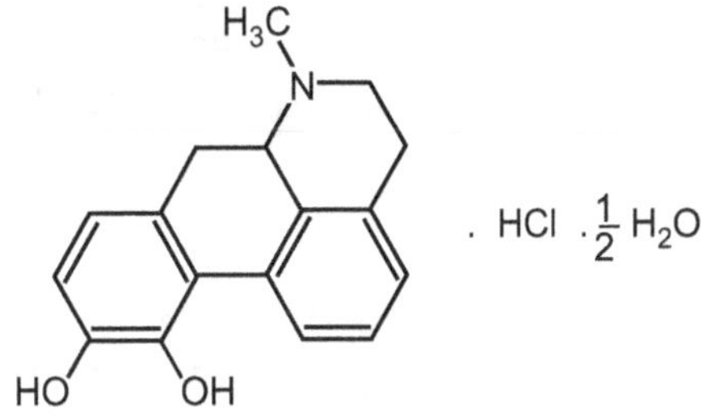

Apomorphine hydrochloride

1.2 OPIUM ALKALOIDS

Opium contains 25% by weight alkaloidal compounds. The opium alkaloids can be divided chemically into two distinct classes :

(a) Phenanthrenes : e.g. morphine, codeine and thebaine.

(b) Benzylisoquinolines : e.g. papaverine and noscapine.

Opium alkaloids :

(a) Phenanthrenes :

(1) Morphine, R = – H; R' = – H

(2) Codeine; R = – CH$_3$; R' = – H

(3) Thebaine; R = – CH$_3$; R' = – CH$_3$,
    A double bond between C$_5$ and C$_6$.

(b) Benzylisoquinolines :

Papaverine

Noscapine

Opioids act as agonists of endogenous substances known as endorphins (a group of morphine like peptides), interacting with stereospecific binding sites or receptors in the brain and other tissues. Enkephalins represent the simplest members of endorphins. They are located in short interneurons predominantly in the areas of the CNS which are related to the perception pain, movement, mood behaviour and to the regulation of neuroendocrinological functions.

Opioid mediated inhibition of transmitter release in various mammalian cells has been reported to involve either a reduction in the influx of Ca^{++} through activation of k$^-$ receptors or an increased outward K$^+$ conductance through Ca^{++} activated K$^+$ channels following activation of either µ or σ receptors. The inflow of potassium ions hyperpolarizes the membrane potential. This results in decrease in neurone excitability.

Opioids have been shown to inhibit either basal or neurotransmitter-stimulated increases in adenylate cyclase activity in several areas of the mammalian CNS. The mechanism for opioid inhibition of adenylate cyclase appears to involve stimulation of a high affinity membrane associated GIPase, reflecting an activation of the guanine nucleotide regulatory binding protein, G.

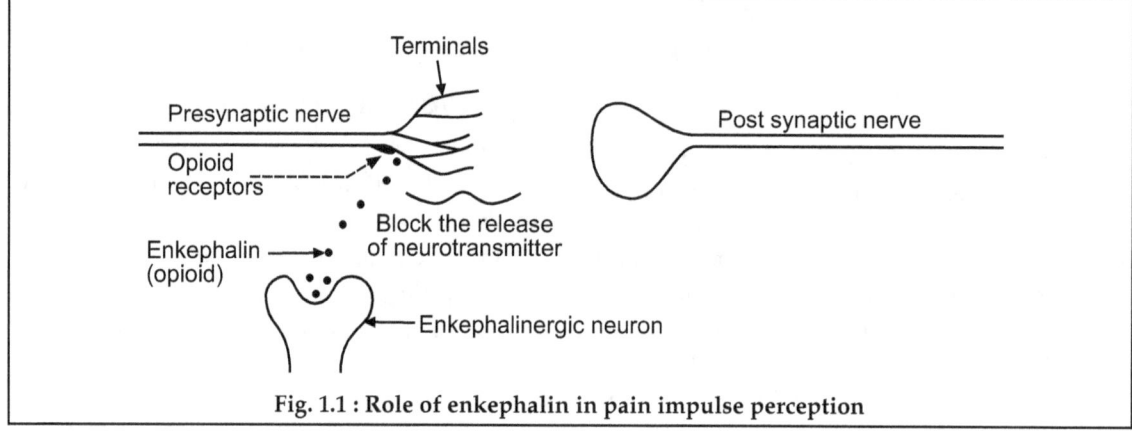

Fig. 1.1 : Role of enkephalin in pain impulse perception

Thus, under the influence of enkephalin, pre-synaptic terminals fail to release neuro-transmitter in the synaptic cleft and pain impulse is not received by post-synaptic neuron. The opioid mediated fall in cyclic AMP levels also contributes to produce analgesia.

It is assumed that all opioids (morphine like drugs) produce their effects by mimicking the actions of endogenous enkephalins.

1.3 OPIOID RECEPTORS

Morphine causes analgesia by selectively acting on receptors situated both in the higher centers and the spinal cord. The existence of an opioid receptor is supported by :

(1) SAR of morphine like compounds.

(2) Close structural similarities between opioid agonists and antagonists.

(3) Competitive inhibition of actions of morphine agonists by narcotic antagonists.

The ideal narcotic analgesic structure is represented by Morphine.

Morphine

The structural features which are recognised to be essential for the perfect fit of a narcotic analgesic on receptors are represented by A, B, C and D.

where, A = Phenyl or aromatic portion
　　　B = Quaternary carbon
　　　C = Ethylene bridge
　　　D = Tertiary nitrogen

Beckett and Casy (1954) proposed that an opioid receptor is composed of three prominent parts.

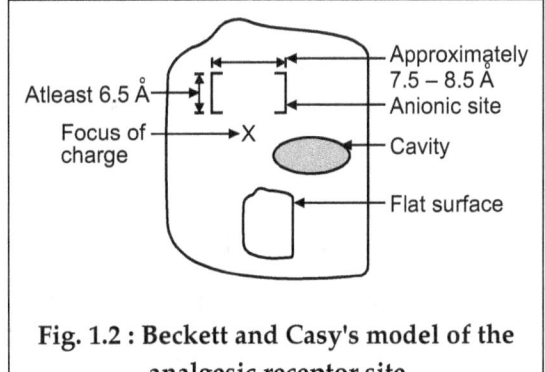

Fig. 1.2 : Beckett and Casy's model of the analgesic receptor site

(1) A flattened part which holds the aromatic portion of an analgesic molecule through van der Waal's forces.

(2) A cavity or a hollow portion which entraps the ethylene bridge.

(3) An anionic site which holds the tertiary nitrogen which is assumed to be ionised at physiological pH. The pKa values of most of analgesics fall in the range of 7.8 - 8.9 so that tertiary nitrogen is equally present in ionized and un-ionized forms at physiological pH. The drug crosses the blood-brain barrier as the free base while interacts with the receptor in ionic form.

The fact that these sites do not bind other substances and are saturated by even very low concentrations of opioids explains the highly stereospecific orientation of these three components of opioid receptors.

Similarly GTP, GDP and the non–hydro-lyzable analogue Gpp (NH)1, reduce agonist affinity while divalent ions such as magnesium increase agonist affinity. Sodium ions and Gpp (NH)p were found to decrease the binding of agonists to μ sites more effectively than to δ sites with binding to κ sites least affected.

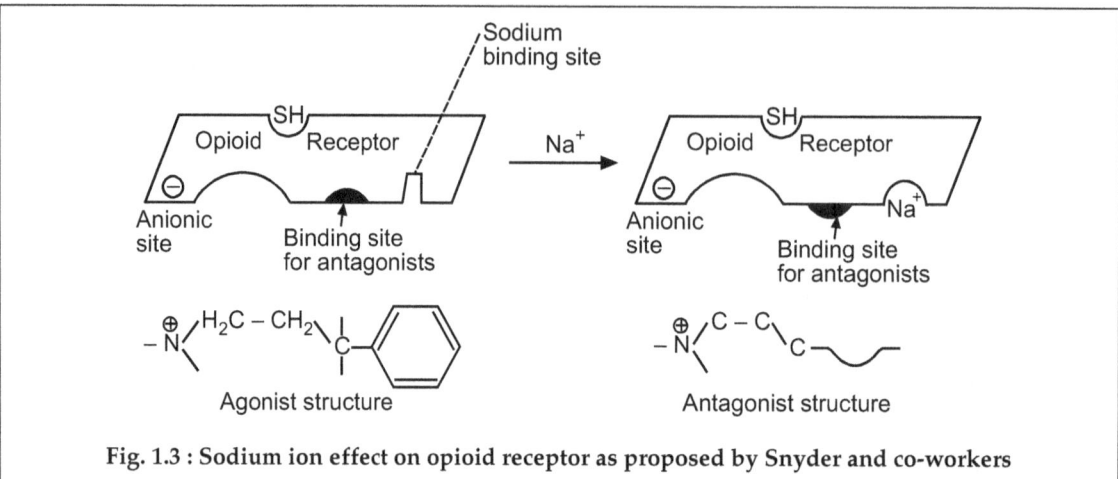

Fig. 1.3 : Sodium ion effect on opioid receptor as proposed by Snyder and co-workers

The narcotic antagonists competitively inhibit the access and binding of morphine agonists to the opioid receptors but lack the intrinsic activity (ability to initiate the biological response).

The irregular distribution of these opioid receptors in the various regions of central nervous system explains the untoward effects associated with the opioids; like, euphoria, sedative and emetic actions.

Sodium ions are reported to reduce the affinity of opioid receptors for agonists and to increase the affinity for narcotic antagonists. It is suggested that Na^+ protects the sulfhydryl group of receptors from the alkylating agents by changing the conformation at opioid receptors. And while doing so, Na^+ ions modify the opioid binding sites, which are now more suitable for binding of antagonist molecules than that of the agonists.

No other ion showed this selectivity. Na^+ ion effect is used to distinguish pure agonist, antagonist and mixed agonist-antagonist.

Sodium index - IC_{Na}^{50}/IC_{50} : It is the ratio of concentration of test drug required to inhibit by 50% the stereospecific binding of standard tagged, pure antagonist in presence of sodium ion.

For pure antagonist index will be in range of 1-2 (ideally 1).

For pure agonist it is 10-60 and for mixed agonist - antagonist the ratio is 3-7.

Molecular Dissection of Morphine :

Morphine is a complex pentacyclic skeleton which was considered to be responsible for a number of adverse effects associated with morphine skeleton. Hence, attempts were made to identify the pharmaco-dynamically essential part through the application of molecular dissection concept. In this attempt, various components of the skeleton are gradually removed one by one. Since the resulting new skeletons were found to retain the activity, the part removed, was considered non–essential for the analgesic activity. Various series which can be obtained through the application of molecular

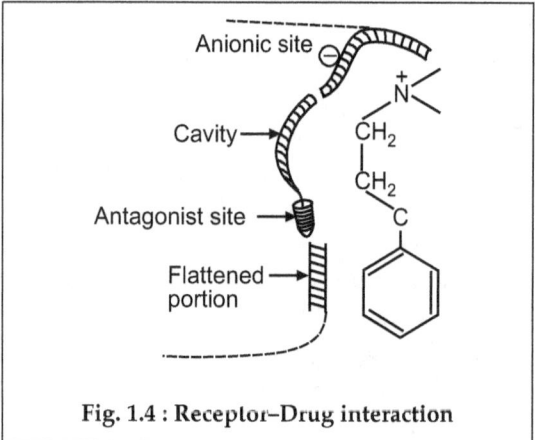

Fig. 1.4 : Receptor–Drug interaction

dissection concept to morphine, are shown as below.

Morphine

N-Methylmorphinan

Benzomorphan

Meperidine

Bemidone

Prodine

Fentanyl

Methadone

1.4 CHEMISTRY OF OPIOIDS

Though morphine itself is a potent analgesic agent, the serious side effects (like, euphoria, sedation, respiratory depression, addiction and tolerance) associated with morphine, initiated the attempts for modification of this structure, in order to increase the therapeutic usefulness and to widen the difference between desirable action and toxicity syndromes.

The various modifications of the morphine molecule are categorised as :

(1) Early changes on morphine nucleus.

(2) Modifications carried out in 1929 by Small, Eddy and co–workers.

(3) Modifications carried out in 1938 by Eisleb and Schaumann.

(4) Modifications carried out by Grewe in 1946.

Like other simple semisynthetic analogues of morphine (like, codeine, heroin, hydromorphone, hydrocodone) many other classes of chemically distinct opioids have been prepared, some of which have been employed clinically. These include the morphinans, benzomorphans, methadones, phenylpiperidines, propionanilides, and thiambutene and benzimidazole derivatives. All these classes share certain common chara-cteristics with the prototype, morphine, which are shown by heavy lines in the structure of the morphine.

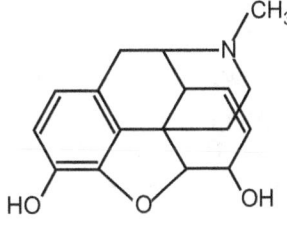

Morphine

1.4.1 Early changes on morphine prior to the study of Small, Eddy and co-workers

The analgesic properties of morphine are found in the (–) enantiomer which has the absolute configuration 5(R), 6(S), 9(R), 13(S), 14(R).

Prior to 1929, many analogues of morphine had been prepared by attempting simpler molecular modifications. Except hydromorphone and hydrocodone, which remain in clinical use, none were found to be superior to morphine.

Simpler Derivatives of Morphine Prior to 1929 :

(A)

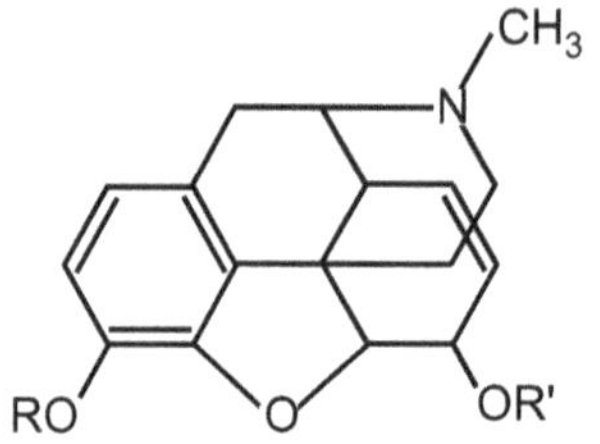

(1) Codeine, R = – CH$_3$; R' = – H

(2) Ethylmorphine; R = – C$_2$H$_5$; R' = – H

(3) Heroin; R = – CH$_3$CO; R' = – CH$_3$CO

Codeine, is only one tenth as analgesic as morphine. This indicates the need of a free phenolic hydroxyl for greater potency. While heroin is more potent despite having a significantly weaker opioid receptor binding affinity. Reasons : (1) Heroin is more lipophilic than morphine. (2) It gets rapidly converted in-vivo to the active metabolite, σ– acetylmorphine and morphine.

(B)

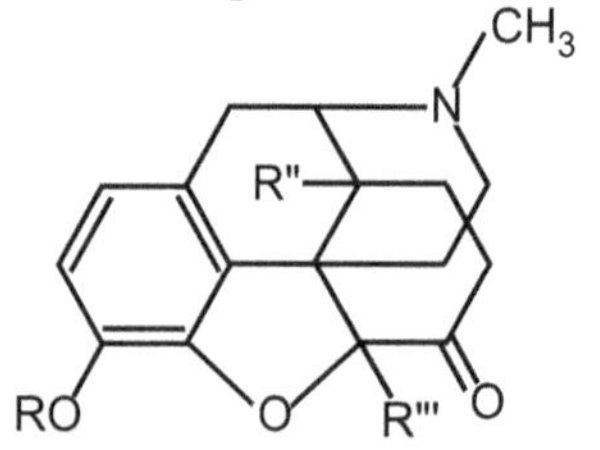

(1) Hydromorphone, R = – H; R" = – H; R''' = – H.

(2) Hydrocodone; R = – CH$_3$; R" = – H; R''' = – H.

(3) Oxycodone; R = – CH$_3$; R" = – OH; R''' = – H.

(4) Methylhydromorphone

     R = – H; R"= – H. R''' = – CH$_3$.

(C)

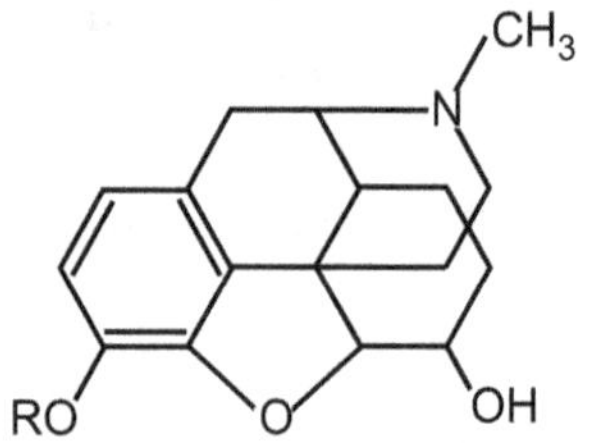

(1) Dihydromorphine; R = H

(2) Dihydrocodeine; R = CH$_3$

All the above compounds were prepared by modifying only the easily changeable peripheral groups and not according to the principles of structure–activity relationship.

1.4.2 Modifications carried out after 1929 by Small, Eddy and co-workers :

Prior to 1929, all morphine analogues had been prepared through non-rational, random search for new drugs.

The first systematic effort had been made by Small, Eddy and co–workers to investigate the structure–activity relationship in morphine molecule during their 10 years synthesis and testing programme, initiated by the National Research Council of United States. Though their studies were far more comprehensive, the principal targets, chosen for modifications in morphine structure were,

(1) The peripheral groups and simple skeletal modifications on alicyclic ring.

(2) The peripheral group and simple skeletal modifications on aromatic ring.

(3) The tertiary nitrogen.

Peripheral Groups on Morphine :

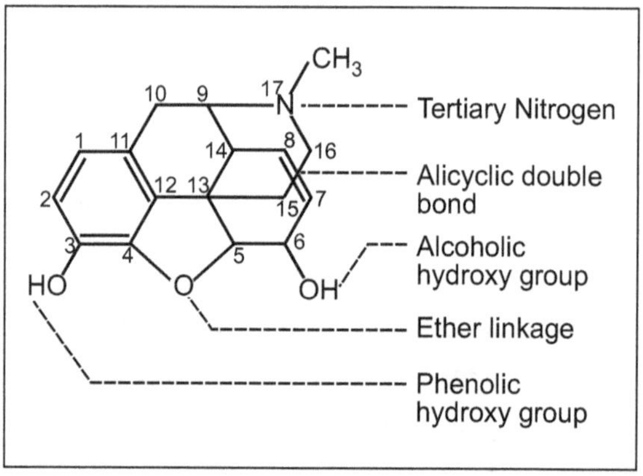

(1) Modifications on alicyclic ring :

(a) The C–6 α–hydroxyl group is methylated, esterified, oxidised, removed or replaced by halogen in order to get more potent analgesics. e.g., codeine, heroin, chloromorphide. But there is also a parallel increase in toxicity.

(b) The C-8 presents the next site for modification :

It has got a hydrogen atom and a double bond. The outcome of catalytic hydrogenation is the compounds dihydrocodeine and dihydromorphine which are the precursors of more potent ketones, dihydrocodeinone and dihydromorphinone. Similarly C–8 β–halo derivatives are found to be more potent analgesics than morphine.

(c) C–14 :

Introduction of 14-OH group in dihydroforms yielded the still more potent 14-hydroxydihydrocodeinone and 14-hydroxydihydromorphinone.

Bridging of C_6 and C_{14} through a ethylene linkage is also tried e.g., etorphine. It is about 200 times more potent than morphine in man.

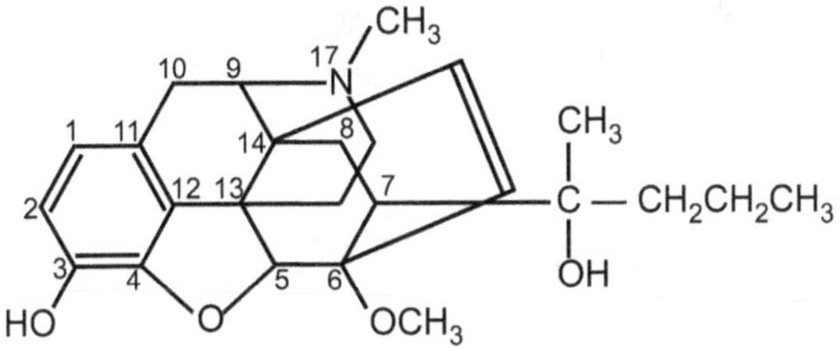

Etorphine

(d) Introduction of any new substituent further, does not enhance the activity. 5–Methyl dihydromorphine and azidomorphines may be the exceptions.

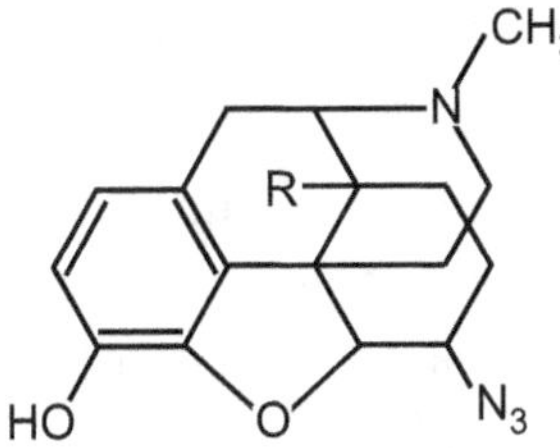

(1) R = – H
(2) R = – OH

Azidomorphines

(2) Modifications on phenyl ring :

(a) An intact benzene ring is, in general, essential for analgesic activity.

(b) Modification of C_3 – phenolic hydroxyl group causes a decrease in analgesic activity.

(c) Any further substitution in phenyl ring generally diminishes activity. The only exception is 1–fluoro codeine which possesses the same analgesic activity as that of codeine.

(3) The tertiary nitrogen :

(a) When R is methyl, n-pentyl or n-hexyl chain, it results into opioid agonists.

(b) The N-phenylethyl group enhances the analgesic activity in desmorphine, codeine and heterocodeine.

(c) N-allyl and N-cycloalkylmethyl functions impart narcotic antagonistic properties to the molecule. e.g.,

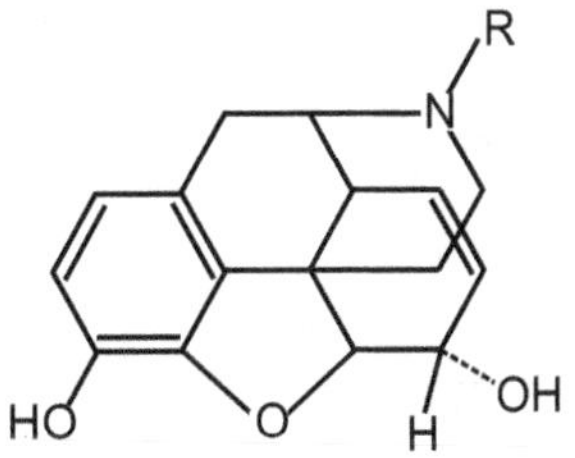

Morphine; R = – CH₃

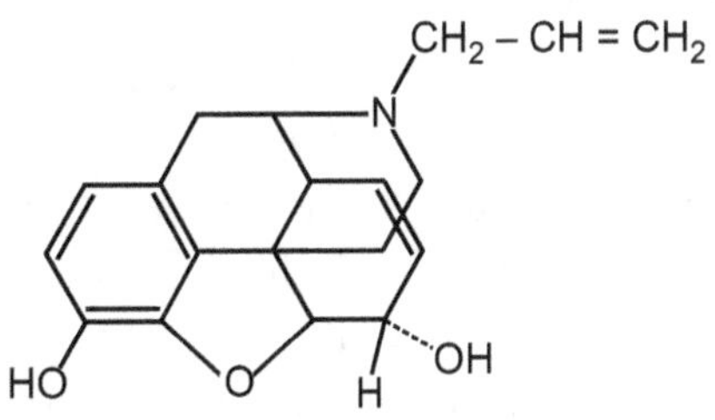

N-allylmorphine (Nalorphine)

Nalorphine was the first clinically useful narcotic antagonist. Its unpleasant psycho-mimetic and hallucinogenic properties preclude its use as analgesic, though it is a potentially valuable non-addict drug with partial agonistic features.

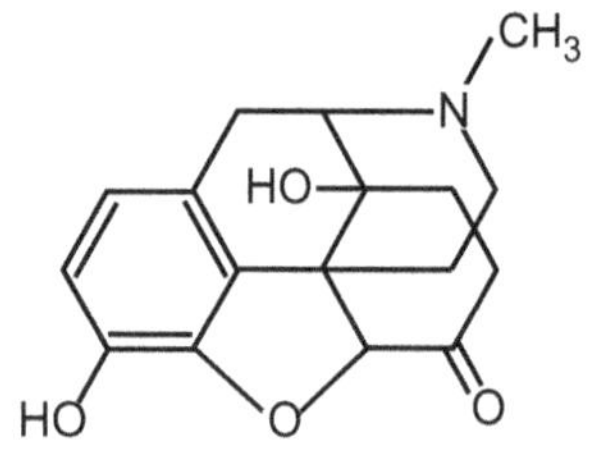

Oxymorphone

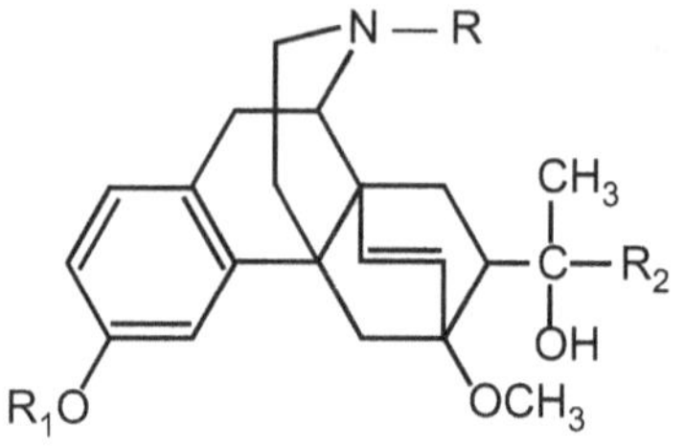

Thebaine; $R_1 = -CH_3$
Oripavine ; $R_1 = -H$

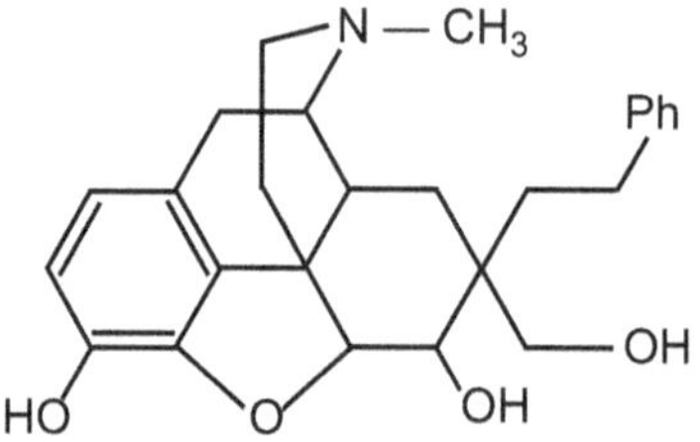

(1) Naloxone : It is a hydrazone of naltrexone. It is a long acting antagonist with a comparable duration of action.

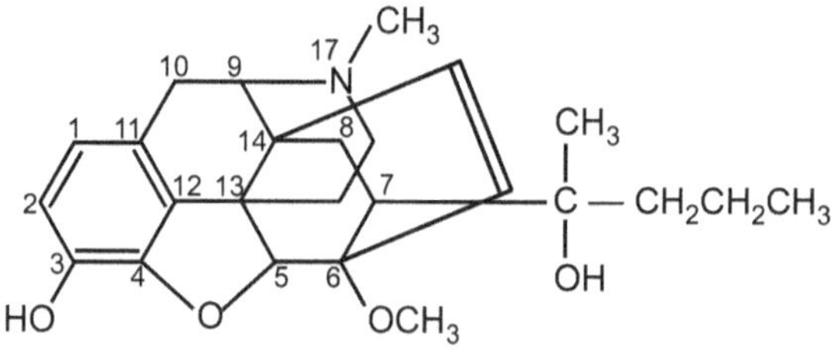

$$R = -CH_2CH = CH_2$$

(2) Naltrexone :

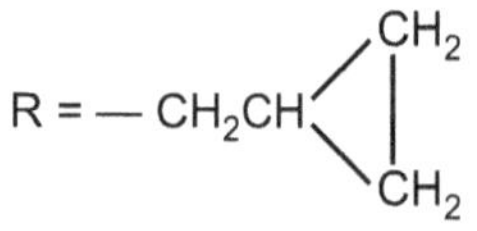

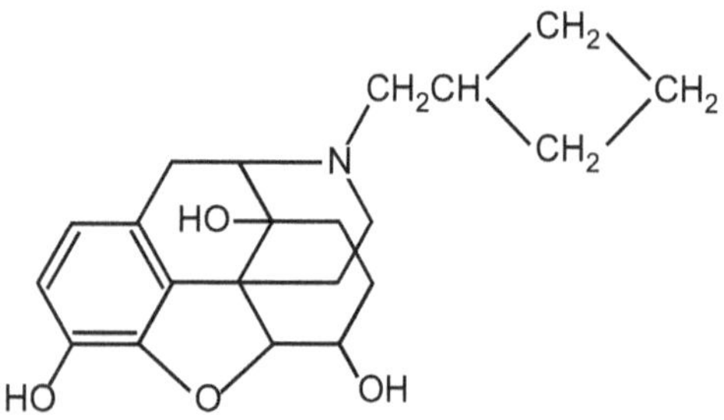

$$R = -CH_2CH \begin{array}{c} CH_2 \\ \backslash \\ CH_2 \end{array}$$

(1)

Nalbuphine

Etorphine (Pure agonist)

Derivatives of Thebaine :

Since most of the opioids discovered in this period (1929 – 38) of morphine prototype, though more potent than morphine, are also associated with the undesirable psychotomimetic effects. So Bentley and Hardy postulated that it might be a more rigid molecular structure which is important to act with a single pain relieving receptor and not with other side-effects evoking centres. This led to the synthesis of thebaine derivatives.

Diel-Alder adducts of the diene system in thebaine are known collectively as oripavines.

This compound (1) is about 700 times more potent than morphine.

(1) Etorphine is a pure agonist (1000 times more potent than morphine). Because of its side-effect profile, its use is restricted to veterany medicine as a sedative for large animals.

(2) Buprenorphine is about 100 times active as morphine as agonist and four times as active as nalorphine as antagonist and is therefore non-addicting and without psychotomimetic effects.

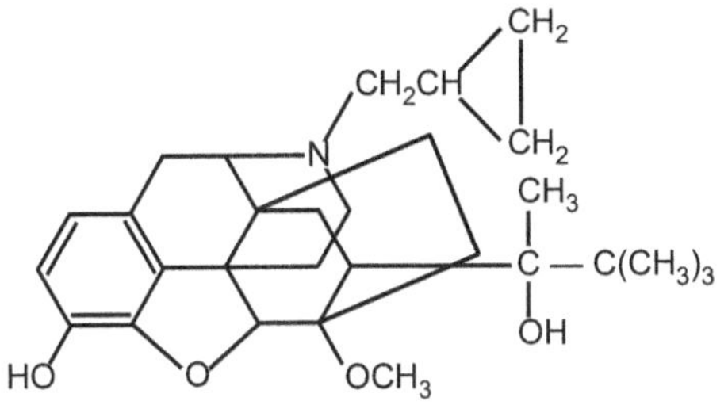

Buprenorphine (Partial agonist)

(3) Diprenorphine is a potent narcotic antagonist (100 times more potent than nalorphine). The additional alkyl substitution at C–7 is able to produce agonist, partial agonist and antagonist which suggests an evidence for an additional lipophilic binding site at the opioid receptor.

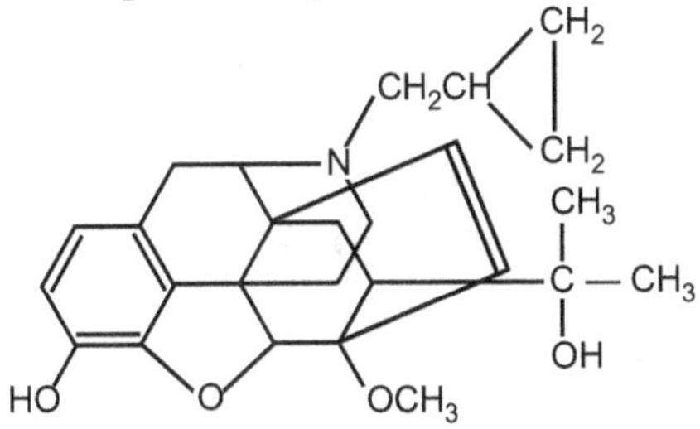

Diprenorphine (Antagonist)

In general, in morphine series, replacement of N-methyl group by larger alkyl groups not only lowers analgesic activity but potentiates narcotic antagonistic properties of the molecule. The only exception to this generalisation, is the N– phenethyl series.

1.4.3 Modifications carried out by Eisleb and Schaumann

The 1930s saw many new antispasmodics of general formulae $ArCO_2 (CH_2)_2 NR_2$, $Ar_2CHCO_2 – (CH_2)NR_2$ and similar structures. The rules of isosterism emerging at that time emphasized that reversed esters could be a good variation to improve anticholinergic activity. This led to synthesis of meperidine by Eisleb in 1930.

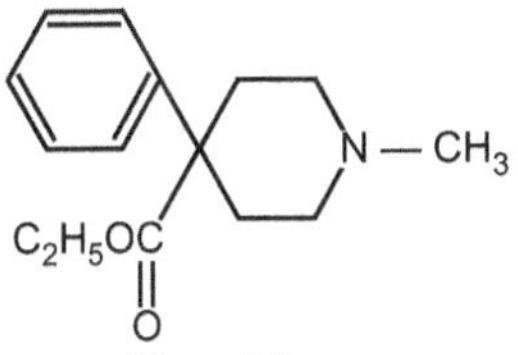

Meperidine

It had lived upto its expectations and had moderate antispasmodic as well as sedative properties. When Schaumann tested it in the cat, he was surprised by an exhibition of Straub's tail, a phenomenon (test for analgesic activity) associated with morphine. Further studies indicated that meperidine had 10–12% of overall activity of morphine. Schaumann succeeded to spot the segment in morphine structure similar to meperidine as a result of molecular dissection.

The discovery of analgesic properties of meperidine opened new avenues for the search of simpler, relatively small, structurally uncomplicated analgesics.

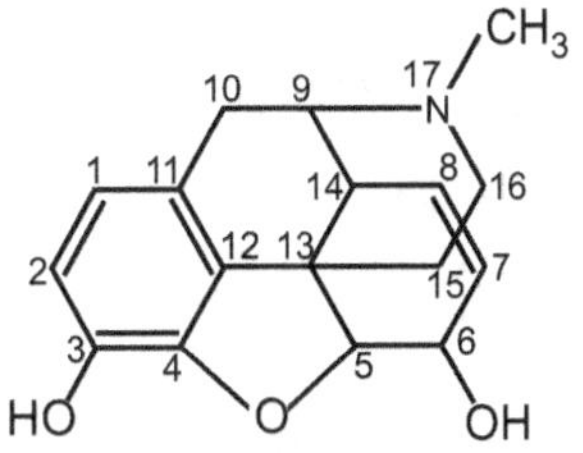

Morphine

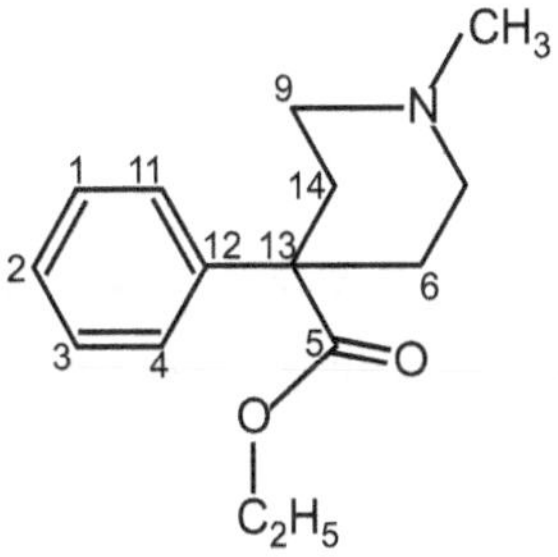

Meperidine

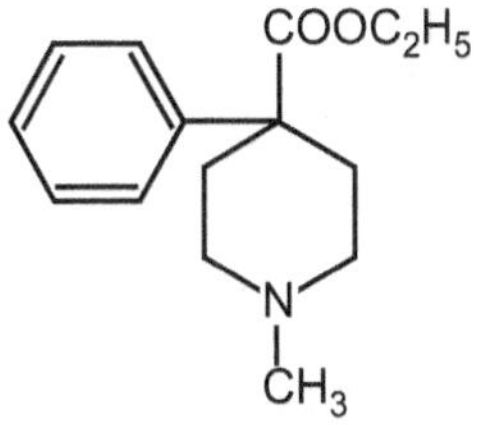

Meperidine

Meperidine was not designed by molecular dissection. It was of "reversed" antispasmodic structure and its analgesic properties were observed during pharmacological work-up.

The various modifications of meperidine and related compounds are vaguely divided into four major categories :

(a) meperidines
(b) bemidones
(c) prodines
(d) fentanyl series

Structure-Activity Relationship :

(1) Replacement of 4-phenyl group by hydrogen, alkyl, aroalkyl or heterocyclic group results in reduced activity.

(2) Many N-substituted analogues of meperidine have been prepared. Anileridine is employed clinically.

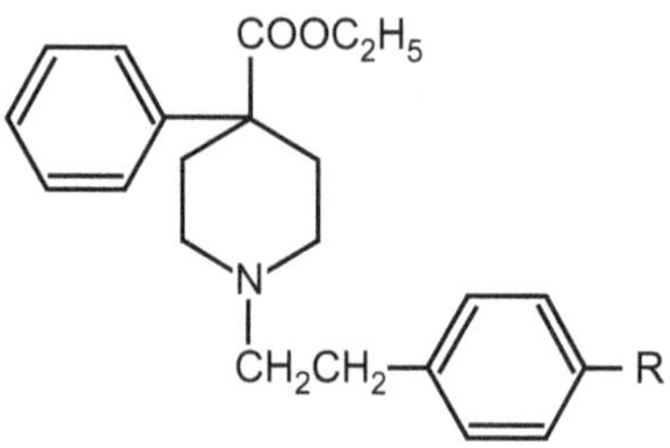

Anileridine : R = – NH$_2$
Pheneridine : R = – H

(3) Replacement of carbethoxyl group (–COOC$_2$H$_5$) by acyloxy group (OCOC$_2$H$_5$) results in better analgesic activity.

(4) The replacement of N-methyl group by various aralkyl groups can increase the analgesic property markedly.

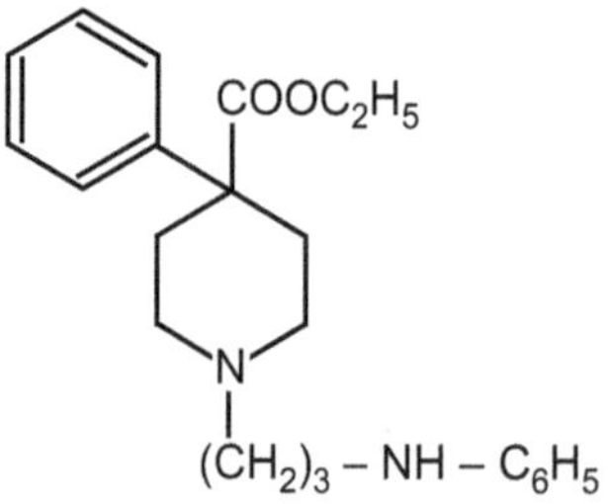

Piminodine

(5) Series of compounds were prepared where piperidine is enlarged to 7-membered azepine ring.

Proheptazine is among the more active analgesic agents in higher ring homologue of meperidine.

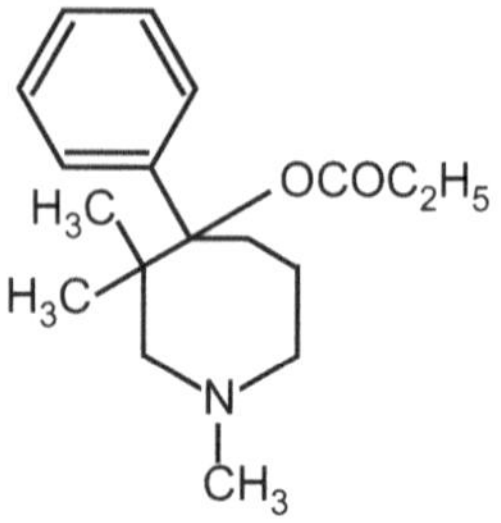

3, 3-Dimethyl-4-phenyl-4-propionoxy hexahydroazepine (proheptazine)

(6) Substitution of the piperidine ring with 5–membered pyrrolidine ring is also successful.

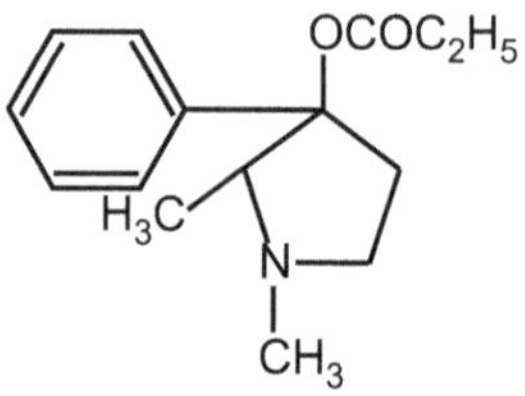

Prodilidene

(7) The presence of m–hydroxyl group in the phenyl ring resembles that of C$_3$ phenolic hydroxyl group in the morphine. Bemidone represents this class.

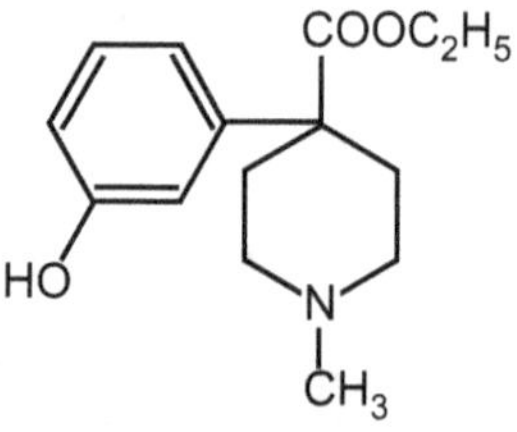

Bemidone

Replacement of the ester moiety by a ketone function in the bemidone, yielded a new series of compounds, ketobemidone.

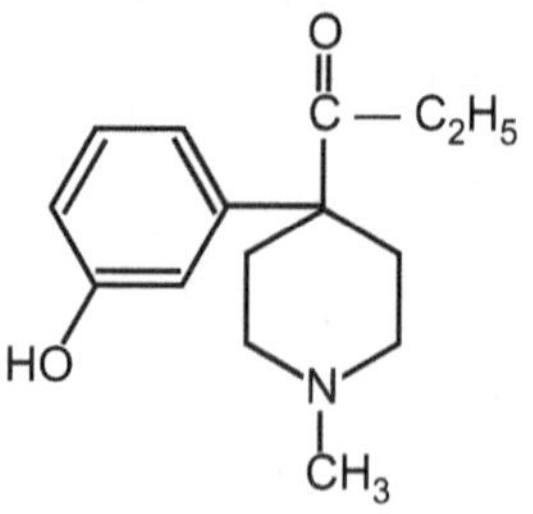

Ketobemidone

(8) Prodines are the reversed esters of meperidines. Here the ester of meperidine ($COOC_2H_5$) is replaced by ($OCOC_2H_5$) propionoxy function.

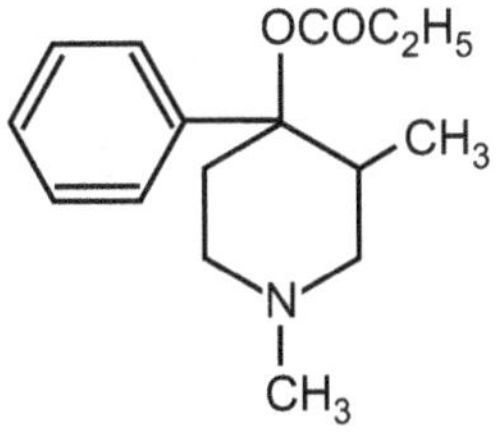

Prodine

(9) In all the above structures, phenyl ring and acyl group are directly attached to the piperidine ring. In fentanyl series, phenyl ring and acyl group are separated from the ring by a nitrogen.

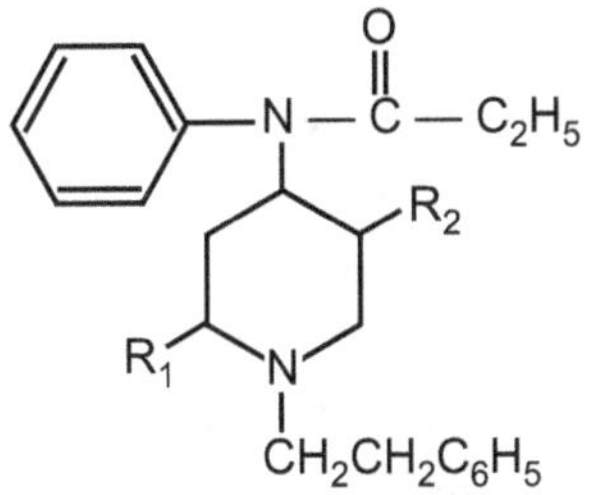

Fentanyl : $R_1 = -H$; $R_2 = -H$
Lofentanyl : $R_1 = -CH_3$; $R_2 = -COOC_2H_5$

Sufentanil is a recent example from fentanyl series.

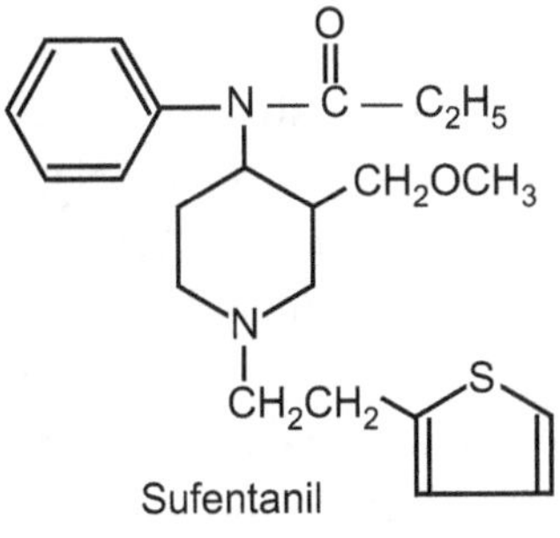

Sufentanil

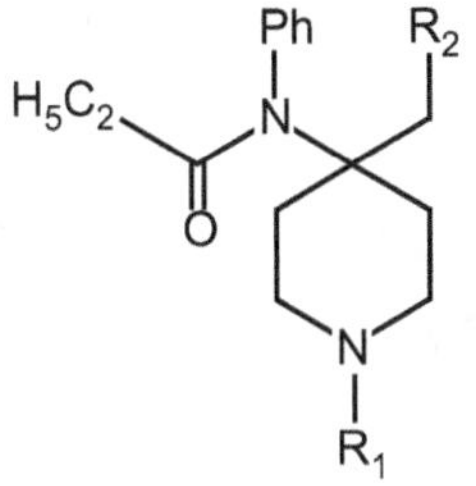

(a) Alfentanyl;

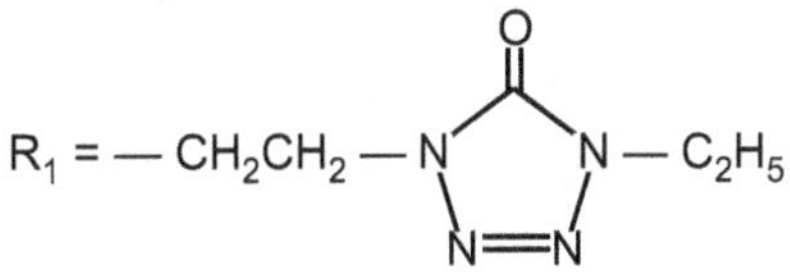

$R_1 = -CH_2CH_2-N$ ... $N-C_2H_5$

$R_2 = -CH_2OCH_3$

(b) Carfentanyl; $R_1 = -CH_2CH_2-Ph$

$R_2 = -CO_2C_2H_5$

Fentanyl is about 500 times as potent as pethidine. Some of the 4, 4-disubstituted piperidines, alfentanyl, sufentanyl and carfentanyl are even more potent. The latter two have a much longer duration of analgesia and respiratory depression and indicate a different therapeutic use e.g. anaesthesia.

Methadone Series :

The further simplification of morphine nucleus by opening of the nitrogen ring, resulted into methadone series of compounds. Methadone, itself possesses analgesic as well as spasmolytic properties.

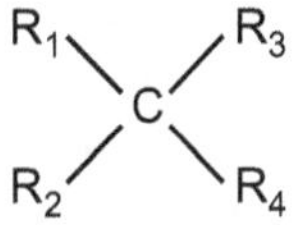

Methadone series

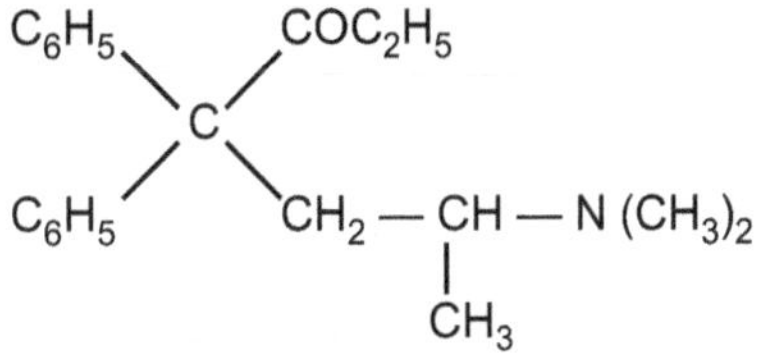

Methadone

The resemblance of methadone structure with meperidine structure can easily be seen.

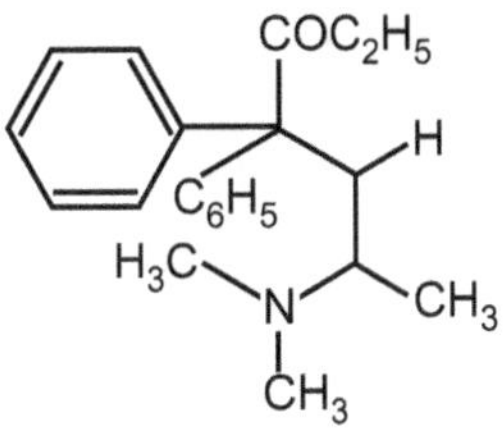

Methadone 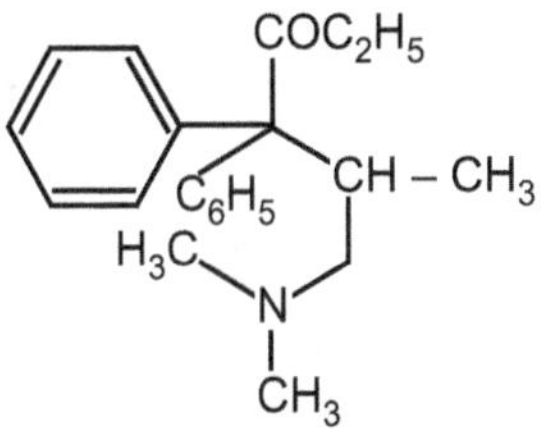   Isomethadone

Structure-Activity Relationship :

(1) Unlike meperidine or bemidone series, the insertion of m-hydroxyl group in one of the phenyl rings of methadone causes a marked decrease in analgesic activity.

(2) The methadone derivatives are generally more potent analgesics (and also more toxic) than the isomethadone analogues.

(3) The replacement of propionyl (COC$_2$H$_5$) group by hydrogen, hydroxyl or acetyloxy, led to decrease in activity.

Similarly attempts were also made to replace the propionyl group by amide functions. e.g. Racemoramide; it is more active than methadone.

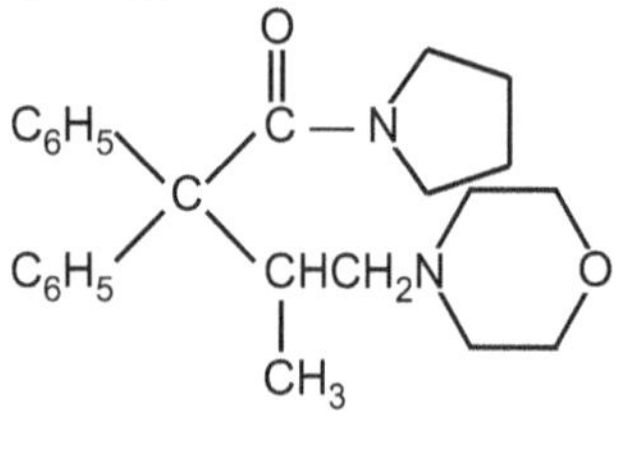

Racemoramide

(4) Removal of any of the two phenyl rings results into decreased activity.

(5) The dimethylamino group is replaced by heterocyclic rings like morpholine and piperidine. The clinically employed agents from this class are :

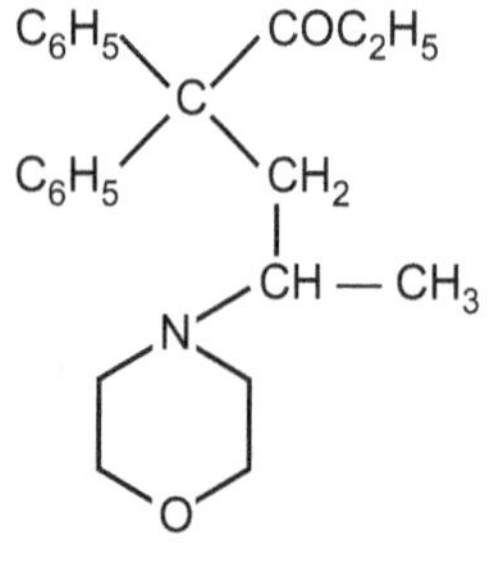

Phenadoxone

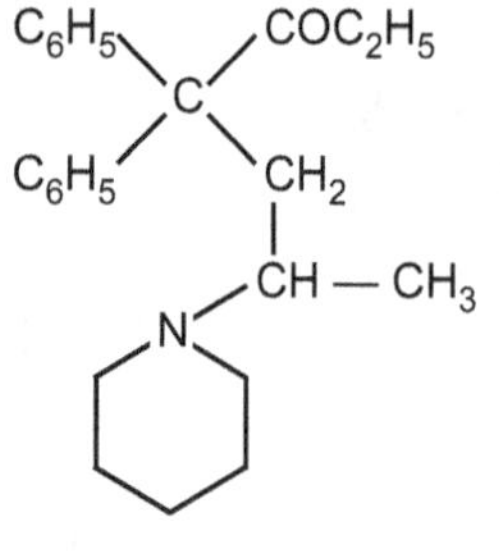

Dipanone

(6) The following are N-demethylated derivatives which are metabolites of methadone analogues in man and are found to retain the analgesic activity.

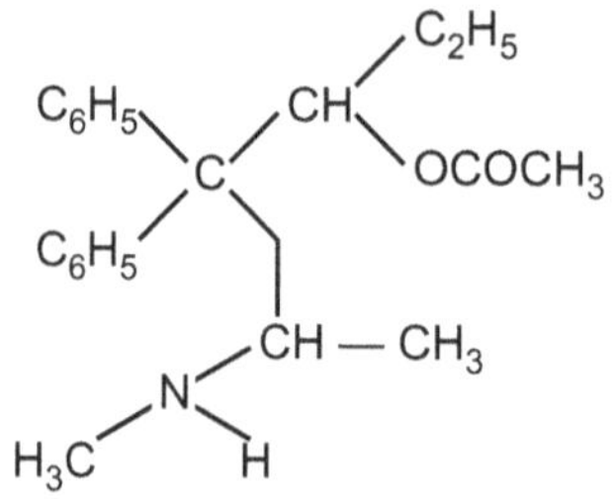

Metabolite of alphacetylmethadol

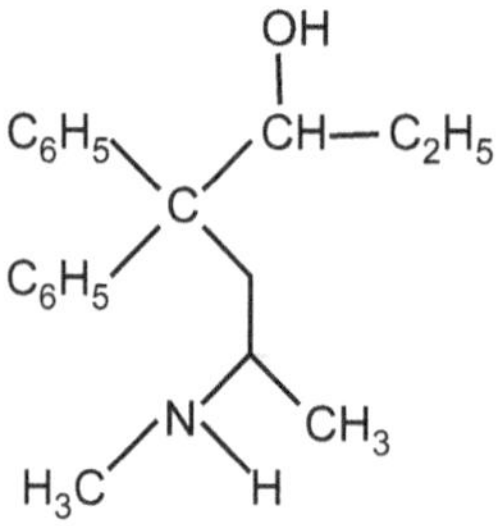

Metabolite of methadone

Molecular modifications of Methadone include : homologation and cyclization of dimethyl-amino group, reduction of CO to –CHOH, removal and relocation of CH$_3$ branching, isosteric replacement of one or both phenyls by thienyl etc. Examples : Replacement of the keto group by an amide group results into dextromoramide. Insertion of an ester oxygen between blocking groups and carbonyl (as well as a benzyl instead of one phenyl) gave dextropropoxyphene. In thiambutene, the blocking thiophene rings converge on an amine chain and instead of an electron rich carbonyl group, a double bond is introduced.

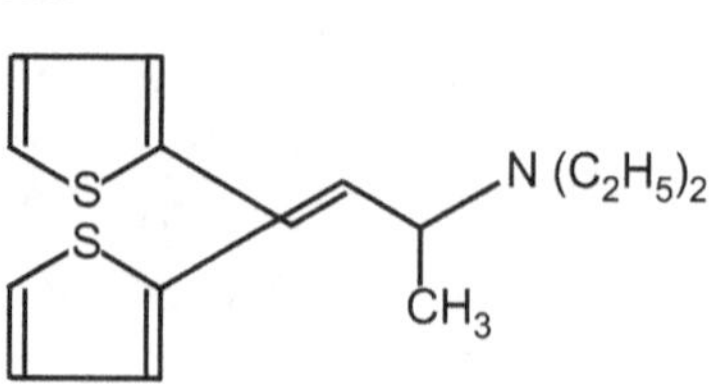

Thiambutene

Table 1.1 : Compounds from methadone series

	Name	R_1	R_2	R_3	R_4
1.	Methadone	$-C_6H_5$	$-C_6H_5$	$-COC_2H_5$	$-CH_2CH(CH_3)N(CH_3)_2$
2.	Isomethadone	$-C_6H_5$	$-C_6H_5$	$-COC_2H_5$	$-CH(CH_3)\ CH_2N\ (CH_3)_2$
3.	Normethadone	$-C_6H_5$	$-C_6H_5$	$-COC_2H_5$	$-CH_2CH_2\ N\ (CH_3)_2$
4.	Alphacetylmethadol	$-C_6H_5$	$-C_6H_5$	$-\underset{\underset{O-COCH_3}{\mid}}{C}HC_2H_5$	$-CH_2CH-(CH_3)N(CH_3)_2$
5.	Dextromoramide	$-C_6H_5$	$-C_6H_5$		
6.	Propoxyphene	$-C_6H_5$	$-CH_2C_6H_5$	$O-\underset{\underset{O}{\parallel}}{C}-C_2H_5$	$-\underset{\underset{CH_3}{\mid}}{C}HCH_2\ N\ (CH_3)_2$

Table 1.2 : Compounds from meperidine series

(R$_6$ = H, except trimeperidine)

	Name	R_1	R_3	R_4	R'_3	R'_4
1.	Meperidine	$-CH_3$	H	$-COOC_2H_5$	H	H
2.	Bemidone	$-CH_3$	H	$-COOC_2H_5$	$-OH$	H
3.	Prodine	$-CH_3$	CH_3	$-OCOC_2H_5$	H	H
4.	Trimeperidine	$-CH_3$ $(R_6 = -CH_3)$	CH_3	$-OCOC_2H_5$	H	H
5.	Diphenoxylate	$-CH_2CH_2\ \underset{\underset{CN}{\mid}}{C}-(C_6H_5)_2$	H	$-COOC_2H_5$	H	H
6.	Loperamide	$-CH_2CH_2\ \underset{\underset{\underset{\parallel}{C}-N(CH_3)_2}{\mid}}{C}-(C_6H_5)_2$	H	$-OH$	H	$-Cl$

1.4.4 Modifications carried out by Grewe in 1946

Various compounds belonging to morphinan and benzomorphan series have been synthesized and tested clinically.

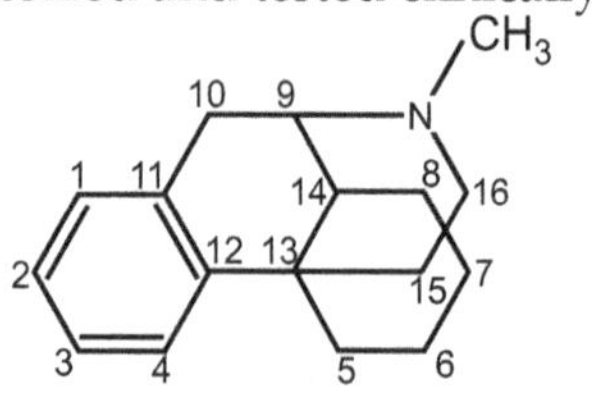

N-methylmorphinan

These compounds lack the ether bridge between the carbon atoms 4 and 5.

Structure-Activity Relationship :

(i) The laevo form of morphinan possesses the analgesic activity while the dextro form (dextro methorphan) is having cough suppressant activity.

(ii) Introduction of a hydroxyl group at C - 3 enhances the analgesic activity.

(iii) The ethers and acylated derivatives of the 3-hydroxyl form also have considerable analgesic activity.

(iv) The 14-hydroxylation results in potent derivatives with both agonist and antagonist properties e.g.

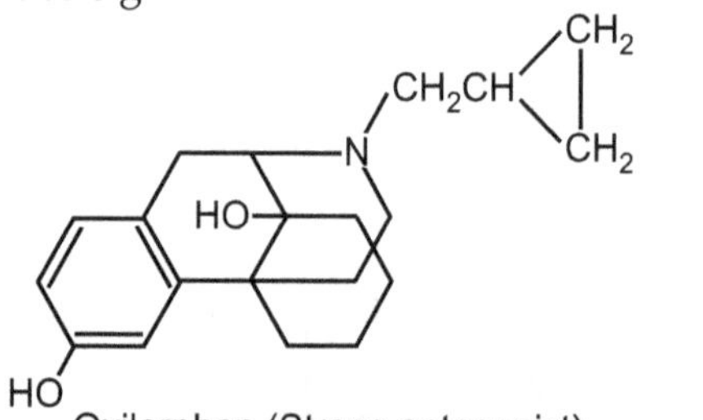

Oxilorphan (Strong antagonist)

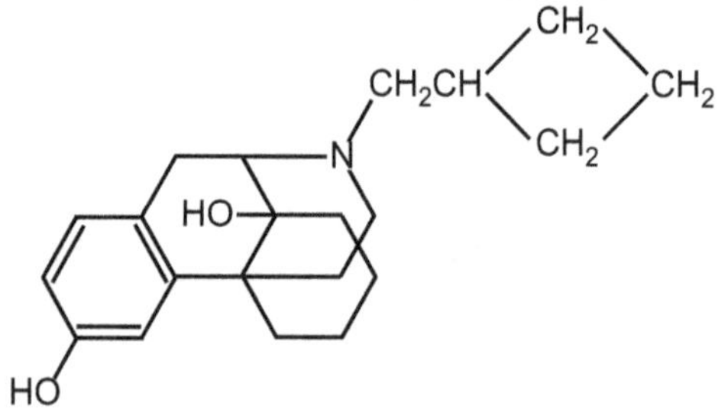

Butorphanol

(v) N-substitution may result into either agonist or antagonist depending upon the nature of substituent e.g., the N - phenylethyl or N-p- amino phenylethyl derivative of levorphanol are potent analgetics. The N-furylethyl and N–acetophenone analogues are also potent analgetics, while N–allyl derivative (cyclorphan) possesses antagonistic properties.

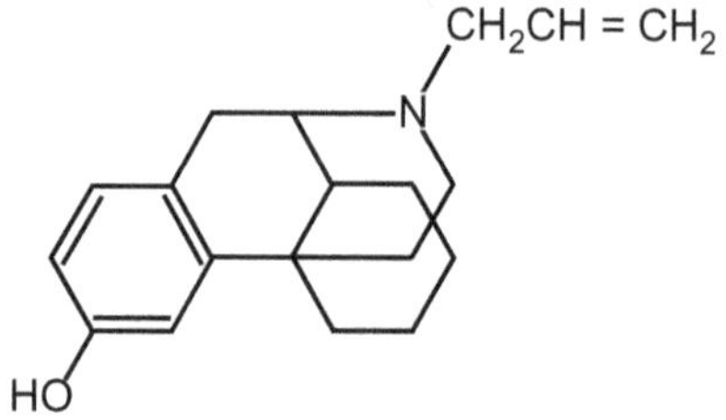

Levallorphan

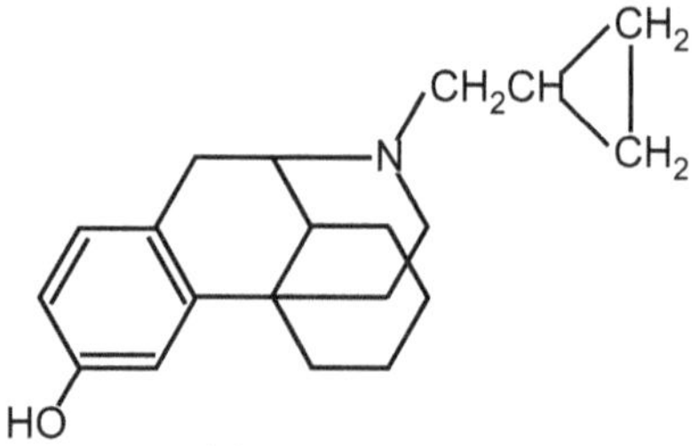

(–) Cyclorphan

1.4.5 Benzomorphans

The fact that, the removal of ether bridge and all the peripheral groups in the alicyclic ring of the morphine did not destroy its analgesic activity, encouraged May and Murphy to synthesize a new series of compounds known as benzomorphans (in which the alicyclic ring was replaced by one or two methyl groups).

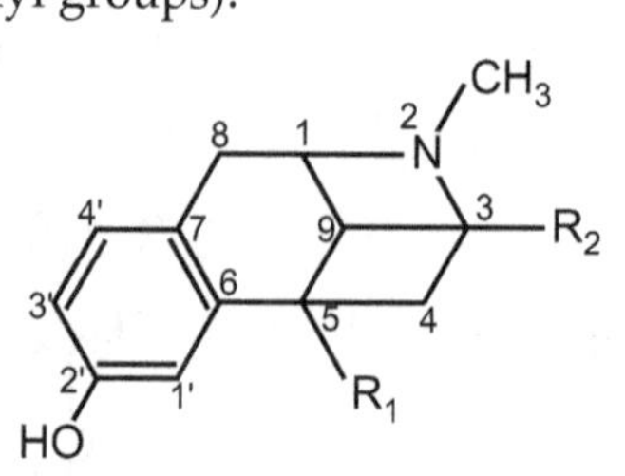

Benzomorphan ($R_1 = R_2 = H$)

Structure-Activity Relationship :

(1) Amongst the various substitutions at position 2', following SAR is observed

$$OH \geq H \geq NH_2, NO_2, F \text{ and } Cl$$

(2) The trimethyl compound $(R_1 = R_2 = CH_3)$ is about 3 times more potent than the dimethyl analogue $(R = H; R_2 = CH_3)$.

(3) Insertion of methyl group at C-9 increases analgesic activity.

(4) Insertion of hydroxyl group at C-9 (which is equivalent to 14-hydroxylation in morphine series) decreases the activity.

(5) The N-phenylethyl analogues always possess greater potency over N-methyl analogues.

(6) A clear-cut separation of analgesic activity and addiction liability can be observed in two isomeric forms (cis and trans) of the same compound, e.g.

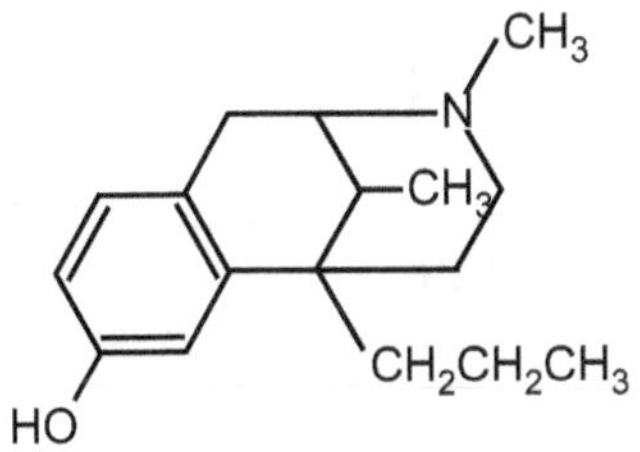

Further separation can also be observed between the enantiomers of the cis-isomer, e.g. (–) isomer is a stronger analgesic without addiction, while (+) isomer is a weak analgesic with high physical dependence capacity.

(7) Pentazocine and cyclazocine are the classic antagonists from benzomorphan series.

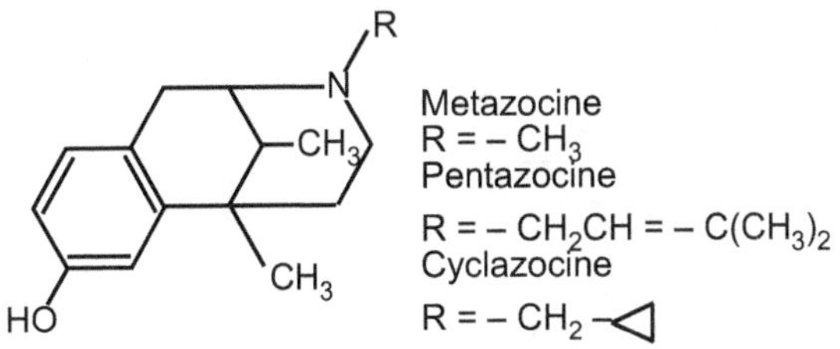

Metazocine
R = – CH₃
Pentazocine
R = – CH₂CH = – C(CH₃)₂
Cyclazocine
R = – CH₂ –◁

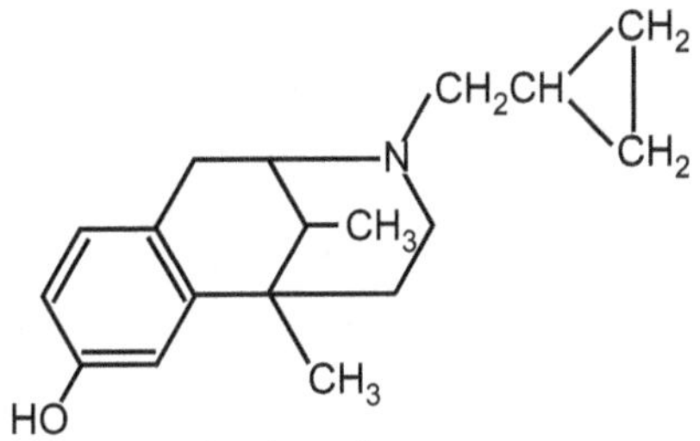

Cyclazocine

Cyclazocine and pentazocine are useful mixed agonist-antagonists. Unfortunately, the former has considerable hallucinogenic properties, although pentazocine is a very useful analgesic.

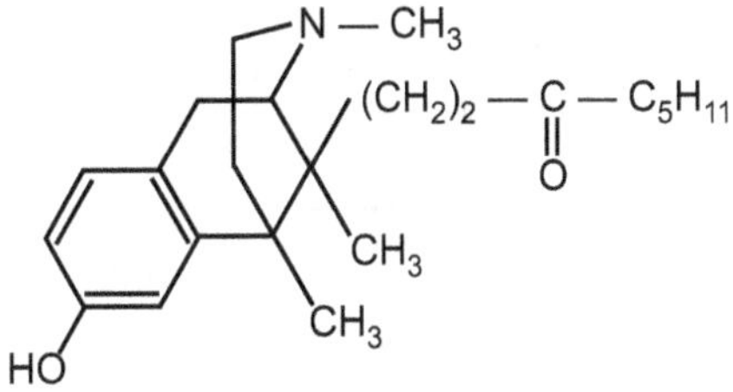

(a) Tonazocine

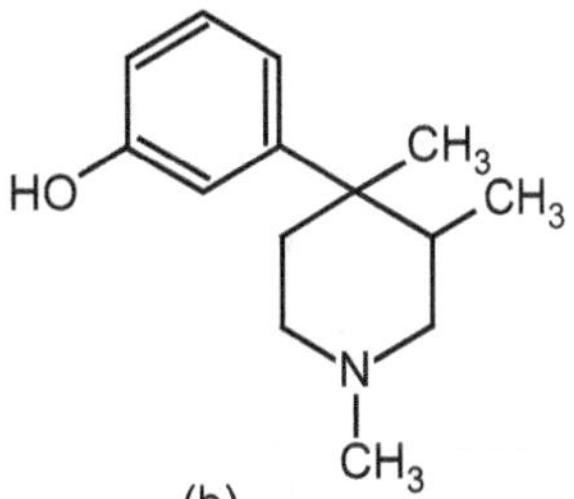

(b)

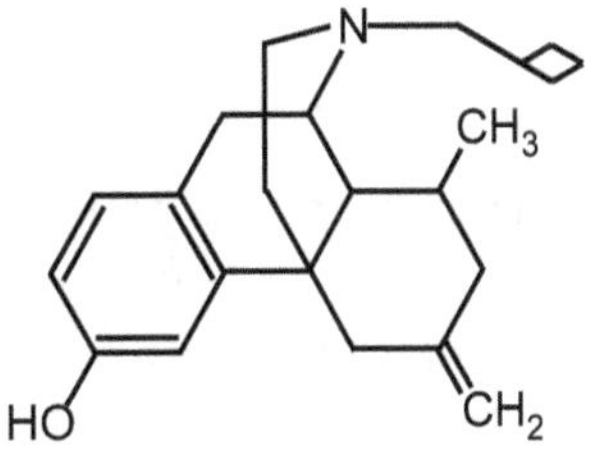

(c) Xorphanol

An N-allyl or an N-cyclopropylmethyl group frequently confers antagonist activity. However, there are numerous exceptions to this. e.g., tonazocine (a) is an antagonist and the 4-phenylpiperidine derivative (b) has greater antagonist potency with an N-methyl than with an N-allyl or N-cyclopropylmethyl substituent. Within the morphine skeleton, a C – 14 hydroxy or alkoxy group and a C – 6 ketone are necessary for pure antagonist activity (e.g. Naloxone). Xorphanol is found to be a partial agonist at the k-receptor and antagonist at the μ-receptor. Snyder has suggested that the steric effects of the C - 14 hydroxyl group of naloxone makes the N-allyl substituent equatorial and this stabilizes the receptor in an antagonist rather than in an agonist conformation. The oripavine derivative, 16 – methyl cyprenorphine is the most selective non-peptide delta antagonist.

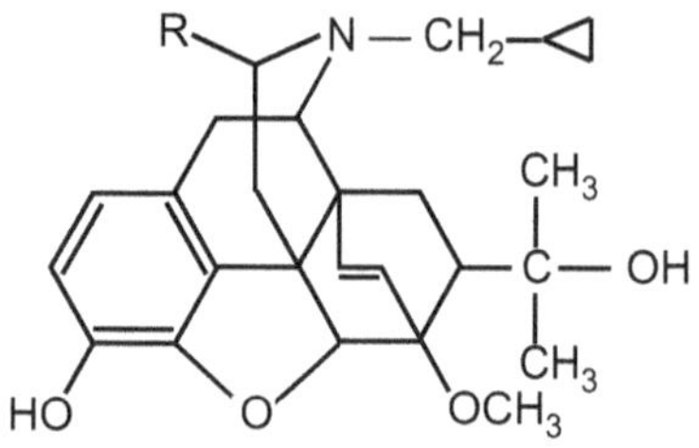

Cyprenorphine (R = H)

(8) Introduction of N-furfuryl group into the benzomorphans have provided a new series of potent agonists and antagonists that are now undergoing clinical evaluation.

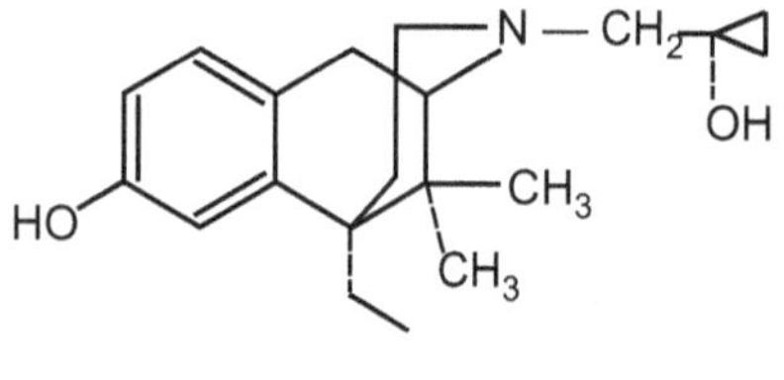

A new benzomorphan, bremazocine is a powerful k – agonist of long duration of addictive properties and respiratory depressant activity. It is about 200 times more active than morphine.

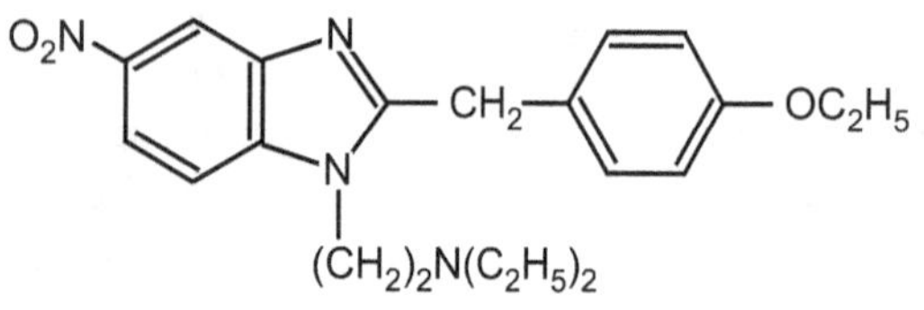

Etonitazene

Etonitazene can be related to morphine. It is a benzimidazole derivative and is highly potent, having about 1000 times activity of morphine.

1.4.6 Antitussive-opioidal agents

A compound synthesized as, and found to be, a narcotic antagonist turned out to be a potent and long lasting antitussive, is (+) butorphanol.

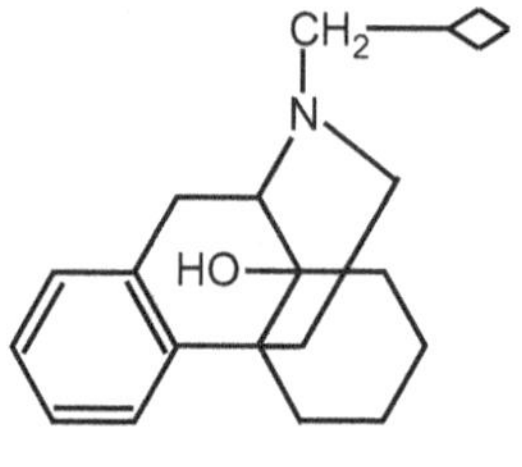

Butorphanol

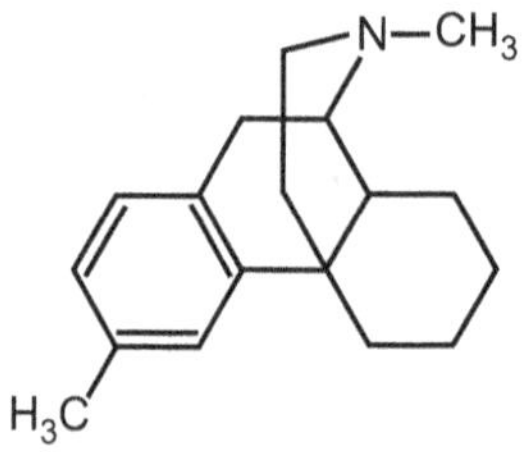

Dimethorphan

The (+) isomer of dimethorphan is essentially devoid of analgesic and additive properties but is effective antitussive agent.

Other examples of antitussive skeletons include :

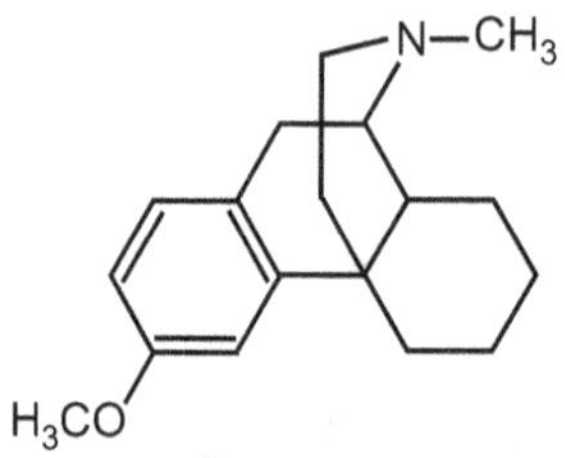

Dextromethorphan

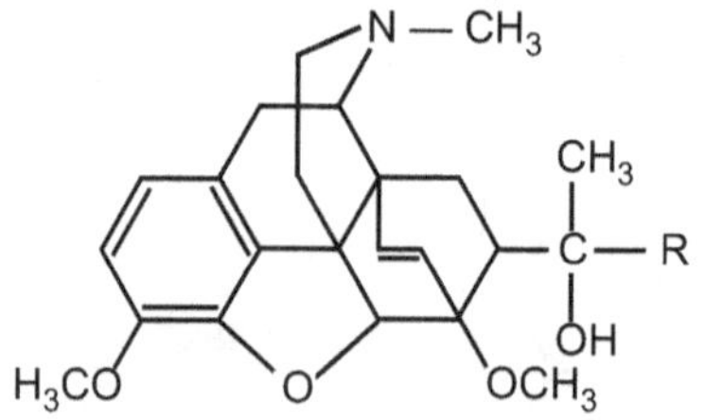

6,14-endo-Ethenotetrahydro-thebaine
(7-substituted-16 methyl)

1.5 NARCOTIC ANTAGONISTS

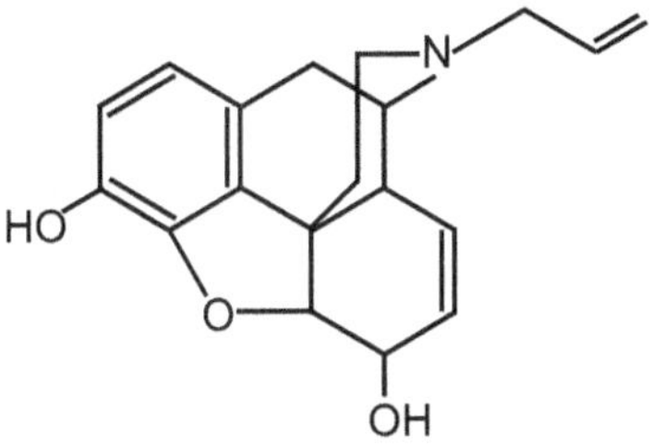

Nalorphine (1940)

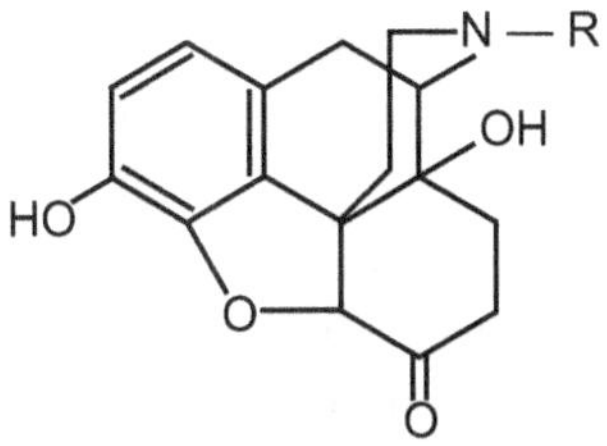

4-Hydroxy morphone

R = ⟍⟋⟍⟋
Naloxone (1961)

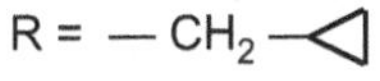

R = — CH$_2$ —◁
Naltrexone

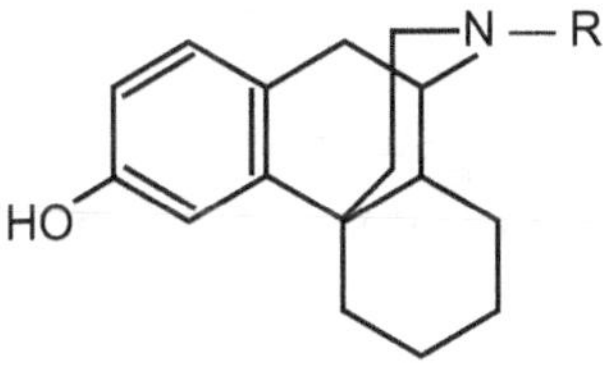

Morphinane

R = ⟍⟋⟍⟋
Levallorphan

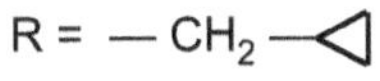

R = — CH$_2$ —◁
Cyclorphan

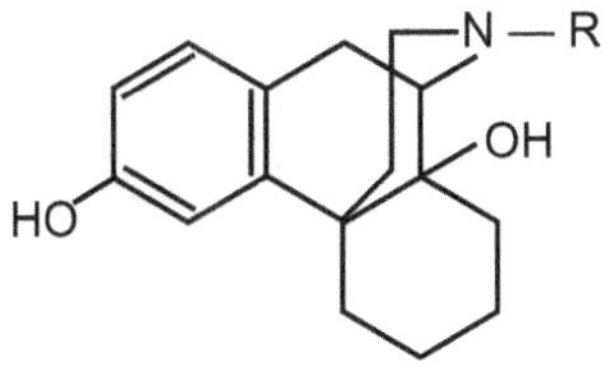

14-Hydroxy morphinane

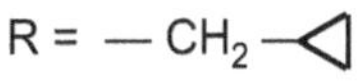

R = — CH$_2$ —◁
Oxilorphan

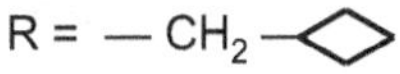

R = — CH$_2$ —◇
Butorphanol

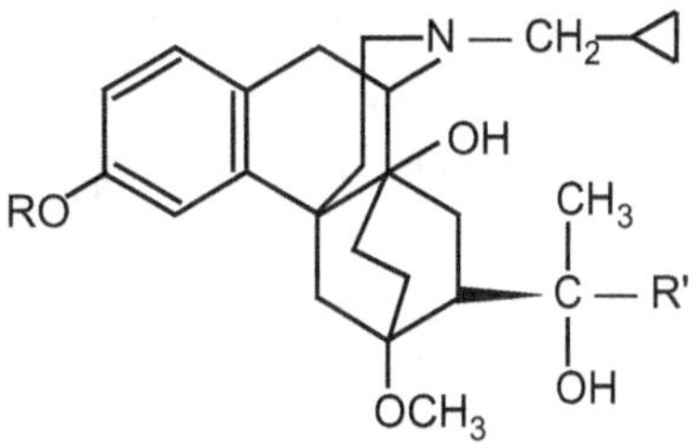

Oripavine

R = — H, R' = — t-Bu
Buprenorphine
R = — CH$_3$, R' = — CH$_3$
Diprenorphine

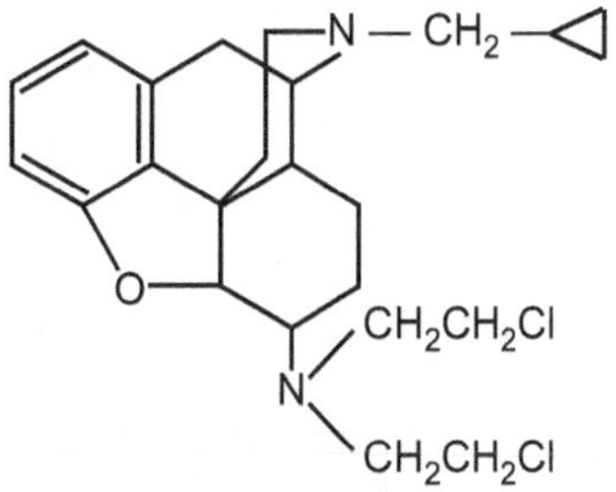

Chlornaltrexamine

Other examples of narcotic antagonists include cyclazocine and pentazocine (benzomorphan series). The recently described chlornaltrexamine, which acts as an irreversible alkylating affinity label on the opiate receptor, can maintain its antagonistic effect for the astonishing period of 3 days.

Narcotic antagonists competitively antagonise the effects of opioid analgetics by binding at several subspecies of opioid receptor.

The original concept of opioid receptor was first postulated from the stereo-selective studies of Beckett and Casy (1954). They proposed a model of opioid receptor. In the early 1970s, biochemical binding experiments with radio labelled naloxone, which antagonises the pharmacological effects of morphine, led to the identification of stereo-specific opioid receptors in mammalian brain tissue. In 1976, Martin classified opioid receptors into three subtypes : μ receptors (morphine-like), k receptors (ketozocine-like) Ethylketozocine, an analgesic that is chemically unrelated to morphine and σ receptors (N-allylnormetazocine-like) on the basis of effects of opioids on respiration, heart rate and locomotor activity.

A steric theory of opiate agonists and antagonists was proposed in 1983 by Martin. This theory helps to understand both agonistic and antagonistic features of opioid. The antagonistic activity of N-allyl or N-cyclopropylmethyl substituent can be explained on the basis of van der Waal's interaction of these substituents with the receptor. This may result in moving the nitrogen away from the position required for agonism.

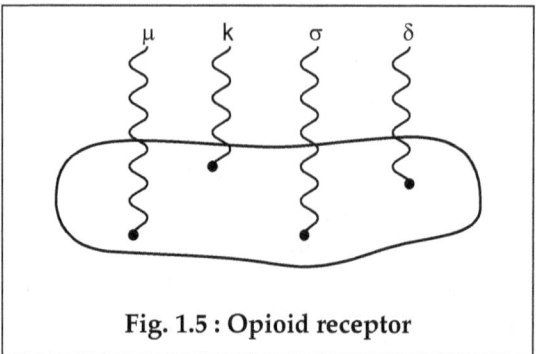

Fig. 1.5 : Opioid receptor

Opioid receptors are a group of G-protein coupled receptors with opioids as ligands. The opioid receptors are ~40% identical to somatostatin receptors.

Martin and Gilbert in 1977 have postulated the existence of three subspecies of

opioid receptors, designated as μ, k and σ. While Lord et al., in 1977 designated δ. It is thought that

(i) μ subspecies are involved in producing : analgesia, respiratory depression, euphoria, addiction, miosis and reduced GI motility.

Tapentadol : It is an opioid analgesic (μ-receptor agonist) with norepinephrine reuptake inhibitory activity.

$$C_2H_5$$

HO⟶...⟶$N(CH_3)_2$

CH_3

(ii) k receptor subspecies are involved in producing : spinal analgesia, sedation and miosis.

(iii) σ subspecies are involved in producing : dysphoria, hallucinations, respiratory stimulation and

(iv) δ subspecies are involved in producing analgesia, antidepressant effects and addiction.

An agonistic or antagonistic activity of the drugs depends only on their relative affinity for these receptor subspecies.

Opiates may cause respiratory depression which is attributed to the stimulation of both μ and δ receptors present in areas of the brain stem associated with control of respiration. Thus, μ and δ agonist appear to alter respiratory function by reducing the responsiveness of both central chemoreceptors in the brain stem and peripheral chemoreceptors in the carotid body to carbon dioxide.

1.6 ENDOGENOUS OPIOIDS

In 1975, Hughes and Kosterlitz isolated extracts from pig brain which had opioid activity similar to that of morphine. This activity was shown to be due to mixture of two pentapetides which they characterized and named Leu enkephalin and Met enkephalin.

The term 'endorphin' (endogenous morphine) is used to describe any endogenous opioid substance including the two enkephalins, e.g. $\alpha-$, $\beta-$, or $\gamma-$ endorphin and dynorphin.

The term 'opioid' is applied to any substance which produces its biological effects through an interaction with any of the three major types of opioid receptor (μ, k or δ) and whose actions are reversed by naloxone. An opiate is an opioid whose chemical structure and biological properties are similar to morphine.

The three families of peptides that have been isolated and identified are the Enkephalins, the Endorphins and the Dynorphins. Met–enkephalin has a sequence of amino acids identical with that of residues 61– 65 of the pituitary hormone β–lipotropin. This fragment itself has a potent opioid activity.

Elevated levels of immunoreactive β–endorphin and enkephalin have been reported in human plasma after exercise and after surgical stress.

Metabolism :

The enkephalins and dynorphin have a much shorter half-life than β–endorphin in-vivo because of faster hydrolysis by a variety of non–specific metallopeptidases. Consequently, β–endorphin is the only endogenous opioid which causes sustained analgesia after i. v. administration to mice. The two major metabolic processes for the enkephalins are the cleavage of Tyr^1-Gly^2 by membrane bound aminopeptidases, which are inhibited by bestatin or kelatorphan, and the hydrolysis of Gly^3-Phe^4 by a variety of metalloendopeptidases including 'enkephalinase', which is inhibited by thiorphan or kelatorphan.

The opioid peptides are formed in the brain, the pituitary gland and in the adrenal medulla by the proteolytic cleavage of three protein precursors; these are preproopiomelanocortin (POMC) [also known as corticotropin-β-lipotropin precursor (ACTH-β-LPH precursor)]; preproenkephalin A (also known as preproenkephalin) and preproenkephalin B (also known as preprodynorphin).

Tyr– Gly– Gly– Phe–Leu
Leu–enkephalin

Tyr– Gly– Gly – Phe– Met
Met–enkephalin

Tyr– Gly– Gly– Phe– Leu– Arg Arg– Ile– Arg– Pro–Lys– Trp– Asp-Asn– Gln
Dynorphin

Tyr-Gly-Gly-Phe-Met-Thr-Ser-Glu-Lys-Ser-Gln-Thr-Pro-Leu-Val-Thr-Leu-Phe-Lys-Asn-Ala-Ile-Ile-Lys-Asn-Ala-Tyr-Lys-Lys-Gly-Gly
β– Endorphin

Tyr-Pro-Trp-Glu-NH₂
Endomorphin-1

$\alpha-$ Endorphin : 1– 16 sequence
$\gamma-$ Endorphin : 1– 17 sequence
$\delta-$ Endorphin : 1– 27 sequence

Tyr-Pro-Glu-Glu-NH₂
Endomorphin-2

Fig. 1.6 : Structures of endogenous opioid peptides

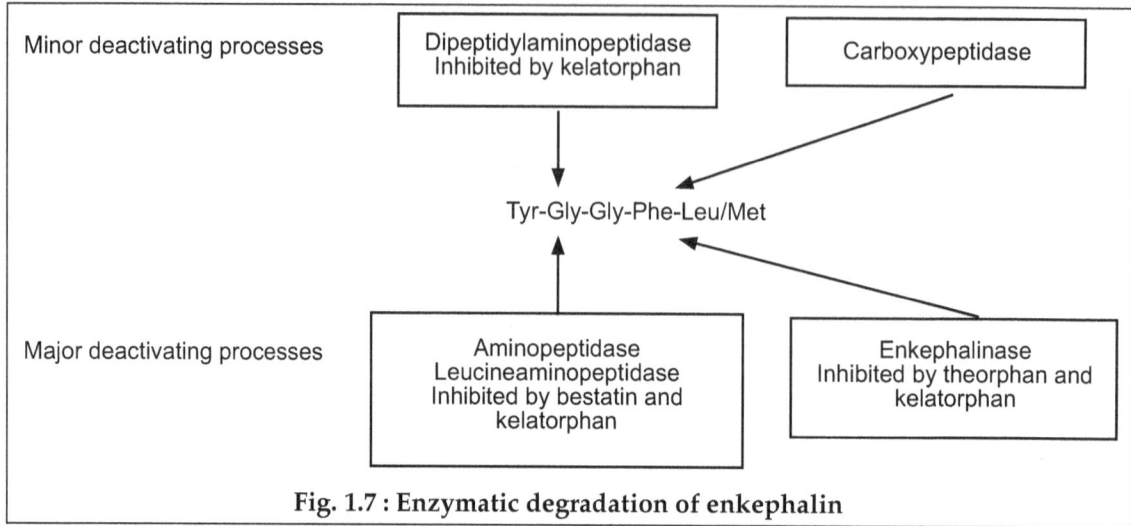

Minor deactivating processes	Dipeptidylaminopeptidase Inhibited by kelatorphan	Carboxypeptidase

Tyr-Gly-Gly-Phe-Leu/Met

Major deactivating processes	Aminopeptidase Leucineaminopeptidase Inhibited by bestatin and kelatorphan	Enkephalinase Inhibited by theorphan and kelatorphan

Fig. 1.7 : Enzymatic degradation of enkephalin

Over 1000 analogues of enkephalines have been synthesized. Greater stability towards metabolizing enzymes can be attained by conversion of the terminal carboxyl to $-CONH_2$, or by inserting a D-amino acid at this position. The tyrosyl group which provides a link between the enkephalins and thebaine derivatives, is an essential feature. A 10.0 ± 1.1 A° distance between the aromatic rings of Tyr[1] and Phe[4] may be important in the design of enkephalins with other aromatic moieties.

Enkephalinase inhibitors might be of use as analgesic drugs, but to date there is little clinical data to support this. Schering and Plough are reported to have developed an orally active enkephalinase inhibitor, Sch-34862, which is currently in clinical trials.

Enkephalin analogue (Tyr– X– Gly– Phe– Y)

Sch - 34862

Other physico-chemical techniques that have been used to study the conformations of the enkephalins lead to the conclusion that the enkephalins are flexible molecules whose conformation depends upon their molecular environment. In aqueous solution at room temperature they may adopt several different conformations.

Table 1.3 : Effect of the position of thiomethylene linkage on the half-life of synthetic Leu-enkephalin derivatives

Structure	Amide bond replaced	Half-life (min) in human serum at pH 7.4 (HPLC assay)	Opioid binding (versus etorphine) (nM) affinity
Tyr-Gly-Gly-Phe-Leu	–	12.5	256
Tyr-ψ (CH$_2$S) Gly-Gly-Phe-Leu	1 - 2	11.8	1060
Tyr-Gly-ψ (CH$_2$S) Gly-Phe-Leu	2 - 3	85.5	–
Tyr-Gly-Gly-ψ (CH$_2$S) Phe-Leu	3 - 4	134	–
Tyr-Gly-Gly-Phe-ψ (CH$_2$S) Leu	4 - 5	318	480

A 70 mg parenteral dose of metkephamid (Tyr – Ala – Gly – Phe – NMeGly – NH$_2$) was equivalent to 100 mg of meperidine in treating post-operative pain. Side-effects included a sensation of heavy limbs, dry mouth, redness of eyes and nasal stuffiness which are different from μ-selective opiate drugs and may be due to the relatively high affinity of metkephamid for δ-receptors.

The δ-selective peptide (Tyr–D–Ala–Gly–Phe–D–Leu) has been found to produce effective analgesia after intrathecal administration to cancer patients who had become tolerant to the analgesic effects of morphine.

The heptapeptide dermorphin was isolated from the skin of the frog Phyllomedusa bicolar.

Classification :

Depending upon the activity, drugs can be classified as :

(a) Pure antagonists : Naloxone

(b) Partial antagonist : Nalorphine, Levallorphan and Cyclazocine

(c) Partial agonists of morphine : Propiram and Profadol.

In particular, the pure agonist molecule can be converted into a partial agonist or a pure antagonist by relatively minor changes in the structure. The most common substitution is that of a larger moiety (like an allyl or methylcyclopropyl group) for the N–methyl group of an opioid.

Dermorphin

1.7 THERAPEUTIC USES OF OPIOID ANTAGONISTS

(1) In the treatment of opioid induced respiratory depression.

(2) Chronic administration of nalorphine along with morphine prevents or minimizes the development of dependence on morphine.

(3) Therapeutic agents in the treatment of compulsive users of opioids.

(4) Reduce the intensity of various untoward effects of opioids, e.g., euphoria, drowsiness, vomiting and muscular incoordination.

(5) An abstinence syndrome characterized by abnormal pain, irritability, cold sweats, diarrhoea, nausea and vomiting. These effects usually last in 4–10 weeks. Nalorphine precipitates the withdrawal symptoms in patients addicted to heroin and methadone.

(6) In acute poisoning due to morphine and related compounds.

Other Narcotic Analgesic Leads :

A chloro homolog of laudanosine, an alkaloid that occurs in opium.

Thiorphan
(Enkephalinase Inhibitor)

Tifluadom
(Kappa receptor agonist)

Aza-cannabinoids : R = – CH$_3$; – CH$_2$C ≡ CH
(Cannabis sativa)

μ receptors = supraspinal analgesia, respiratory depression, miosis, reduced GI-motility and euphoria.

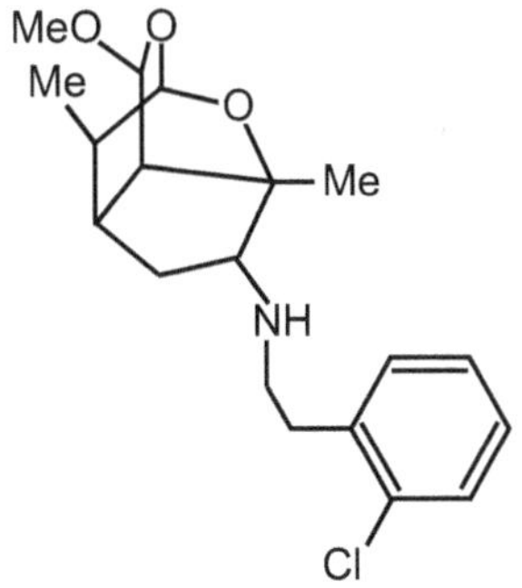

Valorphin (μ-selective agonists)

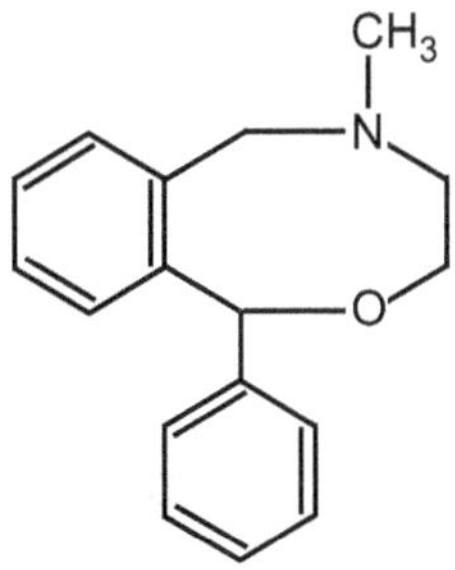

Nefopam

It is a novel analgesic agent having very rapid onset of action. It possesses minimum side-effects.

Table 1.4 : Non-narcotic antitussive agents

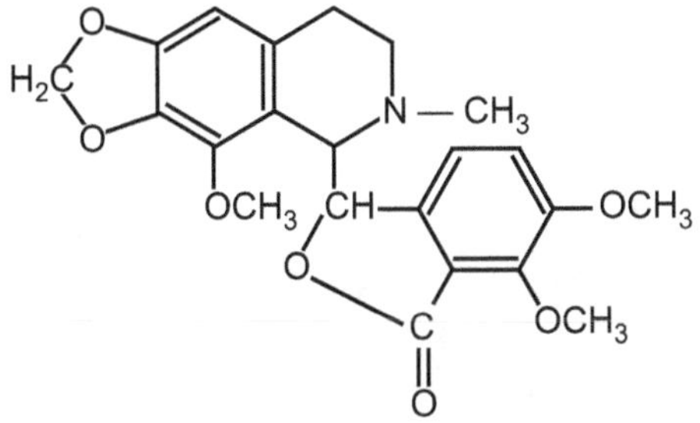

Noscapine

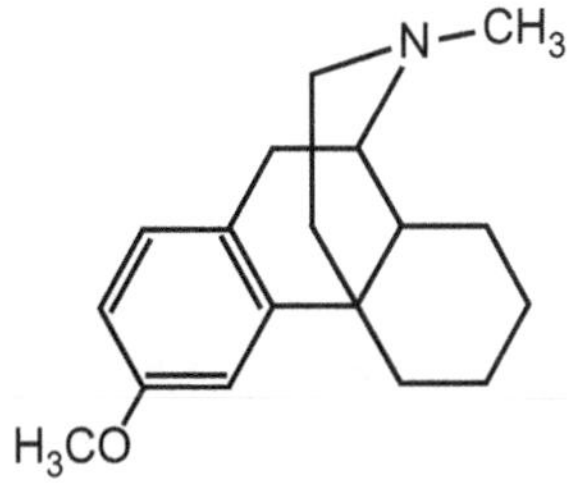

Dextromethorphan

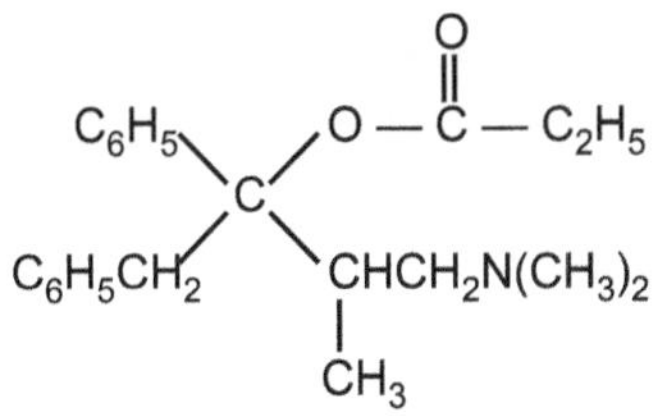

Levopropoxyphene

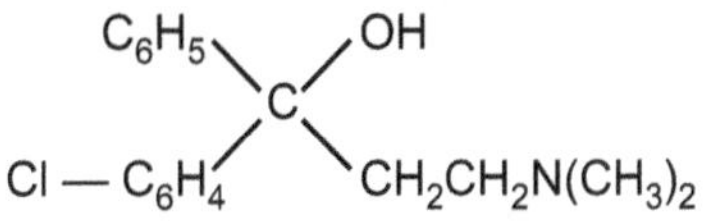

Chlophedianol

Contd...

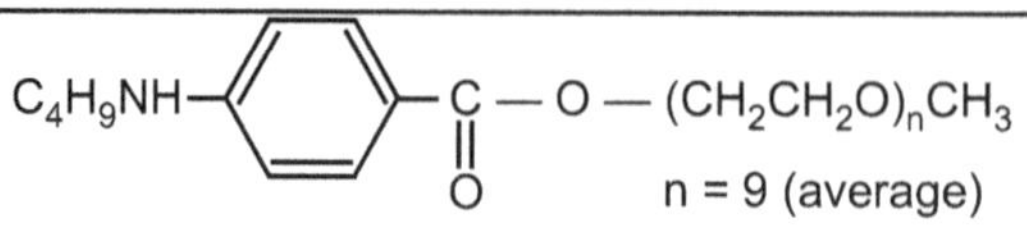

$$C_4H_9NH-\!\!\!\!\bigcirc\!\!\!\!-\overset{}{\underset{O}{C}}-O-(CH_2CH_2O)_nCH_3$$

n = 9 (average)

Benzonatate

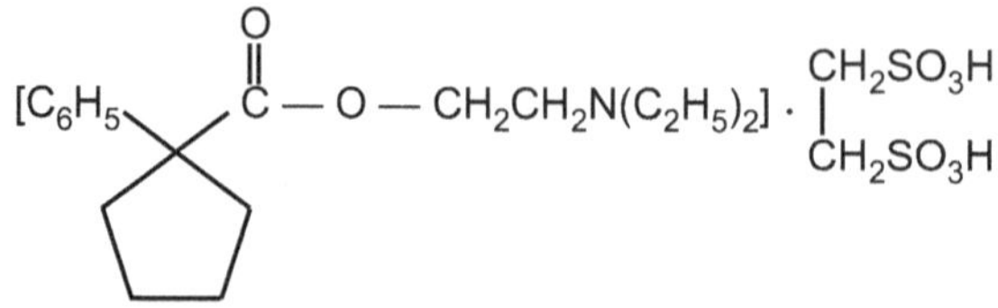

$$[C_6H_5 \diagup \overset{O}{\overset{\|}{C}}-O-CH_2CH_2N(C_2H_5)_2] \cdot \overset{CH_2SO_3H}{\underset{CH_2SO_3H}{|}}$$

Caramiphene Edisylate

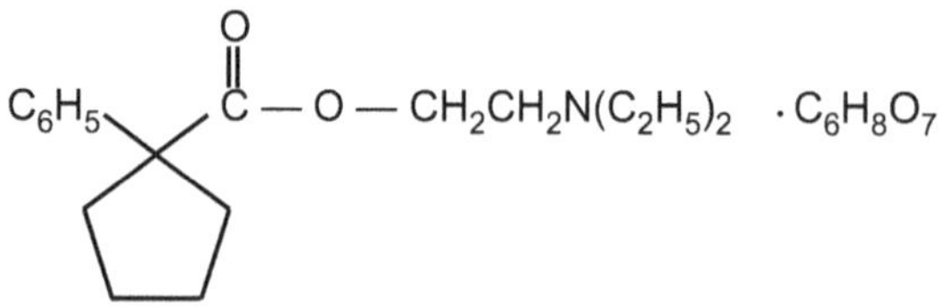

$$C_6H_5 \diagdown \overset{O}{\overset{\|}{C}}-O-CH_2CH_2N(C_2H_5)_2 \quad \cdot C_6H_8O_7$$

Carbetapentane Citrate

Synthesis

(I) Methadone :

(i)

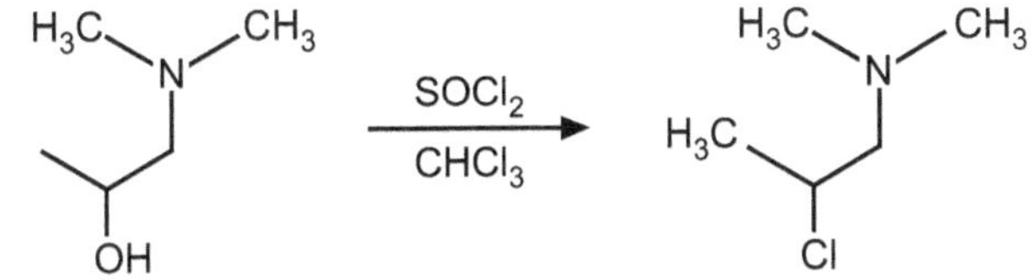

1-Dimethylamino
-2-Propamol

$\xrightarrow[\text{CHCl}_3]{\text{SOCl}_2}$

1-Dimethylamino
-2-Chloropropane

(ii)

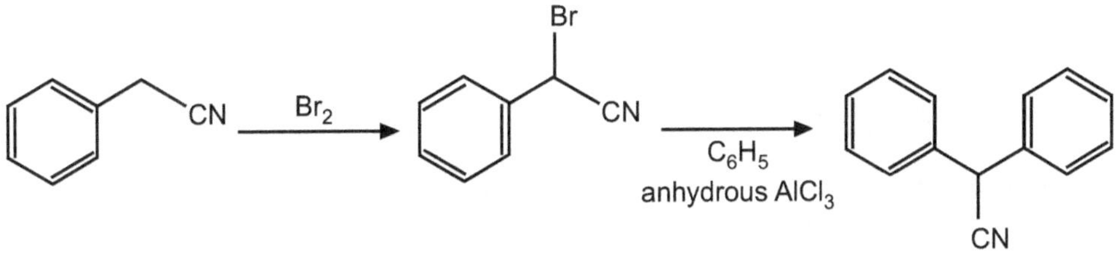

Benzyl cyanide

$\xrightarrow{\text{Br}_2}$

Benzyl bromocyanide

$\xrightarrow[\text{anhydrous AlCl}_3]{\text{C}_6\text{H}_5}$

Diphenyl acetonitrile

(iii)

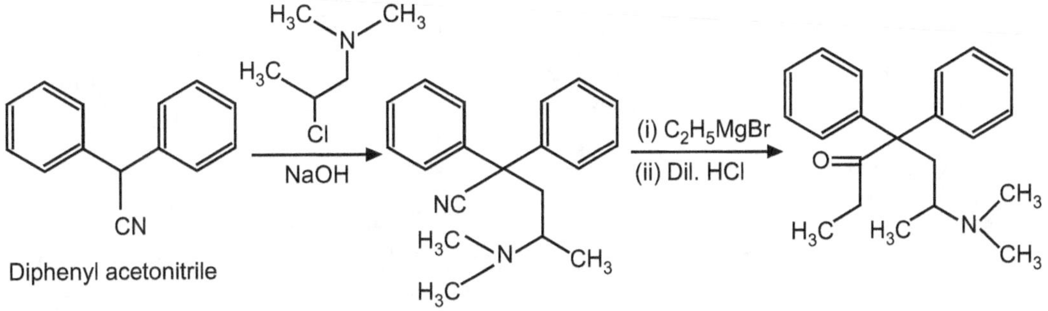

Diphenyl acetonitrile

$\xrightarrow{\text{NaOH}}$

2,2-Diphenyl-3-methyl
4-dimethylaminobutyronitrile

$\xrightarrow{\text{(i) C}_2\text{H}_5\text{MgBr} \\ \text{(ii) Dil. HCl}}$

Methadone

(II) Dextropropoxyphene hydrochloride :

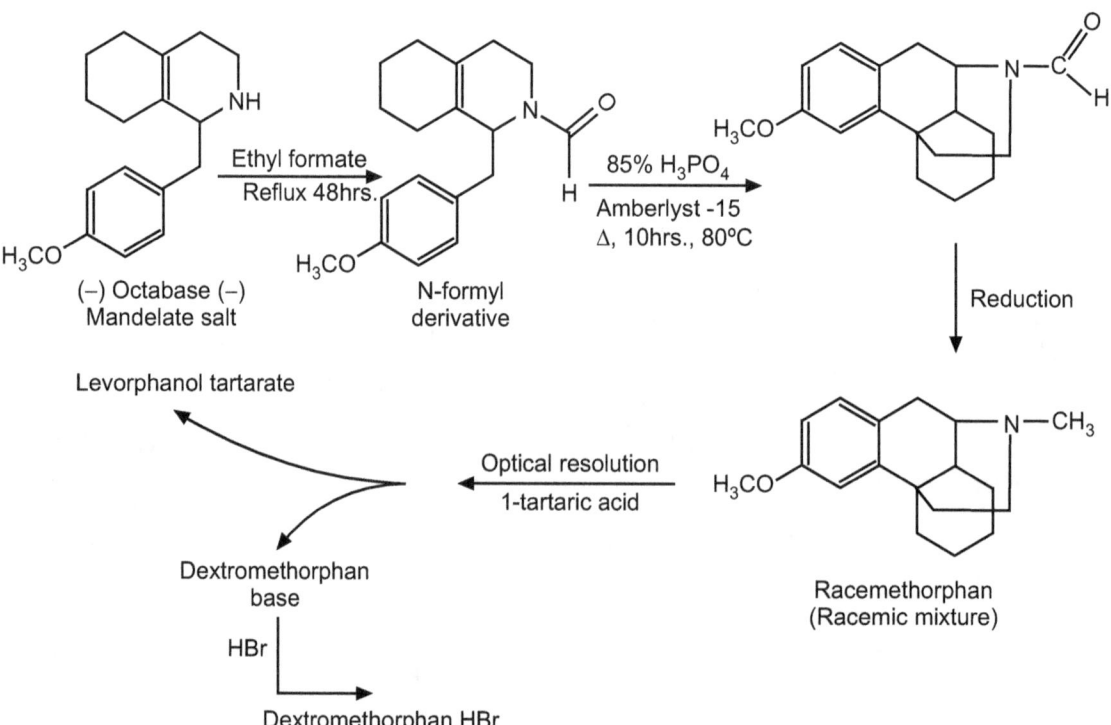

Propiophenone

Mannich base

Dextropropoxyphene hydrochloride

(III) Dextromethorphan :

(–) Octabase (–)
Mandelate salt

N-formyl
derivative

Levorphanol tartarate

Dextromethorphan
base

Dextromethorphan HBr

Racemethorphan
(Racemic mixture)

2

ANTI-INFLAMMATORY ANALGESICS

2.1 INTRODUCTION

Inflammation can be defined as 'a defensive but exaggerated local tissue reaction in response to exogenous or endogenous insult'. It is a complex phenomenon, comprising of biochemical as well as immunological factors. It is recognised by the following symptoms :

(1) Calor (Heat)

(2) Rubor (Redness)

(3) Tumour (Swelling) and

(4) Dolor (Pain).

Tissue damage initiates or activates the local release of various chemotactic factors that provoke directly or indirectly the appearance of the mediators of pain and inflammation. These factors include :

(a) Amines : Histamine, serotonin.

(b) Proteases : Kallikrein, plasmin. Release of lysosomal enzymes usually occurs from mast cells, macrophages, polymorphonuclear leucocytes and platelets.

(c) Prostaglandins.

(d) Hageman factor : It was discovered in 1955, in a preoperative blood of 37 years old patient, John Hageman. This factor is activated when it comes in contact with a foreign surface.

Once activated, Hageman factor is known to act upon a number of macromolecular substrates present in the plasma.

Hageman factor is a serum globular protein (β-globulin) of high molecular weight (110000). The three main functions performed by Hageman factor in the inflammatory reaction can be summarised as :

(a) Generation of thromboplastin activity in the pathways leading to coagulation. It is also termed as coagulation factor XII.

(b) Conversion of plasminogen pre-activator to plasminogen activator in the pathway leading to fibrinolysis.

(c) Conversion of pre-kallikrein in the pathway leading to kinin production.

Kinins are polypeptides formed in blood from inactive precursors called kininogens, induce vasodilation and increase permeability and serve as chemotactic agents for phagocytes.

Bradykinin is the major final biologically active product of the kallikrein-kinin pathway. Bradykinin has been cited as mediating vasodilatation, increasing vascular permeability and producing pain. Bradykinin also increases local lymph flow, another characteristic of local inflammation.

(e) Other factors : These include leucotoxin, leucocytosis promoting factor and lymph node permeability factor.

Blood and interstitial fluids contain three main types of antimicrobial proteins :

(i) **Interferons :** Lymphocytes, macrophages and fibroblasts infected with virus, produce antiviral proteins called interferons.

(ii) **Complement system :** A group of normally inactive proteins in blood plasma and on plasma membrane when get activated, causes cytolysis (bursting) of microbes, promotes phagocytosis and contributes to inflammation.

(iii) **Transferrins :** Iron binding proteins that inhibit growth of certain bacteria by reducing the amount of available iron.

Complement is a complex cascade system comprising about 20 plasma proteins, many of which are enzymes. It helps the ability of antibodies and phagocytes to clear pathogens. This cascade acts as :

- opsonizing pathogens,
- inducing inflammatory responses (release of small peptide mediator which invite increased flow of phagocytes),
- enhancing antibody responses and
- attacking some pathogens directly.

Different components of complement system stimulate histamine release, attract neutrophils by chemotaxis and promote phagocytosis. Some components can also destroy bacteria. A number of complement components mediate various inflammatory effects, in particular C_3a and C_5a. C_5a in particular is chemotactic for neutrophils and increases vascular permeability. Conditions where complement is involved include glomerulonephritis, rheumatoid arthritis, rheumatic fever and drug allergies.

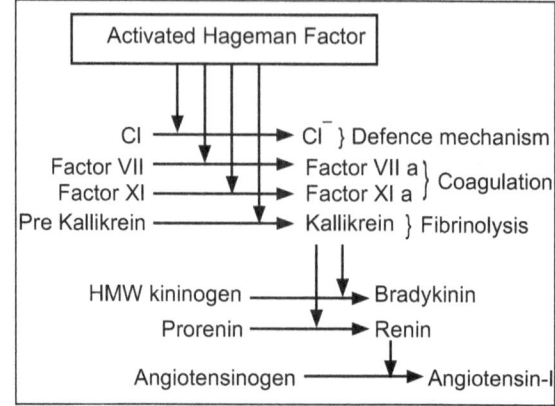

Complement peptides trigger cell function, aid in the recognition of invading pathogens and regulate the phagocytic process via interactions with specific cell surface receptors.

There are five types of WBC (Neutrophils + Lymphocytes + Monocytes + Eosinophils + Basophils). WBC combat pathogens by phagocytosis or immune responses. Several different chemicals released by microbes and inflammed tissues attract phagocyte, this phenomenon called chemotaxis. At site of inflammation, basophils leave capillaries, enter tissues and release granules that contain heparin, histamine and serotonin. Mast cells are fixed and found particularly in connective tissues of skin and mucous membranes of respiratory and GI tracts.

Hydrolytic enzymes are released by cells from intracellular vacuoles (known as lysosomes) during phagocytosis and also during cell death. There are two classes of these enzymes. Those in the first group act at acid pH (3 - 5) and are normally contained within lysosomes that fuse with vacuoles to form secondary phagosomes. The activity of these acid hydrolases is normally intracellular, but on cell death they may well be liberated at the site of inflammation and cause considerable damage.

Lysosomal enzymes are secreted from human neutrophils by cyclic nucleotides, autonomic neurohormones, prostaglandins, glucocorticoids and calcium. Discharge of lysosome granule contents from neutrophils

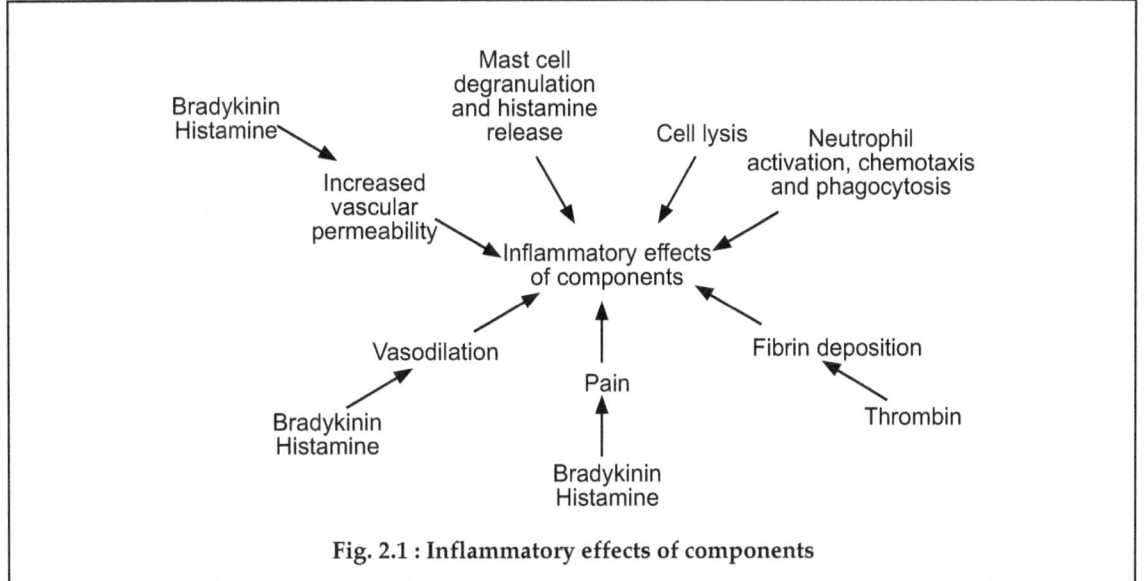

Fig. 2.1 : Inflammatory effects of components

results in the provocation of acute inflammation and connective tissue degradation. Agents that enhance lysosomal enzyme secretion include c-GMP, immune reactants, Ach, $PGF_{2\alpha}$ and Ca^{++} ions. While inhibiting occurs due to accumulation of intracellular c-AMP, epinephrine and several prostaglandins (PGE, PGA).

The second group of hydrolytic enzymes consists of those that act at neutral pH and are contained in cell organelles other than lysosomes. These are probably more important in the early stages of tissue damage during inflammation. Normal phagocytosis seems to involve these neutral pH enzymes; they include collagenase and elastase.

All these mediators cause local vascular response, which is characterized by :

(1) Increased blood flow to the affected area.

(2) Increased vascular permeability which may cause oedema.

(3) Cellular infiltration of platelets and macrophages from the capillaries into the tissue spaces.

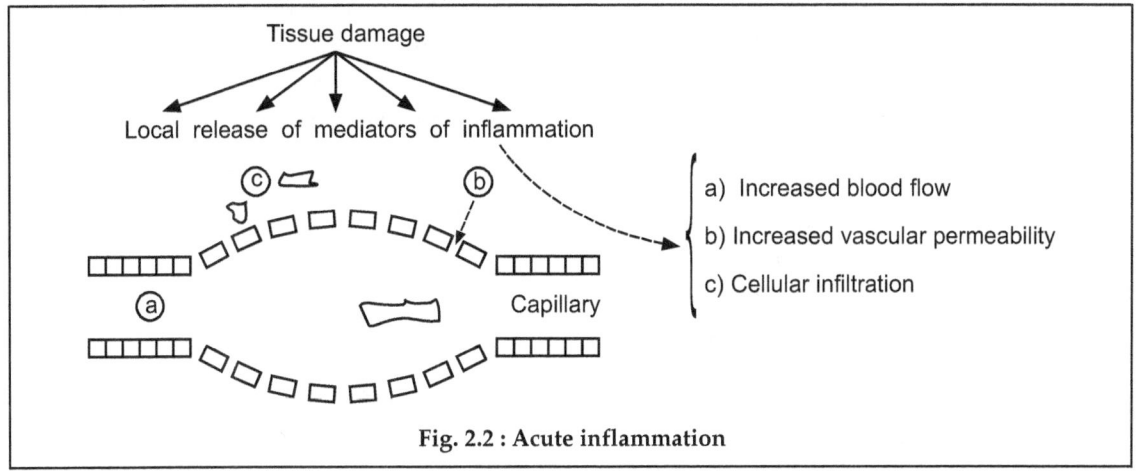

Fig. 2.2 : Acute inflammation

So in brief, the sequence of early events in inflammation may be summarised as :

(a) Initial injury which causes the release of inflammatory mediators.

(b) Vasodilation.

(c) A glycoprotein E-selectin appears on the inner surface of vascular endothelium during inflammation. It induces the adhesion of WBCs by attracting the tetrasaccharide sialyl Lewis X which is displayed on the surfaces of WBCs. After further adhesion the white blood cells are then able to squeeze through gaps between endothelial cells and enter the adjacent tissues to help repair injury. Thus, this increased vascular permeability, results into cellular infiltration.

(d) Migration of phagocytic cells to the inflammed area, resulting into release of lytic enzymes due to rupturing of cellular lysosomal membranes.

An inflammation may be either a primary or a secondary response to the tissue damage. A primary inflammation involves direct and generally acute defence reaction while in the secondary inflammation, it is an indirect consequence of the exaggerated cell physiology, arising due to pathological condition, e.g., rheumatoid arthritis.

The anti-inflammatory analgesic agents, also popularly known as non-steroidal anti-inflammatory drugs are associated with analgesic and antipyretic activities. The peripheral nerve fibres which conduct pain impulses may be categorised as :

(a) The large myelinated A fibres that conduct fast, more intense and precise pain.

(b) The myelinated B fibres that conduct pain impulses of medium intensity, and

(c) Unmyelinated C fibres that conduct slow and diffused pain.

The drugs covered in this chapter, have an ability to inhibit the synthesis of thromboxane and prostaglandins. This fact was first discovered by Vane in 1971, who assigned the therapeutic as well as adverse effects of aspirin-like drugs to their ability to prevent prostaglandin biosynthesis.

Considerable evidence has supported the concept that non-steroidal anti-inflammatory analgesic drugs act by inhibiting the biosynthesis of prostaglandins which are the basic cause behind pain, fever and inflammatory conditions. They have the ability to sensitise the pain receptors to mechanical and chemical stimulation. The biosynthesis of prostaglandins is catalysed by microsomal enzymes present in almost every mammalian cell type, except erythrocytes.

Prostaglandins are a group of cyclopentane derivatives formed from poly-unsaturated fatty acids by most mammalian tissues. The basic structure of all prostaglandins contains about 20 carbon atoms having a cyclopentane ring with two adjacent side-chains.

Arachidonic acid serves as a precursor for biosynthesis of prostaglandins in humans. Arachidonic acid is probably stored in the phospholipid fraction of the cell. The biosynthetic route for the formation of various prostaglandins is shown in Fig. 2.3.

Prostaglandin release has been demonstrated under a variety of conditions, for example, at the sites of inflammation (skin, joints, eye, white cells); during anaphylactic reactions; in platelets during aggregation; in the cerebral ventricles during fever, in subcutaneous fat during lipolysis and in the uterus during labour or during menstruation.

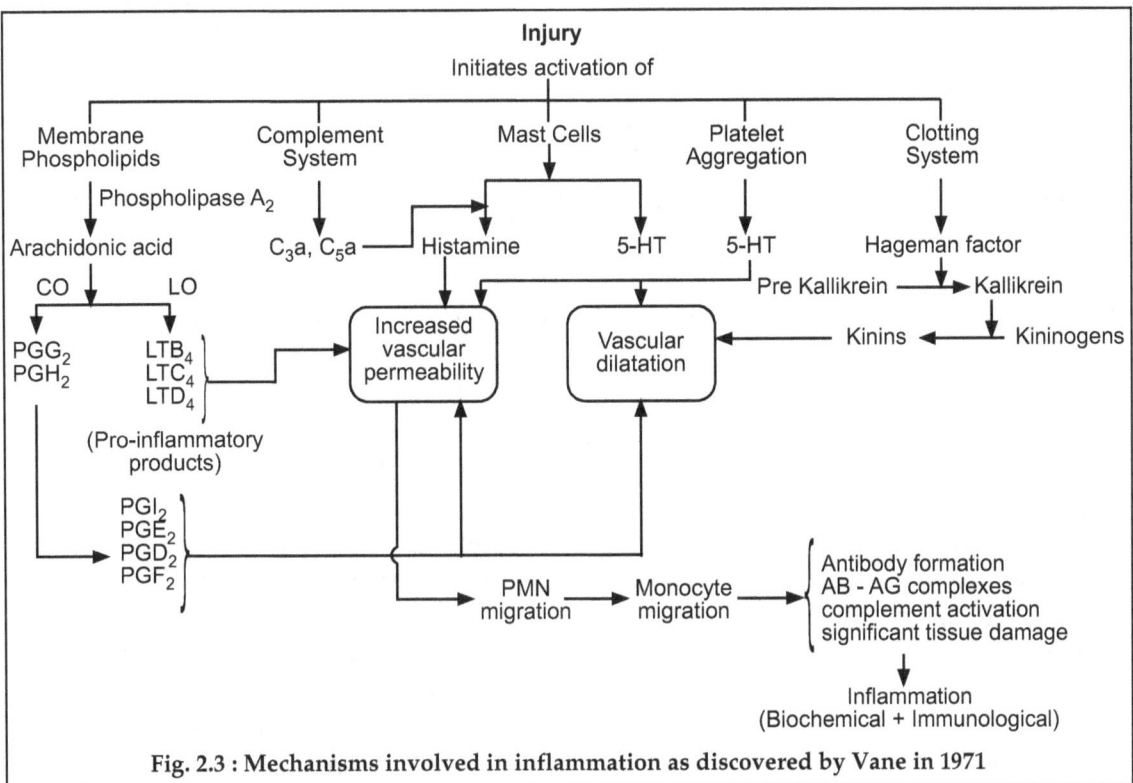

Fig. 2.3 : Mechanisms involved in inflammation as discovered by Vane in 1971

Prostaglandins potentiate the early inflammatory response, causing vasodilation, increased permeability, facilitating cellular infiltration and sensitising the pain receptors. The non-steroidal anti-inflammatory analgesics do not act centrally to intervene in the perception of the pain. They act peripherally to inhibit both, the synthesis and release of prostaglandins. Thus, they have minimum CNS side-effects. They neither induce mood alterations nor have a tendency to cause drug dependence. Thus, morphine like drugs act on CNS while these drugs act mainly peripherally at the site of origin of pain.

An elevation of body temperature is usually seen in many infectious diseases. It is also often associated with the inflammatory process. The centre for control of body temperature is located in the hypothalamus. An elevation of the body temperature occurs due to the attack of pyrogenic substances on this regulatory centre. Pyrogens are the metabolic products of bacteria and leucocytes. They induce changes in the normal regulatory process of body temperature resulting into reduced heat loss by peripheral vasoconstriction associated with an increase in the heat production. The net result is a rise in body temperature.

Prostaglandin E_1 is known to be a potent pyrogen (fever inducing) and PGE_2 causes pain, oedema, fever and reddening of the skin.

In an inflammatory disorder, the endogenous pyrogen apparently passes into the CNS and stimulates the release of prostaglandin-like substances from some specific sites within the brain. The non-steroidal anti-inflammatory analgesic agents have antipyretic activity. They block the synthesis and release of these substances, followed by peripheral vasodilation and increase sweating, resulting into considerable heat loss from the body. This brings down the body temperature to normal.

Anti-inflammatory agents are believed to act by disrupting the arachidonic acid cascade. These drugs are widely used for the treatment of minor pain and also for the management of oedema and the tissue damage resulting from arthritis.

They also provide relief to the patient from the emotional trauma of fever, pain and insomnia. Besides inhibiting the cyclooxygenase enzymes involved in prostaglandin biosynthesis, they also interfere with a variety of other enzymes. The inhibition of cyclooxygenase enzyme is probably only one of several mechanisms for the anti-inflammatory activity of these drugs, since indomethacin does not block this enzyme. The adverse effects, in part, can be accounted on this basis. The major adverse-effects common to different classes of these drugs are as follows :

(a) Except para amino phenol derivatives, these drugs produce gastrointestinal side-effects. In the untreated normal person, the GIT-membrane is protected from mucosal damage by prostaglandins like PGI_2 and PGE_2. These drugs inhibit the synthesis of gastric prostaglandins and expose the mucosal membrane to increased gastric acid attack resulting into gastric or intestinal ulceration.

(b) Their ability to inhibit the biosynthesis of prostaglandins enables them to prevent the formation of thromboxane A_2, a potent aggregating agent. Thus, treatment with non-steroidal anti-inflammatory drugs leads to increase in the bleeding time.

It revealed that medium dose of aspirin (75-325 mg daily) produced reductions of about a quarter in heart attack, stroke or other arterial diseases such as angina or peripheral vascular diseases. A long term therapy is beneficial in almost all patients with suspected heart attack or unstable angina or with any history of heart attack, stroke, angina, arterial bypass surgery or angioplasty, or other occlusive diseases of the blood vessels, irrespective of age, hypertension or diabetes. Higher doses do not increase the antiplatelet effect but onset of action is quicker. Because side-effects are possible, long-term aspirin intake may even do more harm than good in low-risk individual. Therefore, treatment of normal people with prophylactic aspirin is not recommended. However, it is rather suggested that advice on a healthy life-style would be of greater benefits to the patient.

(c) The gestation or spontaneous labour is found to be prolonged.

(d) Due to their higher affinity for plasma proteins, these agents cause easy displacement of other plasma protein-bound drugs. This may lead to a sudden, unexpected rise in the plasma concentration of co-administered drug resulting in potentially dangerous effects.

(e) In some individuals, hypersensitivity reaction may be seen during therapy which is characterized by oedema, generalised urticaria and sometimes bronchial asthma. Epinephrine is usually used to control such hypersensitivity reaction.

The anti-inflammatory analgesics popularly known as non-narcotic analgesic agents are also associated with antipyretic property. The prototype of this class is aspirin, and hence, though this class comprises the chemically unrelated heterogenous group of compounds, these compounds are often referred to as 'aspirin-like' drugs. They are valuable for the non-specific relief of pain of mild to moderate intensities, like headache, arthritis, neuralgia, dysmenorrhea etc. Due to their ability to inhibit the synthesis and release of thromboxane A_2 (platelet aggregating factor), some of these agents are also useful in the treatment of diseases characterized by platelet hyperaggregation such as, coronary artery disease, myocardial infarction etc.

Their use in rheumatism is, however, symptomatic only. The remission of rheumatoid or osteoarthritis requires corticosteroid treatment, often combined with the use of penicillamine, antimalarials, gold compounds (e.g., auranofin) or immuno-suppressive agents.

Their effectiveness in various inflammatory conditions is due to their ability to inhibit the biosynthesis of prostaglandins. Aspirin itself inactivates the cyclooxygenase enzyme by acetylating serine group at its active site. With the exception of indomethacin, the aspirin-like drugs irreversibly inhibit the cyclooxygenase enzymes.

Besides this, some of these agents have an ability to speed up the breakdown of muco-polysaccharides, in addition to inhibiting its synthesis. They also stabilise the lysosomes and cool down other mediators of inflammation.

Some of 'aspirin-like' drugs have uricosuric effect (i.e., promote excretion of uric acid) and hence may be useful in the treatment of gout.

2.2 CLASSIFICATION

The various analgesic-antipyretic anti-inflammatory agents can be classified as :

Non-Steroidal Anti-inflammatory Drugs

Acidic drugs　Basic drugs　Non-acidic drugs

　　　　　e.g., Timegadine　e.g. Indoxole

　　　　　inhibits neutrophil　　　Nictindole

　　　　　degranulation and

　　　　　superoxide production

→　Salicylates : Salicylic acid (1838), Aspirin (1899)

→　Para amino phenols : Paracetamol

→　Pyrazolones : Phenylbutazones Suxibuzone

→　Indole acetic acids : Indomethacin, Clamidoxic acid

→　Propionic acids : Ibuprofen, Naproxen

→　Aryl anthranilic acids : Meclofenamic acid, Tolfenamic acid

→　Miscellaneous agents : Piroxicam, Tenoxicam

2.3 SALICYLIC ACID DERIVATIVES

Salicylic acid was first used in rheumatic fever by Mac Lagan in 1877. The salicylic acid derivatives are most widely employed to treat arthritis.

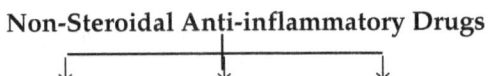

Salicylic acid

The aspirin like drugs are mild analgesics and are effective against pain of low to moderate intensity.

Table 2.1 : Salicylic acid derivatives

Name	R_1	R_2	Year of introduction
1. Salicylic acid	H	H	1838
2. Methyl salicylate	CH_3	H	1844
3. Sodium salicylate	Na^+	H	1875
4. Phenyl salicylate	C_6H_5	H	1886
5. Acetyl salicylic acid (Aspirin)	H	$COCH_3$	1899

Since, salicylic acid is so irritating, (that it can only be used externally) various derivatives have been synthesized for systemic use. These derivatives can broadly be divided into :

(i) Esters of salicylic acid :

Important landmarks of Aspirin:

The antipyretic (fever reducing) property of the bark of the Willow tree (Salix alba) was known to the ancient Greeks.

Sr. No.	Year	Landmarks
1.	1763	Edward Stone noticed that chewing the bark of the willow tree helped to relieve the symptoms of malaria – chills and fever.
2.	1827	The active ingredient in willow bark, **salicin,** was isolated.
3.	1838	Raffaele Pivia, an Italian Chemist, hydrolyzes **salicin** to produce glucose and **salicyl alcohol**. He further oxidizes salicyl alcohol to salicylic acid, establishing a connection between that substance and the active ingredient in willow bark.
4.	1843	A related compound, **methyl salicylate** was found by the French chemist, Auguste Cahours and the American chemist, William Proctor, to be a major constituent of oil of wintergreen, which was extracted from the leaves of the wintergreen plant.
5.	1853	Charles Gerhardt of Strasbourg replaced the OH of salicylic acid with an acetyl group using acetic anhydride, the first synthesis of **acetyl salicylic acid**, which was later called aspirin.
6.	1859-1993	During this period, salicylic acid which is moderately strong acid ($pK_a = 3$) was widely used as a medicine. The acid burned the mouth. Efforts to moderate the effects of its acidity resulted in the administration of the sodium salt of salicylic acid, sodium salicylate. The salt, however has an unpleasant taste.
7.	**1893**	In an effort to find a less unpleasant way to administer salicylic acid. Felix Haffman, a chemist working for the Bayer pharmaceutical company in Germany, reinvestigated the acetylation reaction first conducted by Gerhardt in 1853. Hoffman's father was rheumatic, which added a personal motivation for finding such a substitute. The synthetic material called **aspirin** lacked the strong acidity of the salicylic acid and the unpleasant taste of its sodium salt.

(ii) Salicylate esters of organic acids :

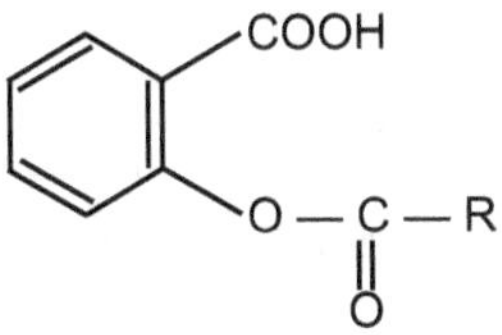

(iii) Phenoxy derivatives :

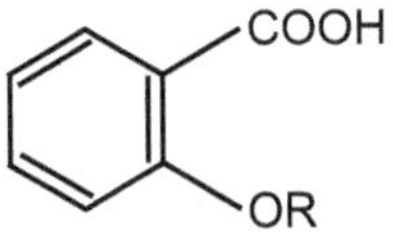

(i) Esters of salicylic acid : The alkyl and aryl esters are used externally, mainly as counter irritants. These compounds have very little analgesic value e.g.

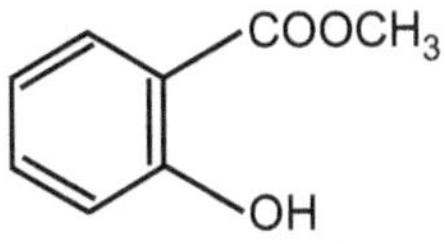

Methyl salicylate

Salicylic acid is moderately strong acid (pKa = 3.0). It burns the mouth. Efforts to dilute the effects of its acidity resulted in sodium salicylate. It has however an unpleasant taste.

A few inorganic salicylates are used internally as analgesics. These compounds vary in their stomach irritation property.

These include the following salts of salicylic acid :

(a) Sodium salicylate

(b) Sodium thiosalicylate

(c) Magnesium salicylate

(d) Choline salicylate

(e) Less commonly used

(i) Ammonium salicylate

(ii) Lithium salicylate

(iii) Strontium salicylate.

(ii) Salicylate esters of organic acids : Examples from this class are :

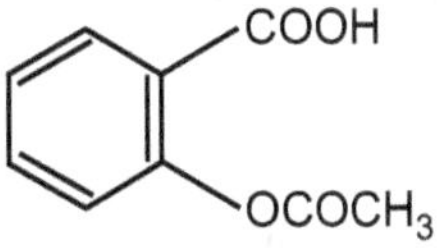

Aspirin

Aspirin lacks the strong acidity of salicylic acid and unpleasant taste of its sodium salt. It is still the most extensively employed analgesic-antipyretic and anti-inflammatory agent associated with few untoward effects like allergic reactions (asthma and urticaria) and gastric irritation (due to its hydrolysis to salicylic acid).

The name was coined by adding an "a" for acetyl to spirin for Spiraea, the plant species from which salicylic acid was once prepared.

The following salts of aspirin appear to have fewer undesirable side effects and to induce analgesia faster than aspirin.

(a) Aluminium aspirin

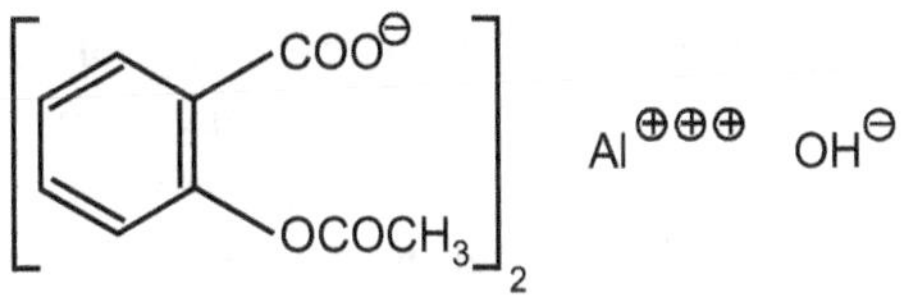

(b) Calcium aspirin

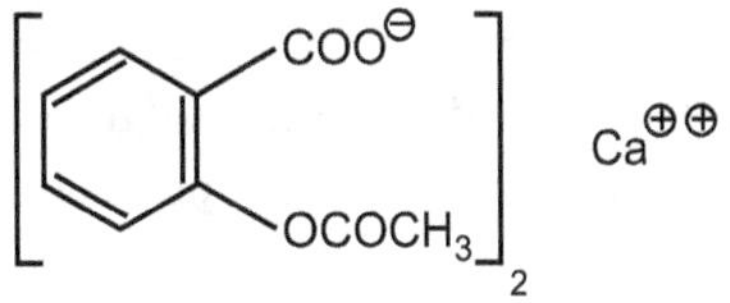

Other compounds of interest are :

(1) Carbethyl salicylate : It is an ester of ethyl salicylate and carbonic acid and this is a combination of a type I and type II derivatives of salicylic acid.

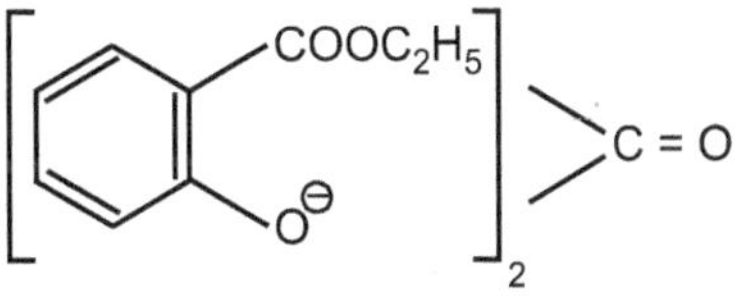

(2) Salicylamide : It gets excreted more rapidly than other salicylates and exerts a moderately quicker and deeper analgesic effect than does aspirin.

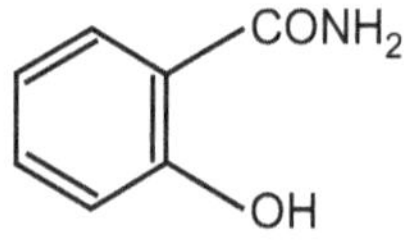

Salicylamide

Structure-Activity Relationship :

(a) Various substitutions on the carboxyl or hydroxyl group result into change in potency as well as toxicity.

(b) The ortho position of the OH group is an important feature for the action of the salicylates.

(c) Benzoic acid, though much weaker, shares many of the actions of salicylic acid.

(d) Various approaches have been made towards the design of a superior analogue. e.g.,

(1) Trilisate (Choline Magnesium Trisalicylate): It is a complex salt of salicylic acid with choline and magnesium which possesses longer duration of action and lesser gastrointestinal irritation than aspirin.

(2) Trolamine salicylate : It is a topical analgesic used in sunscreen. The salicyclic acid possesses both the sun protection effect (by absorbing UV radiation) and analgesic effect. Triethanolamine neutralizes the acidity of salicyclic acid.

(3) Benorylate : It is the N-acetylamino-phenol ester of aspirin.

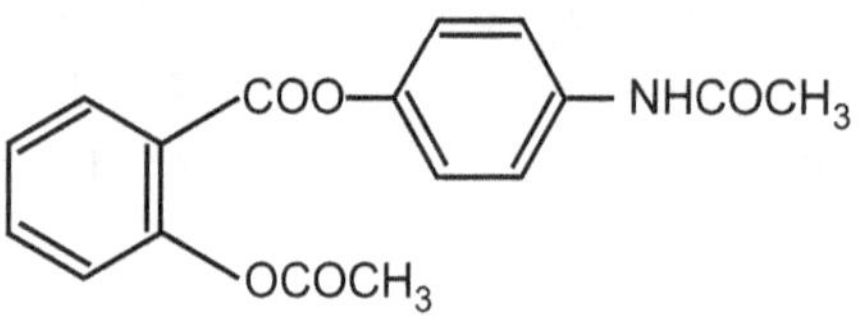

Benorylate

(4) Diflunisal (1971) : It is recently introduced for clinical use in some parts of the world. It has a long duration of action.

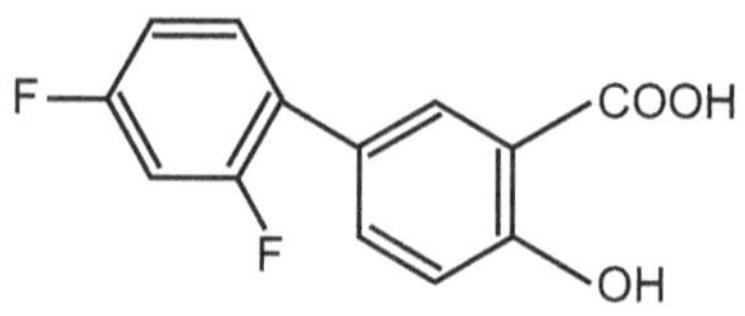

5-(2,4-difluorophenyl) salicyclic acid

(5) Fendosal : It possesses an analgesic activity comparable to that of diflunisal.

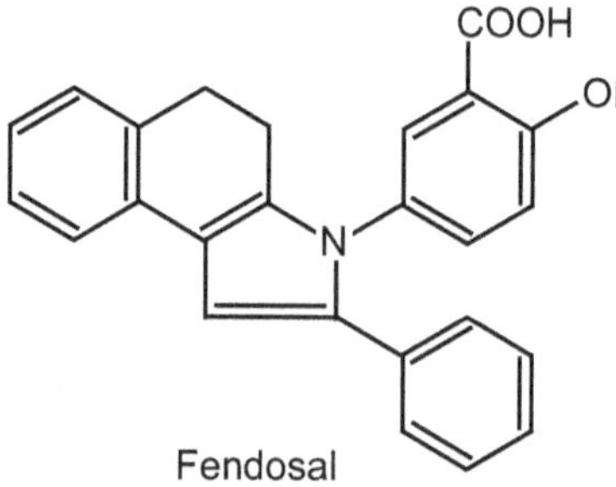

Fendosal

(6) Mesalazine (5-aminosalicylic acid) : It is a bowel specific anti-inflammatory drug used to treat inflammation of the digestive tract ulcerative colitis. It is considered as active metabolite of sulfasalazine.

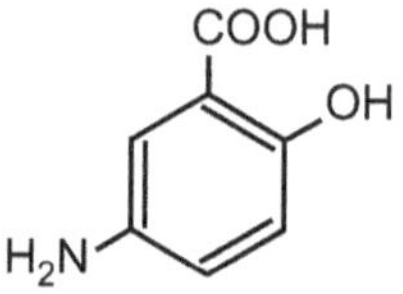

(7) Salsalate : It is the ester formed between two salicylic acid molecules. Since, it is relatively insoluble in the stomach and is not absorbed until it reaches the small intestine, it is said to cause less gastric irritation.

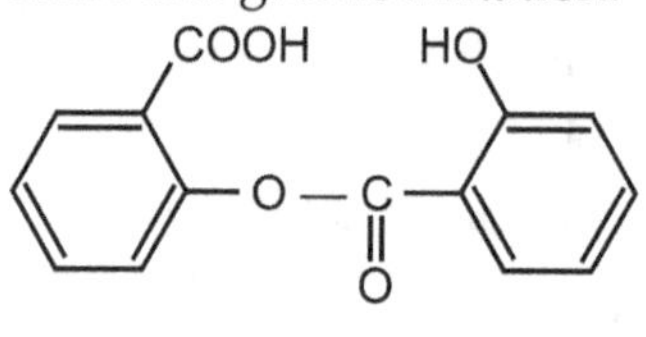

Salsalate

(8) Flufenisal : With the introduction of a hydrophobic group (F) at 5' position, the compound became more potent, longer acting and with less gastric irritation.

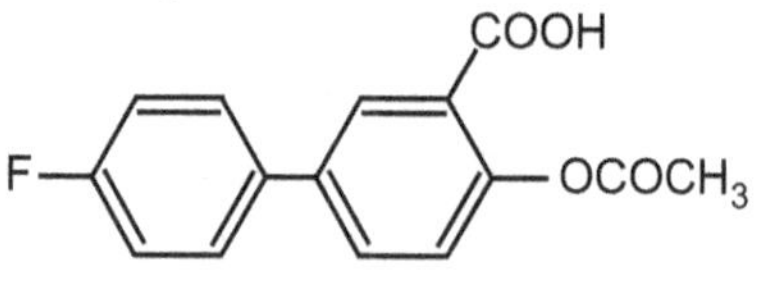

Flufenisal

Local Actions :

Salicylic acid and methyl salicylate, since, both are too irritant to the gastric mucosa internally; these compounds are used for topical applications due to their keratolytic, antiseptic and fungistatic actions.

Salol Principle :

Salol, (phenyl salicylate) was introduced by Nencki in 1886. It is an ester of two toxic substances like phenol and salicylic acid.

When both the components (i.e., alcohol and acid) of an ester are active compounds, the ester is called as True salol or Full salol e.g. phenyl salicylate (salol) and β-naphthol benzoate (betol). When only one component of the ester (either alcoholic or acidic part) is active, toxic or corrosive compound, the ester is referred to as a partial salol e.g. methyl salicylate and thymol carbonate.

2.4 PARA-AMINO PHENOL DERIVATIVES

Since, p-amino phenol is the metabolite of aniline (aniline also possesses antipyretic activity) these analgesics are also being called as "coal tar analgesics". The only agents of interest, from this class are :

NHCOCH$_3$ NHCOCH$_3$ NHCOCH$_3$

OH   OC$_2$H$_5$

Acetanilide   Paracetamol   Phenacetin

Acetanilide is metabolised into paracetamol and aniline. The toxicity of the latter compound discouraged its use in therapeutics.

The p-amino phenol derivatives are analgesics and antipyretics. They do not have anti-inflammatory activity. They are safe in children and patients with ulcers. However, they are hepatotoxic.

2.5 PYRAZOLONE DERIVATIVES

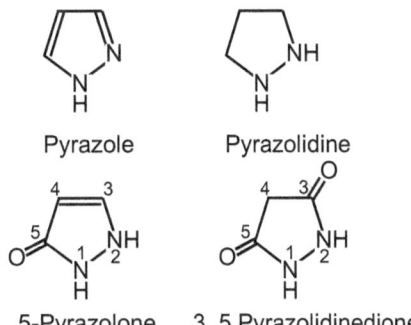

Pyrazole   Pyrazolidine

5-Pyrazolone   3, 5 Pyrazolidinedione

(a) 5-Pyrazolone derivatives :

Compound	R$_2$	R$_4$
Antipyrine	–CH$_3$	H
Aminopyrine	–CH$_3$	–N (CH$_3$)$_2$
Dipyrone	–CH$_3$	$-\underset{\underset{CH_3}{\vert}}{N}- CH_2 SO_3 Na$

Antipyrine is the parent drug from this category. Its modification further resulted into the introduction of aminopyrine and dipyrone in clinical use.

Antipyrine and aminopyrine have analgesic, antipyretic and antirheumatic activities. Fatal agranulocytosis caused by dipyrone and aminopyrine has limited their usefulness. The patient is at high risk of infection due to low count of granulocytes (i.e. neutrophils, basophils and eosinophils).

Aminopyrine is no longer an official drug. Chemically, aminopyrine is N-phenyl-N-alkyl-substituted pyrazoline-3-one. Being considered as structural analogue of quinine, the antipyretic action of aminopyrine was discovered. Due to haematological toxicity search for improved analogue of aminopyrine lead to phenylbutazone.

(b) 3, 5-Pyrazolidinedione derivatives :

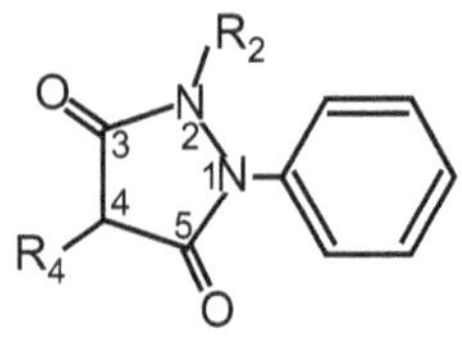

(1) Phenylbutazone

$R_2 = - C_6H_5, R_4 = - n - C_4H_9$

(2) Oxyphenbutazone

$R_2 = - p - OHC_6H_4; R_4 = - n - C_4H_9$

(3) Sulfinpyrazone

$R_2 = - C_6H_5; R_4 = - CH_2CH_2 SC_6H_5$

↓

O

To eliminate GI-disorders and occasional agranulocytosis, the n-butyl group of phenyl-butazone may be replaced by $(CH_2)_2SOC_6H_5$ which increases analgesic activity and uricosuric activity in sulfinpyrazone.

Phenylbutazone, although analgesic itself, was originally developed as a solubilizer, for the insoluble aminopyrine. Compared with phenyl butazone, oxyphenbutazone is an equally potent anti-inflammatory analgesic but is slightly less toxic.

Phenylbutazone completely undergoes metabolism by liver microsomal enzymes to (a) oxyphenbutazone and (b) γ-hydroxy-phenylbutazone. Other compounds of interest from this series are :

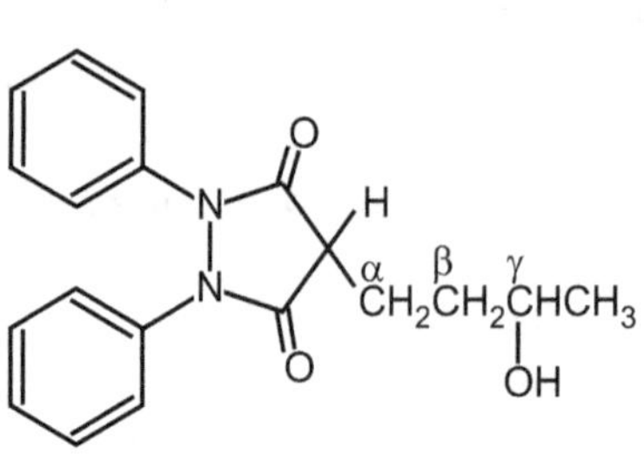

γ-Hydroxyphenylbutazone

(a) **Kebuzone :** It has similar properties and actions as that of phenylbutazone.

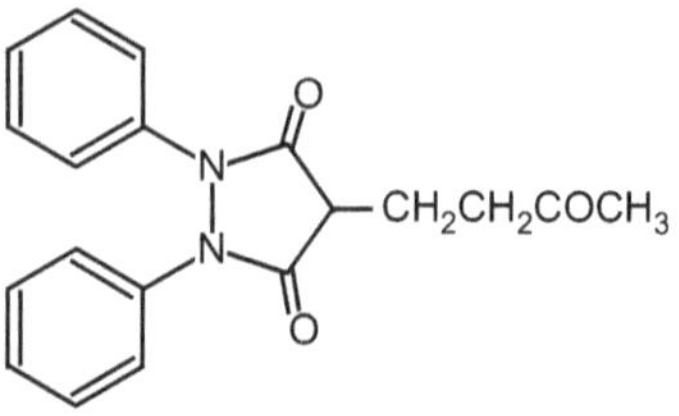

Kebuzone

(b) **Propyphenozone**

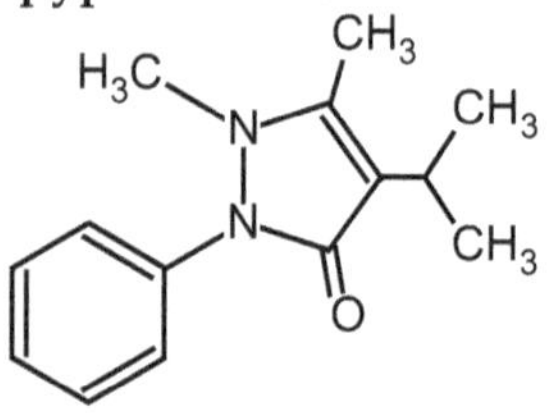

Propyphenazone

(c) **Phenazone :**

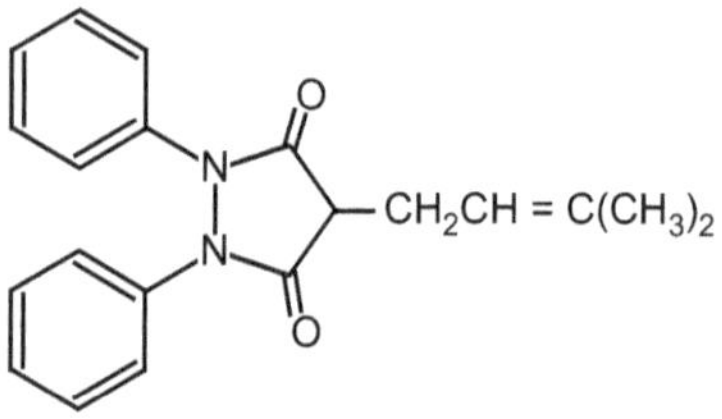

(d) **Azapropazone :** It is a pyrazolo benzotriazinedione derivative, having similar activity as that of phenylbutazone.

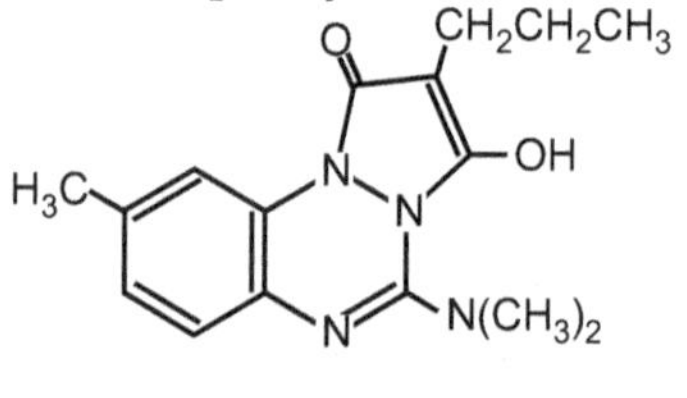

Azapropazone

SAR for pyrazolidine diones :

(i) Activity decreases if nibutyl group at C_4 is replaced by propyl or allyl group.

(ii) Substitution (e.g. CH_3, Cl, NO_2, OH) only at para position in phenyl ring retains the activity.

(iii) Replacement of nitrogen in pyrazolidines with oxygen yields equipment isoxazole analog.

(iv) Analogs with lower pKa value passes shower plasma half life.

(v) Substitution at C_4 by methyl group destroys anti-inflammatory activity.

(vi) The most active analog has log P value of 0.7.

2.6 INDOMETHACIN AND OTHER ARYLACETIC ACID DERIVATIVES

The possibility that 5-hydroxytryptamine might be an important mediator of inflammation led to the discovery of indomethacin, after the laboratory evaluation of 350 indole derivatives.

Introduced in 1964, indomethacin is a powerful anti-inflammatory analgesic agent.

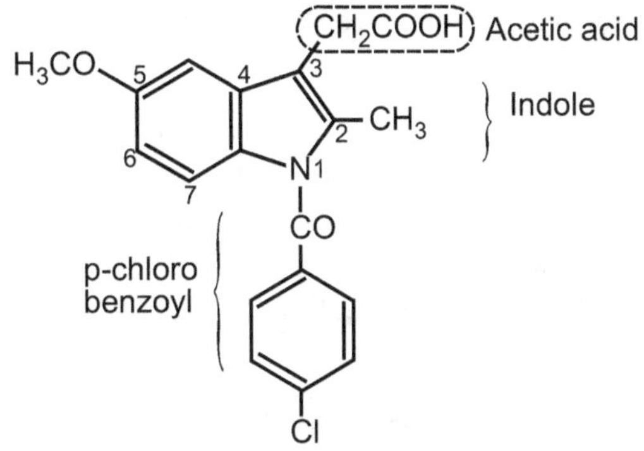

Indomethacin

In man, it is largely metabolised by O-demethylation and N-deacylation. Excretion is facilitated by conjugation with glucuronic acid.

The most frequent side-effects include peptic ulceration, blood disorders, severe frontal headache and GIT disturbances.

Structure-Activity Relationship :

(1) The following substituents generally give expected activities :

(a) Indole substituents :

　5-Methoxy, F, $(CH_3)_2N$;

　5-Methoxy-6-F; 2-Methyl

(b) Benzoyl substituents :

　CF_3 or SCH_3 at para position provides greatest anti-inflammatory activity :

　　p – Cl, F or CH_3S

(c) Acetic acid substituents :

　　α-CH_3, CO_2CH_3

(2) The carboxyl group is necessary for anti-inflammatory activity. The more acidic the carboxyl group, the greater the antirheumatic activity.

(3) N-substitution of indole derivative increases anti-inflammatory activity in the order benzoyl > alkyl > H.

(4) The 1-indene isostere has activity similar to that of indomethacin.

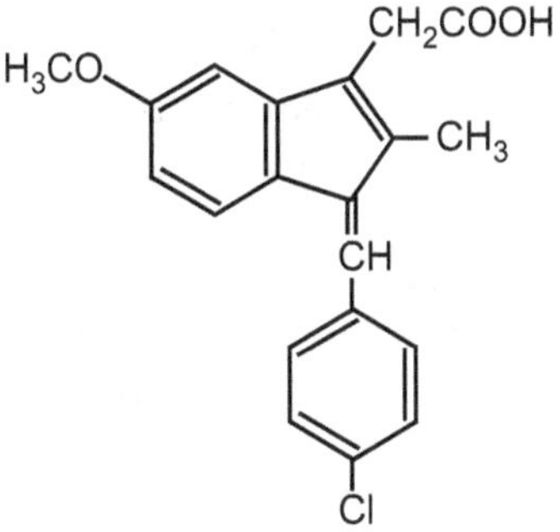

The study of SAR of this class resulted in the development of the following clinically used agents.

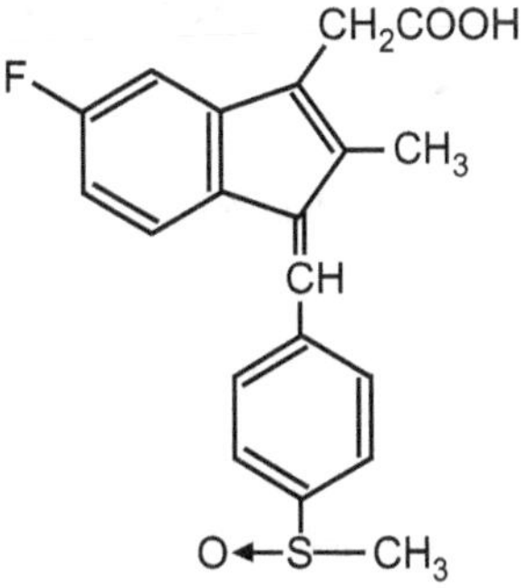

Sulindac

Sulindac is a pro-drug, the active form being its reduced sulfide (–S CH_3) derivative. It is also an indene isostere, substituted by F in the indene and by methylsylphoxide in phenyl group.

　$OCH_3 > (CH_3) N > CH_3 > H$ at 5-position

Pyrroleacetic Acid Derivatives :

(1) Tolmetin

(2) Zomepirac

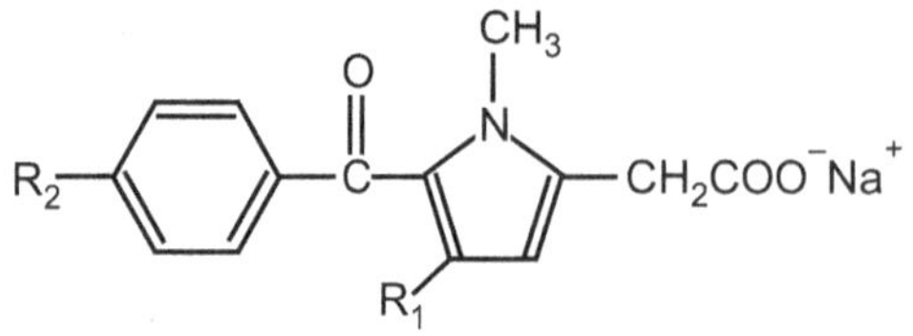

Tolmetin : $R_1 = - H$; $R_2 = - CH_3$

Zomepirac : $R_1 = - CH_3$; $R_2 = - Cl$

2.7 PHENYLACETIC ACID AND PROPIONIC ACID DERIVATIVES

Numerous phenylacetic acid and propionic acid derivatives have been synthesized and found to possess anti-inflammatory activity. The most commonly employed agents from this class are :

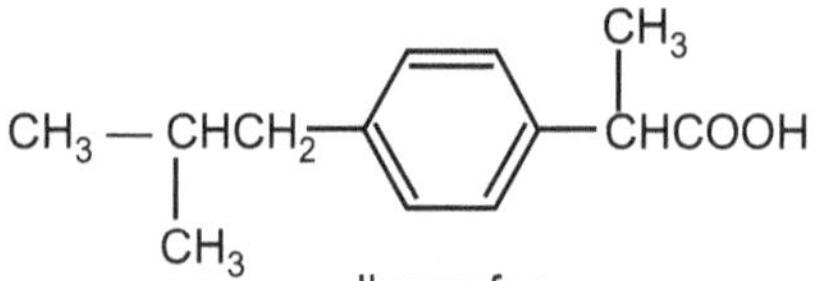

Ibuprofen

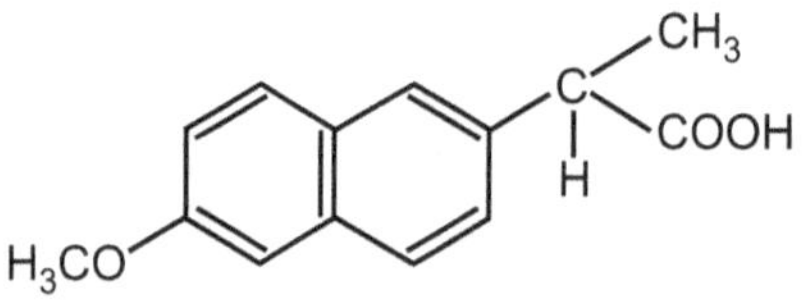

Naproxen

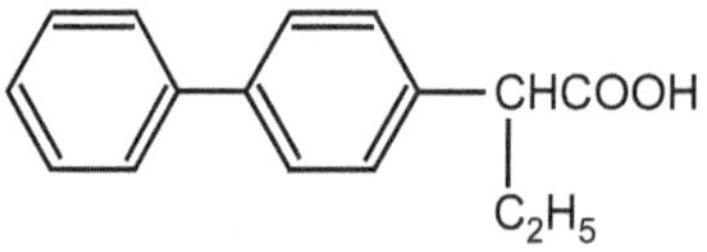

Namoxyrate

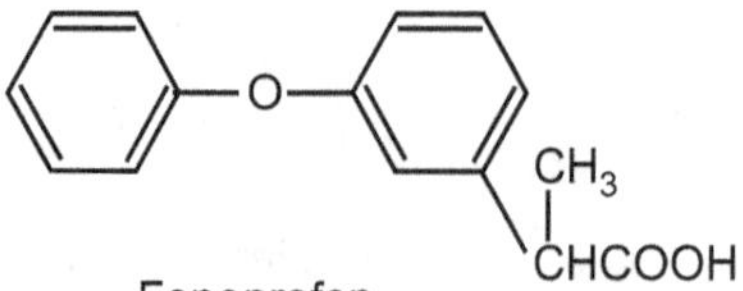

Fenoprofen

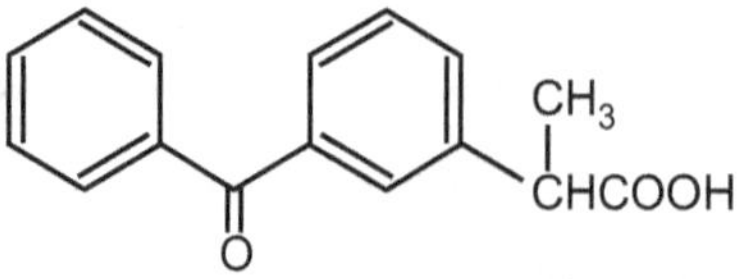

Ketoprofen

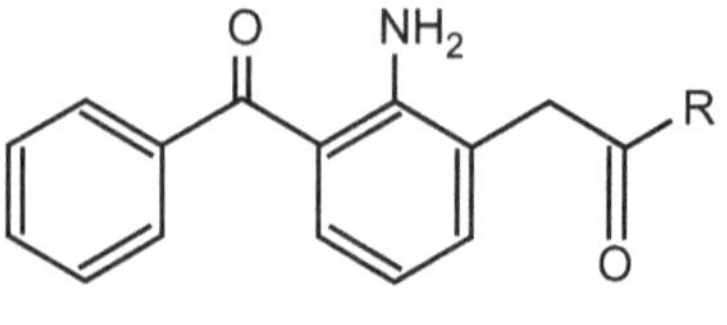

Nepafenac (R = –NH$_2$)

Amfenac (R = – OH)

It is a prodrug. After topical ocular dosing, nepafenac penetrates the cornea and is converted by ocular tissue hydrolases to amfenac, a non-steroidal anti-inflammatory drug.

Indomethacin, piroxicam and ibuprofen inhibit PG - synthesis by macrophages (present in inflammatory exudates as well as by syncoviocytes and chondrocytes which contribute to inflammation of joint) almost to the same extent.

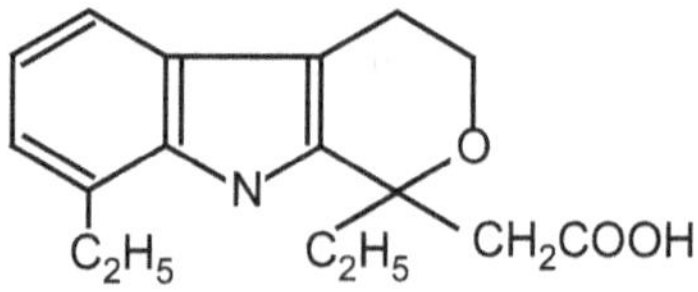

Etodolac (1991)

Etodolac is also suggested for the treatment of osteoporosis. It is a potent anti-inflammatory drug with a high gastric tolerance. The apparent elimination half-life is 7 hours.

It extensively binds to plasma-proteins. Etodolac is found to possess potent anti-inflammatory, anti-arthritic and analgesic activity. It is superior to other NSAIDs in having less faecal blood loss. Chemically, it is 1, 8 - diethyl - 1, 3, 4, 9 - tetrahydro pyrano [3, 4-b] indole -1- acetic acid. In man, a dose of 200 mg per day is suggested as minimum effective dose for the relief of active rheumatoid arthritis.

Several other arylacetic acid derivatives are under clinical trials. These include alcofenac, fenclofenac, pirprofen, prodolic acid, ketoprofen and oxepinac.

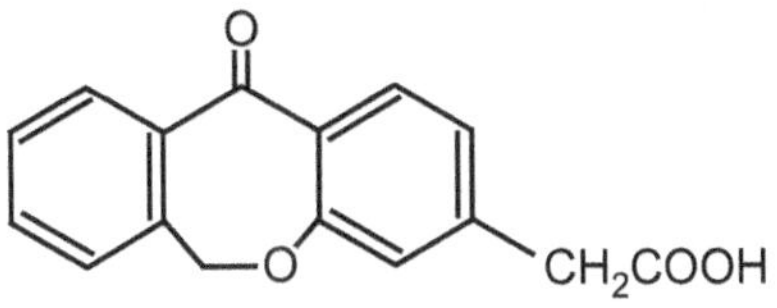

Oxepinac

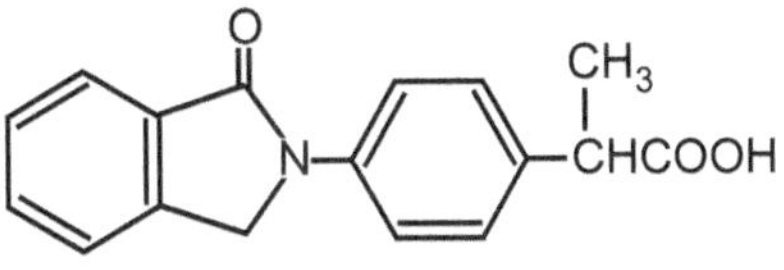

Indoprofen

A hybrid of fenamate and phenylacetic acid is diclofenac.

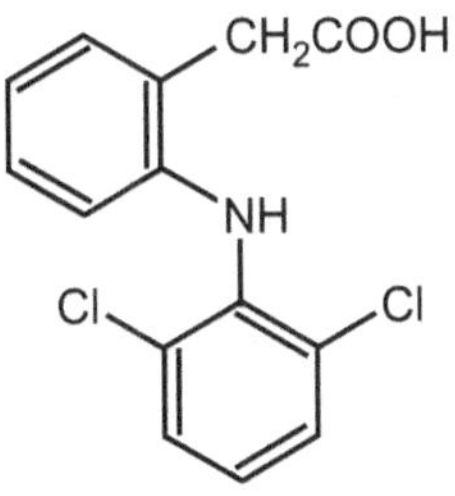

Diclofenac

Replacement of carboxyl group by an ester, alcohol, amide, hydroxamic acid (NHOH) or tetrazole (CHN$_4$) generally produces less active compound. Among enantiomers, activity usually resides in the S(+) isomer.

The metabolism of substituted phenyl acetic acids involves mainly aromatic or aliphatic hydroxylation followed by glucuronide conjugation at the hydroxyl and/or carboxyl group.

2.8 FENAMATES OR DERIVATIVES OF N-ARYLANTHRANILIC ACID

Replacing phenolic OH of salicylic acid by an aryl substituted amino group which results in isosters of aryl ethers of salicylic acid. Fenamates are a family of N-arylanthranilic acids, which are nitrogen analogues of salicylic acid.

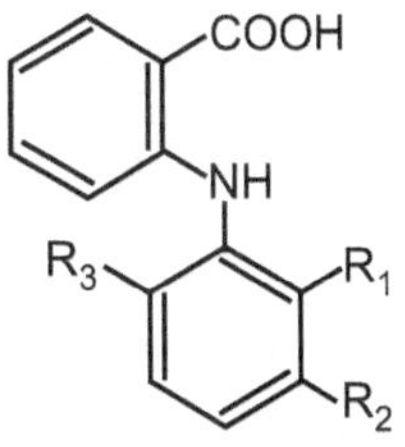

N-arylanthranilic acid

(R$_3$ = H; except in meclofenamic acid)

Mefenamic acid, flufenamic acid and meclofenamic acid are the clinically useful fenamates.

(1) Mefenamic acid : R$_1$ = R$_2$ = − CH$_3$

(2) Flufenamic acid : R$_1$ = − H, R$_2$ = − CF$_3$

(3) Meclofenamic acid :
R$_1$ = − Cl, R$_2$ = − CH$_3$, R$_3$ = − Cl

Mefenamic acid has moderate anti-inflammatory activity and mainly used as a short term analgesic. Diarrhoea, drowsiness and headache are among the principal side-effects.

It is also used in the management of primary dysmenorrhea, which is thought to be caused by excessive concentrations of prostaglandins.

The following heterocyclic isosters of fenamates are under clinical trials.

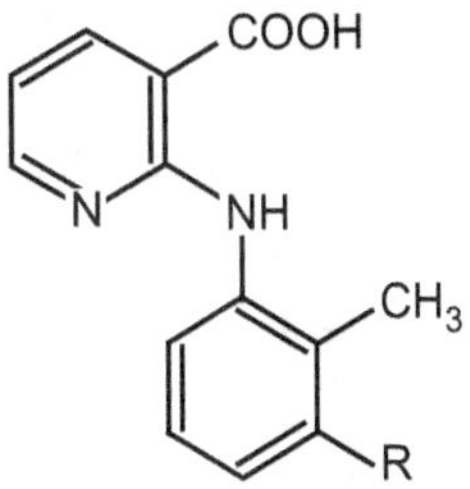

(i) Clonixin : R = − Cl

(ii) Flunixin : R = − CF$_3$

Substituted aza analogues :

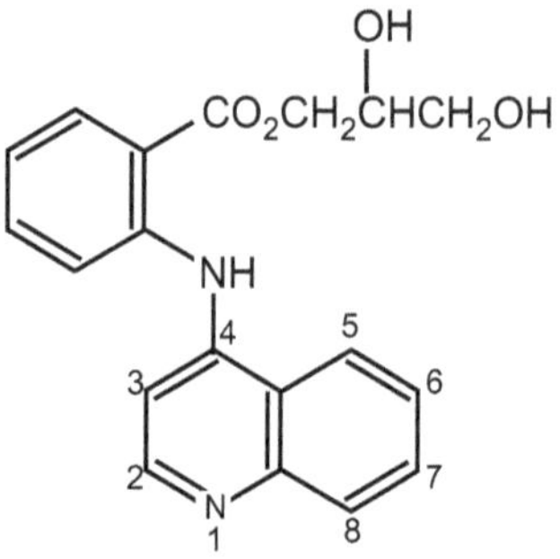

Glafenine : 7-Cl

Floctafenine : 8-CF$_3$

Glafenine is a combination of 7-chloro-quinoline and anthranilic acid. These compounds possess only weak anti-inflammatory activities.

High incidences of anaphylactic reactions and acute renal failure have led to the withdrawal of glafenine in most of the countries.

2.9 MISCELLANEOUS AGENTS

(a) Many o-hydroxy aromatic carboxy-lates have been tried (salicylic acid) in which benzene ring of salicylic acid is replaced by other aromatic or quasiaromatic nuclei. The group of oxicams represents N-aryl-carboxamides of 4-hydroxy-1, 2-benzothiazine 1, 1-dioxides. e.g., piroxicam.

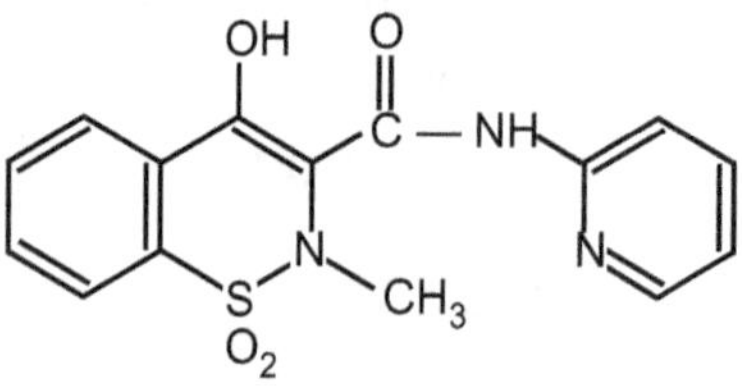

Piroxican
Pfizer (Feldene)
Log P = 0.26, pKa = 4.6

1. The initial compounds, isoquinoline carboxanilides showed AI potency similar to phenylbutazone. The enhanced acid properties of these cyclic β - diketones were responsible in part for their biological activities.

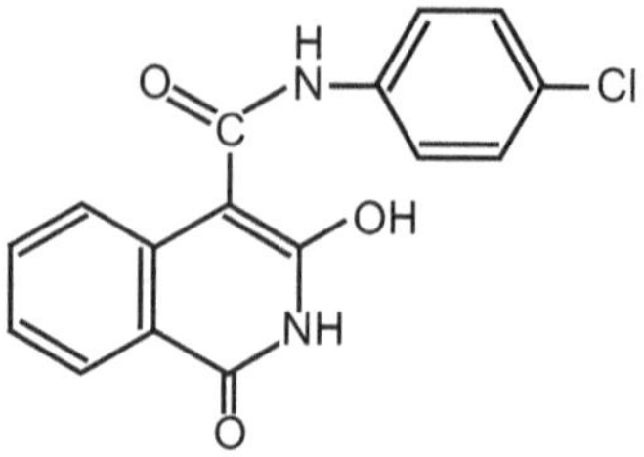

Tesicam

Metabolic studies in animal suggested that chlorine substituted at 4-position of the phenyl ring extended the half-life and duration of action.

2. 2H - 1, 2 - benzothiazine - 3 (4H) - one - 1, 1-dioxides as bioesters of tesicam was synthesized. This series did not prove fruitful. Consequently, the isomeric carboxamides of the 4 - hydroxy - 2H - 1, 2 - benzothiazine - 1, 1 - dioxide were prepared.

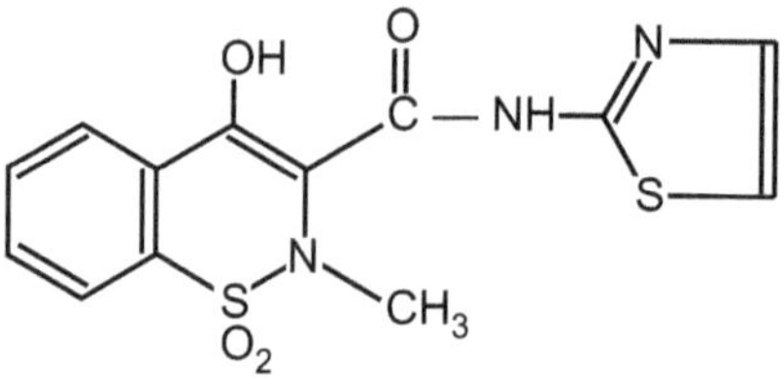

Sudoxicam

Sudoxicam is more potent than testicam and has a longer duration of action.

3. Further research led to piroxicam which has a half-life of 45 hours.

4. The tautomeric structures impart further stability to the enolate anion. Such stabilization of the enolate anion would thereby contribute to a further increase in the acidity of the conjugated acid.

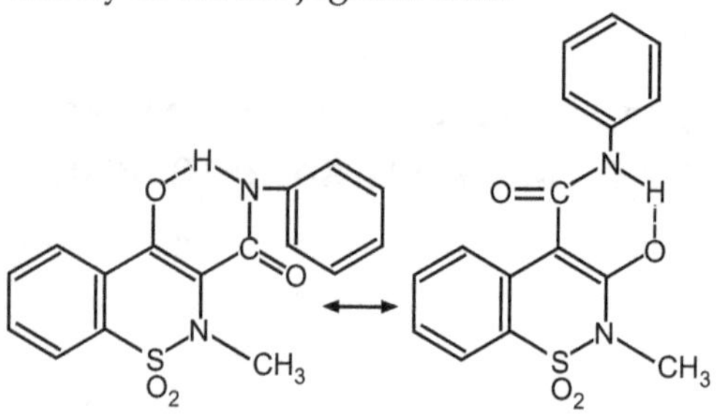

III　　　　　　　　IV

V　　　　　　VI

5. It is assumed that first step of the reaction involves a reduction of the enzymatic Fe^{+++} to Fe^{++} by abstracting H-atom at C_9 of arachidonic acid to give a delocalised radical which reacts with molecular oxygen. This results into formation of superoxide anion which is metabolised to reactive oxygen species including H_2O_2, hydroxyl radical and singlet oxygen. These reactive oxygen species are thought to contribute to the inflammatory process and tissue destruction.

Piroxicam and tolmetin are recently developed promising agents having good analgesic-antipyretic and anti-inflammatory activities. Both these agents have an ability to inhibit cyclo-oxygenase enzyme. They are rapidly and completely absorbed from GIT, and get extensively bound to plasma-proteins.

Tolmetin

Piroxicam is metabolised mainly by hydroxylation in the pyridyl ring followed by glucuronide conjugation, while tolmetin metabolism occurs by the oxidation of para methyl group to COOH. The metabolites are excreted in urine in both, free and conjugated forms. Piroxicam is better tolerated agent, having long half-life.

Both these drugs cause gastric erosions and increase in the bleeding time. The most frequent adverse effects include nausea, vomiting, epigastric pain, anxiety, skin rash, gastric and peptic ulceration.

Meloxicam : It is structurally related to piroxicam and belongs to oxicam family.

SAR for Oxicams :

(i) The nitrogen of benzithiazine having CH_3 substituent and electron with drawing groups. (C_1, CF_3) on anilide phenyl ring increase anti-inflammatory activity.

(ii) The introduction of a heterocyclic ring in the amide oxide chain significantly increase the activity. Sudoxicam is more potent than indomethacin.

(iii) The benzothiazines having pKa range of 6 to 8 have more activity.

(b) Gold compounds : The clinically used agents from this category include aurothioglucose, auranofin and gold sodium thiomalate. In all these agents, the gold is directly attached to sulphur. Hence, these compounds are supposed to act by the inhibition of vital sulfhydryl systems in the body. Gold gets accumulated in the lysosomes where it inhibits the activity of acid phosphatase, β-glucuronidase and cathepsin enzymes which have catalytic role in various inflammatory disorders.

In addition, gold compounds inhibit the synthesis of connective tissues. Hence, they can be used in the treatment of rheumatoid arthritis in patients who do not respond well to the therapy with aspirin-like drugs.

They are usually administered by intramuscular route, since the absorption from oral route is erratic and incomplete. They are extensively bound to plasma-proteins. Their

Aurothioglucose   Auranofin   Gold sodium thiomalate

onset of action is slow and signs of inflammation are reduced in intensity gradually. The slow rate of excretion of gold compounds can be enhanced by concomitant administration of sulfhydryl agents like, penicillamine and dimercaprol. They are primarily excreted in urine and faeces.

The adverse effects associated with gold therapy include cutaneous reactions, aplastic anaemia, leucopenia, agranulocytosis, thrombocytopenia, nephrosis, hepatitis and peripheral neuritis. They are contraindicated in patients with anaemia, renal disease, hepatic dysfunction and in pregnancy.

(c) D-penicillamine : Only D-isomer is clinically used in the treatment of rheumatoid arthritis because L-penicillamine is reported to cause optic neuritis due to its anti-pyridoxine activity. Being a metabolite of penicillin, it has a structural resemblance with cysteine. In certain cases, combination of D-penicillamine with aspirin-like drugs may give better results. It alongwith a disulphide metabolite is excreted in urine and faeces. Due to its high toxicity, it should not be used frequently or for a long-term treatment.

(d) Abatacept : It is a fusion protein composed of an immunoglobulin fused to the extra cellular domain of CTLA-4, a molecule capable of binding B7. It is used in delaying the progressing of structural damage and reducing symptoms of rheumatoid arthritis. It is also beneficial in the treatment of psoriasis and in organ transplantation.

(e) Leflunomide : It is a pyrimidine synthesis inhibitor used to treat rheumatoid arthritis and psoriatic arthritis.

(f) Other agents which have beneficial effects in the treatment of inflammatory disorders include :

(i) Antimalarial agents : Chloroquine and hydroxy chloroquine.

(ii) Glucocorticoids

(iii) Immunosuppressive agents : Azathioprine, cyclophosphamide.

(iv) Sulphonamides : Diflumidone.

2.10 MECHANISM OF ACTION OF NON-STEROIDAL ANTI-INFLAMMATORY AGENTS (NSAIDs)

(a) Biosynthesis of prostaglandins : The biochemical effects of NSAIDs include inhibition of lysosomal membrane stabilization, inhibition of the biosynthesis of mucopolysaccharides, uncoupling oxidative phosphorylation, fibrinolytic activity, sulfhydryl disulfide stabilization, collagenase production and at times suppression of lymphocytic functions.

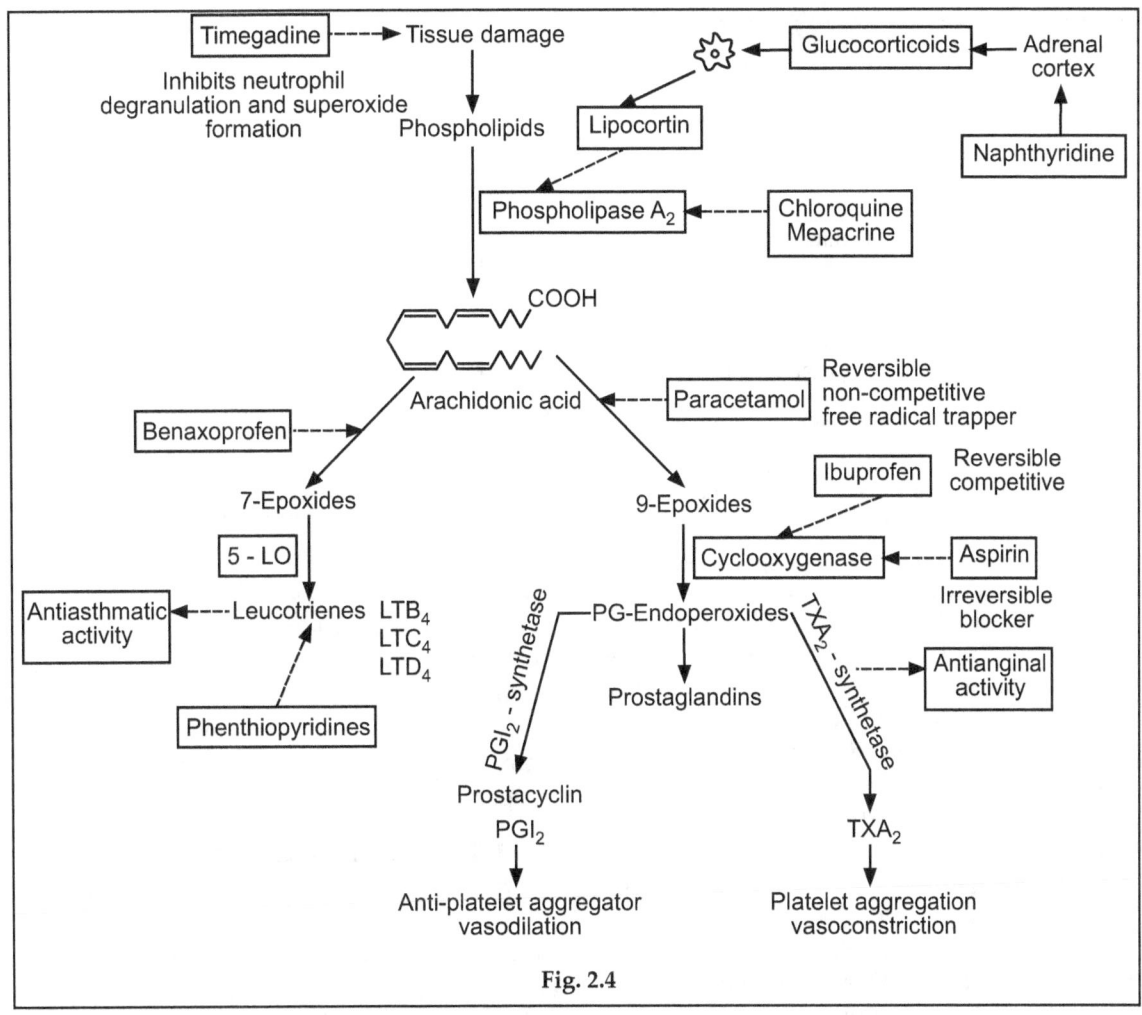

Fig. 2.4

Cyclooxygenase catalyses two enzymatic processes (1) The incorporation of oxygen in a dioxygenase step to form PGG_2 and (2) the subsequent peroxidation to PGH_2. The reaction is initiated by the stereospecific abstraction of hydrogen at C_{13} followed by oxygen attack at C_{11} and C_{15} and ring closure between C_8 and C_{12} in next reaction. The presence of hematin and molecular oxygen is required. Most of NSAIDs act by inhibiting cyclooxygenase by preventing the abstraction of hydrogen from C_{13} and therefore blocking peroxidation at C_{11} and C_{15}. This action is highly specific, for similar abstraction and

peroxidation reactions at other points in the fatty acid molecule are not inhibited.

On the basis of mechanism of action, these chemically diversified NSAIDs can be broadly divided into :

(a) Reversible competitive inhibitors : Examples of this class are fatty acids, closely related to the substrate which have a comparable affinity for the cyclooxygenase (CO) and lipooxygenase (LO) enzymes but are not converted to oxygenated inflammatory products of CO pathway (i.e., prostaglandins) and LO pathway (leucotrienes). Ibuprofen has a binding affinity for cyclooxygenase similar

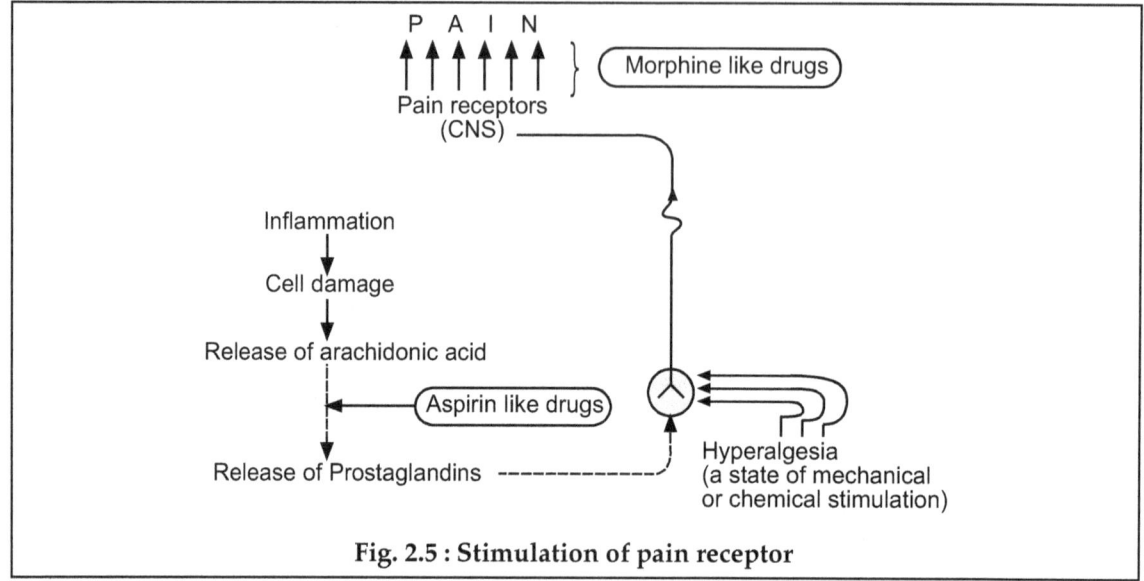

Fig. 2.5 : Stimulation of pain receptor

to that of arachidonic acid. The carboxyl function of aryl acidic NSAIDs is said to resemble the terminal carboxyl of arachidonic acid while the planar hydrophobic groups bind to the enzyme to prevent hydrogen abstraction at C-13. The presence of aryl halogen is supposed to enhance this activity due to its lipophilicity.

(b) Reversible non-competitive inhibitors : The reversible non-competitive inhibitors have anti-oxidant or radical trapping properties. During inflammation, a continual presence of lipid peroxides induces a free radical chain reaction that sustains cyclooxygenase activity. This can be blocked by an addition of radical scavengers or anti-oxidants (e.g. paracetamol) which acts as reversible non-competitive inhibitors.

(c) Irreversible inhibitors : The irreversible inactivation of cyclooxygenase is done by aspirin through the transacetylation of the lysyl amino group in the enzyme which is important for its activity. As salicylic acid is chemically incapable of acylating the enzyme, the anti-inflammatory action of salicylic acid may depend more on other mechanisms such as inhibition of leukocyte emegration and lysosomal stabilization.

Aspirin like drugs block this release of prostaglandins in the brain, followed by peripheral vasodilation and increased sweating resulting into considerable heat loss from the body. This brings down the body temperature to its normal.

2.11 TREATMENT OF GOUT

Gout is a term representing a heterogenous group of genetic and acquired diseases manifested by hyperuricemia and a characteristic acute inflammatory arthritis induced by crystals of monosodium urate monohydrate. Some patients develop aggregated deposits of these crystals (tophi) in and around the joints of the extremities that can lead to severe cripping. Many patients develop a chronic interstitial nephropathy. In addition, uric acid urolithiasis is common in gout. Primarily gout is chiefly a disease of adult men. The frequency of gout is increased in patients taking diuretics, especially of the thiazide group. Gout in all of its forms makes up about 5% of arthritis cases. Humans lack uricase, therefore, uric acid is the end product of purine metabolism. In normal subjects, approximately one third of uric acid disposed of each day is degraded by bacteria in the gut and two third is excreted unchanged by kidney. Both increased purine biosynthesis and decreased renal excretion of uric acid play important roles in the pathogenesis of primary hyperuricemia.

Once the uric acid is filtered by renal glomeruli, it is almost completely reabsorbed into circulation from proximal tubules. In normal circumstances, some of the reabsorbed uric acid is again driven back into the urine by distal tubules. Due to low solubility of undissociated form of urates, the crystals of sodium urate (the end product of purine metabolism) get deposited in the joint cavities and on articular cartilages. Their deposition initiates inflammatory reactions which involve local infiltration of phagocytes that, after ingestion of urate also release chemotactic substances and probably lactic acid. Lactic acid further loweres down the pH of the surrounding medium, resulting into further deposition of uric acid. The phagocytosis of urate crystals releases a glycoprotein which is responsible to produce acute gouty arthritis. An acute attack of gout occurs as a result of an inflammatory reaction. Usually, small joints are affected before larger ones.

Uricosuric agents enhance the rate of excretion of uric acid by reducing the rate of its tubular reabsorption. They thus relieve the signs and symptoms of acute attack of gout and offer symptomatic relief in this condition. Phenylbutazone is such a uricosuric agent.

(a) Colchicine :

It is an alkaloid obtained from colchicum autumnale. It was clinically introduced for the treatment of acute attacks of gout in 1763 by Von Storck.

It does not possess analgesic activity. In inflammatory disorders, it is effective only against acute gouty arthritis. It neither effectively inhibit the prostaglandin biosynthesis nor it influences the tubular reabsorption of uric acid. It probably acts to inhibit the release of lactic acid during phagocytosis of the urate crystals. Its central effects include, depression of the respiratory centers, central vasomotor stimulation and antipyretic action.

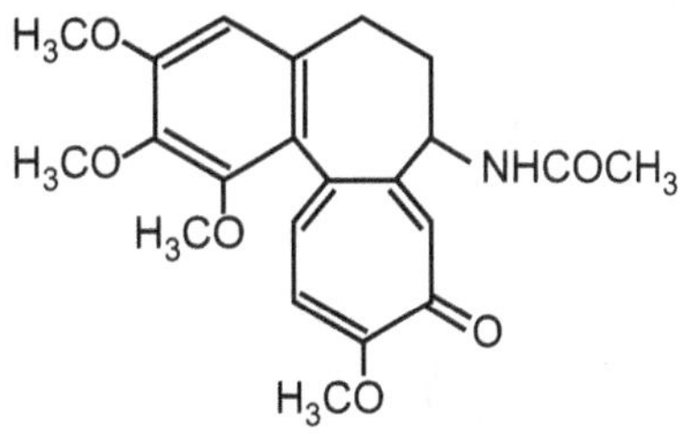

Colchicine

The alkaloid is readily absorbed from GIT and by intravenous route. The drug alongwith its metabolites is mainly excreted through urine and faeces.

The adverse effects are mild and include nausea, vomiting, diarrhoea, abdominal pain and leucopenia. These effects appear in the dose-dependent fashion and are reversed, if treatment is discontinued. In severe toxicity, death usually results due to respiratory arrest.

(b) Allopurinol :

Chemically, it resembles in structure with hypoxanthine. It inhibits the formation of uric acid by competitively antagonising xanthine oxidase enzyme which catalyses the conversion of hypoxanthine to xanthine the precursor for uric acid synthesis. Due to the structural similarity, it competes with hypoxanthine which is the substrate for xanthine oxidase enzyme. At higher concentration, due to the non-specific nature of the enzyme, it acts as non-competitive inhibitor. Instead of hypoxanthine, allopurinol is attacked by xanthine oxidase and is converted primarily to oxypurinol which is also effective enzyme inhibitor. Thus by inhibiting the uric acid formation, it lowers down hyperuricemia and prevents the formation of uric acid stones. In order to enhance therapeutic effectiveness, allopurinol may sometimes be combined with uricosuric agent.

The adverse reactions include, nausea, vomiting, diarrhoea, gastric irritation, headache, fever, drowsiness, and cutaneous reactions. In some patients, hypersensitivity reactions may also be seen.

Allopurinol　　　　　　　Oxypurinol

Febuxostat : It is a xanthine oxidase inhibitor used in the treatment of hyperuricemia and gout.

The pKa of uric acid is 5.6. The solubility of undissociated urates is usually low. Hence, their solubility can be increased by inducing their ionisation.

Hence, alkalinization of urine is one of the effective ways to minimise the intra-renal urate deposition.

Probenecid and sulfinpyrazone also mobilise the uric acid. They are also useful agents in the treatment of chronic gout disorders though they lack analgesic and anti-inflammatory activities.

Recent strategies adopted to minimize the side effects of NSAIDs include the use of the dual LOX/COX inhibitors, the use of selective COX-2 inhibitors and the use of hybrid molecules made up of non-selective or selective COX inhibitors together with a nitric oxide releasing function. Recent data revealed serious cardiovascular side effects to selective COX-2 inhibitors. In addition, such drugs only minimize the development of new gastric ulcers but do not affect the existing ones. The strategy invovling the use of hybrid molecules made up of non-selective COX inhibitors together with a nitric oxide donar, constitute one of the most promising approaches,

because nitric oxide supports several endogeneous GIT defence mechanisms, including increase in mucus, bicarbonate secretions, increase in mucosal blood flow and inhibition of activation of proinflammatory cells. Moreover because of the beneficial cardiovascular effects of NO, such drugs are expected to be devoid of the potential adverse CVS effects associated with the use of selective COX-2 inhibitors. Among those NO-NSAIDs that came into clinical trials are nitroaspirin, nitronaproxene, nitroketoprofen, nitroibuprofen etc. Among the nitirc oxide donors adopted to prove the validity of this principle are furoxans, oximes, hydrazides and organic nitrates.

This may be due to a reduction in the level of the desirable platelet aggregation inhibitor and vasodilatory prostacyclin (PGI$_2$) in conjunction with an increased level of the undesirable potent platelet activator and aggregator thromoboxane A2 (TxA$_2$).

At nanomolar concentrations NO reversibly activates soluble guanylate cyclase by 400 fold, catalyzing the conversion of GTP to c-GMP. Elevation of c-GMP relaxes vascular smooth muscles, inhibits platelet aggregation and adhesion and blocks the adhesion of white cells to blood vessel walls. Similarly, NO acts as a critical mediator of gastrointestinal mucosal defense, exerting many of the same actions as prostaglandins in the GIT.

Inhibition of 5-lipo-oxygenase results in the decrease of autocoids which are involved in the pathophysiological produciton of gastrointensional ulceration and also promote inflammation due to chemotactic effects. Hence, the discovery of novel dual and selective inhibors of COX-2 and 5-LO has led to a new generation of NSAIDs.

Recently developed NSAIDs

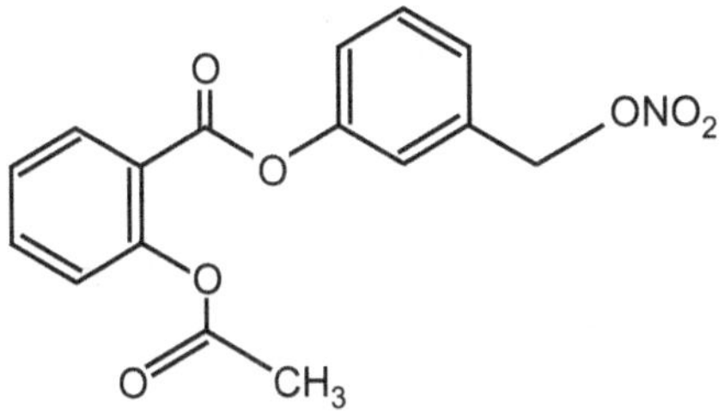

NO-aspirin

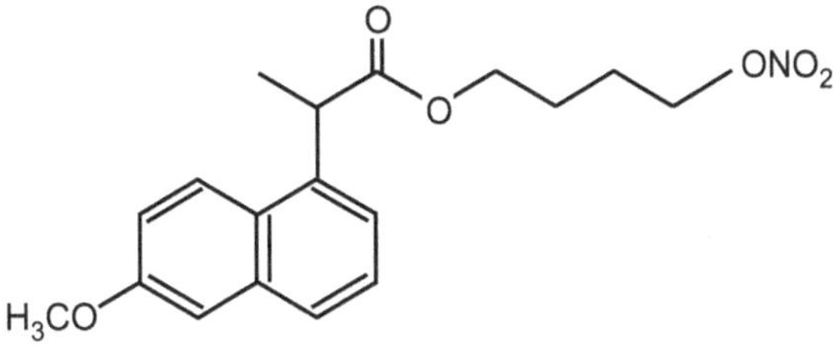

NO-naproxen

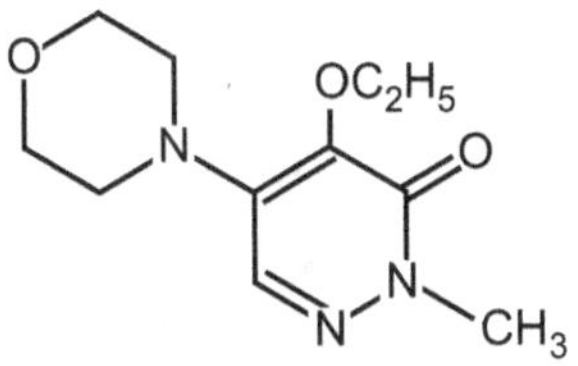

Emarfazone

(Japan, Nandran)

(inhibits vascular permeability and
release of bradykinin)

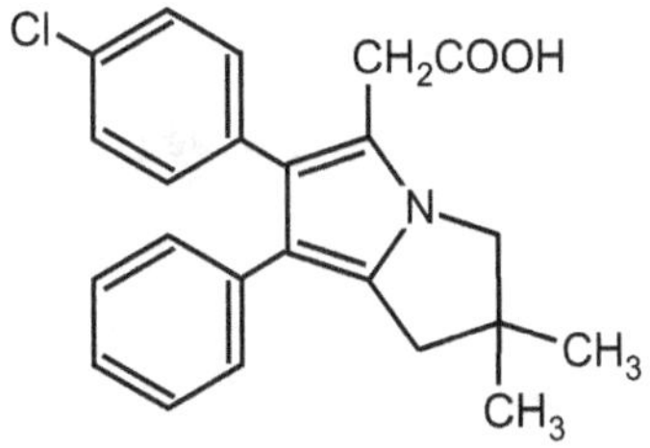

Licofelone

(dual COX/LOX inhibitor)

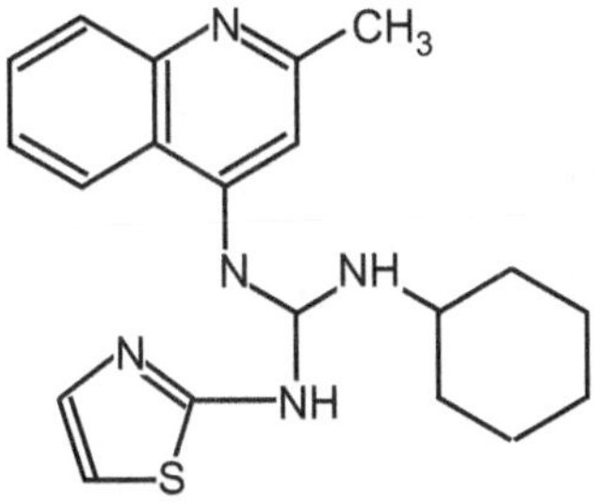

Timegadine (1983)

(inhibits neutrophil degranulation
and superoxide production)

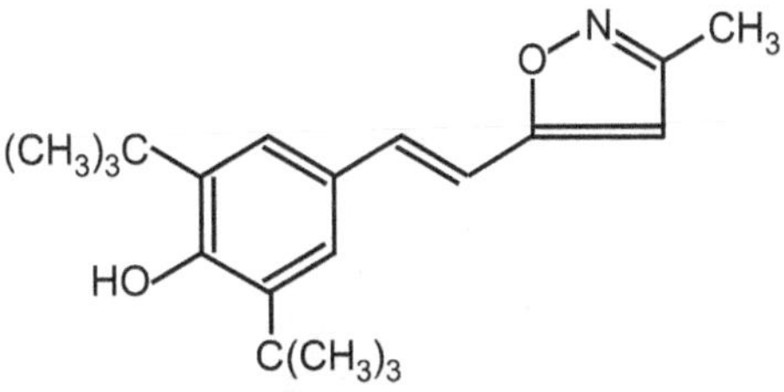

Isoxazole (1993)

(dual inhibitor of CO & 5-LO)

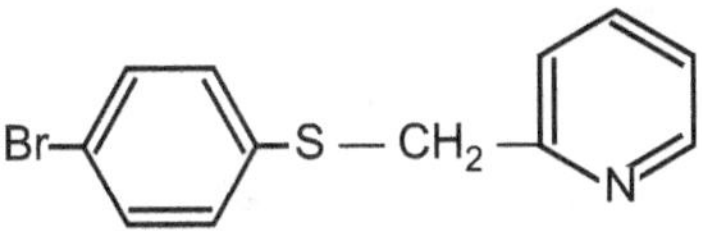

Phenthiopyridine (1987)

(inhibits immune complex
induced inflammation)

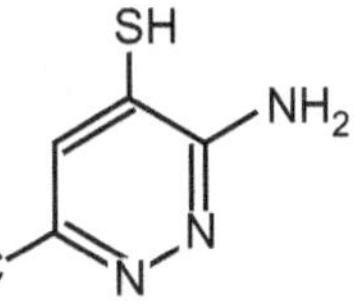

ES-1007 (Germany)

(central mode of action)

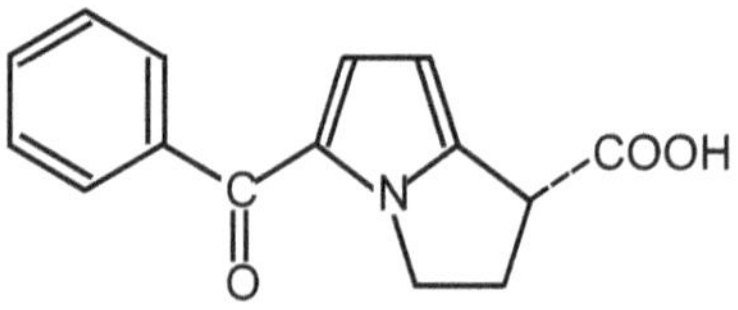

Ketorolac (1990)

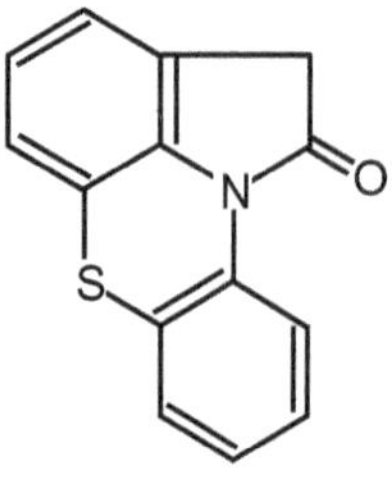

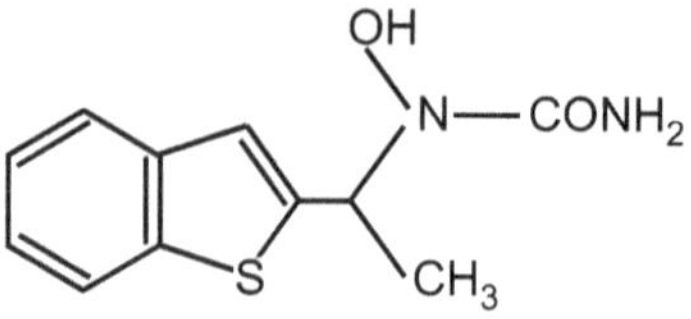

Zileuton
(It blocks leukotriene synthesis)

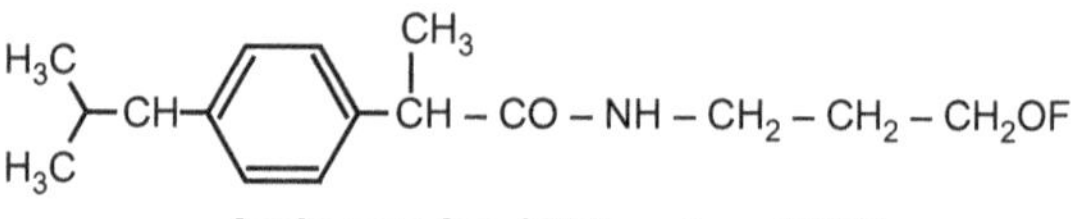

Oxindole carboxamide (1989)

(dual inhibitor of CO and 5-LO)

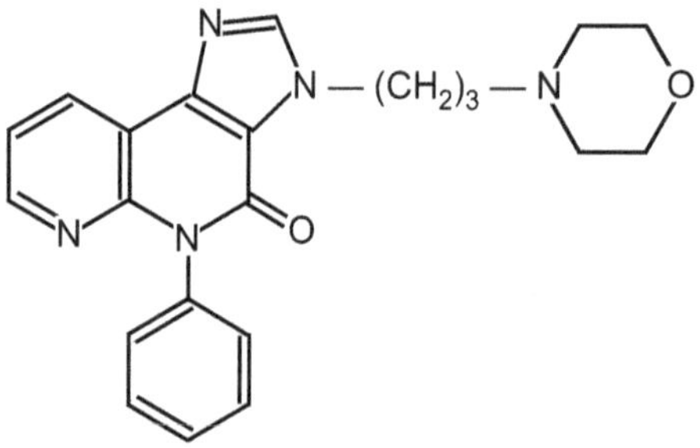

Aminoprofen (Aldounion, 1990)

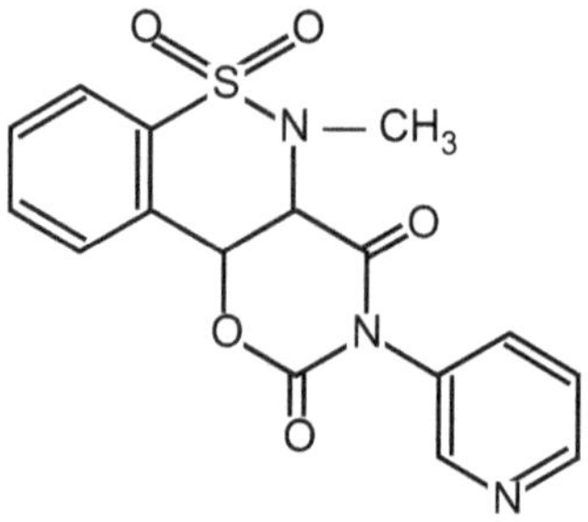

Naphthyridine (1994)

(induces release of endogenous
Glucocorticoids)

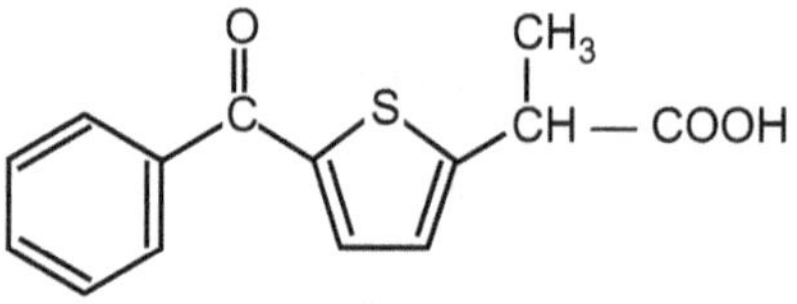

Droxicam (Abbott, 1990)

Tiaprofenic acid

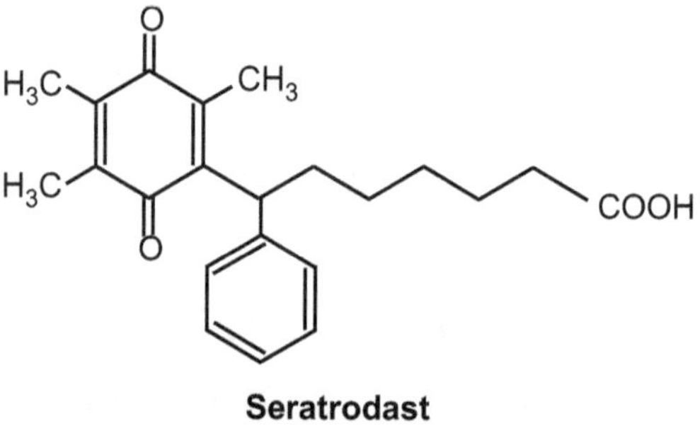

Seratrodast
(It blocks thromboxane receptors)

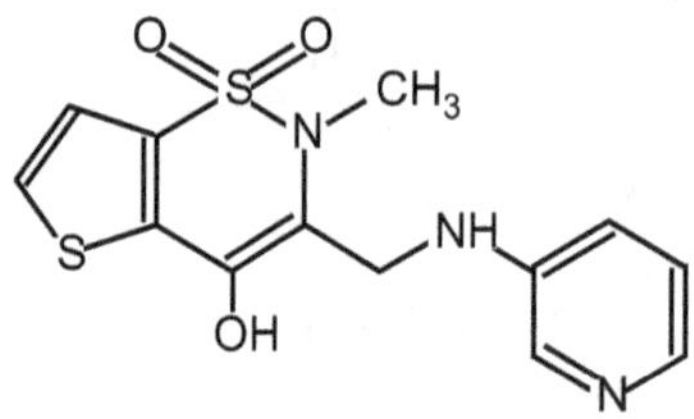

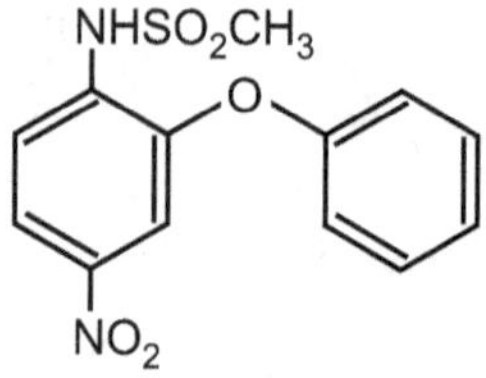

Tenoxicam (Hoffmann-La-Roche, 1987)

Nimesulide
(Preferential COX-2 inhibitor)

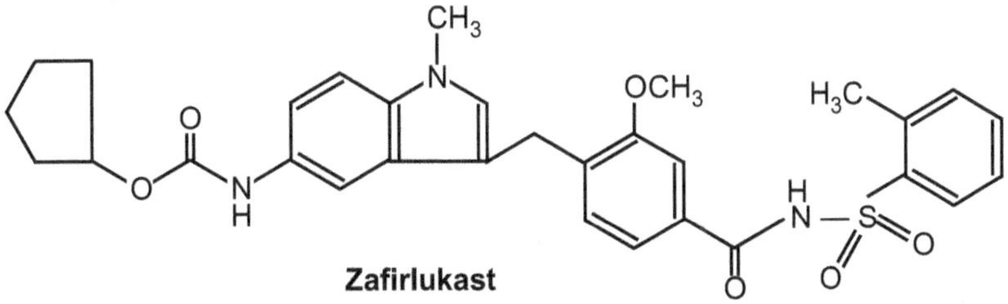

Zafirlukast

(It blocks leukotriene receptor)

Thromboxane synthase inhibitors : Low doses of aspirin impair platelet TXA_2 synthesis with no effect on formation of prostacyclin by the vascular endothelium. Aspirin acetylates the CO and therefore the inhibitory effect remains effective until new enzyme is produced. Whereas the vascular endothelium is capable of generating new enzyme, the platelets do not have the biochemical machinery necessary for protein synthesis. Therefore, the ability of platelets to form TXA_2 is blocked while prostacyclin synthesis recontinue after exposure to aspirin. This explains the anti-thrombotic activity of aspirin. Other specific thromboxane synthase inhibitors include :

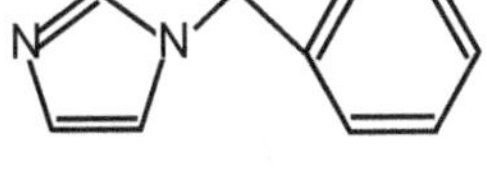

Sumatriptan : It is a selective $5HT_1$-receptor agonist used in the treatment of migrane attack. It belongs to triptan class. It affects a natural chemical (serotonin) that constricts blood vessels in the brain. It may also block other pain pathways in the brain. Other examples include zolmitriptan, naratriptan, rizatriptan, eletriptan, almotriptan and frovatriptan.

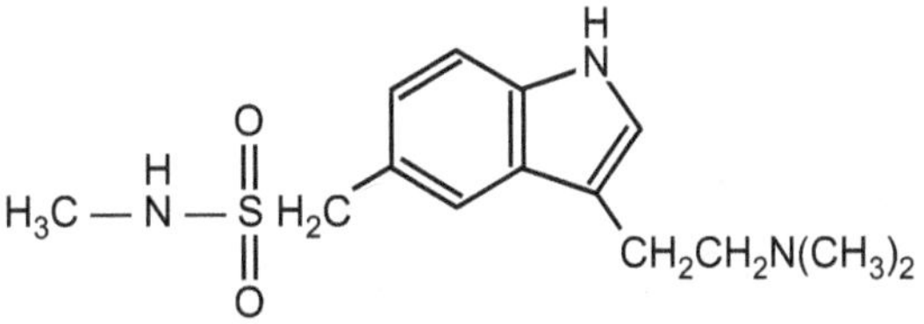

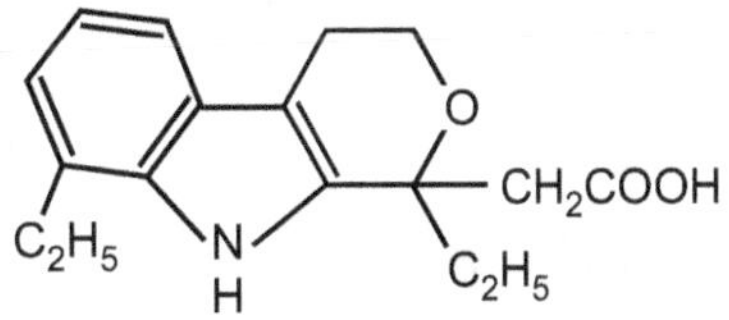

Etodolac (1991)

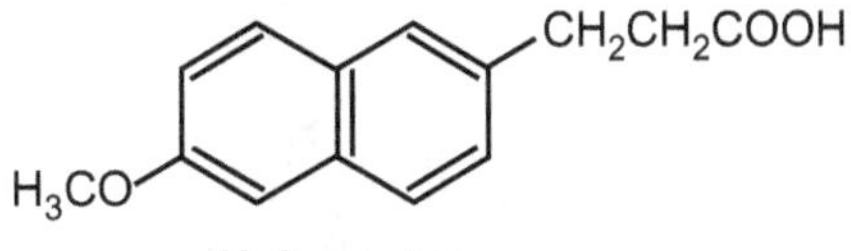

Nabumetone
(Naproxen derivative)

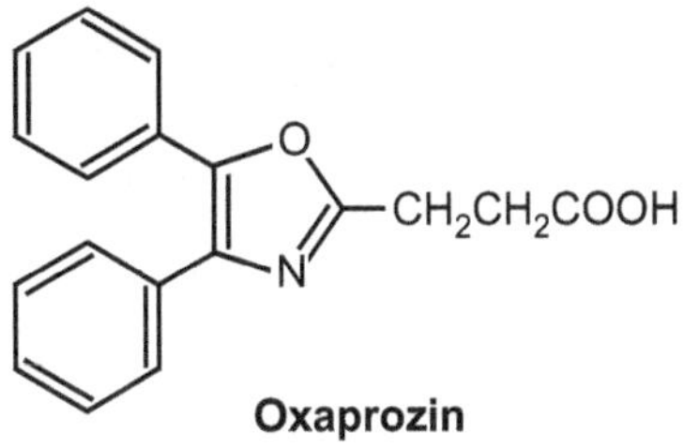

Benzyl imidazole

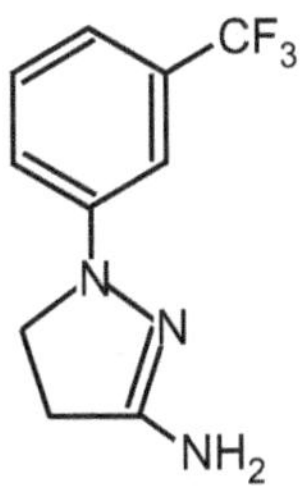

BW 755 C

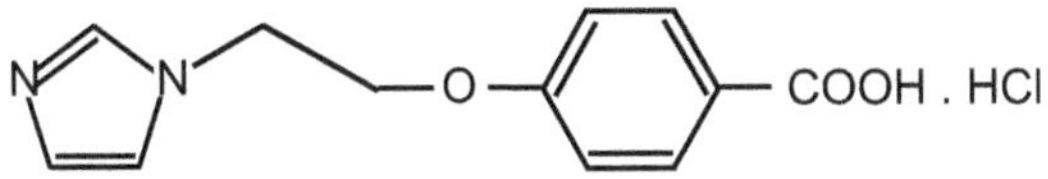

Dazoxiben

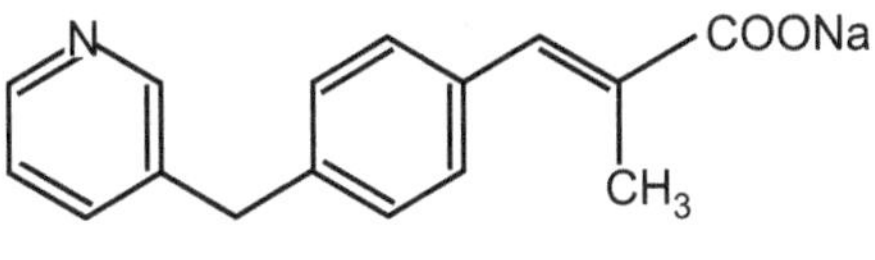

OKY 1518

Oxaprozin

COX-2 selective inhibitors :

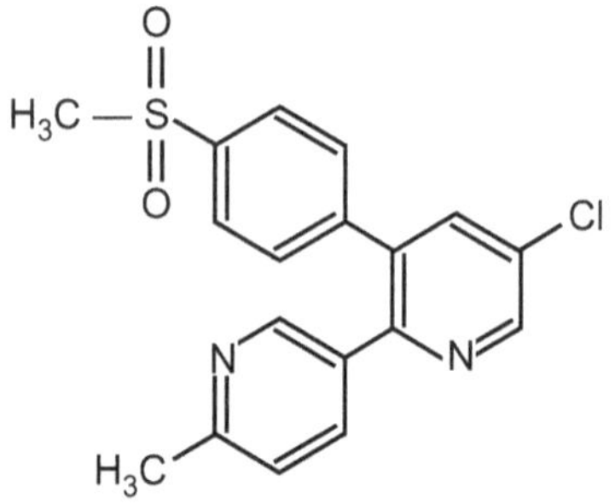

Etoricoxib

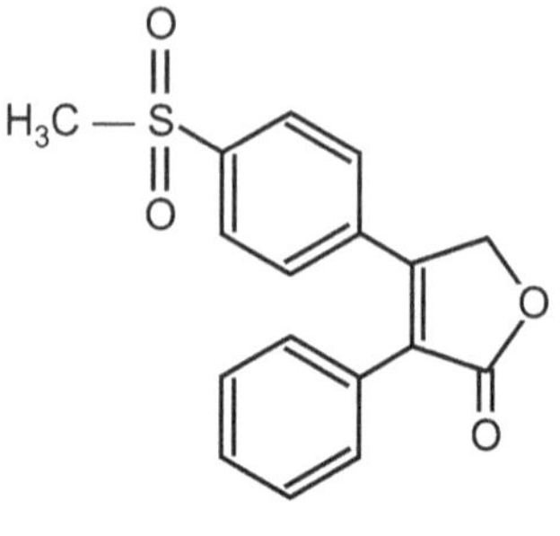

Rofecoxib (Merck)
withdrawn in 2004

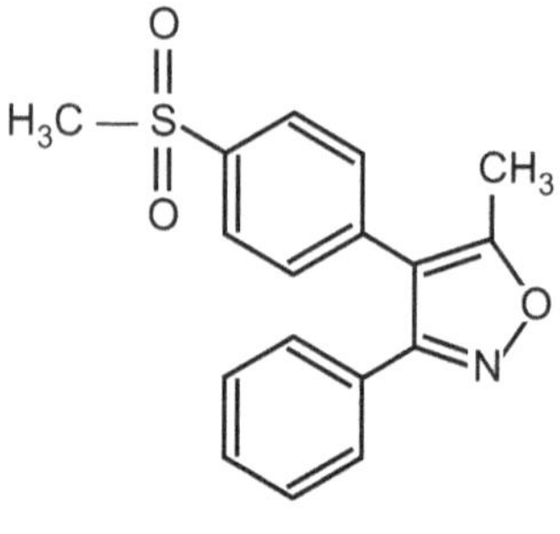

Valdecoxib (Searle)
withdrawn in 2005

Application of bio-isosterism in selective COX₂-inhibitors.

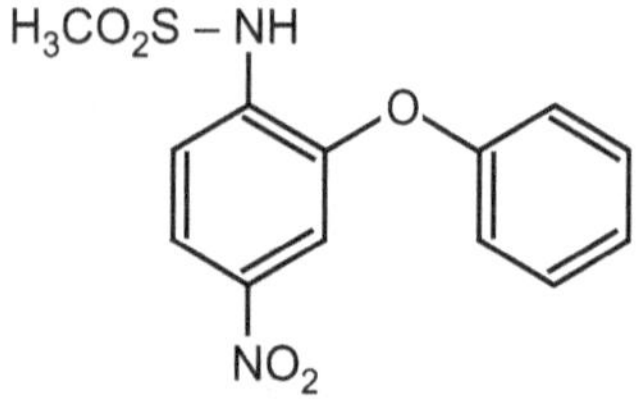

Nimesulide

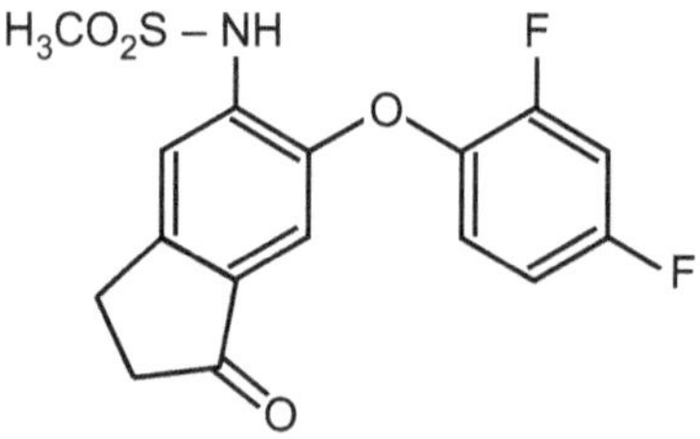

Flosulide

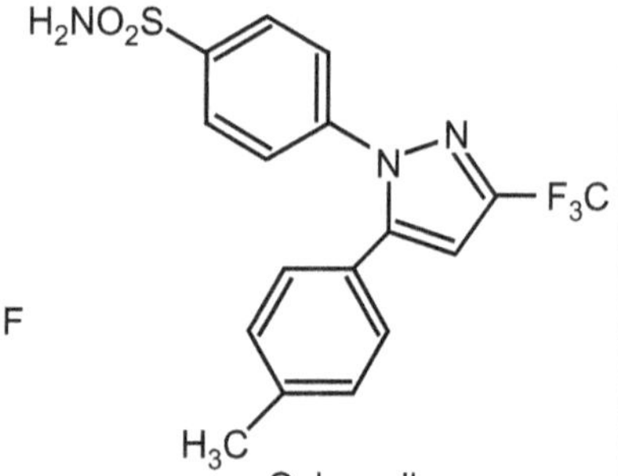

Celecoxib

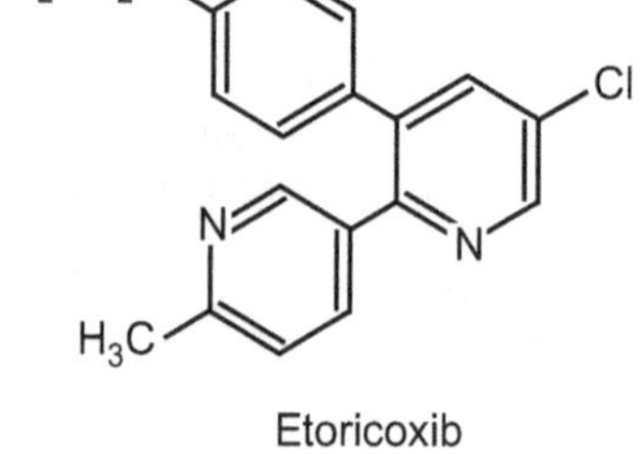

Etoricoxib

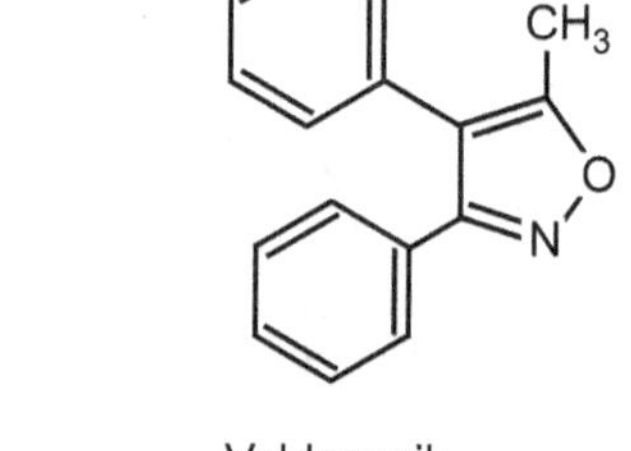

Valdecoxib

Synthesis

(I) Ibuprofen :

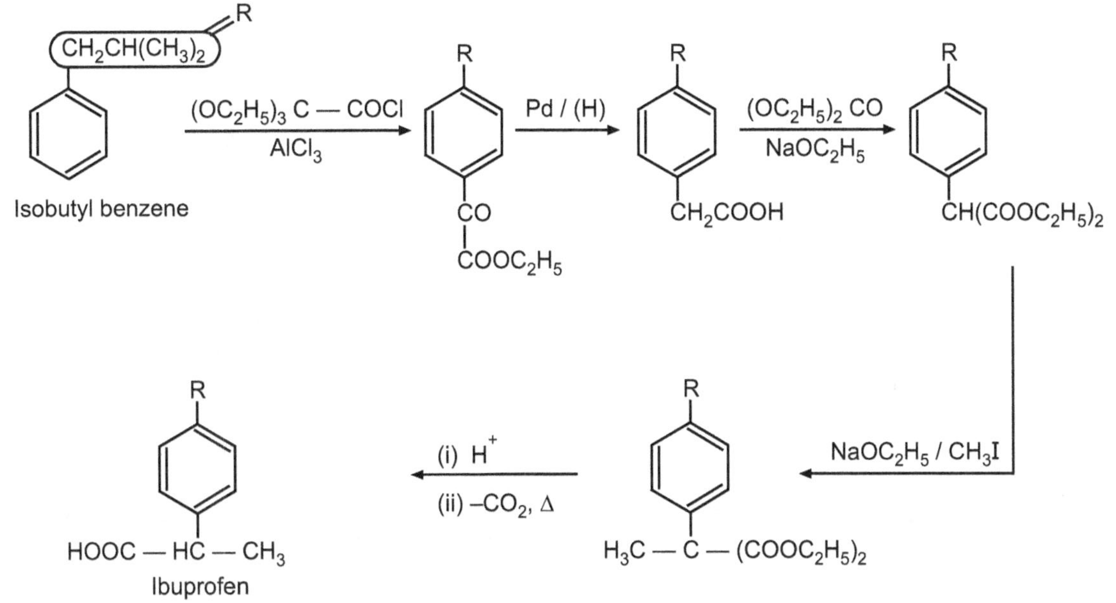
R
$CH_2CH(CH_3)_2$
$(OC_2H_5)_3$ C — COCl
$AlCl_3$
Isobutyl benzene
CO
$COOC_2H_5$
Pd / (H)
CH_2COOH
$(OC_2H_5)_2$ CO
$NaOC_2H_5$
$CH(COOC_2H_5)_2$
$NaOC_2H_5$ / CH_3I
H_3C — C — $(COOC_2H_5)_2$
(i) H^+
(ii) $-CO_2$, Δ
HOOC — HC — CH_3
Ibuprofen

(II) Diclofenac:

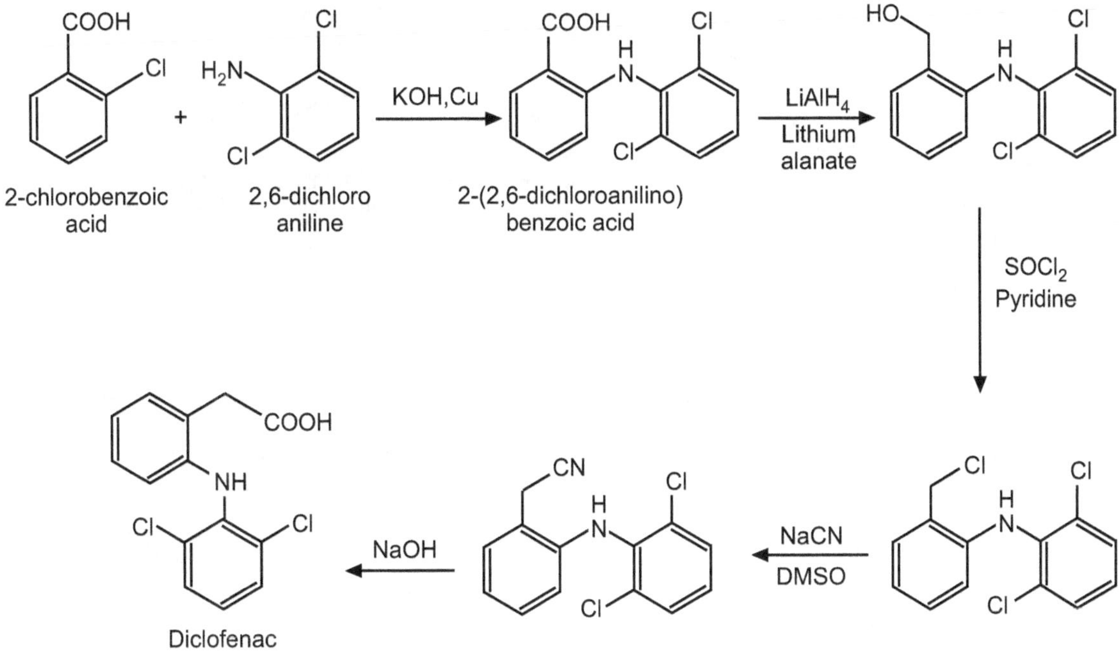
COOH
Cl
H_2N
2-chlorobenzoic acid
2,6-dichloro aniline
KOH,Cu
H
N
2-(2,6-dichloroanilino) benzoic acid
$LiAlH_4$
Lithium alanate
HO
$SOCl_2$
Pyridine
NaCN
DMSO
CN
NaOH
NH
COOH
Diclofenac

(III) Paracetamol :

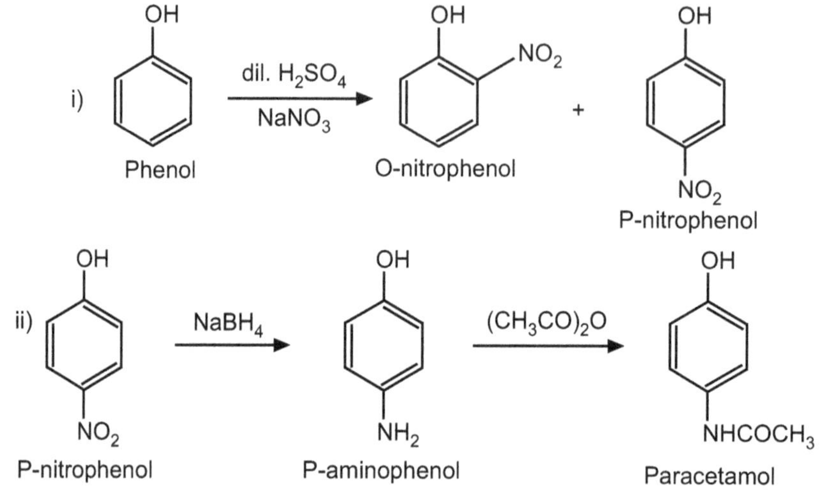

i)

Phenol　$\xrightarrow[\text{NaNO}_3]{\text{dil. H}_2\text{SO}_4}$　O-nitrophenol　+　P-nitrophenol

ii)

P-nitrophenol　$\xrightarrow{\text{NaBH}_4}$　P-aminophenol　$\xrightarrow{(\text{CH}_3\text{CO})_2\text{O}}$　Paracetamol

(IV) Piroxicam :

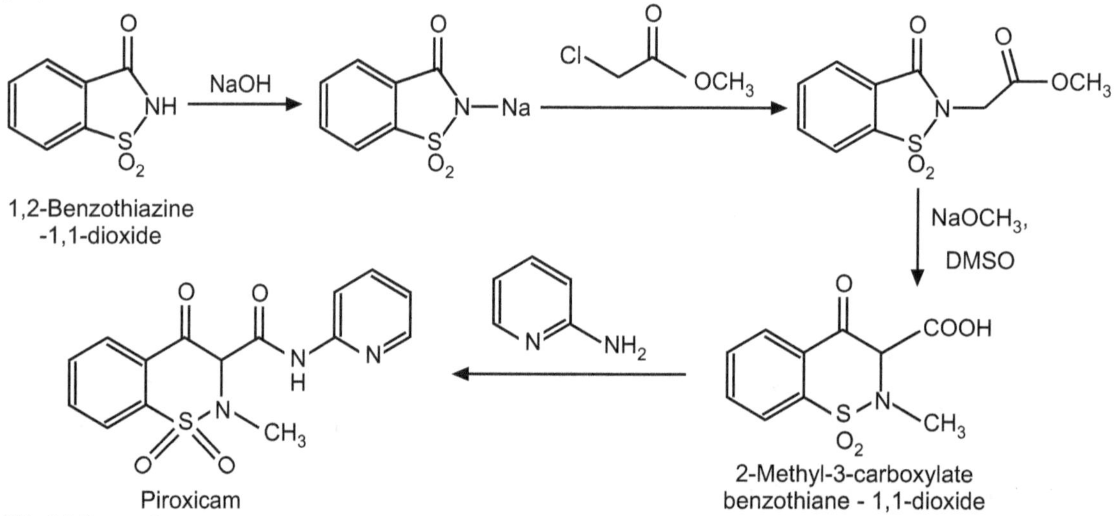

1,2-Benzothiazine-1,1-dioxide　$\xrightarrow{\text{NaOH}}$　(N–Na salt)　$\xrightarrow{\text{Cl}\text{CH}_2\text{COOCH}_3}$　(N–CH$_2$COOCH$_3$)

$\xrightarrow[\text{DMSO}]{\text{NaOCH}_3,}$

2-Methyl-3-carboxylate benzothiane - 1,1-dioxide

Piroxicam　$\xleftarrow{\text{2-amino pyridine}}$

(V) Nabumetone:

2-(bromomethyl)-6-methoxynaphthalene　$\xrightarrow[\substack{\text{K}_2\text{CO}_3/\text{CH}_3\text{COCH}_3 \\ \text{Reflux, 3 hrs.}}]{\text{CH}_3\text{COCH}^-\text{COOC}_2\text{H}_5,\text{Na}^+}$　Ethyl 2-acetyl-3-(6-methoxy-2-naphthyl) propionate

$\xrightarrow[\substack{\text{Aq. KOH} \\ \text{reflux. 6 hrs.}}]{\text{Hydrolysis}}$

Nabumetone

❖ ❖ ❖

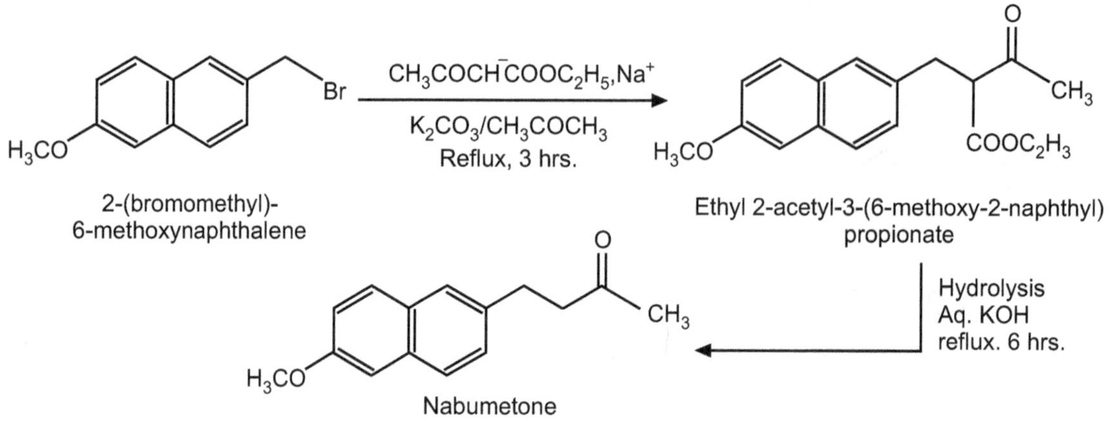

3

AUTACOIDS

3.1 ANTIHISTAMINIC AGENTS

A number of substances with widely differing structures and with diversified pharmacological activities are normally present in the body. These include histamine, serotonin, prostaglandins, angiotensin, endothelins, nitric oxide eicosanoids bradykinin, kallidin etc. Since their pharmacological activities do not permit to call them as hormones or neurohormones, they are grouped together in a class, known as autacoid [Greek word : autos (self) and akos (medicinal agent or remedy)]. Though autacoids play an important role in the body's economical system, their physiological functions can not be stated with assurance.

Histamine is widely distributed in plants and animal tissues. Due to its wide-spread occurrence in body tissues, it was named histamine which means 'tissue amine'. It was first discovered in 1907 by Windaus and Vogt. Its vasodepressor effect was reported in 1910 by Dale et al. In 1927, it was first isolated from liver and lung tissues. It is found to be involved in the diversified physiological processes. It is released in body usually, in response to tissue injury, inflammation, and allergic or hypersensitivity reactions.

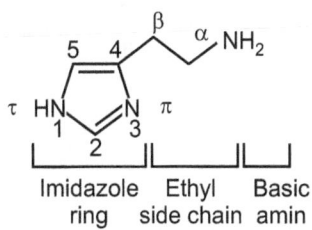

Imidazole Ethyl Basic
ring side chain amin

Histamine is comprised of an imidazole ring connected to an amino group through ethylene bridge. Both, imidazole ring and amino group are basic and get protonated under acidic condition. Chemically, it is β–imidazolyl ethylamine. The structural features of histamine permit it to exist in ionic, tautomeric and conformeric forms which constantly get interconverted to each other. These forms differ mainly in the electronic charge distribution and in the position of hydrogen atoms.

	Mole Percentage of Species at pH 7.4
$pK_{a2} = 5.94$ Dication	3.3
Monocation	96.2
Unionized	0.4
$pK_{a1} = 9.75$ $pK_{a3} = 14$ Anion	~0

There are many drugs with histamine like properties. These drugs may contain the following molecular fragments.

$$-N = C - CH_2 - CH_2 - NH_2$$

or

$$= N - \overset{||}{C} - CH_2 - CH_2 - NH_2$$

These fragments seem to be necessary for attack of histamine on receptor centers of target cells.

3.2 BIOSYNTHESIS, STORAGE AND CATABOLISM

The major source of histamine in body appears to be decarboxylation of the naturally occurring amino acid, histidine, under the influence of L-histidine decarboxylase. It is highly specific enzyme whose activity is governed by histamine itself, through negative feedback inhibition mechanism. This conversion utilises pyridoxal-5-phosphate as a coenzyme. Histidine is also converted to histamine by a pathway of minor importance that is catalysed by non-specific enzyme, aromatic-L-amino acid decarboxylase (dopa decarboxylase). Almost all mammalian tissues contain varying amounts of histidine, L-histidine decarboxylase and enzymes that metabolise histamine. The higher concentration of histamine, however, is found in the skin, intestinal mucosa, lungs and bone marrow. These are the organs which are exposed to external environment. In brain, histamine is present in significant amount.

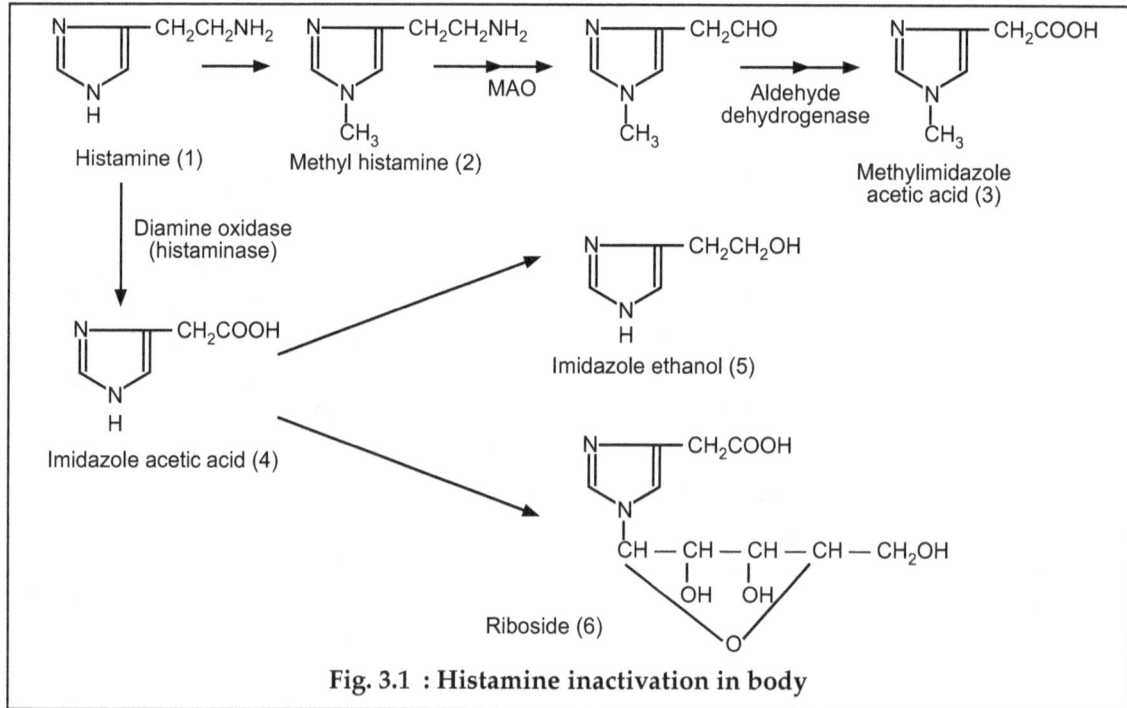

Fig. 3.1 : Histamine inactivation in body

The tissue fixed mast cells and blood basophils (circulating counterparts of mast cells) are the principal cells where histamine is synthesised and is stored in secretory granules. Besides mast cells, histamine is also present in skin, gastric mucosa and CNS where it is biosynthesized and stored in non-mast cells. Here histamine usually undergoes rapid turnover and is released, rather than stored. It is this histamine which is probably of greater physiological importance.

Some histamine is also synthesized in the gut lumen by bacteria. But most of it, is inactivated during absorption in the gastrointestinal mucosa, liver and lungs to N-acetyl histamine.

Fig. 3.1 shows the principal pathways by which histamine is inactivated in the body.

Except (2) and (3), rest of the metabolites of histamine retain little or no physiological activity. In general, conjugation reactions rarely utilise ribose as a substrate. Histamine seems to be among such rare compounds, which are biotransformed through the conjugation with ribose moiety. Acetylation and N-demethylation are other metabolic pathways of minor importance. Urine serves as the principal vehicle for the excretion of these inactive products.

Specific as well as non-specific enzymes are involved in the inactivation of liberated histamine into the body. Imidazole-N-methyl transferase is present in the tissues but not in blood whereas diamine oxidase is present in high concentration in intestine, kidney, liver and thoracic duct lymph. It also utilises other diamines as its substrates. It is mainly inhibited by antimalarial drugs.

3.3 HISTAMINE RELEASE

Under normal conditions, much of the body's store of histamine remains in an inactive form within the tissues. The tissue bound mast cells and basophils are the principal cells for histamine storage. Thus almost every organ is supplied with blood containing histamine, released by basophils. Within the secretory granules of mast cells and basophils, histamine is stored with a heparin-protein complex, to which it is loosely bound with ionic forces. The sensitisation of mast cell is caused by an antigen when it interacts (through bridge formation) with two membrane-bound antibody (immunoglobin) molecules resulting into initiation of a chain of events that ends into an expulsion of the contents of secretory granules by the process of exocytosis. It is Ca^{++} and Mg^{++} ion dependent and energy required metabolic process. Histamine is released from its heparin-protein complex by an exchange program, probably involving calcium ions. Cyclic AMP inhibits the release of histamine, presumably by closing the calcium channels while c-GMP facilitates the calcium influx and induces histamine release.

The concentration of c-AMP is governed by the membrane-bound adenylate cyclase enzyme which is activated by norepinephrine (α-adrenergic agonist), epinephrine (β-adrenergic agonist), prostaglandins and by histamine (negative feedback inhibition by activation of H_2-receptor) itself, while the concentration of c-GMP is governed by another membrane bound guanylate cyclase enzyme which is activated by cholinergic agonists. Both these second messengers control the breakdown of phosphatidyl-inositides and the generation of phosphorylated derivatives of inositol which are involved in the regulation of calcium channels.

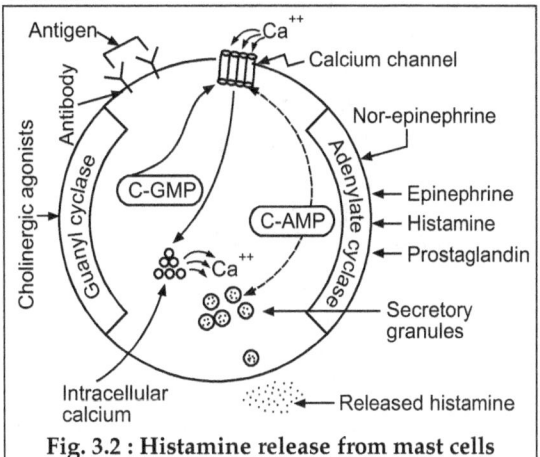

Fig. 3.2 : Histamine release from mast cells

The intracellular concentration of free calcium is important for the exocytotic release of histamine. In certain cases, non-exocytotic mechanism may also be involved in the release of histamine. These include morphological changes in the mast cells resulting into mast cell lysis or physical displacement of histamine. Chlorpromazine may cause the histamine release from mast cells by a cytotoxic mechanism.

Since, activation of H_2-receptor sites on mast cell membrane, results into elevation of c-AMP, all physiological actions of histamine that are initiated by H_2-receptor activation, will be associated with elevated intracellular c-AMP level. Similarly the physiological actions of histamine that are due to H_1-receptor activation in general may then be associated with elevated intracellular c-GMP levels.

In hypersensitivity reaction, the mast cell is sensitised by an interaction of specific antigen with the cell bound antibody (IgE or reagin), resulting into degranulation and subsequent release of granular contents. Histamine is released along with other autacoids like, plasmakinins, angiotensin, prostaglandins, serotonin, platelet activating factor, slow releasing substance of anaphylaxis (SRS-A) and eosinophill chemotactic factor. These chemical mediators lead to pathologic responses such as increased vascular permeability, change in smooth muscle tone and increased secretion of mucous.

There are two different mechanisms that trigger the release of mediators from mast cells. The first triggering mechanism is atopic or IgE-mediated. This mechanism involves allergen specific IgE antibodies attached to receptor sites on mast cells (and also basophils) thereby sensitising them. These cell-bound IgE antibodies act like a trigger or fuse.

The other broad category of mast cell triggering mechanism is called non-atopic or non-immune. These non-lgE mediated mechanisms act directly or indirectly on the mast cells or target cell membrane to bring about the same results release of histamine and other mediators and consequent pathologic responses as occur with atopic triggering. Some of the non-immune triggers are acetylcholine, complement components, oestrogen, prostaglandins, chemicals, drugs, conditions and events such as weather changes, respiratory infections, air pollution, anxiety and stress.

3.4 HISTAMINE LIBERATION

Histamine release may be increased in urticarial reactions, mastocytosis and basophilia. Similarly in certain patients, many drugs may produce hyper-sensitivity reactions by sensitising mast cells. In some cases, these drugs or their metabolic products may act as antigen while few of them can directly or indirectly activate the calcium ion channel. This may result into an eventual expulsion of the granular contents of the mast cells which include heparin and other mediators of anaphylaxis along with histamine.

Chlortetracycline, morphine, pethidine, amphetamine, tolazoline, d-tubocurarine and atropine are some of the drugs which cause the histamine release. Hence, these drugs are termed as histamine liberators. They do not deplete histamine stores from non-mast cells.

3.5 PHYSIOLOGICAL ACTIONS OF HISTAMINE

(1) An ability of histamine to dilate the capillaries and to increase their permeability, suggests its basic role in the beginning of the inflammatory reactions.

(2) In allergic reactions, (antigen-antibody), histamine plays a role along with other autacoids.

(3) Histamine exerts a variety of actions on the cardiovascular system.

(4) A "nascent" histamine refers to biosynthesis of histamine that can be provoked when needed. It is made but not stored. It may play a role in anabolic processes.

(5) Histamine is unevenly distributed in the brain and may also act as a central neurotransmitter.

(6) Histamine stimulates sensory nerves in the skin and if these sensory impulses continue into CNS to sufficient intensity, this results into itching or pain sensation.

(7) By causing the dilation of intracranial blood vessels, histamine causes an intense headache.

(8) It causes contraction of smooth muscles of GIT. This action, coupled with its stimulatory action on the secretion of gastric hydrochloric acid, causes epigastric distress, nausea, vomiting and diarrhoea.

(9) Excessive histamine release may cause peptic ulceration and asthmatic conditions.

(10) Histamine when injected into the skin, it produces dilation of both the capillaries and the neighbouring arterioles which is associated with an increased permeability of these vessels and the increased exudation of tissue fluid (giving rise to a weal). These three effects i.e., dilation of capillaries, formation of weal and dilation of the arterioles constitute the term 'triple response'.

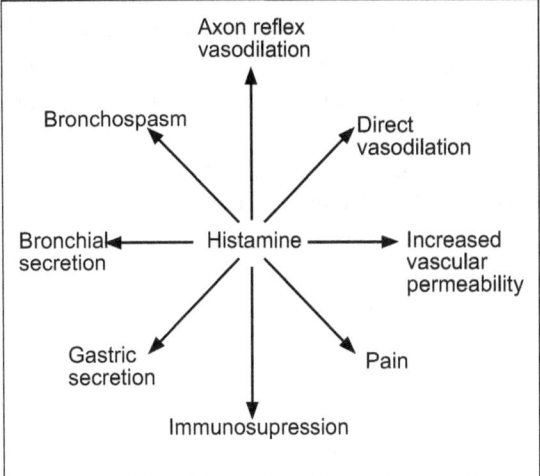

Fig. 3.3 : Physiological actions of histamine

3.6 HISTAMINE AGONISTIC ACTIVITY

3.6.1 Modifications of the Imidazole Moiety of Histamine

(a) Replacement of the imidazole moiety by other heterocyclic ring structures : Replacement of the imidazole moiety of histamine by other aromatic heterocyclic ring structures leads to several relatively selective H_1-receptor agonists, and some interesting observations concerning the mechanism of action at the H_1-receptor can be made.

When the imidazole ring is, for example, replaced by a 2-thiazole ring, a H_1-receptor selectivity is encountered. The corresponding 3- and 4-pyridyl analogues are both inactive (Durant et al., 1975; Ganellin, 1982), indicating the demand for a nitrogen atom neighbouring the ethylamine side-chain.

CH$_2$CH$_2$NH$_2$ CH$_2$CH$_2$NH$_2$

1, 3-thiazole

CH$_2$CH$_2$NH$_2$ CH$_2$CH$_2$NH$_2$

H_1-receptor agonists

In summary, these observations clearly showed that for H_1-receptor agonism, a nitrogen next to the ethylamine side-chain is sufficient. A tautomeric N^π - N^τ system as in histamine itself is not necessary.

(b) Substitution at the imidazole ring : The 5-alkyl-substituted histamine derivatives are therefore relatively H_2-receptor selective agents. Methyl substitution at position 2 leads to a rather potent and selective H_1-receptor agonist. Methylation of the two N atoms clearly shows that the lone pair of the N^π atom of histamine is essential for H_1-receptor agonism, whereas an N^π - N^τ tautomeric system is not a prerequisite. Moreover, substitution on the other two positions resulted in both selective H_1- and H_2-receptor agonists. Whereas, 5-alkyl substitution is in favour of H_2-receptor agonism (by decreasing H_1 effect), 2-substitution yields quite potent and also selective H_1-receptor agonists. Very interesting is the observation that some 2-phenylhistamine derivatives are highly potent compounds, whereas the saturated analogue is inactive. This might indicate that an extra aromatic binding site is involved in the binding of the 2-phenyl-histamines to the H_1-receptor.

3.6.2 Modification of the Ethylamine Side-chain of Histamine

(a) **α- and β-substitution :** Introduction of substituents into the ethylamine side-chain has not resulted in very interesting results. Methylation at the α- or β-position leads to a reduction in H_1-receptor activity.

(b) **Substitution of the amino group :** The terminal amino group is the only position in the histamine molecule that allows the introduction of a methyl group without concomitant reduction in agonistic activity (Hepp and Schunack, 1980). The addition of a single methyl group yields N-α-methyl-histamine. This compound is approximately equipotent with histamine itself. A second methyl group, however, is also well tolerated. Higher alkyl substituents are not well tolerated at terminal NH_2.

(c) **Replacement of the ethylamine side-chain by other basic groups :** Besides simple substitution of the ethylamine side-chain at the α- or β-carbon atoms and the terminal amino groups, more drastic changes in this part of the molecule have also been performed.

For example, Schunack et al. have incorporated the ethylamine side-chain into several rigid or semirigid ring structures.

α = 1.0
pD_2 = 6.6

α = 0

α = 1.0
pD_2 = 4.5

α = 0

α = 0.78
pD_2 = 4.44

α = 0.94
pD_2 = 3.97

3.7 ANTIALLERGIC AGENTS (CLASSIC ANTI-HISTAMINES)

Histamine binding to the H_1-receptor can cause stimulation of smooth muscle and produce allergic and hypersensitivity reactions such as hay fever, pruritus (itching), contact and atopic dermatitis, drug rashes, urticaria (oedematous patches of skin) and anaphylactic shock. Antihistamines are used widely to treat these symptoms.

3.7.1 First-generation Agents

According to the chemical features they share, these agents are classified as :

1. Ethylenediamine derivatives
2. Aminoalkyl ether analogues
3. Cyclic basic chain analogues
4. Monoaminopropyl analogues
5. Tricyclic ring system
6. Newer agents.

Classical H_1-Receptor Antagonists :

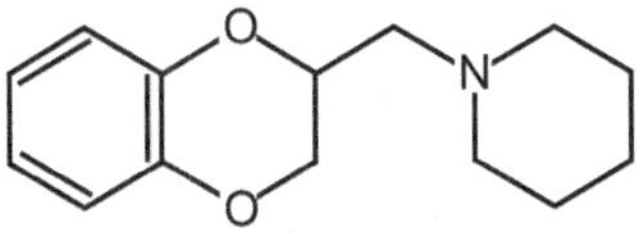

Piperoxan

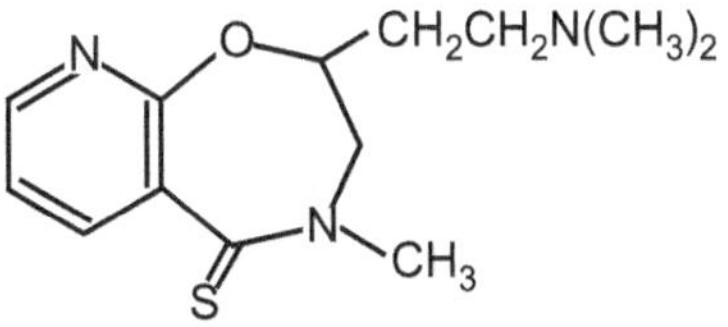
N
O
$CH_2CH_2N(CH_3)_2$
N
CH_3
S

Rocastine

Research on antihistaminic drugs was initiated in 1933 in France by Bovet (Rome, Italy) and Fourneau who reported that piperoxan protects the animals from bronchial spasm induced by aerosolized histamine. Rocastine has been described as a rapid acting, non-sedating H_1-antagonist where no CNS activity was observed.

Genesis:

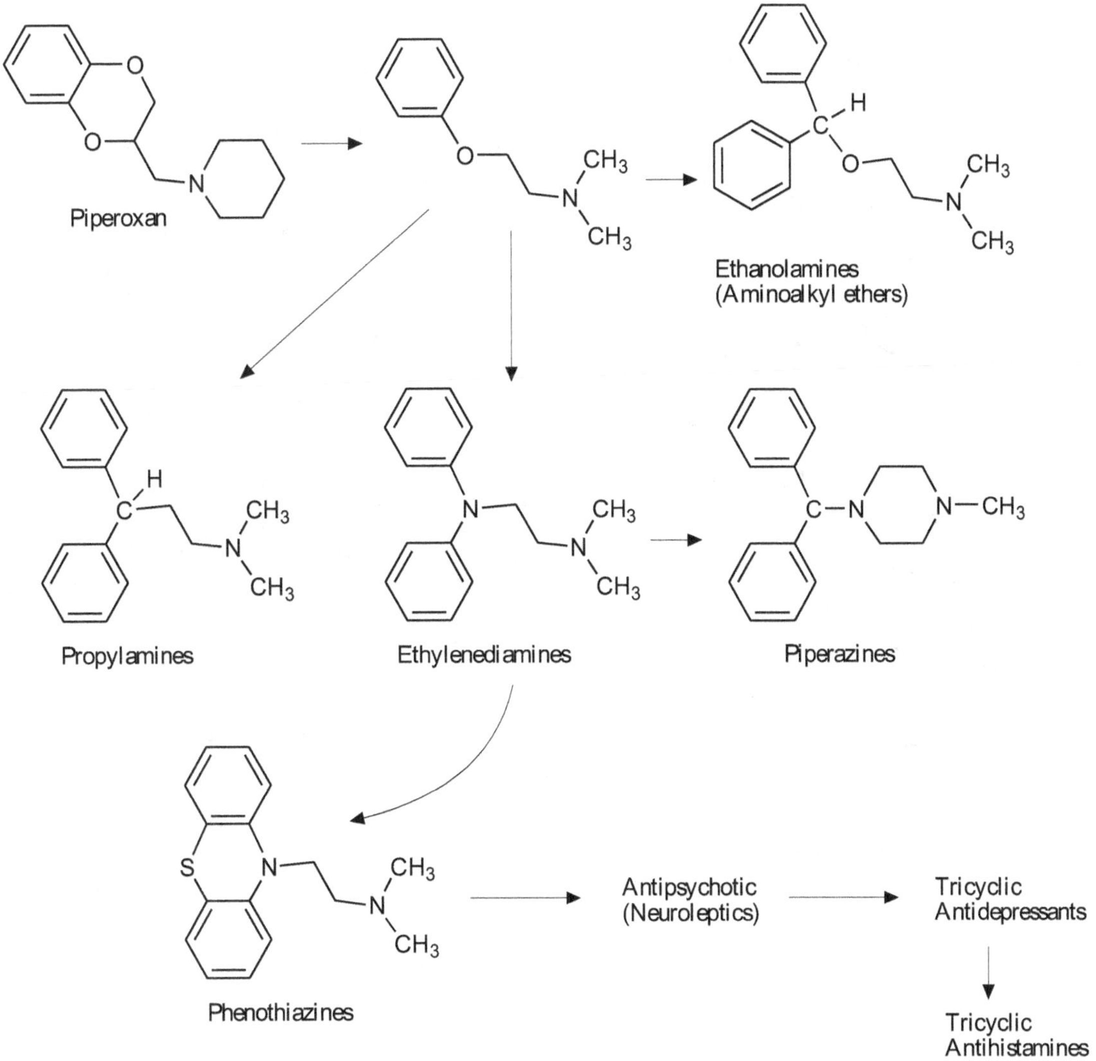
Piperoxan
Ethanolamines
(Aminoalkyl ethers)
Propylamines
Ethylenediamines
Piperazines
Phenothiazines
Antipsychotic
(Neuroleptics)
Tricyclic
Antidepressants
Tricyclic
Antihistamines

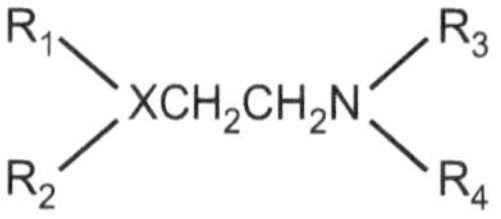

General formula

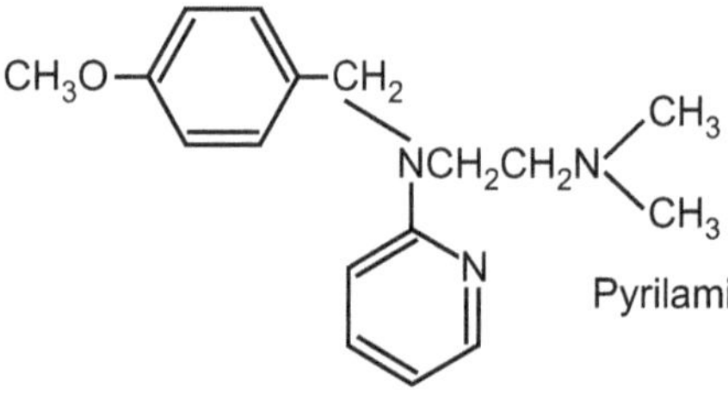

Pyrilamine

Ethylenediamines

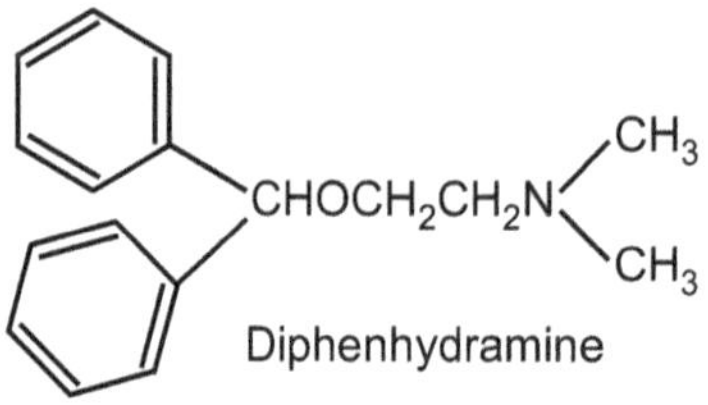

Diphenhydramine

Aminoalkyl ethers

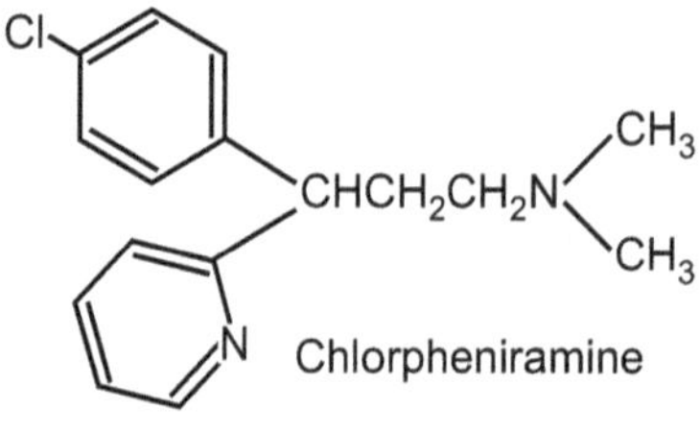

Chlorpheniramine

Aminopropyl compounds

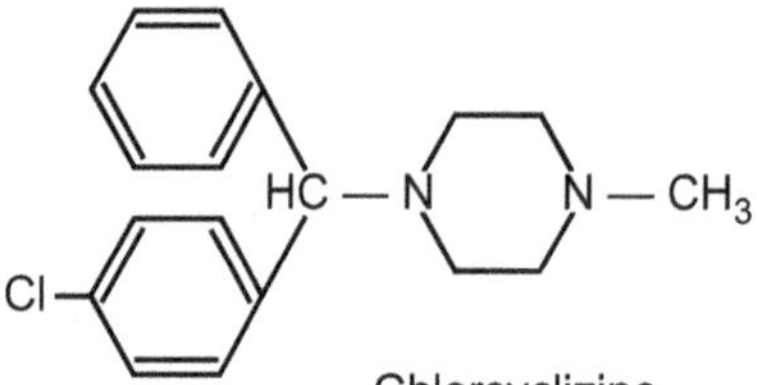

Chlorcyclizine

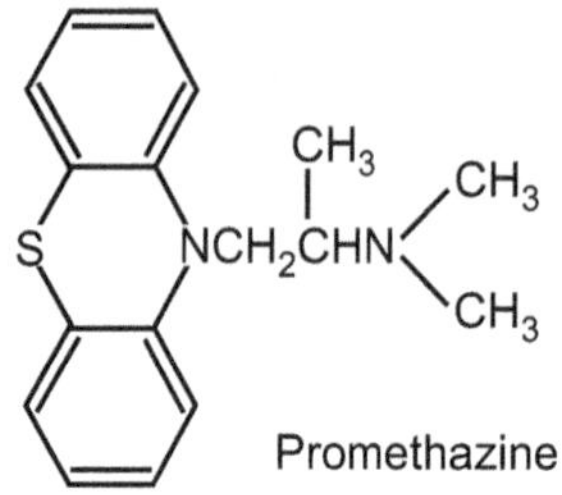

Promethazine

Tricyclic structures

A disubstituted terminal group (usually a dimethylamino group) is connected to an atom X via a short carbon chain. The chain can be saturated, unsaturated, branched or part of a ring system, whereas X can be an oxygen, nitrogen or carbon atom; X links the side-chain to an "aromatic head". This aromatic head generally contains two aromatic rings (e.g. phenyl, benzyl, 2-pyridyl), which may be fused.

Substitution of the aromatic ring can influence the H_1-receptor antagonistic activity. Whereas ortho-substitution is highly undesirable, meta-substitution is either ineffective or unfavourable, and para-substitution in only one of the rings can increase the biological activity if the substituent is lipophilic (e.g. Cl, CH_3) or has electron-releasing properties (e.g. OCH_3).

Structure-Activity Relationship :

Like histamine, most of the classic antihistamines may be described by a substituted ethylamine moiety i.e.

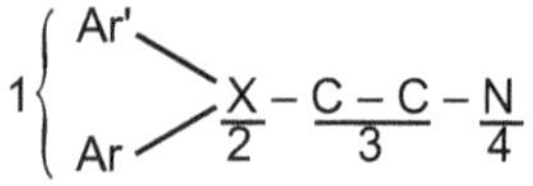

(1) Aryl groups :

In the above structure, Ar is aryl (including phenyl and heteroaryl group like 2-pyridyl) and Ar' is aryl or aryl methyl group.

Sometimes, the two aromatic rings are bridged, which constitutes tricyclic ring derivatives.

(2) Nature of X :

The nature of 'X' provides the basis of chemical classification of classic anti-histamines e.g.

when X = Oxygen (Aminoalkyl ether analogue)

when X = Nitrogen (Ethylene-diamine derivative)

when X = Carbon (Mono aminopropyl analogue)

(3) The alkyl chain :

Most of the structures of classic antihistamines contain an ethylene chain. Extension or branching of this chain results in a less active compound (promethazine is possibly an exception). Homologation has played an important role in the development of neuroleptic and tricyclic anti-depressants from anti-histaminics. All contain, in general, the chain –C–C–NR$_2$, and although some of them have a neuroleptic component, antipsychotic activity is not unveiled in most cases until the carbon chain is lengthened to C$_3$– NR$_2$.

(4) Terminal nitrogen atom :

In general, the terminal N atom should be a 3° amine for maximum activity. Unlike many anticholinergics and local anaesthetics, here the dimethylamine derivatives are found to possess better antagonist activity. The terminal nitrogen may be a part of heterocyclic

ring as in antazoline and in chlorcyclizine, and still retains high antihistaminic activity.

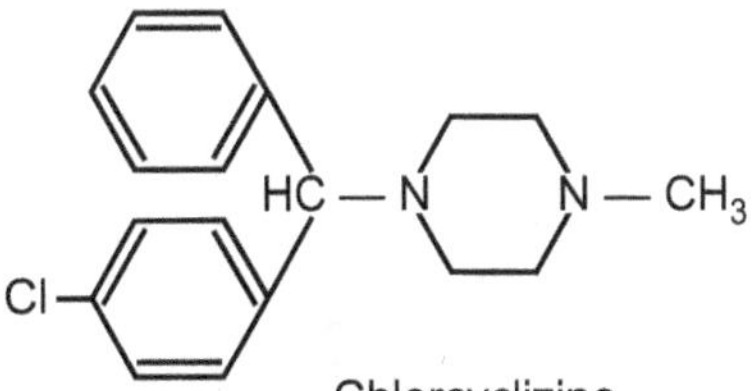

Chlorcyclizine

However, substitutions on the Ar groups, replacement of the aliphatic dimethylamino group with small basic heterocyclic rings, increased branching on ethylene chain and substitutions between X and N, all modify the potency, metabolism, ability to reach the site of action, toxicity and side reactions in-vivo.

5.   Since, the structures of anti-histamines have a close resemblance with structures of cholinergic blocking agents, most of the classic anti-histamines do exhibit anticholinergic activity. The reverse is also true.

Table 3.1 : Antiallergic agents or Classic Anti-histamine agents

(1) Ethylenediamine derivatives :

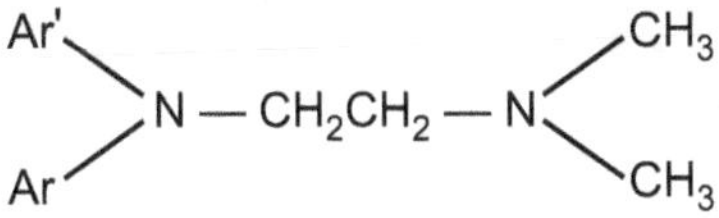

	Name	Ar'	Ar
1.	Pyrilamine	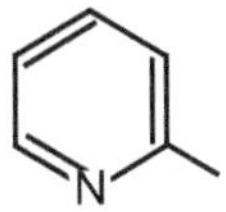	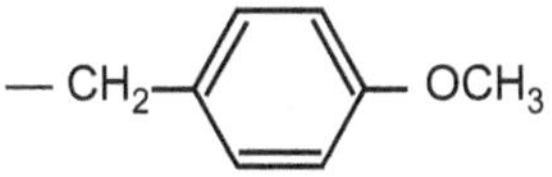
2.	Tripelennamine	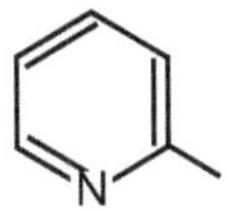	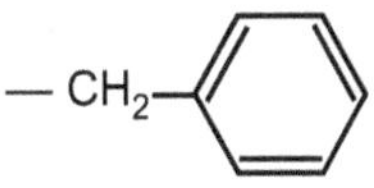
3.	Methapyrilene	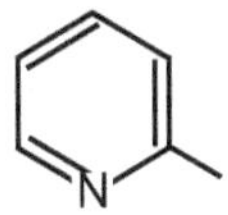	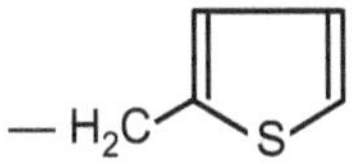
4.	Thonzylamine	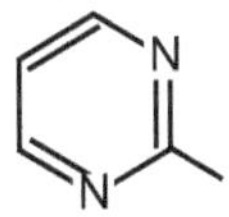	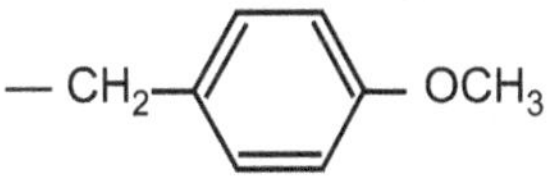

(2) Aminoalkyl ether analogues :

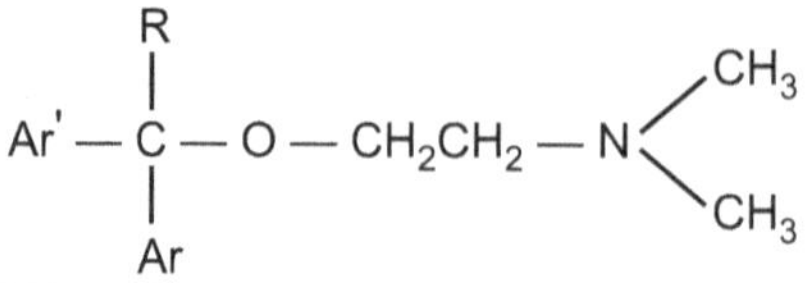

$$Ar' - \underset{\underset{Ar}{|}}{\overset{\overset{R}{|}}{C}} - O - CH_2CH_2 - N \overset{CH_3}{\underset{CH_3}{\big\langle}}$$

Name	Ar'	Ar	R
1. Diphenhydramine (Benadryl; 1946)	$- C_6H_5$	$- C_6H_5$	H
2. Bromodiphenhydramine	$- C_6H_5$	p-bromophenyl	H
3. Doxylamine	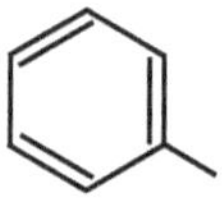	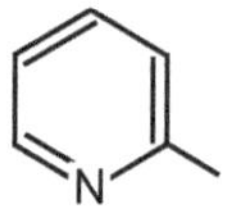	$- CH_3$
4. Carbinoxamine	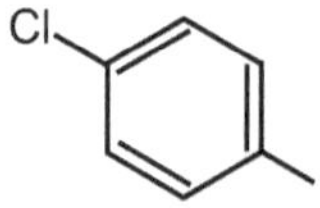	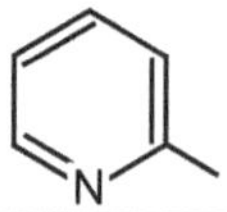	H

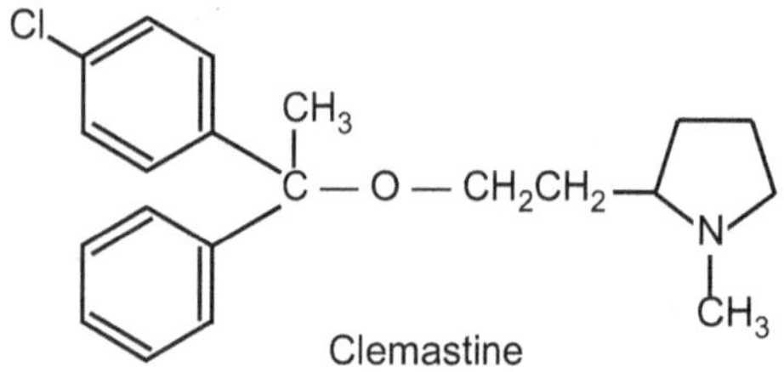

Clemastine

Diphenhydramine +

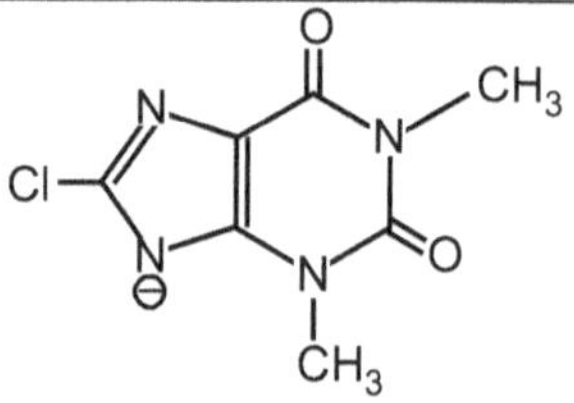

8-chlorotheophylline

Dimenhydrinate (8-chlorotheophylline added to counteract drowsiness)

(3) Cyclic basic chain analogues :

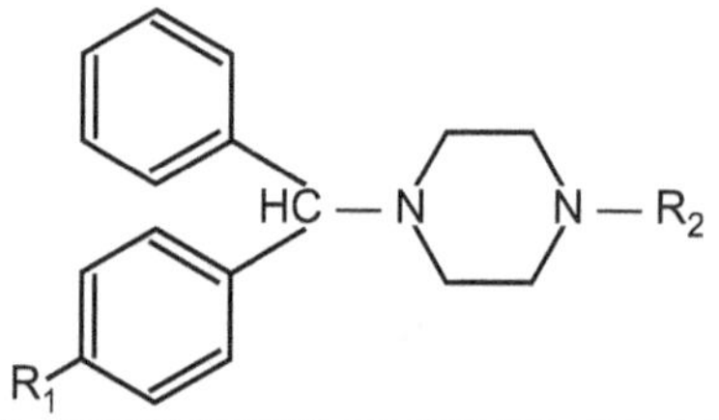

$$HC - N \overset{\frown}{\underset{\smile}{}} N - R_2$$

Name	R_1	R_2
1. Cyclizine	H	$- CH_3$
2. Chlorocyclizine	$- Cl$	$- CH_3$
3. Buclizine	$- Cl$	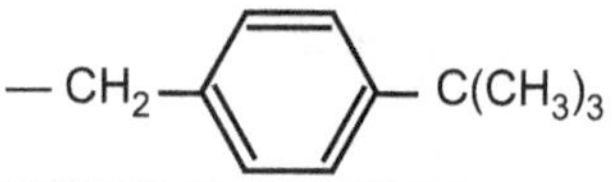 $- CH_2 - C_6H_4 - C(CH_3)_3$
4. Meclizine	$- Cl$	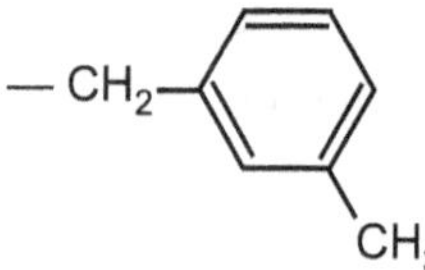 $- CH_2 - C_6H_4 - CH_3$

(4) Monoaminopropyl analogues :

(a)

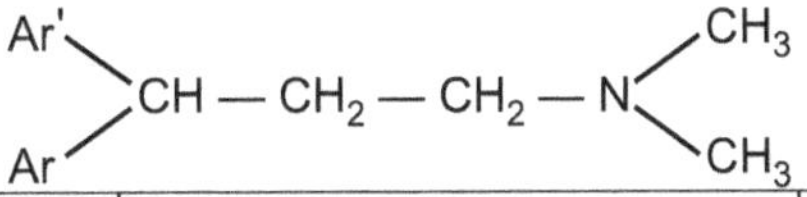

	Name	Ar'	Ar
1.	Pheniramine	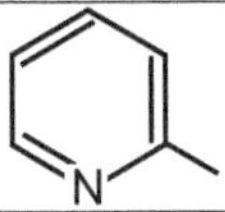	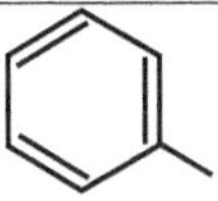
2.	Chlorpheniramine	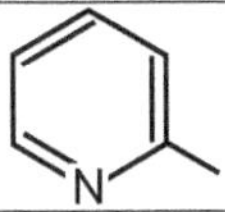	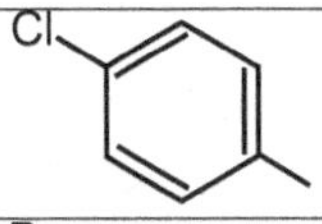
3.	Brompheniramine	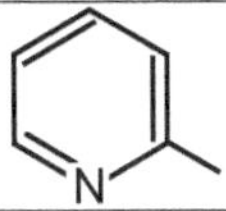	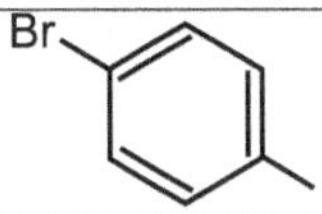

(b)

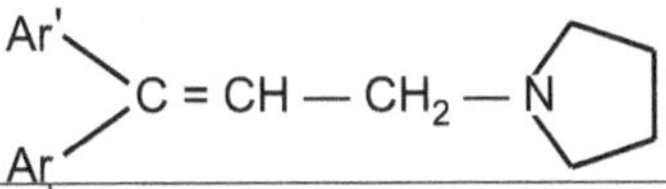

	Name	Ar'	Ar
1.	Triprolidine	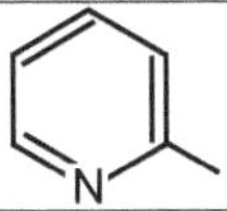	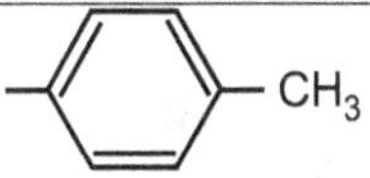
2.	Pyrrobutamine	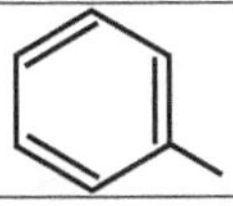	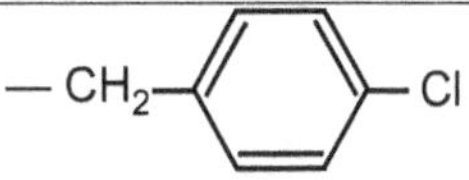

(5) Tricyclic ring systems : (Phenothiazine analogues) :

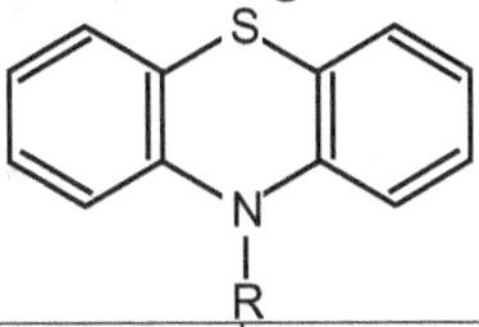

	Name	R
1.	Promethazine	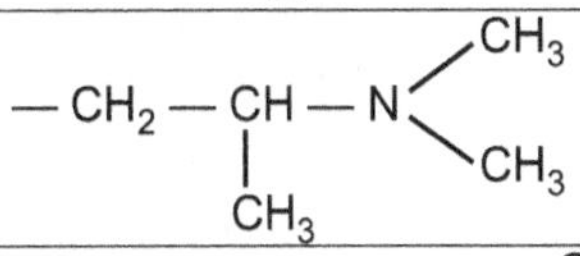 $- CH_2 - CH - N \begin{smallmatrix} CH_3 \\ CH_3 \end{smallmatrix}$ with CH_3 on middle carbon
2.	Trimeprazine	$- CH_2 - CH - CH_2 - N \begin{smallmatrix} CH_3 \\ CH_3 \end{smallmatrix}$ with CH_3 on second carbon
3.	Methdilazine	$- CH_2 - CH$ attached to pyrrolidine ring $CH_2 - CH_2 / CH_2 - N - CH_3$

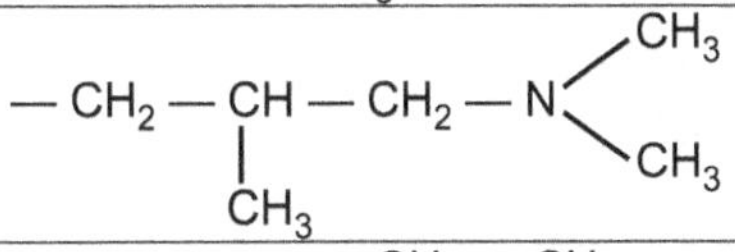

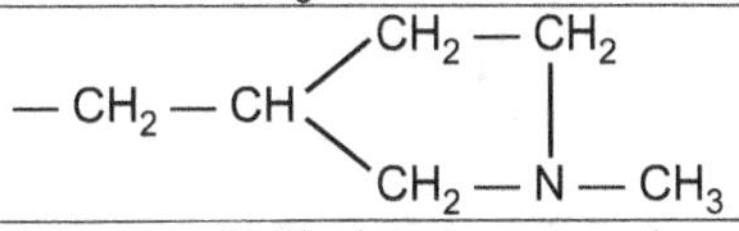

Phenothiazines : Extension of dialkylaminoethylene chain to dialkylaminopropylene is not conclusive to antihistaminic activity but promotes neuroleptic activity. In chlorprothixene, trans-isomer in which the amino alkyl group lies on the side of unsubstituted aromatic ring is more anti-histaminic than the cis isomer, while reverse is true for neuroleptic activity.

(6) Miscellaneous agents :

(a)

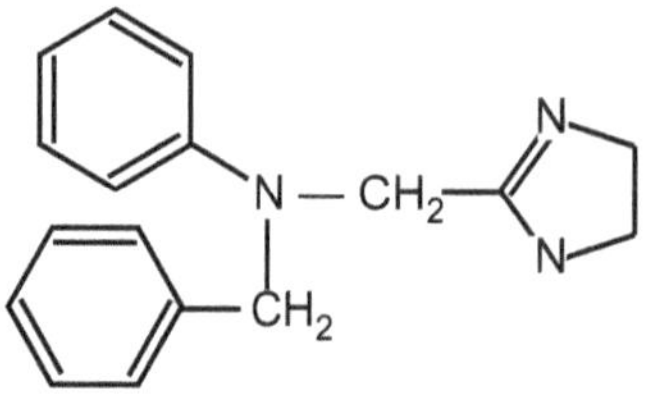

Antazoline

(b) Dibenzepines:

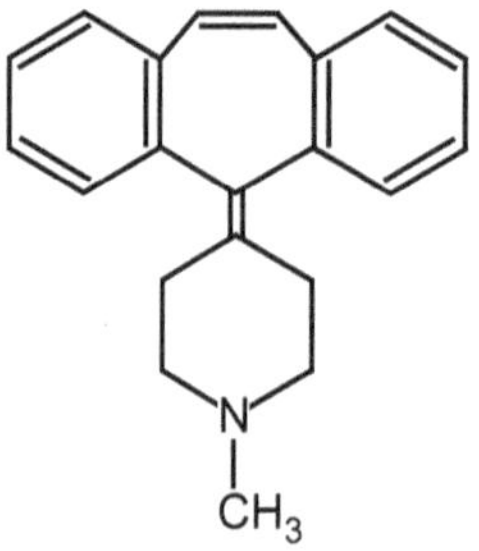

Periactin (Cyproheptadine)

It has antihistaminic, anticholinergic and local anasthetic properties.

(c)

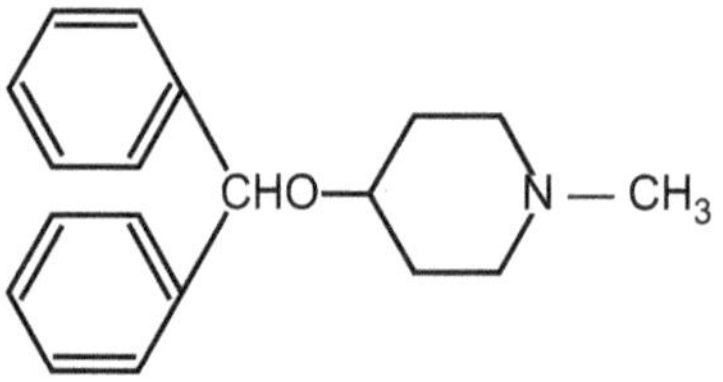

Diphenylpyraline

In diphenylpyraline, the basic side-chain of diphenhydramine is tied back so as to link the benzhydryl ether group with N-methyl piperidine in the 4th position.

(d)

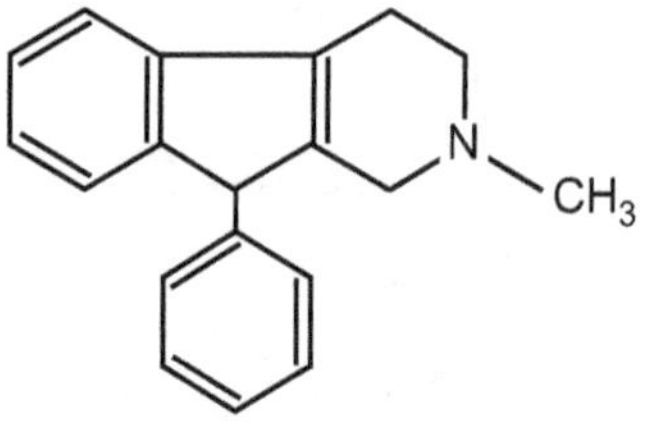

Phenindamine
(1940)

(e)

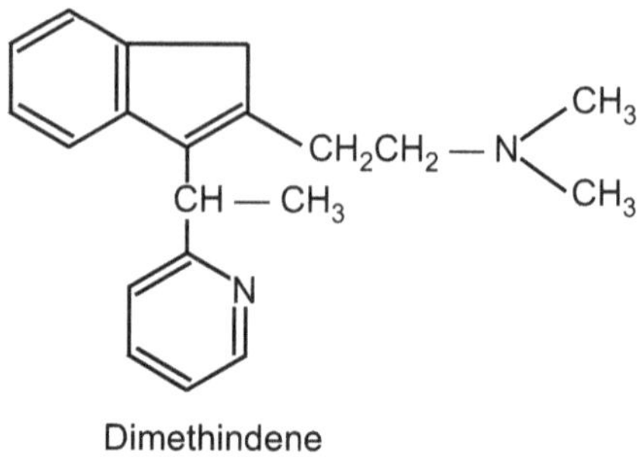

Dimethindene

(f)

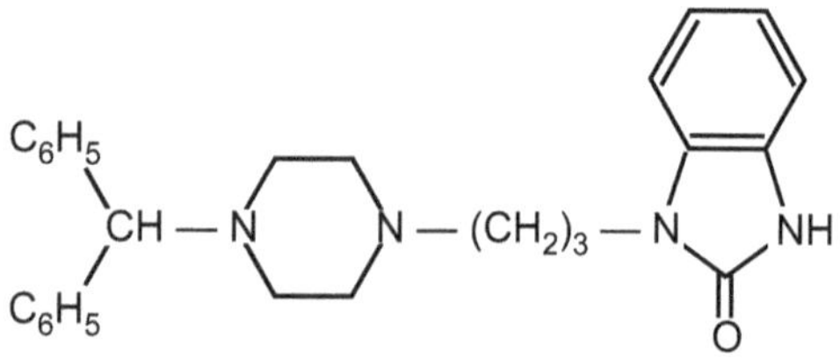

Oxatomide
(Janssen pharma, 1975)

An innovative drug with a combined H_1-5HT-leukotriene antagonism is oxatomide. It is usable in asthma, where ordinary H_1-antagonists are not appropriate.

(g)

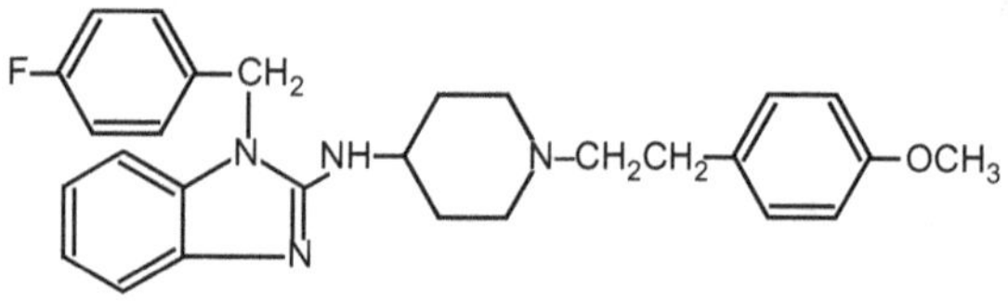

Astemizole

Astemizole (1977) : Astemizole is also metabolized by CYP3A4 and has similar problems of cardiotoxicity (QT interval prolongation and arrhythmias) when administered with CYP3A4 inhibitors and has been removed from the market (1999).

Astemizole and terfenadine are non-sedative H_1-blockers. These are quite polar molecule and cannot cross BBB to reach central H-receptors. Astemizole is especially long acting.

(h) Levocabastine (1979):

Astemizole's profile led to research on compounds containing the 4-phenyl piperidine ring (like terfenadine). Unlike Astemisole, it has a fast onset and a long duration.

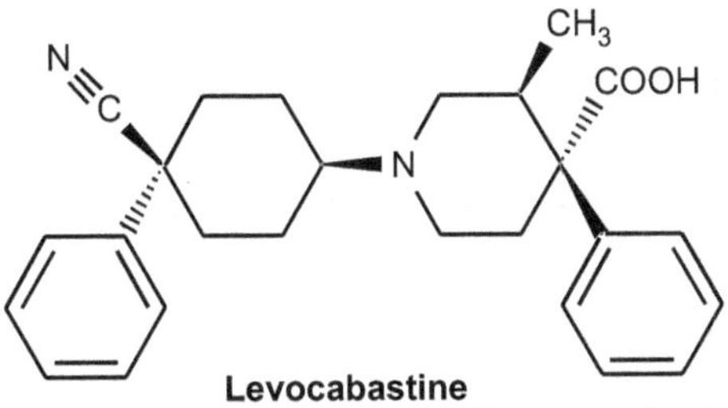

Levocabastine

(i) Mizolastine :

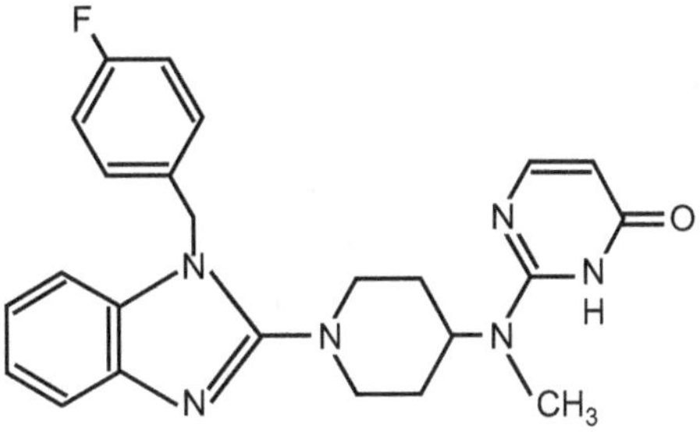

Mizolastine

It is a non-sedative antihistamine. It is effective in allergic rhinitis and urticaria by single daily dose. It blocks H_1-receptors.

(7) Newer agents under investigation :

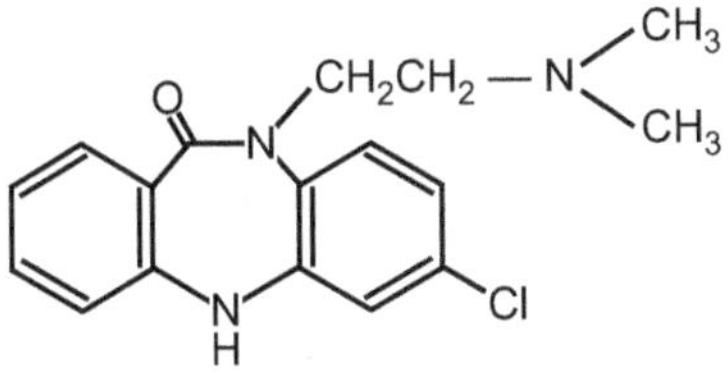

Tarpane

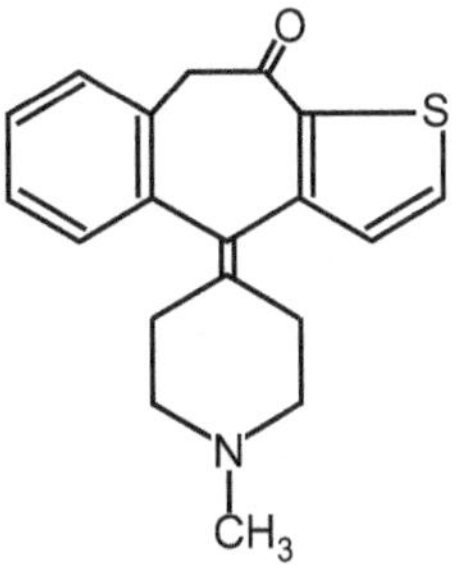

Ketotifene

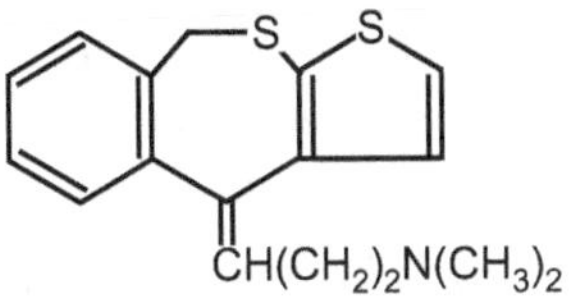

Dithiadene

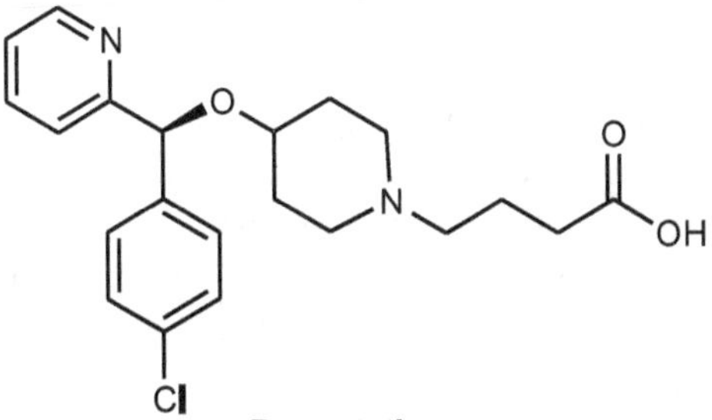

Bepostatine

Bepostatine (Bepreve) is a relatively new drug in this class approved in Japan for systemic (oral) use for the treatment of allergic rhinitis and uriticaria/puritus in July 2000 and January 2002, respectively.

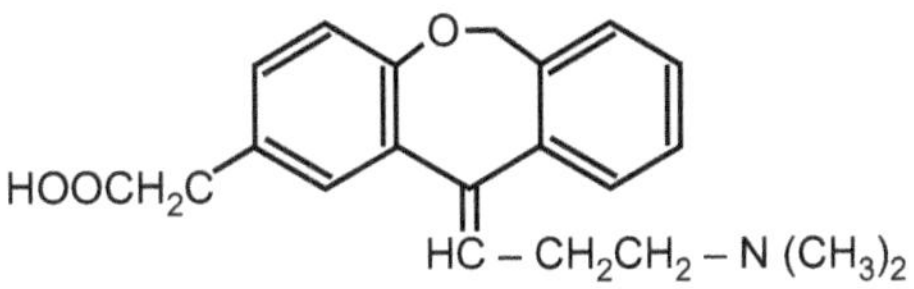

Olopatadine

Olopatadine : It is an antihistaminic and mast cell stabilizer. It is used to treat iching associated with allergic conjunctivitis.

(j) Azelastine :

Azelastine is a potent second generation selective H_1-receptor antagonist used to treat allergic rhinitis (nasal spray) and allergic conjunctivities (eye drop). It has (1) Antihistaminic effect, (2) Mast cell stabilizing and (3) Anti-inflammatory effect.

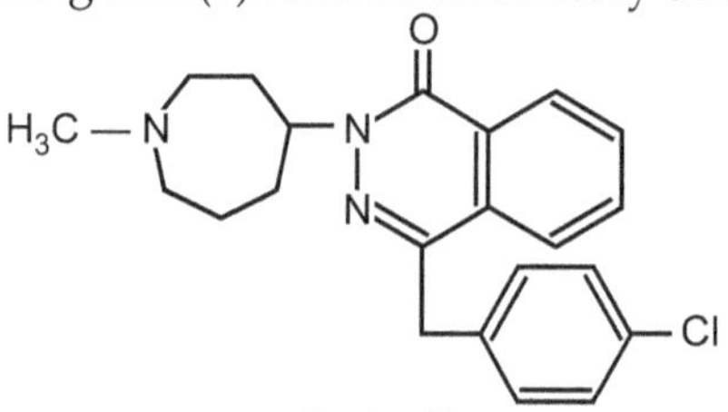

Azelastine

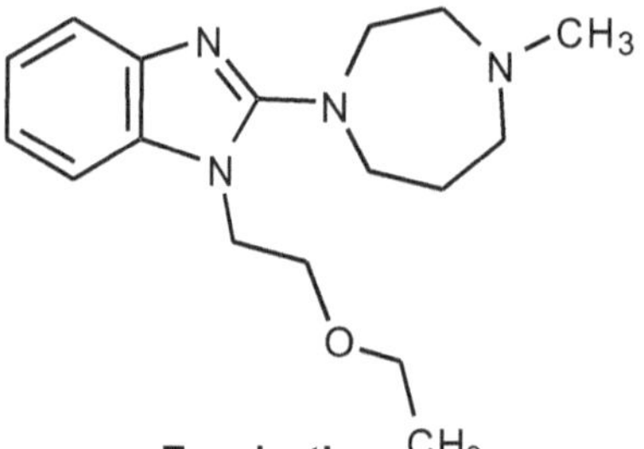

Emedastine

Emedastine is an ophthalmic H_1 antagonist, mast cell stabilizer.

(k) Cromolyn Sodium :

It is a derivative of khellin, a vasodilatory benzopyrone isolated from the umbelliferous plant Ammivisnaga. Cromolyn belongs to a completely novel class of compounds which bring about their antihistaminic effects by the suppression of release of autacoids during antigen-antibody interaction.

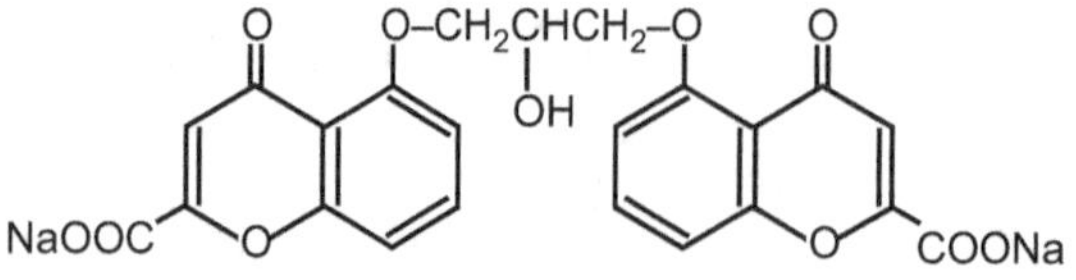

Cromolyn Sodium

It bears neither a structural relationship to other commonly used anti-histaminic compounds nor it possesses a smooth muscle relaxant or bronchodilatory activity.

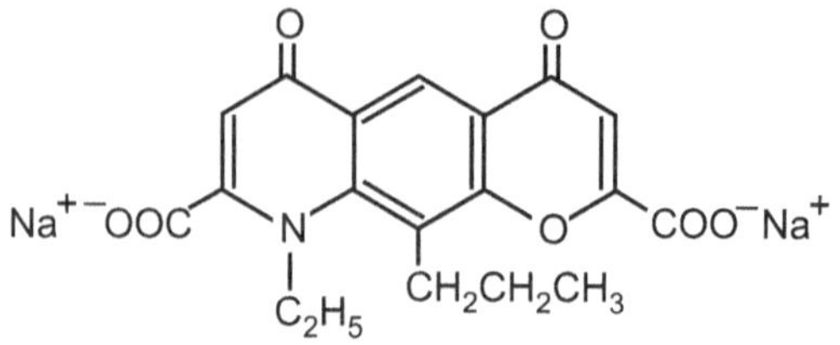

Nedocromil-Na

It is structurally related to cromolyn but has superior and broader pharmacological actions in the treatment of asthma. It is a mast cell stabilizer.

Nedocromil : Na and Na-cromoglycate seem to act by phosphorylating a mast cell protein and thereby stabilize the cell, preventing its disruption.

Bronchial asthma and allergic rhinitis are diseases where sodium chromoglycate is the only drug for prophylaxis. Being a mast-cell stabilizer, it can be used only in the adults, that too in inhalation form only. Ketotifene is an orally active agent with similar action, having prophylactic properties. It is a tricyclic derivative of benzocyclo heptathiophine skeleton. It is useful in cases of bronchial asthma with Type I hypersensitivity as well as allergic rhinitis. It has a limited use in acute attack. It has got antiallergic, antiasthmatic and anti-anaphylactic properties.

It inhibits antigen induced release of chemical mediators, especially SRS-A, histamine. Optimization of β_2-receptor expression by reducing its tachyphylaxis results into asthma prophylactic activity while optimisation of H_1-blockade activity results into anti-allergic action.

The structures of various classic anti-histaminic agents reveal the fact that the agents from other therapeutic class also exhibit considerable anti-histaminic activity e.g., Phenoxybenzamine (an adrenaline blocking agent), many local anaesthetics, tranquillizers (phenothiazines) and diphenylmethane derivatives (atropine like drugs and the antiparkinsonian agents).

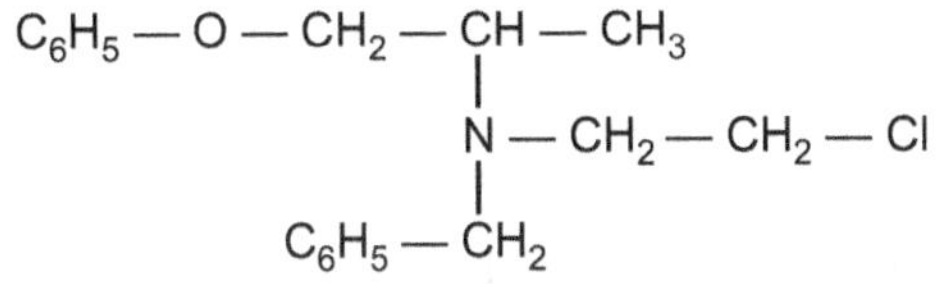

$$C_6H_5 - O - CH_2 - CH - CH_3$$
$$| \quad N - CH_2 - CH_2 - Cl$$
$$| \quad C_6H_5 - CH_2$$

Phenoxybenzamine

Forced by limited usefulness due to unwanted side-effects, non-sedative H_1-antagonists were developed. These new non-sedative H_1-antagonists originate from several classical H_1-antagonists but sometimes also comprises new and unexpected structural elements.

In contrast to the classical H_1-antagonists, the new developed compounds do not easily cross the blood brain barrier and therefore act only peripherically. Some of the new H_1-antagonists (e.g. astemizol, etirizine, loratadine) are now in clinical use and appear to be of value for treating allergic conditions.

Sedation is the side-effect of the first generation H_1-antihistamines. Several antihistaminics have been derived from classical structures that have reduced ability to penetrate the CNS. They have little or no sedative side effects. These are collectively referred to as the second generation (non-sedating) H_1-receptor antagonists.

3.7.2 Second-generation Agents

(Non-sedative Antihistaminics)

The advantages of this class include :

(i)   Poor CNS penetration

(ii) Reduced sedation

(iii) Prolonged duration of action

(iv) Lacks anticholinergic side effects.

(a) Piperazines:

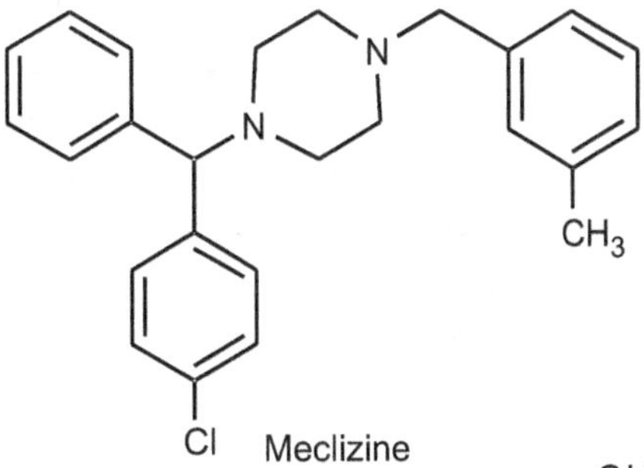

Meclizine

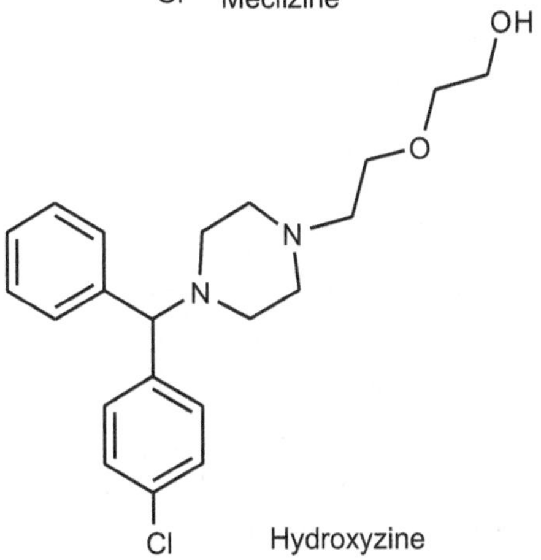

Hydroxyzine

Both nitrogens are basic; the terminal nitrogen is more basic due to less steric hindrance and no electron withdrawing groups in the vicinity.

They have moderate potency with a slow onset and prolong duration of action, moderate sedation and low anticholinergic effects.

They also possess peripheral and central antinausea activity, thus they are used as antiemetic, antivertigo and antinausea products.

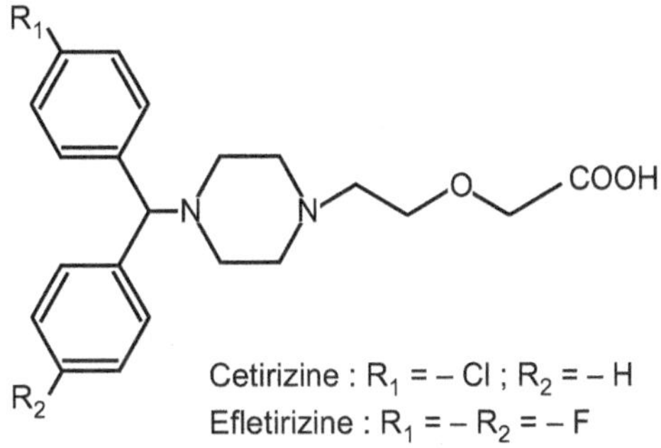

Cetirizine : $R_1 = -Cl$; $R_2 = -H$
Efletirizine : $R_1 = -R_2 = -F$

Cetrizine is an excellent example of the second generation histamine H_1-receptor antagonist which is carboxylated metabolite of hydroxyzine. It is a long acting drug and free from central sedation and antimuscarinic activity. It is used for the symptomatic relief of hypersensitivity reactions.

(b) Piperidines:

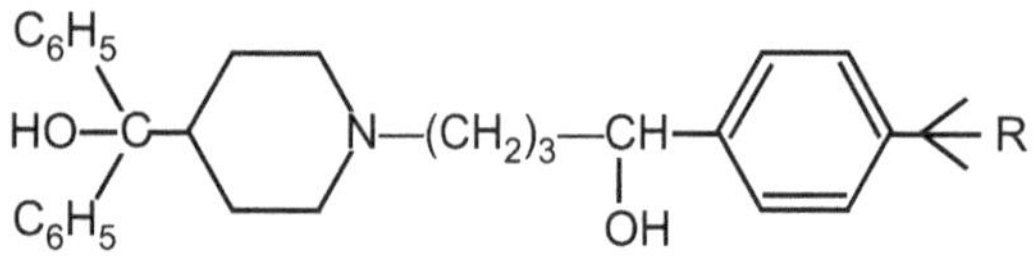

Terfenadine　: R = –CH$_3$ (1985)

Fexofenadine : R = –COOH

It is a butyrophenone derivative having anti-histaminic activity without sedative action used in the treatment of seasonal and perennial allergic rhinitis.

Terfenadine 1985 was discontinued when it became apparent that there was a high frequency of heart arrythmia associated with the drug. In patients with compromised liver metabolism or when the presence of other drugs limit the metabolism of terfenadine, persistent levels result in the observed arrythmias.

Fexofenadine is a metabolite and is the activated form responsible for antihistamine activity. Therefore, the fexofenadine replaced terfenadine (1997).

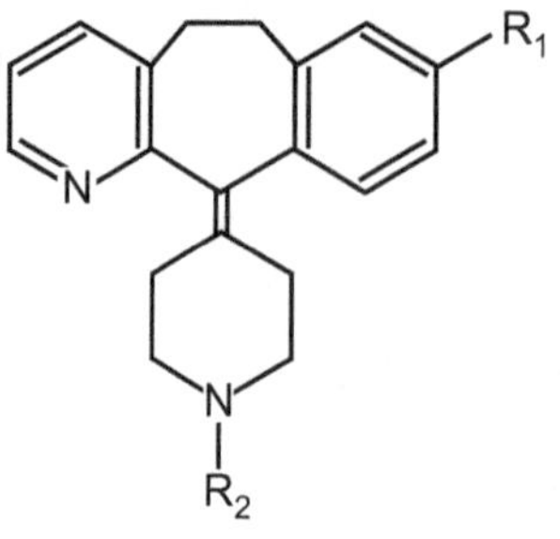

Azatadine :　R_1 = – H; R_2 = – CH$_2$

Loratadine :　R_1 = – Cl, R_2 = – COOC$_2$H$_5$

Azatadine (1983; I^{st} generation) is cyproheptadiene analog where a phenyl has been replaced by a 2-pyridyl and the double bond has been saturated. It also has antiserotonin and high anticholinergic potency and thus similar side effects.

Loratadine : It is a second generation H_1-receptor antagonist used in the treatment of allergic rhinitis and urticaria. Unlike most classical antihistamines, it is devoid of CNS depressant (e.g., drowsiness) effect. It is a prodrug, metabolized to an active metabolite, desloratadine.

Acrivastine is a non-seditive second generation H_1-receptor antagonist used in the treatment of allergies and hay fever.

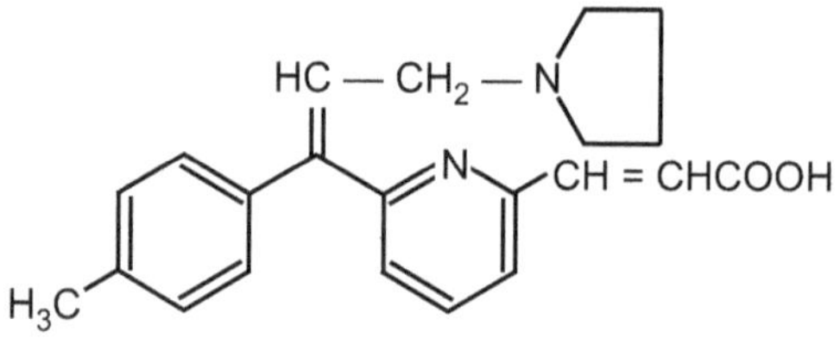

Acrivastine

(2nd generation drug)

3.8　MECHANISM OF ACTION OF CLASSIC ANTI-HISTAMINIC AGENTS (ANTIALLERGIC AGENTS)

Since histamine alone, is not responsible for allergic and anaphylactic conditions, the antihistamines do not necessarily antagonise all the symptoms of above reactions.

Anti-histamines seem to act as antiallergic agents by more than one mechanisms.

(i) By those whose pharmacological actions are opposite to that of histamine.

(ii) Those that prevent the access of histamine to its receptors by competitive antagonism.

Some anti-histamines also antagonise serotonin and bradykinin which are released along with histamine during anaphylaxis reaction. The classic anti-histamines act competitively. Some of them probably fit fairly snugly on the histamine receptor but others can only occupy the minimal area of the receptor-surface thereby, preventing the access of histamine through the steric hindrance. The receptor antagonist complex, like receptor histamine complex is a reversible reaction but unlike the latter, when antagonist binds to the receptor, it has no intrinsic activity. These competitive antagonists are not very effective if they are given after an anaphylactic attack has begun, hence substances whose actions are opposite to histamine, like adrenaline, are much more useful in these conditions.

It is also possible that histamine and its antagonists do not bind with the same site on the receptor. Such binding is called as allosteric binding and may cause a small reversible molecular perturbation in the receptor, resulting into a change in structural and chemical nature of the active site to which histamine normally binds. In such case, histamine may not be able to bind the changed active site or, if it does bind, it may not exhibit an intrinsic activity.

3.9 FATE OF ANTI-HISTAMINES IN THE BODY

Metabolite formation depends upon the chemical nature of anti-histamine and age, sex and animal species in which the drug is studied. Generally small animals exhibit simpler excretion patterns. Metabolism occurs through typical metabolic reactions like N-dealkylation, deamination, side chain degradation, ring hydroxylation and oxidation. Prolonged administration leads to an enhanced activity of liver microsomal enzymes, resulting into increased metabolism of the anti-histamines.

3.10 SIDE EFFECTS

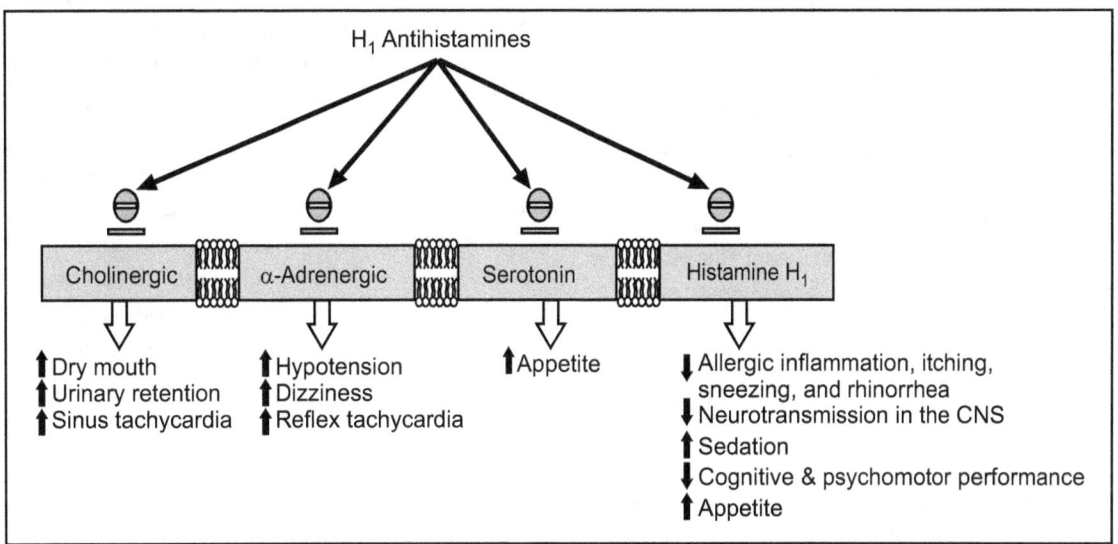

3.11 THERAPEUTIC USEFULNESS OF CLASSIC ANTI-HISTAMINES

(1) Histamine induced contraction of smooth muscle and increase in capillary permeability can be antagonised via H_1-receptor blockade, resulting in an improvement of asthmatic conditions and a reduction in formation of oedema and cutaneous wheal. The classical H_1-receptor antagonists, however, are usually ineffective in bronchial asthma, but they can successfully be employed in the treatment of allergic rhinitis (allergic inflammation of nasal airways), conjunctivitis and dermatitis (rash or irritation of skin) effects.

(2) As hypnotic and rarely as local anaesthetics e.g., promethazine and diphenhydramine.

(3) In the treatment of Parkinsonism, e.g., orphenadine and diphenhydramine.

(4) In motion sickness.

(5) In cardiac arrhythmias, e.g., antazoline, diphenhydramine.

(6) As antiemetic in cases where, vomiting is caused by histamine liberation from the damaged cells.

(7) Due to their atropine-like action, they have been used in cough mixtures.

Even though the general term, anti-histaminic implies the inhibition of the actions of histamine, certain prominent actions of histamine such as, the stimulation of gastric acid secretion, relaxation of uterus and positive inotropic effect on heart (i.e., increase in force of contraction and heart rate) of guinea pig were not blocked by the classic anti-histamines.

Histamine is a powerful stimulator of hydrochloric acid secretion by the oxyntic cells of gastric mucosa. The large doses of histamine also augment the secretion of pepsin and serves as a chemical mediator for the secretory action of substances like gastrin and methylxanthines. It has been established that gastric mucosa possesses high levels of histamine.

In 1966 Ash and Schild hypothesized (on the evidence parallel to the Ahlquist's hypothesis for the existence of two different adrenaline receptors) that histamine should act via atleast two distinct receptor subtypes. James W. Black and co-workers from Glaxo Smith Kline (foremely SK & F) suggested that the histamine responses which are blocked by classic anti-histamines be classified as H_1-receptor responses while those blocked by newer agents (or not blocked by classic anti-histamines) be classed as H_2 responses. These H_2-receptor antagonists of histamine are also termed as anti-secretory drugs.

3.12 ANTI-SECRETORY DRUGS (H_2-ANTAGONISTS)

One of the compounds showing weak H_2-antagonist activity, guanylhistamine, was the point of departure in the development of these drugs. Extension of the side chain was found to increase the H_2-blocking activity, but some agonist effects were retained. When the very basic guanidino group was replaced by the neutral thiourea, burimamide was obtained. Although effective, it lacks oral effectiveness. The addition of a 4-CH_3 group further improved binding to H_2-receptor. Introduction of electron withdrawing sulphur atom into the side-chain reduced the ring pKa. The proportion of the cationic form was decreased and the tele-tautomer became predominant. Reduced ionisation improved the membrane permeability of molecule. Oral absorption (metiamide) was excellent. It is 10 times potent than burimamide. However, metiamide still showed some side effects, in the form of haematological and kidney damage, which were attributed to thiourea group.

Since, 4-methyl histamine shows a weak but noticeable inhibition of the secretion of gastric acid, it was chosen to study the proton tautomerism in its imidazole ring as well as the steric interaction between 4-CH$_3$ group and α-CH$_2$ of side chain. The personal experience of investigators with guanidines suggested the replacement of thiourea group by a guanidine unit [– NHC (= NH) NHR] but it increases basicity and reduces activity. Hence, basicity would be decreased by introducing an electron withdrawing group into the guanidine group e.g. – NHC (= NNO$_2$) NHR or – NHC (= N – CN) NHR. Hence, cyanoguanidine [H$_2$NC (= NCN) NH$_2$] was compared directly with thiourea. Such a side-chain was introduced into 4-methyl imidazole resulting into cimetidine.

A satisfactory replacement was found by substituting another electron withdrawing group on guanidine while retaining appropriate pKa. A cyano group proved suitable and resulted into development of safe and effective cimetidine. Lately, it has become clear that an imidazole nucleus is not absolutely necessary for H$_2$-blocking activity. The furan derivative ranitidine and famotidine were found to be more active.

Since, none of these compounds is lipid soluble, they do not produce any sedative action, as they cannot cross BBB.

Burimamide was the first selective H$_2$-antagonist produced by modification of histamine (Black et al 1972).

Burimamide

Burimamide was poorly absorbed orally and better absorption and higher activities were achieved by introducing a methyl group in the ring to yield metiamide.

Metiamide

Replacement of the thione (= S) sulphur atom of metiamide by a cyanoimino group yielded a potent H$_2$-antagonist, cimitidine.

Cimitidine

Another recently introduced potent H$_2$-antagonist is ranitidine.

Ranitidine

Ranitidine is a nitroethane derivative of furan and on molar basis, it is five times more potent than cemitidine.

Famotidine

It differs in having a thiazole nucleus rather than a furan or imidazoline ring . It is 20 times more potent than cimetidine and 7.5 times more potent than ranitidine in inhibiting basal and pentagastrin stimulated gastric acid secretion.

H$_2$-blockers are generally very polar compounds with pronounced H-bonding ability. They are very hydrophilic and don't enter the brain in more than tiny amounts.

The first brain-penetrating H_2-blocker is Zolantidine (SK & F 95282). However, the physiological role of CNS H_2-receptors is not known.

Other H_2-blockers :

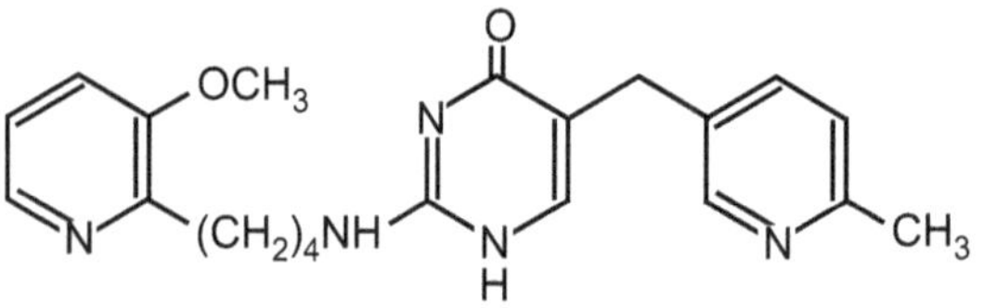

Icotidine

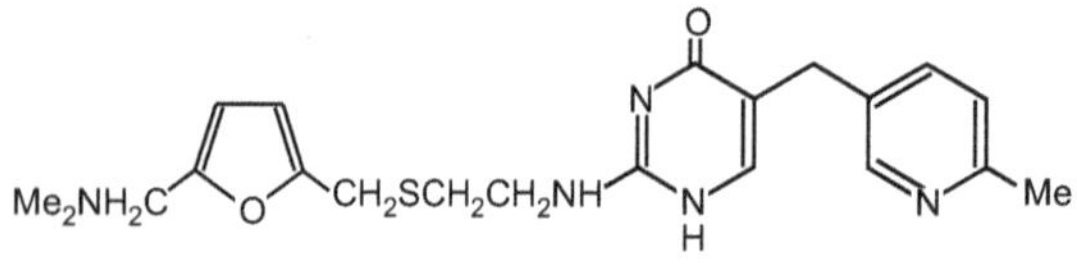

Lupitidine

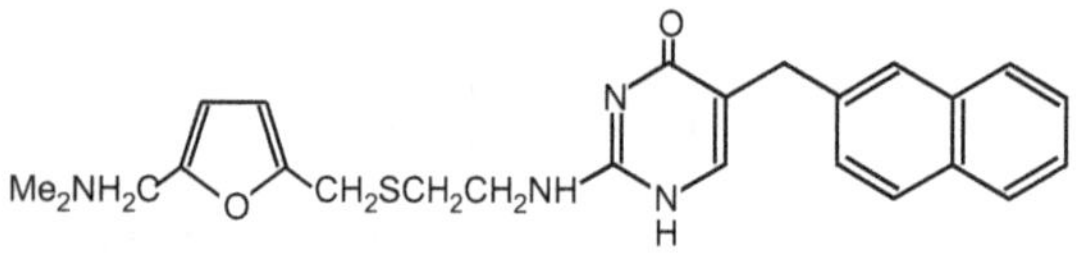

SK & F 93619

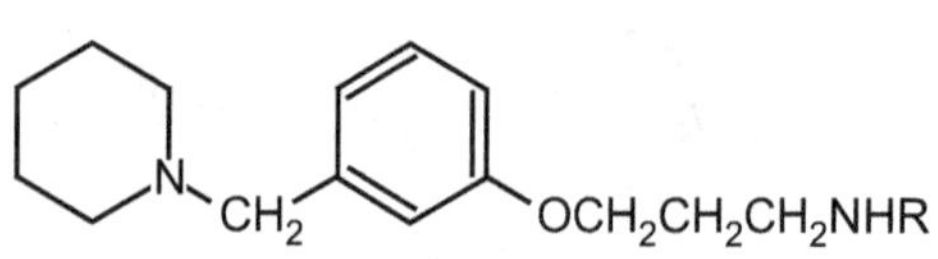

Zolantidine ; R =

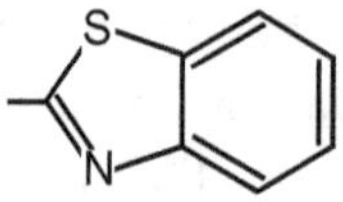

Roxatidine; R = —$COCH_2OCOCH_3$

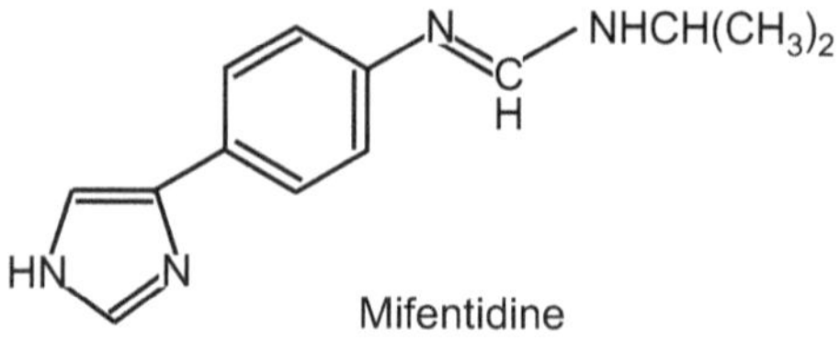

Mifentidine

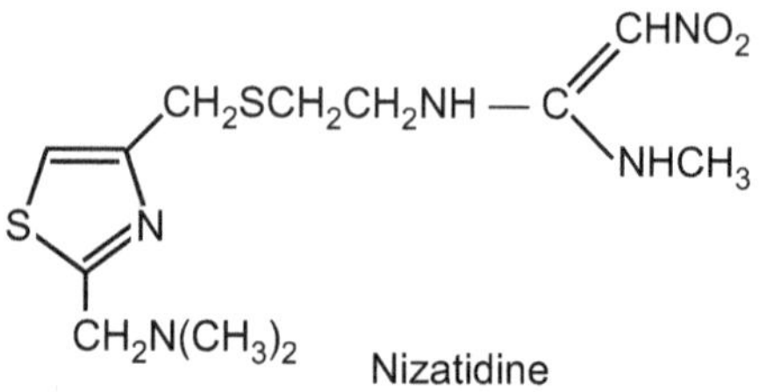

Nizatidine

Nizatidine is a (thiazole instead of furan) derivative of Ranitidine.

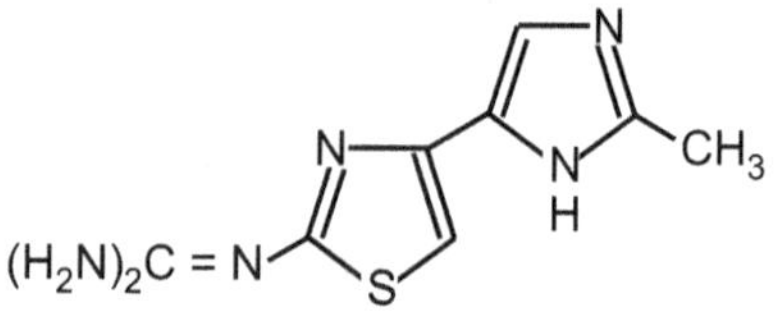

Zaltidine

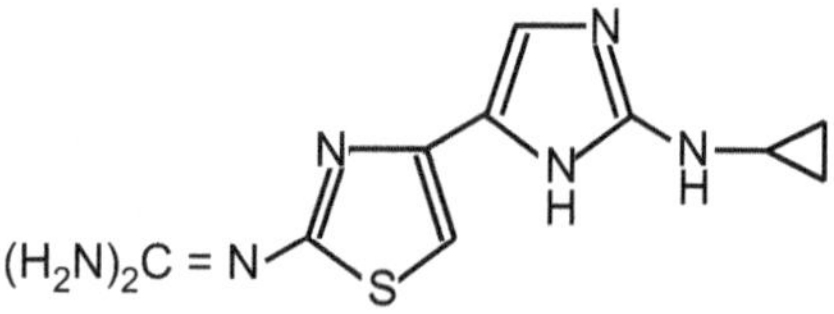

III-195

Schunack described a new class of compounds in which H_1-receptor antagonism is combined with histamine H_2-receptor agonism (e.g. VUF 8531).

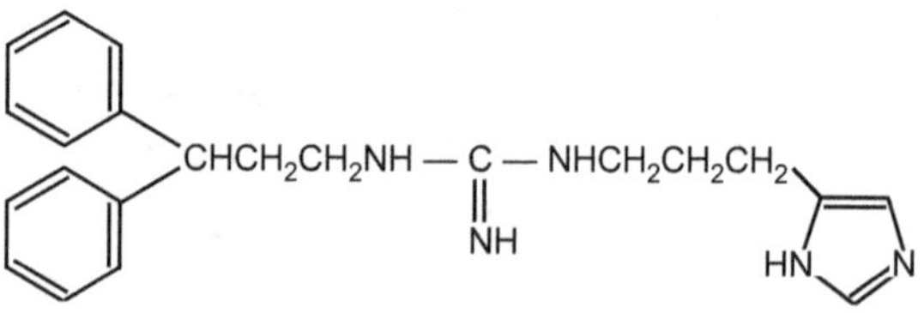

VUF 8531

The compounds concerned are derivatives of the potent H_2-receptor agonist impromidine, in which the 5-methylimidazole moiety has been replaced by the aromatic part of the classical H_1-receptor antagonists.

3.13 H$_2$-RECEPTOR AGONISTS

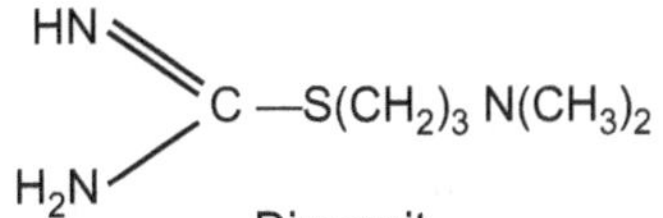

Dimaprit

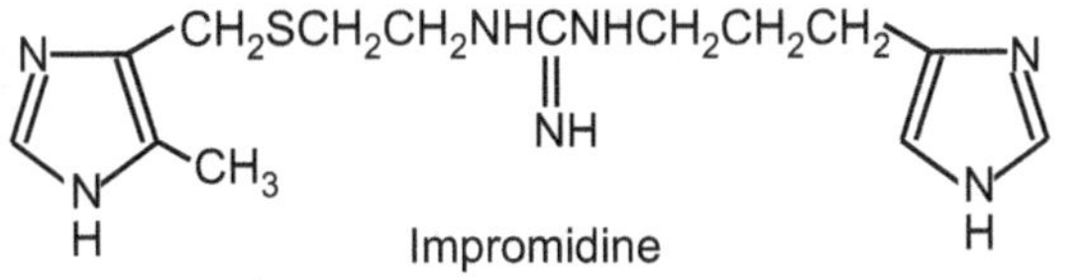

Impromidine

A substantial contribution the elucidation of the structure-activity relationships of H$_2$ agonists occurred when it was established that dimaprit may interact with the H$_2$-receptor through its S- and N-atoms instead of its two N-atoms of the isothiourea system. Undoubtedly, this observation has opened the possibility to design new H$_2$-agonists.

An additional class of H$_2$-agonists is formed by the impromidine analogues with the guanidinopropylimidazole moiety as a characteristic feature.

From a therapeutic point of view, selective H$_2$-agonists may become useful in the treatment of heart failure and catecholamine-insensitive cardiomyopathy.

Structure-Activity Relationship :

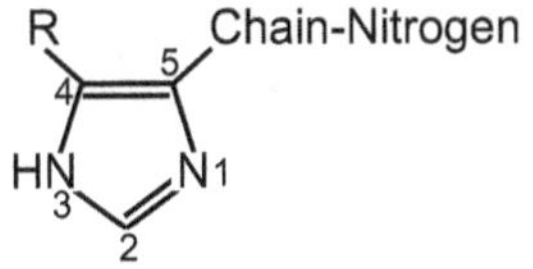

H$_2$ - Antagonist

Unlike the H$_1$-blockers which are typically lipophilic amines, H$_2$-blockers such as cimetidine are very polar. Furthermore, H$_2$-blockers have longer uncharged side chains unrelated to the protonated dialkylaminoalkyl side chains found in H$_1$-blockers. In H$_2$-blocker structure, the imidazole ring is believed to be important for receptor recognition.

(1) Imidazole ring substitutions :

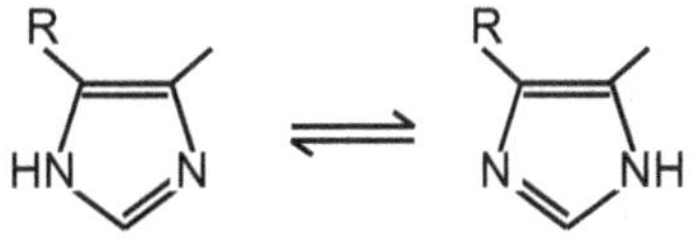

(I)　　　　(II)

The imidazole ring exists in above two tautomeric forms. The form (I) seems to be necessary for maximal H$_2$-antagonistic activity. In most cases, when R = CH$_3$, activity is potentiated.

(2) Chain :

A chain of four carbon atoms is optimal for the activity. A shorter chain, drastically lowers antagonist activity. The chain should contain an electron withdrawing substituent. An isosteric thioether (–S–) link in place of methylene group (–CH$_2$–) leads to more active compounds.

(3) The terminal nitrogen group :

The terminal N-group should be a polar, non-basic substituent for maximal antagonist activity. Though a positively charged group binds more tightly to the receptor, it leads to an agonist activity rather than an antagonist activity.

3.14 MECHANISM OF ACTION

Mucous secreted by the gastric mucous cells combined with surface epithelial bicarbonate secretion contributes to a barrier (the mucous - bicarbonate barrier) that prevents gastric acid and pepsin from damaging the gastric mucosa. While the luminal pH is acidic, the pH adjacent to the epithelial cell membrane is near neutral due to epithelial bicarbonate production and the presence of the mucous layer.

In humans, the parietal cell secretion is estimated to contain approximately 149 meq / litre HCl.

The parietal cell is pyramidal or triangular in shape, relatively large (approximately 25 µm in diameter) and the basal side bulges into the lamina propria. H^+/K^+ -ATPase is located within the cell membrane. The parietal cell also contains an unusually large number of mitochondria occupying approximately 30 - 40 % of the cytoplasm. These are necessary for the high level of oxidative function involved in gastric acid secretion.

The gastric mucosa also secretes small quantities of HCO_3. At the luminal membrane there is a Cl^-/HCO_3^- exchange stimulated by glucagon as well as active HCO_3^- transporter that is chloride independent and stimulated by prostaglandins and c-AMP. Hydrogen ions are secreted into the gastric lumen by an active transport pump, the H^+/K^+ ATPase pump. H^+ ions for the pump are made available by carbonic anhydrase which catalyses the formation of H_2CO_3 from CO_2 and H_2O. The H_2CO_3 dissociates to $H^+ + HCO_3^-$. To maintain intracellular neutrality as H^+ is secreted into the canaliculus (from where H^+ is released through H^+/K^+-ATPase pump). HCO_3^- is exchanged for Cl^- across the basolateral membrane. The resulting increased intracellular Cl^- drives through chloride conductive pathways across the luminal surface of the cell. The overall process generates HCl secretion that is followed by passive H_2O flow.

Since, the parietal cell secretes H^+ ions from the intracellular canaliculus using H^+/K^+-ATPase pump, intracellular K^+ concentration develops. High intracellular K^+ and Na^+ concentrations are maintained by $Na^+ - K^+$-ATPase at the basolateral membrane, while K^+ also moves through conductive pathways into the lumen thereby providing K^+ for H^+/K^+- ATPase.

Three separate receptors have been identified on the parietal cells that mediate HCl secretion. These receptor types interact with histamine, gastrin and acetylcholine. Stimulation of parietal cell function is linked to either c-AMP-dependent (e.g. H_2-receptor) or calcium-dependent mechanisms.

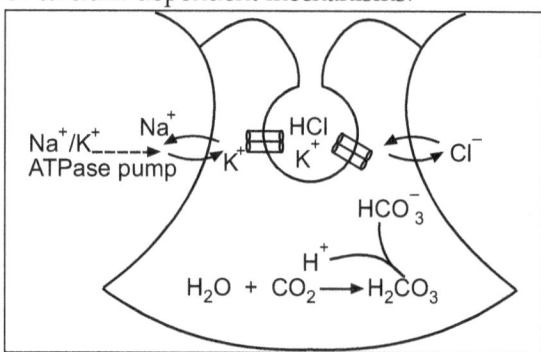

The cholinergic and gastrin stimulation are associated with increases in intracellular calcium. Proglumide which blocks the gastrin receptor, has anti-secretory properties in-vitro but its in-vivo potency is low.

Since H_2-receptor antagonists are potent inhibitors of all stimulants of gastric acid secretion, histamine may be considered as a single common final mediator of acid secretion on the parietal cells.

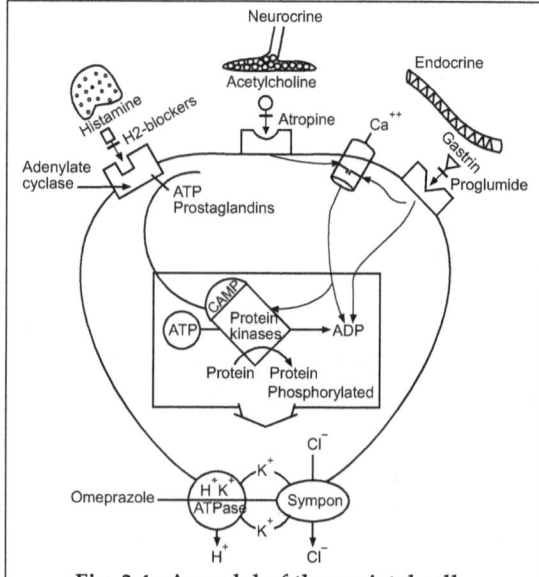

Fig. 3.4 : A model of the parietal cell representing the pathways of acid secretion

The current hypothesis states that the H_2-antagonists simply inhibit the direct actions of histamine (by forming some sort of reversible complex with the H_2-receptors) on acid secretion.

The responses to stimulation of histamine H_2-receptors are mediated through the activation of adenylate cyclase, providing yet another analogy between histamine H_2- and adrenaline β-receptors.

3.15 INHIBITORS OF H⁺- K⁺-ATPase PUMP

The proton pump is a α, β-heterodimeric enzyme. The gastric acid secretion is regulated by the functioning of H⁺ - K⁺ ATPase pump present in the parietal cell membrane (1970). It works just similar to Na⁺-K⁺- ATPase pump and exchanges proton for K⁺- ions.

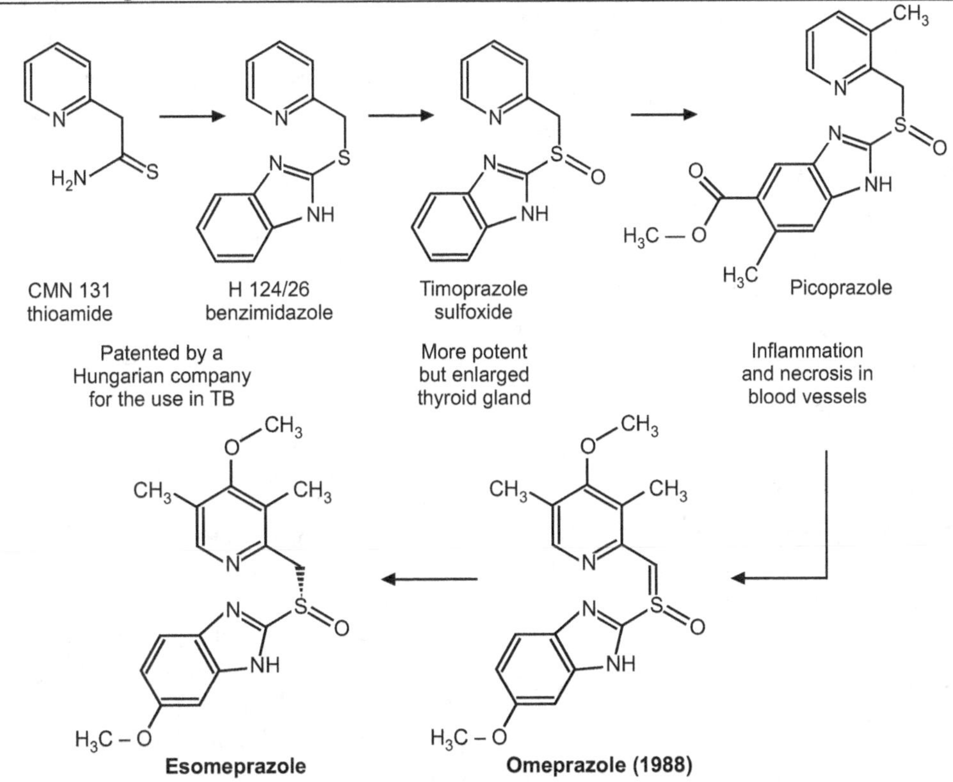

CMN 131
thioamide

Patented by a
Hungarian company
for the use in TB

H 124/26
benzimidazole

Timoprazole
sulfoxide

More potent
but enlarged
thyroid gland

Picoprazole

Inflammation
and necrosis in
blood vessels

Esomeprazole

Omeprazole (1988)

- In 1977, the proton pump was discovered to be the final step in acid secretion.
- In the early 1980s, it was shown that the substituted benzimidazoles blocked the proton pump.
- Since, weak bases accumulate in the acidic compartment, substituents were added to the pyridine ring to obtain a pKa that maximized the accumulation in the parietal cell.
- The resulting compound was called Omeprazole (1976).
- Omeprazole was originally marketed as Losec but renamed Prilosec to avoid confusion with Lasix.
- The higher pKa also increases the rate of acid mediated conversion to the active species.
- Substitution in the benzimidozole ring made the compound more stable to conversion at neutral pH and eliminated thyroid enlargement effect.
- Intramolecular transfer of a proton occurs prior to the nucleophilic attack.
- Electron donor (OCH_3) to the pyridine ring enhanced the rate of attack of the C_2 thereby promoting formation of the active species (*Sulfenamide*).

3.16 ABSORPTION, FATE AND EXCRETION

Cimetidine and ranitidine are the clinically used agents from this category. By oral route, they are rapidly and completely absorbed. However, the presence of antacid may interfere in their absorption pattern. Both these drugs get widely distributed in the body. Cimetidine is reported to cross placental barrier. Metabolism of cimetidine yields chiefly sulphoxide and 5 – hydroxymethyl derivatives while N-oxide, S-oxide and desmethyl derivatives are obtained upon ranitidine metabolism. Most of the administered dose of cimetidine appears in the urine as the mixture of unchanged (free and conjugated) and its metabolite forms. Minor quantity may be eliminated in stool.

Adverse effects are few and of mild nature. These include nausea, diarrhoea, constipation, headache, skin rashes and dizziness. Due to their antiandrogenic effect, they may cause sexual dysfunction. Ranitidine is devoid of this effect. Cimetidine may also cause leukopenia. It also depresses the activity of metabolising enzyme and may thus potentiate the effects of other concomitantly administered drugs.

3.17 THERAPEUTIC USES

These drugs have inhibitory effect on gastric acid secretion. Hence, they are highly effective in treating conditions characterised by hyper secretion of gastric acid. Thus, they create a favourable environment for rapid healing of gastric and duodenal erosions.

Antacids are commonly used along with H_2-receptor blocking agents in the treatment of peptic ulcer.

Pantoprazole (1994)

Lansoprazole (1991)

Rabeprazole (1999)

Rabeprazole is a prodrug. It turns into active sulphenamide form in the acid environment of parietal cells. It is used in the treatment of stomach ulcers and zollinger-ellison syndrome.

It is effective orally as well as parenterally and inhibits ATPase pump in the reversible fashion. Its clinical usefulness promoted further the development of drugs from this category.

i) Higher pKa value of the pyridine helps to facilitate entry of the drug (lipophilic) to accumulate within the parietal cell thereby increasing the rate of acid mediated conversion to the active (ionic) form.

ii) In general, fluoro substituent is found to block metabolism at the point where it is attached. Addition of trifluoromethyl group to benzimidazole moiety led to a series of very active compounds. Later, the more balanced fluoroalkoxy substituent instead of trifluoromethyl group led to highly active and longer acting drugs.

Dexlansoprazole : It is a proton pump inhibitor (enantiomer of lansoprazole) used in the treatment and maintenance of patients with erosive oesophagitis and non-erosive gastro-oesophageal reflux disease.

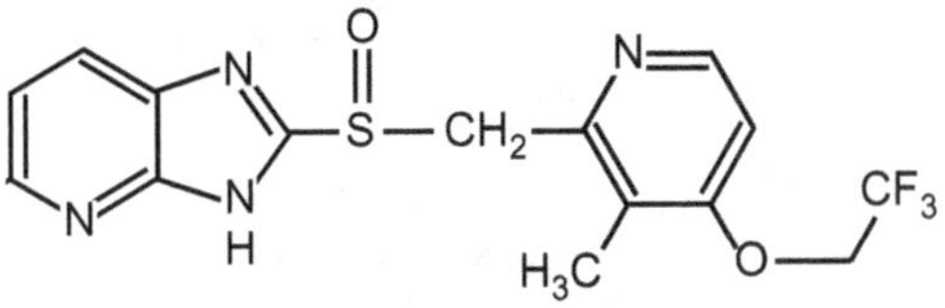

Dexlansoprazole

PPIs are prodrugs which in acidic condition, get converted into cyclic sulfenamides.

PPI chemically are divided into :

(a) Benzimidazole linked to substituted pyridine; e.g. Omeprazole.

(b) Imidazopyridine linked to substituted pyridine e.g. Tenatoprazole.

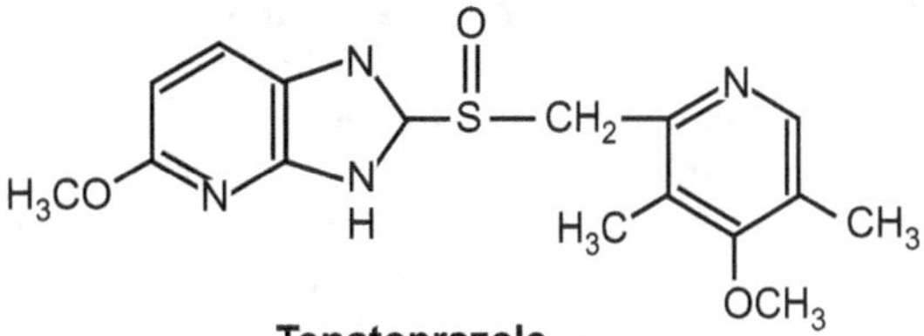

Tenatoprazole

Mechanisms of Action :

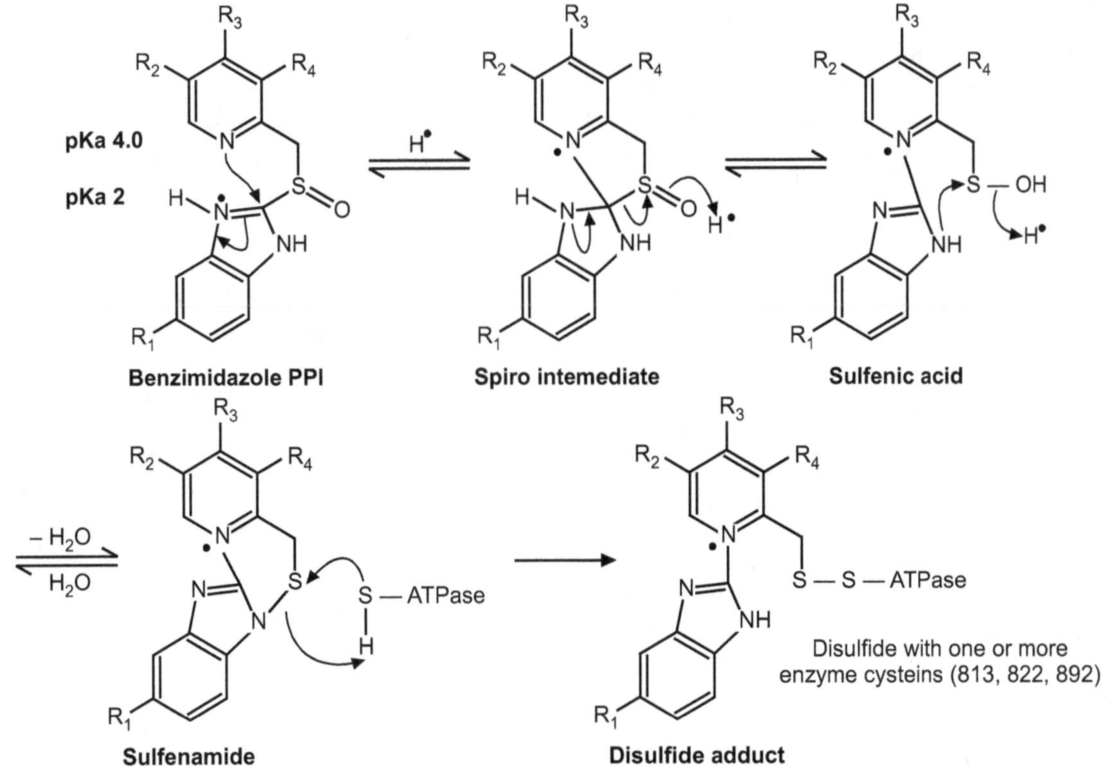
pKa 4.0
pKa 2
Benzimidazole PPI
Spiro intemediate
Sulfenic acid
– H_2O
H_2O
S — ATPase
S — S — ATPase
Disulfide with one or more enzyme cysteins (813, 822, 892)
Sulfenamide
Disulfide adduct

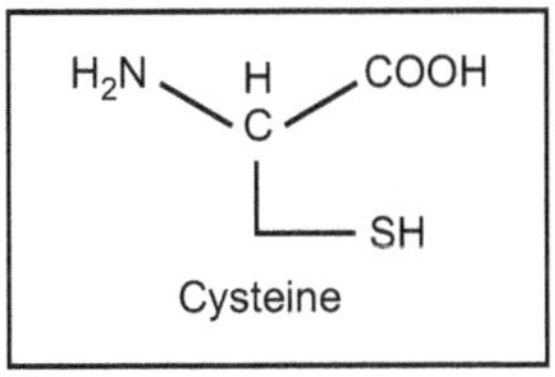
Cysteine

3.18 H₃-RECEPTOR

Histamine is both a local hormone and a neurotransmitter. Histaminergic pathways in the CNS have been described in detail. The activity pattern of a neuronal system is governed by several elements : action potential, transmitter release, interaction of transmitters with post-synaptic receptor (s), inactivation routes including neuronal reuptake and interaction with presynaptic receptors. In 1983, a presynaptic inhibitory autoreceptor for histamine was described. Presynaptic receptors modulate the release of a neurotransmitter in a quantitative sense (autoreceptor).

These seem to be presynaptic autoreceptors, controlling histamine release and synthesis. They are activated by histamine concentrations. Their blockade may potentially lead to increased blood flow and metabolism combined with a central arousal, whereas their stimulation (or inhibition of central H_2 receptors) could have an anticonvulsant or sedative effect.

Immepip
H₃-receptor agonist

Selective H₃-receptor agonists :

These include R (α)-methylhistamine, S (α)-methylhistamine, Imetit, Immepip.

Selective H₃-receptor agonists do not have any therapeutic use except as research tools. While H₃-receptor antagonists may be used to sleep disorders (narcolepsy) and neuropathic pain. They have stimulant and nootropic effects. They increase histamine release in the brain and improve wakefulness, attention and learning.

H₃-receptors were **first indentifier** pharmacologically in 1983. They are primarily found in brain and are inhibitory autoreceptors which modulate the release of histamine. Activation of H₃-receptors affects cognition, the sleep wake cycle, obesity and epilepsy.

Selective H₃-receptor antagonists :

These include thioperamide, clobenpropit, ciproxifan, iodoproxyfan, iodophenpropit, carboperamide, betahistine etc.

Thioperamide
H₃-receptor antagonist

Clobenpropit

Ciproxifan

Peripheral H₃-receptor activation has been shown to inhibit gastric acid secretion induced by food and pentagastrin in cats, dogs and rabbits.

The benefecial effects of H₃-receptor agonists in neurogenic inflammation and in migraine is also suggested. Certain types of arrythmias are shown to be inhibited by H₃-receptor stimulation.

While H₃-receptor antagonists like ciproxifan, has been shown to enhance wakefulness in cats and rats. H₃-receptor stimulation or blockade, thus, is suggested to be a novel approach to the treatment of sleep disorders such as hypersomnia or narcolepsy and to promote wakefulness in vigilance deficits.

Narcolepsy includes excessive daytime sleepiness, persistent tiredness and lack of energy. While cognitive disorders may include inability to focus, solve problems, process information, communicate, memory impairment.

Hence, H₃-receptor antagonists are used in the treatment of narcolepsy, dementia and cognitive disorders.

3.19 EICOSANOIDS

Eicosanoids are signaling molecules derived by oxidation of 20 carbon omega-3 (ω-3) or omega-6 (ω-6) fatty acids as detailed below :

(a) 8, 11, 14 eicosatrienoic acid

(dihomo-7-linolenic acid)

(b) 5, 8, 11, 14-eicosatetraenoic acid or arachidonic acid, an ω-6 fatty acid with four double bonds.

(c) 5, 8, 11, 14, 17-eicosapentaenoic acid an ω-3 fatty acid with five double bonds.

The fatty acid is named by the location of the first double bond, counted from the CH_3 end in omega (ω) or lower side chain. The ω-3 fatty acid possesses double bond at the 3rd C-atom from the end of carbon chain.

The important categories of eicosanoids include

- Prostanoids (e.g. prostaglandins, prostacyclins, thromboxanes.

- Leucotrienes (LT)

- Eoxins (EX) and lipoxins

Prostaglandins were originally shown to be synthesized in the prostate gland thromboxanes from platelets (thrombocytes) and leucotrienes from leucocytes. Lipoxins are potent inflammation modulating eicosanoid derivatives.

Eicosanoids work like local hormone. They are extremely potent at very dilute concentrations. They act on cells close to their site of production through receptors mediated G-protein linked signaling pathways. Eicosanoids rapidly undergo metabolism so they are not able to travel very far. Hence, eicosanoids are not stored within cells but are synthesized as required. They play a regulatory role chiefly in inflammation (predominantly those of joints, skin and eyes); pain, fever, immunity, blood clotting and certain respiratory and reproductive processes. Most eicosanoids are produced from arachidonic acid.

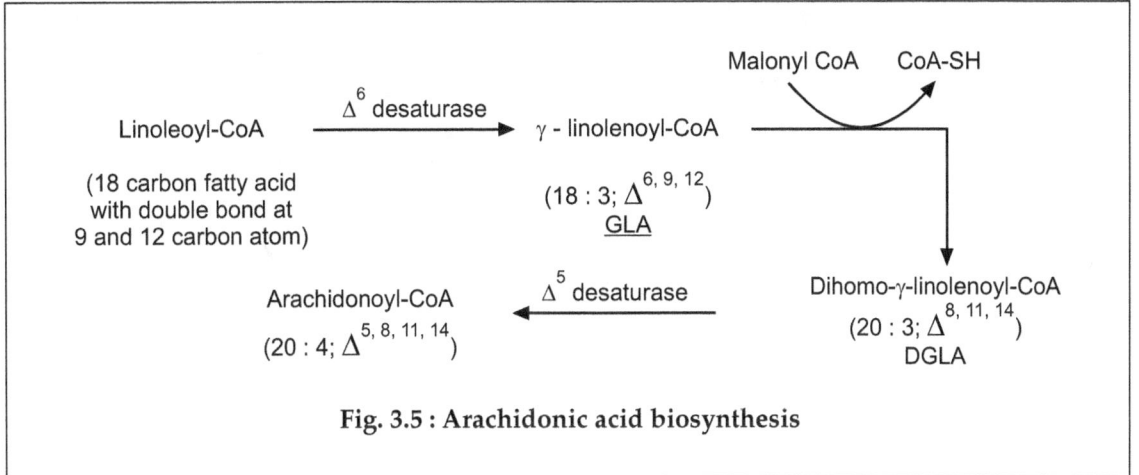

Fig. 3.5 : Arachidonic acid biosynthesis

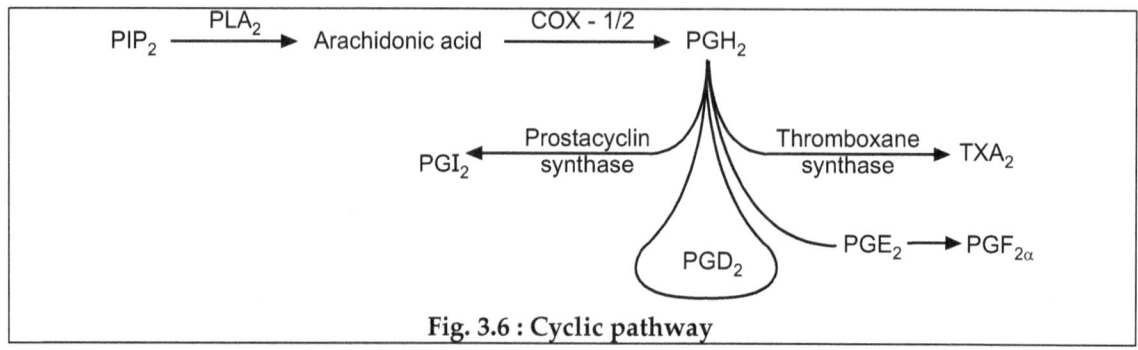

Fig. 3.6 : Cyclic pathway

Biosynthesis of Eicosanoids :

Two main pathways involved in the biosynthesis of eicosanoids include.

(i) Cyclic pathway : The prostaglandins (PGs) and thromboxanes (TX) are synthesized by the cyclic pathway. Numerous stimuli (e.g., epinephrine, thrombin and bradykinin) activate phospholipase A_2 enzyme (PLA_2) which hydrolyzes arachidonic acid from cell membrane phospholipids. Arachidonic acid is converted to PGH_2 by cyclo-oxygenase (or prostaglandin G/H synthase or prostaglandin endoperoxide synthase) enzyme.

(ii) Linear Pathway : It is mediated through the action of arachidonate lipooxygenase (e.g. 5-LO, 12-LO and 15-LO). The 5-LO is responsible for synthesis of leukotrienes in white blood cells, mast cells, lung, spleen, brain and heart. While 12-LO and 15-LO are involved in the synthesis of the lipoxins.

Eicosanoids Receptors :

Each of the eicosanoids functions through the activation of the G-protein coupled receptor (GPCR) family. There are atleast 10 characterized prostaglandin receptors. For example

(i) **DP receptors** : bind with prostaglandin $D_1/D_2/D_3$.

(ii) **EP receptors** : bind with prostaglandin $E_1/E_2/E_3$.

(iii) **FP receptors** : bind with prostaglandin $F_1/F_2/F_3$.

(iv) **IP receptors** : bind with prostacyclin (PGI_2).

(v) **TP receptors** : bind with thromboxanes.

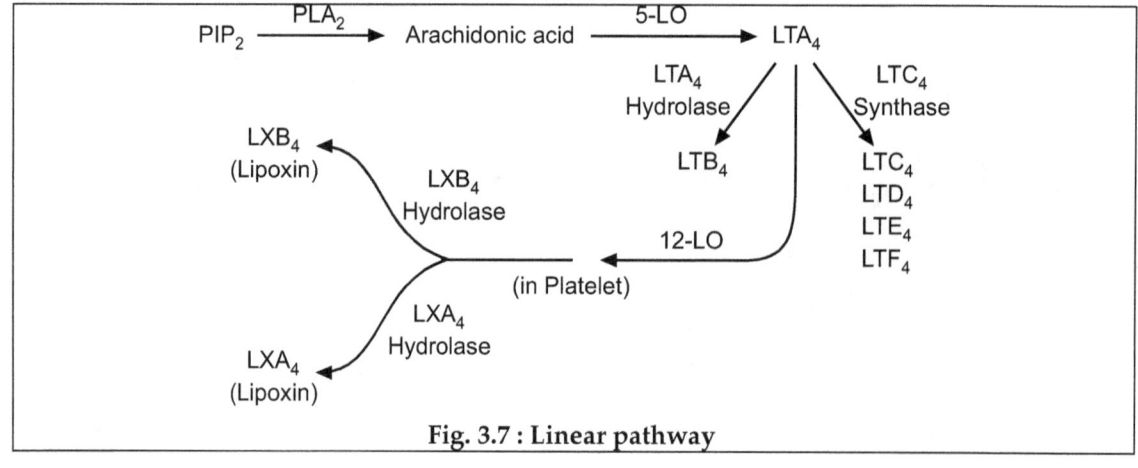

Fig. 3.7 : Linear pathway

3.20 PROSTAGLANDIN ANALOGS

The prostaglandins (PGs) are unsaturated fatty acid derivatives containing 20 carbon atoms. All the prostaglandins are formed in the animal body by ring closure and oxygenation of essential polyunsaturated fatty acids such as arachidonic acid.

In the reproductive system, PGE_1 and PGE_2 increase the contraction of the pregnant uterus, but inhibit the motility and tone of the non-pregnant uterus and intravaginally used to induce therapeutic abortion. PGF_2 increases the motility of both sperm and uterince tubes.

In the GIT, prostaglandins increase motility and diminish gastric acidity. They increase renal blood flow, inducing a sodium and water diuresis and also redistribute blood from medulla to cortex, thus antagonising renin production.

In 1933, Maurice Goldblatt and Von Euler independently found that a humoral principle present in the human seminal fluid leads to both smooth muscle contraction and vaso-constriction. Euler (1935) identified the lipids soluble nature of that component and gave the name, prostaglandin to these substances with the belief that the biologically active substance found in the human semen was a secretion of the prostate gland. He defined prostaglandin as a "lipid soluble smooth muscle stimulating and blood pressure lowering factor with acidic properties in human seminal fluid and some accessory genital glands of man and sheep".

The work on the identification of prosta-glandins was commenced by Bergstrom (1949). He recognized the presence of more than one unsaturated hydroxy fatty acid in partially purified prostaglandin extracts. The isolation in pure crystalline form from sheep vesicular glands of the first two prostaglandins, now called prostaglandin E_1 (PGE_1) and prostaglandin $F_{1\alpha}$ ($PGF_{1\alpha}$) was reported by Bergstrom and Sjovall in 1957. Later, additional compounds having related structures were isolated from different organs. The natural prostaglandins are hydroxylated C_{20}^- polyunsaturated fatty acids having extensive and varied activities in mammalian system, such as :

(a) stimulating or relaxing uterine smooth muscles,

(b) constriction of bronchi,

(c) lowering or raising blood pressure,

(d) inhibiting gastric secretions,

(e) mediating inflammation,

(f) promoting sodium ion excretion, and

(g) inducing labour.

Thus, they qualify to be called as 'local hormones'.

Occurrence :

Although prostaglandins were first discovered in seminal plasma and in vesicular glands, their distribution is not restricted to the male accessory genital glands and their secretions. Prostaglandins are known to be distributed widely in mammals. They can be extracted from most animal tissues. The total prostaglandin production in the adult human is 1 to 2 mg per day.

Human seminal fluid contains the highest concentration and the greatest number of prostaglandins (about 31 prostaglandins). Similarly sheep prostate contains PGE_1, PGE_2, PGE_3 and $PGF_{1\alpha}$. The table 3.1 shows some of the tissues and fluids in which prostaglandins are present.

Table 3.2 : Prostaglandins present in human tissues

	Source	Prostaglandins
1.	Bronchi	PGE_2, $PGF_{2\alpha}$
2.	Cardiac muscle	PGE_2
3.	Cervical sympathetic nerve	PGE_2, $PGF_{2\alpha}$
4.	Endometrium (lung)	PGE_2, $PGF_{2\alpha}$
5.	Maternal venous blood during labour	PGE_2, $PGF_{2\alpha}$
6.	Menstrual fluid	PGE_2, $PGF_{2\alpha}$
7.	Placental blood vessels	PGE_1, PGE_2, $PGF_{1\alpha}$, $PGF_{2\alpha}$
8	Semen	PGA_1, PGA_2, PGB_1, PGB_2, PGE_1, PGE_2, PGE_3, $PGF_{1\alpha}$, $PGF_{2\alpha}$
9.	Stomach mucosa	PGE_2
10.	Vagus nerve	PGE_2, $PGF_{2\alpha}$

Nomenclature and Chemistry of Prostaglandins :

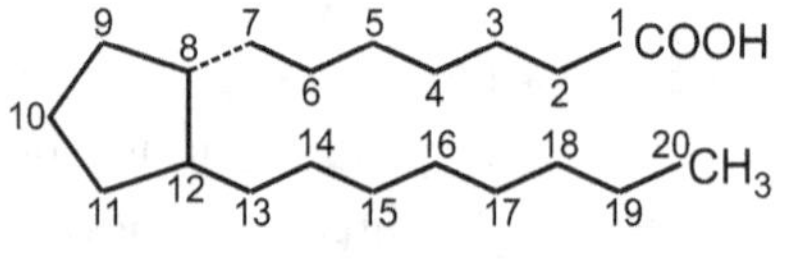

Prostanoic acid

Structurally prostaglandins are derivatives of prostanoic acid and have a cyclopentane ring with two side-chains attached to adjacent carbon atoms.

Systematic nomenclature of prostaglandins is based upon the hypothetical parent 'prostanoic acid' numbered as shown. With the increasing number and types of prostaglandins coming out, it became virtually essential to define the norms of nomenclature and classification of prostaglandins.

The present classification is based upon the nature of

(a) cyclopentane ring

(b) two adjacent side-chains and

(c) configuration of newly introduced functional group.

(a) Nature of the Cyclopentane Ring :

Depending upon the nature of functional groups present, the cyclopentane ring may be categorised into :

(i) A-type cyclopentane ring contains 10, 11 - unsaturated 9-ketone function

(ii) B-type cyclopentane ring contains 8, 12 - unsaturated 9-ketone function

(iii) C-type cyclopentane ring contains 11, 12 -unsaturated 9- ketone function

(iv) E-type cyclopentane ring contains β-hydroxy ketone system

(v) F-type cyclopentane ring contains 1, 3 - diol system.

PGA and PGB were so called because of their stability in acids and bases respectively. The names of other prostaglandins were based on the separation procedures, i.e. PGE partitioned into ether and PGF into phosphate (Fosfat in Swedish) buffer. Other types like PGC, PGD, PGG and PGH have also been described.

(b) Nature of Adjacent Side-chains :

Two side-chains are attached to the cyclopentane ring at carbon atoms 8 and 12. The upper side-chain having carboxyl (– COOH) group at its terminal, is termed as carboxylhexyl or α-side-chain while the lower side-chain (attached to C_{12}) having hydroxyl at C_{15} is called as hydroxyoctyl (ω) side-chain. Compounds in these groups, are further characterized by a subscript 1, 2 or 3 depending on the number of double bonds in the side-chains. The side-chains may contain as many as 3 to 4 double bonds.

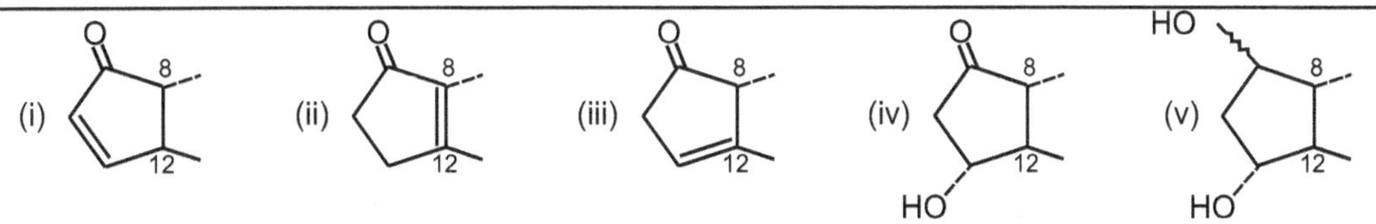

| (i) A-type | (ii) B-type | (iii) C-type (Unstable) | (iv) E-type | (v) F-type |

For example,

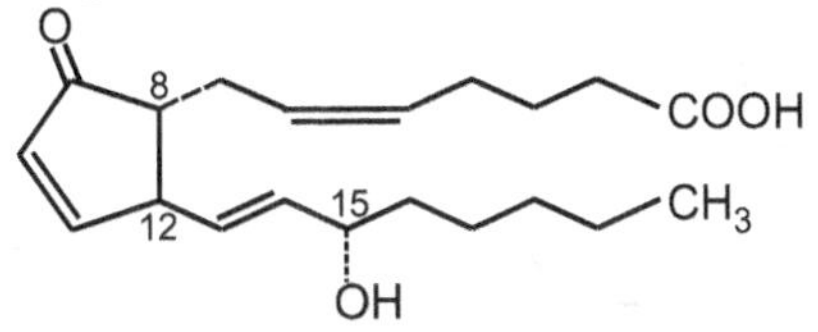

(I)

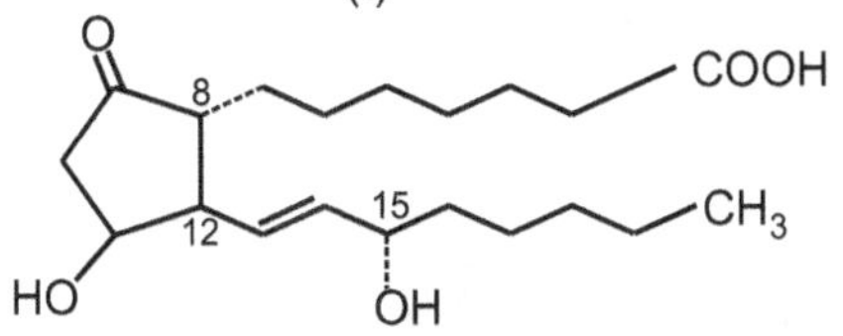

(II)

In the above structures, (I) contains cyclo-pentane ring of type A and two double bonds in the side-chains. Hence, the name will be PGA_2. While, the structure (II) contains the cyclopentane ring of type E and only one double bond in the side-chain. Hence, it can be named as PGE_1.

In all the natural prostaglandins, the upper side-chain is attached to the cyclopentane ring through an α-bond (i.e., projecting behind the plane of the ring) and is shown by a dotted line. Similarly the naturally occurring prostaglandins possess an α-hydroxyl group at C_{15} atom. Any change in this configuration must be specified by adding epi- as a prefix to the name alongwith the number of carbon atom at which this change has occurred.

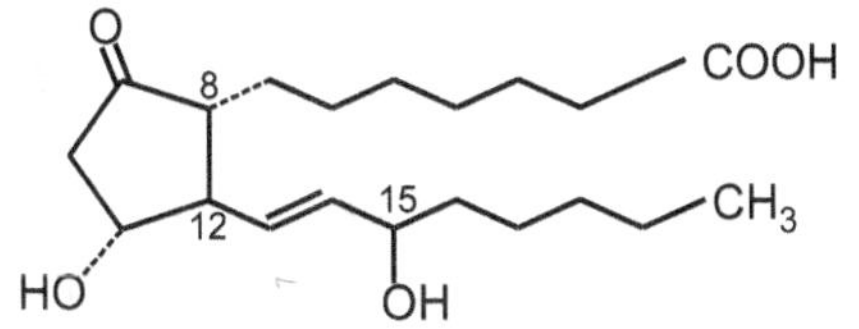

15 - epi PGE_1

(c) **Nature of the Configuration :**

This parameter is needed to define the configuration of newly introduced functional group in the molecule. The literature prior to 1968 was extended by Anderson (1969) to designate further possible isomers and the optical antipodes. For example, PGE can be converted to PGF by reducing the C_9-ketone to a hydroxyl group. Thus, the PGF group can be further divided into PGF_α and PGF_β types, depending on whether the hydroxyl at C_9 is behind the plane (α) or above the plane (β) of the ring.

The generic name, eicosanoids is given to a class containing prostaglandins, leukotrienes and related compounds because the basic skeleton is of 20-carbon fatty acid containing 3, 4 or 5 double bonds. In man, arachidonic acid (precursor of prostaglandins) is either derived from dietary linoleic acid or is ingested as a dietary constituent. Thromboxanes (TX) contain a six member oxane ring instead of the cyclopentane ring of prostaglandins. While prostacyclin (PGI_2) has a double-ring structure in addition to a cyclopentane ring.

Hydroperoxy eicosatetraenoic acids (HPETEs) are obtained from arachidonic acid by the attack of lipooxygenase enzymes. The HPETEs are unstable intermediates and are further metabolised by a variety of enzymes. All HPETEs may be converted to their corresponding hydroxy fatty acid (HETE) either by a peroxidase or non-enzymatically. Similarly, leukocytes convert 15-HPETE to trihydroxylated metabolites called lipoxins.

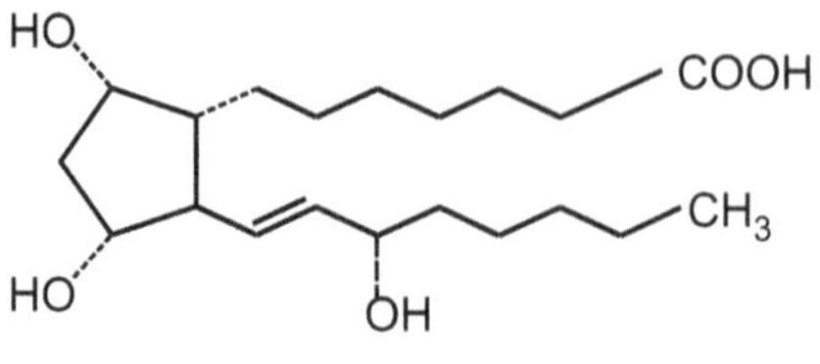

PGF$_{1\alpha}$

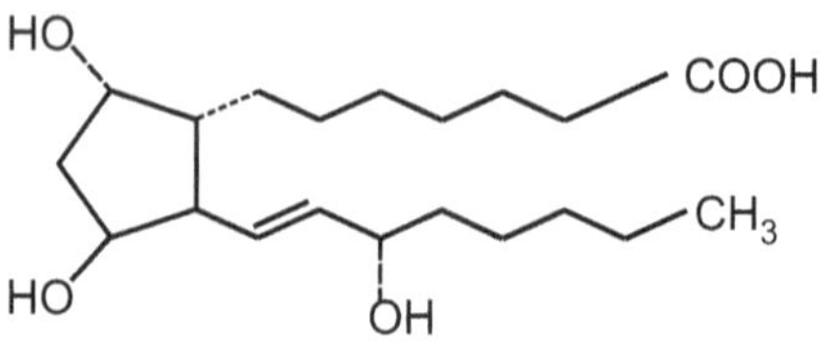

PGF$_{1\beta}$

Biosynthesis and Metabolism of Prostaglandins :

Prostaglandins are synthesized enzymatically from certain open chain C$_{20}$ unsaturated fatty acids which include

(a) 8, 11, 14 eicosatrienoic acid
　(dihomo-7-linolenic acid)

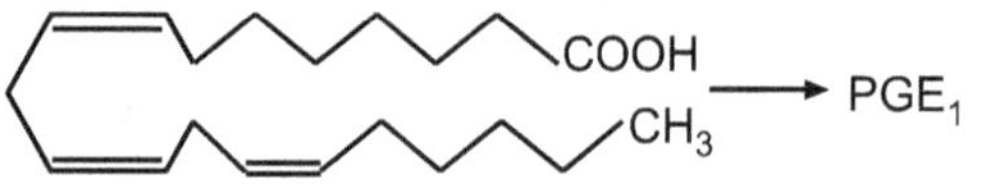

COOH
CH$_3$ ⟶ PGE$_1$

(b) 5, 8, 11, 14-eicosatetraenoic acid or arachidonic acid

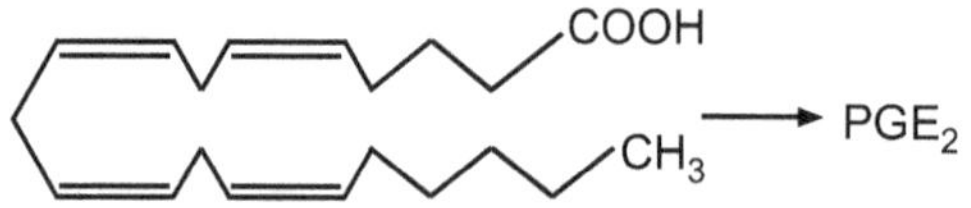

COOH
CH$_3$ ⟶ PGE$_2$

(c) 5, 8, 11, 14, 17-eicosapentaenoic acid

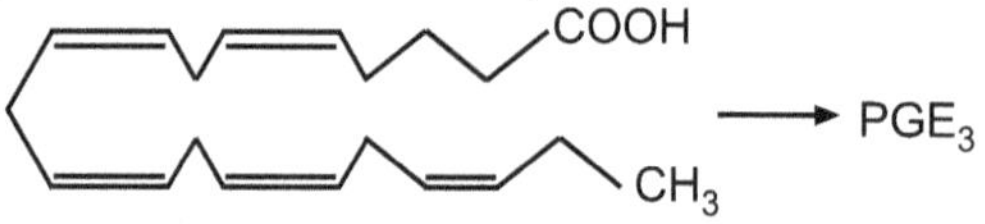

COOH
CH$_3$ ⟶ PGE$_3$

These acids are precursors of the in-vivo prostaglandin synthesis.

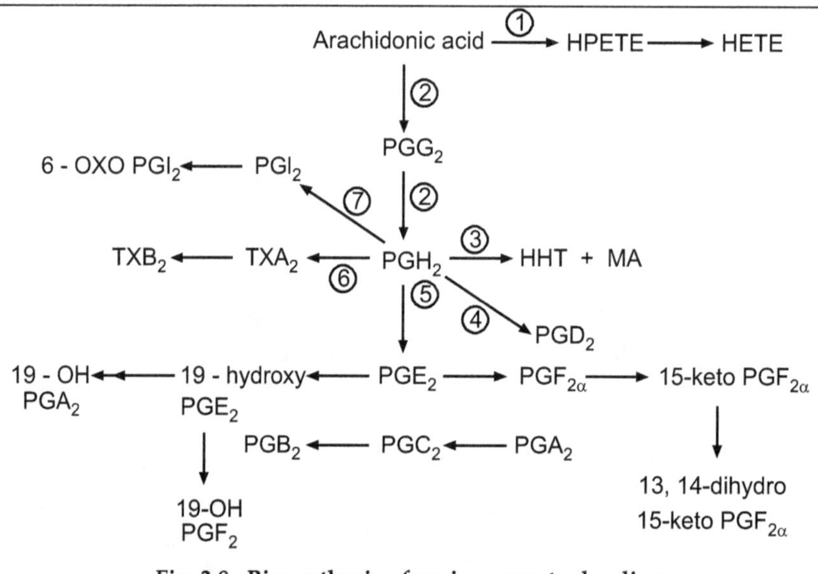

Fig. 3.8 : Biosynthesis of various prostaglandins

where, HHT: 12 - L - hydroxyl - 5, 8, 11 - heptadecatrienoic acid; MA : Malondialdehyde; HETE: 12 - L - hydroxy - 5, 8, 10, 14 - eicosatetraenoic acid; HPETE : 12 - L – hydroperoxide analogue

Enzymes involved in the biosynthesis of prostaglandins :

(1) lipo-oxygenase; (2) cycloxygenase (PG-endoperoxide synthetase); (3) serum albumin glutathione-s-transferase; (4) PG-endoperoxide reductase; (5) PG-endoperoxide-E-isomerase; (6) PG-endo-thromboxane A isomerase (thromboxane A2 synthetase); (7) PG- endoperoxide I isomerase.

Pharmacological Actions of Prostaglandins :

Prostaglandins have been extensively studied because of their profound effects on physiological processes. All such important biological effects of prostaglandins include :

(a) Gastrointestinal system :

Prostaglandins are found to exert the following actions on GIT system :

(i) decrease the gastric acid secretion.

(ii) increase the non-acid secretion in rats.

(iii) induce contraction of smooth muscles.

(b) Urinary system :

Specifically PGE_2 and $PGF_{2\alpha}$ increase bladder activity and help to maintain blood flow.

(c) Bronchial and tracheal smooth muscles :

Some prostaglandins (e.g. PGA, PGE_1, PGE_2) relax the bronchial smooth muscles while PGF induces bronchoconstriction.

(d) Reproductive system :

Prostaglandins increase the rate of synthesis and release of testosterone. Hence, PG - deficiency in male may lead to infertility. They stimulate myometrial smooth muscles that leads to uterine contraction (e.g. $PGF_{2\alpha}$). Hence, clinically it may be used to induce abortion.

(e) Cardiovascular system :

Prostaglandin endoperoxide and TXA_2 cause platelet aggergation and vasoconstriction. While PGI_2 (prostacyclin) decreases platelet aggeregation and leads to vasodilation. Similarly PGE_2 and PGA_2 produce peripheral vasodilation and they may be used in the treatment of hypertension.

(f) Nervous system :

Prostaglandins affect mood, behaviour, brain excitability and EEG-pattern. The CNS-effects vary from CNS-depression to excitation. However, they do not influence A.N.S. functioning.

Metabolism of Prostaglandins :

Gastric tissue easily metabolise prosta-glandins, as shown in the rat. Only about 0.1% of prostaglandins in the lumen reaches the serosal surface unaltered but it is not known which metabolites are formed. Besides this, other possible sites of PG-metabolism include liver, kidney, lungs, adrenal glands and uterus. For example, in lungs the 15-hydroxyl group of prostaglandins E_1, E_2, A_2 and $F_{2\alpha}$ are metabolised by means of an enzyme system thought to involve 15-hydroxy prostaglandin dehydrogenase.

The 15-keto compound is then reduced to the 13, 14-dihydro derivative, a reaction catalyzed by prostaglandin Δ^{13} - reductase. Subsequent steps involve β and ω oxidation of the side-chains of the prostaglandins, giving rise to a polar dicarboxylic acid, which is excreted in the urine.

Table 3.2: Active Prostaglandins

Substance	Observed biological activity
PGD_2	Weak inhibitor of platelet aggregation.
PGE_1	Vasodilation. Inhibitor of platelet aggregation. Bronchodilatation. Stimulate contraction of Gl smooth muscle.
PGE_2	Stimulate hyperalgesic response. Renal vasodilation. Stimulate uterine smooth muscle contraction. Reduce secretion of stomach acid.
PGF_2	Stimulate uterine smooth muscle contraction. Stimulate breakdown of corpus luteum in animal.
PGI_2	Potent inhibitor of platelet aggregation. Potent vasodilator.

Prostaglandin Antagonists :

The receptor sites at which prostaglandins act in isolated segments of gastrointestinal muscle have been investigated mainly by the use of selective pharmacological antagonists. It was found that PGE_1 and PGE_2 inhibit the circular muscle of the human, guinea pig and rat gut by acting at sites on the muscle which are different from α- and β-adrenoceptors. The excitatory receptors appear to differ from receptors for acetylcholine, 5-hydroxy tryptamine and histamine. The excitatory (longitudinal muscle) and inhibitory (circular muscle) PGE receptors, therefore, appear to be different. The prostaglandin antagonists SC-19220 and polyphloretin phosphate antagonize the excitatory effects of PGE and PGF compounds but not the inhibitory (circular muscle) effects of PGE compounds.

Certain compounds inhibit prostaglandin synthesis by competitive antagonism. This ability is due to their structural resemblance with prostaglandin precursors. They include, (1) 8, 12, 14 - eicosatrienoic acid and (2) 5, 8, 12, 14-eicosatetranoic acid.

Besides these, gold, silver, zinc and cupric ions inhibit the prostaglandin synthesis. Non-steroidal anti-inflammatory drugs inhibit the cycloxygenase enzymes.

Other important prostaglandin-antagonists include

(a)

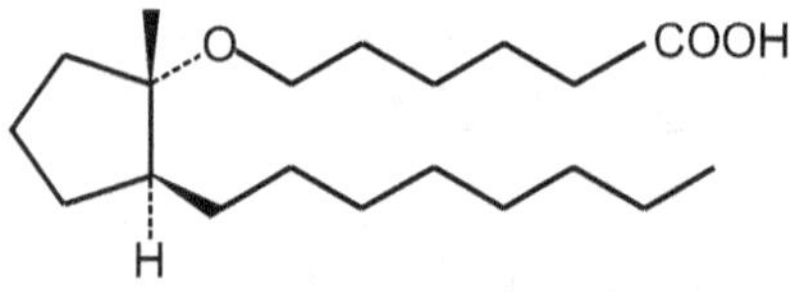

7-oxa prostanoic acid

(b)

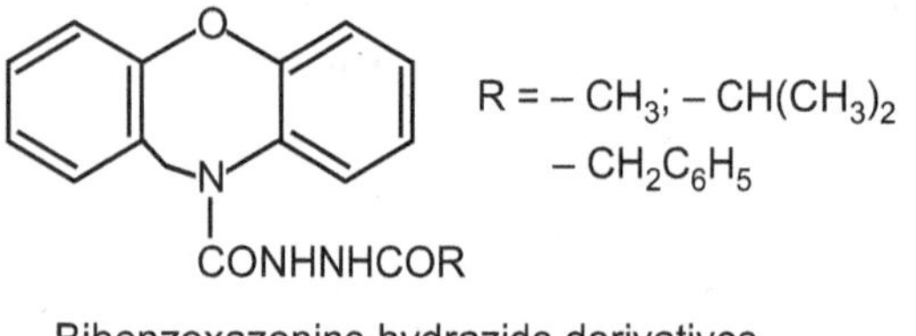

R = – CH_3; – $CH(CH_3)_2$
    – $CH_2C_6H_5$

CONHNHCOR

Bibenzoxazepine hydrazide derivatives

(c)

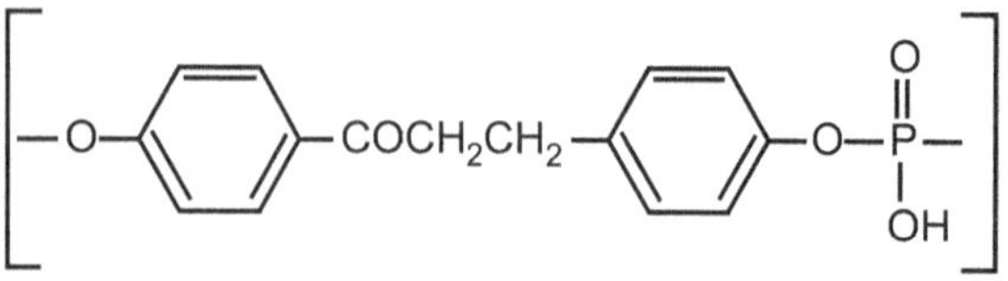

Polyphloretin phosphate

(d) Other drugs like morphine, quinidine and procaine were also reported to have antagonistic actions.

Clinically used Prostaglandin Analogs :

These have been based on modification of the structure of natural prostaglandins (mainly PGE_1 and PGE_2), to increase resistance to metabolism, or achieve a lower incidence of side-effects at therapeutic doses. Some, notably enprostil - have relatively long half-lives. The main prostaglandin analogs are listed below.

(a) Arbaprostil :

It is an analog of 15-methyl PGE_2. It is rapidly absorbed and eliminated with a short half-life. Doses of approximately 2 μg/kg produce more than 60% inhibition of basal and stimulated acid output in humans. Anti-secretory doses of arbaprostil (150 μg 4 times a day) heal duodenal ulcers but lower cytoprotective doses (10 μg to 25 μg about 4 times a day) are ineffective. Arbaprostil may inhibit gastrin release and has been shown to protect against aspirin induced gastric injury in doses of 0.6 μg/kg/ day.

(b) Trimoprostil :

It is 11-methyl analog of PGE_2 which is well absorbed. Doses in the range 7.5-10 μg/kg reduce the basal acid secretion while doses upto 40 μg/kg inhibit meal stimulated acid for upto 3 hours. Doses in the anti-secretory range (2 mg/day and upward) reduce aspirin injury. Trimoprostil stimulates gastric bicarbonate secretion. When given, 750 μg 4 times daily, it is less effective at healing duodenal ulcers and gastric ulcers than cimetidine, 200 mg 3 times daily and 400 mg at night.

(c) Misoprostol :

Both ulcer healing and pain relief effects of misoprostol are dose dependent in the doses of 100 mg 4 times daily or more. Misoprostol, 200 μg 4 times daily, was of similar efficacy to cimetidine, 300 mg 3 times daily, in healing duodenal ulcers and gastric ulcers over 4 weeks.

Misoprostol is a methyl ester of 15-methyl PGE_1. It is rapidly absorbed after oral admini-stration. It is rapidly de-esterified to free acid, binds to albumin and is concentrated in gastrointestinal, hepatic and renal tissues. It is rapidly oxidized and eliminated with a half-life of about 1.5 hours. It has been shown to inhibit basal, daytime and overnight acid secretion and that stimulated by histamine, betazole, pentagastrin, tetragastrin and caffeine. It helps to reduce alcohol injury in man and produces a substantial dose-dependent rise in duodenal bicarbonate secretion.

(d) Rioprostil :

This is a methyl PGE_1 derivative, orally well absorbed with a short half-life. Doses of 300 to 600 μg reduced basal and stimulated acid secretion and pepsin output. It also prevents gastric bleeding and promotes healing rate. With this dosing regimen, diarrhoea and abdominal pain were said to be infrequent.

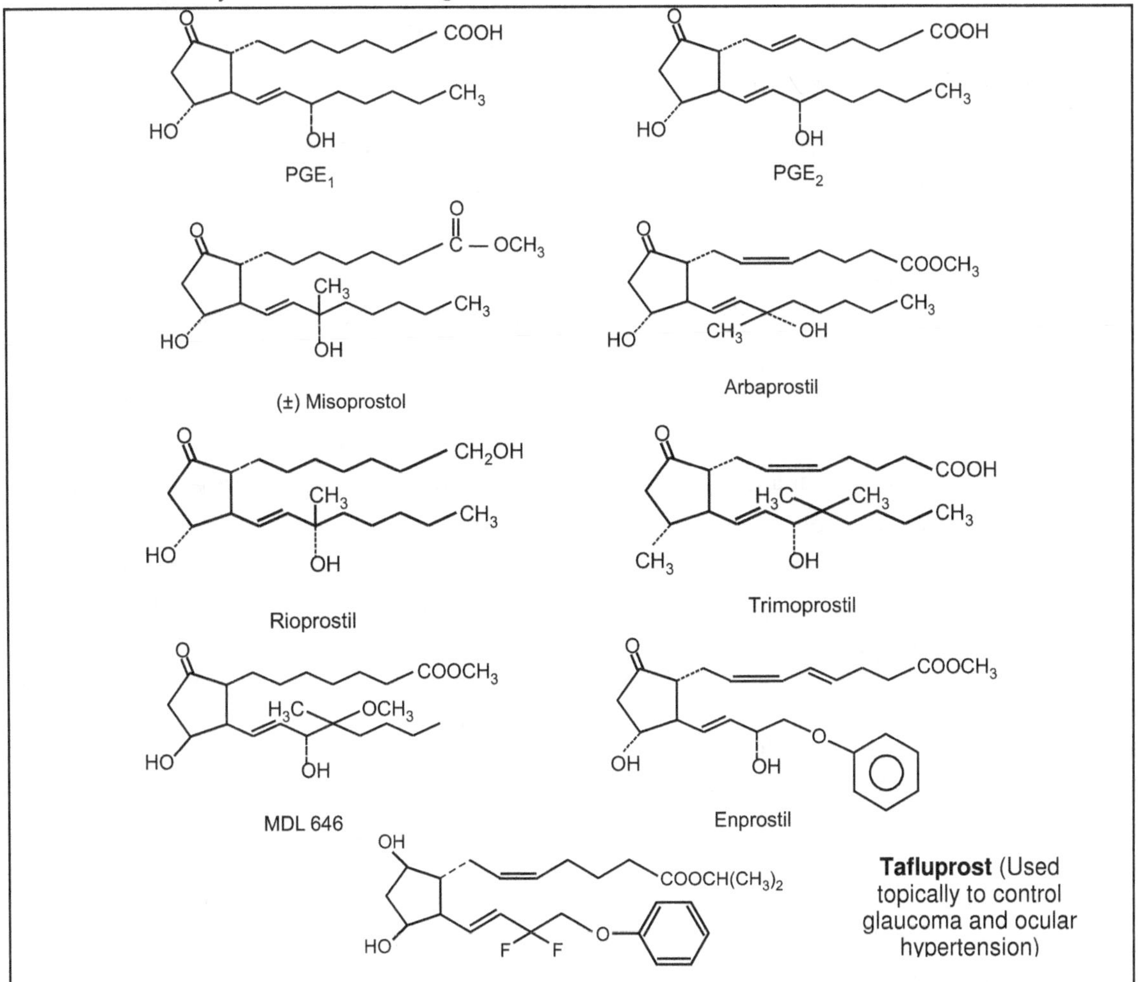

Fig. 3.9 : Some prostaglandin analogs

(e) MDL-646 :

This is a PGE$_1$ - derivative which has local protective effects on gastric mucosa. Single doses of MDL in the range of 800-1200 μg reduced basal acidity but had much less effect on stimulated acid output.

(f) Treprostinil : It is a synthetic analogue of prostacyclin (PGI₂). It is indicated for the treatment of pulmonary arterial hypertension.

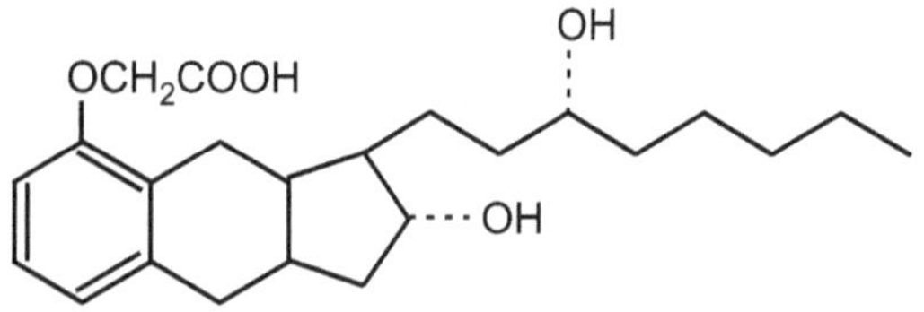

Treprostinil

(g) Travoprost : It is a synthetic PGF$_{2\alpha}$ analogue used in the treatment of glaucoma or ocular hypertension. It reduces the intraocular pressure by increasing the outflow of aqueous fluid from the eyes.

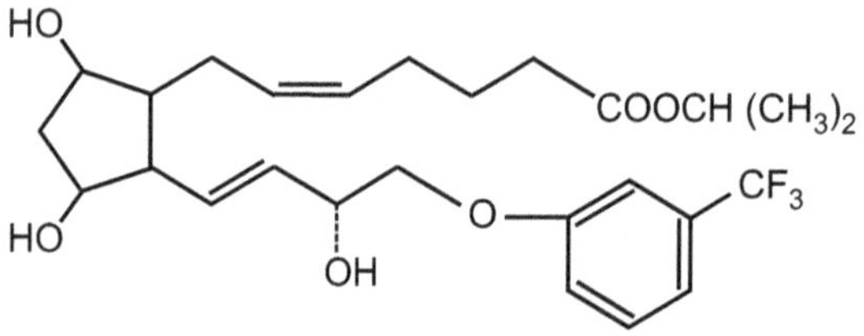

(h) Bimatoprost : It is prostaglandin analogue used to control glaucoma and ocular hypertension.

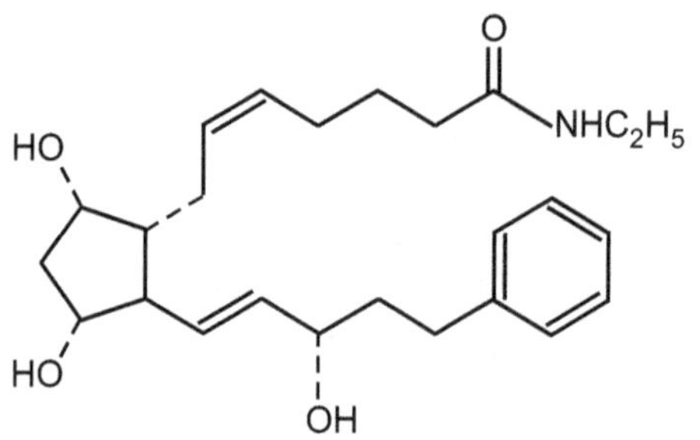

(i) Latanoprost : It is an analogue of PGF$_{2\alpha}$. It works by increasing the outflow of aqueous fluid from the eyes. It is used topically to control progression of glaucoma or ocular hypertension by reducing intraocular pressure.

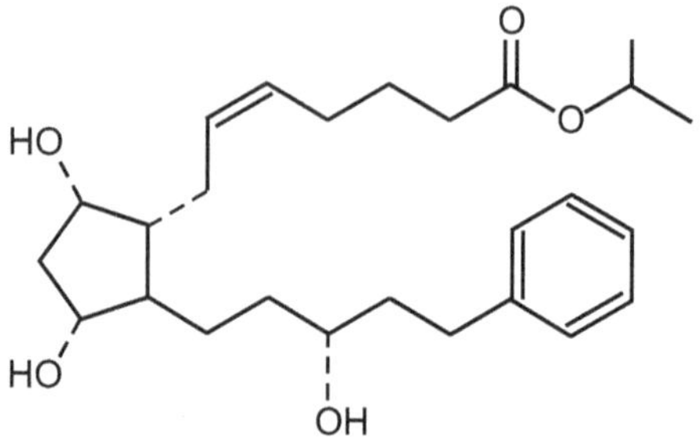

(j) Enprostil :

About 35-140 μg per day of enprostil heals duodenal ulcers and gastric ulcers. However, daily doses of 70 μg are less effective than ranitidine 300 mg in healing duodenal ulcers. Maintenance treatment with enprostil, 35 μg at night is less effective in duodenal ulcer patients than ranitidine 150 mg.

(k) Prostacyclin :

It caused a reduction in duodenal ulcer size in a dose of 5 μg/kg/h infused for 5 hours per day over 6 days. It also increases gastric bicarbonate secretion but does not affect pentagastrin stimulated acid secretion.

(l) FCE 20700 :

This is a new PGE$_2$ derivative (11-deoxy-13, 14-dehydro-16 (S) - methyl PGE$_2$ methyl ester) in doses of 1 and 2 mg produces a small but significant dose related inhibition of acid secretion.

Many of the available ulcer healing drugs (sucralfate, carbenoxolone, bismuth chelate etc.), which do not affect acid are able to enhance prostaglandin level. Other prostaglandin analogs include carboprost, cloprostenol sodium, dinoprost (prostin F₂), dinoprostane (prostine E₂), epoprostenol sodium (prostacyclin), fluprostenol sodium, prostalene and sulprostone.

Table 3.3 : Clinically used Prostaglandins

Chemical abbreviation	Generic name	Trade name	Abortification	Bronchial smooth muscle	Platelets	Blood vessel
PGE_2	Dinoprostone	Prostin E_2	12-20 weeks	Dilation	–	Dilation
$PGF_{2\alpha}$	Dinoprost	Prostin $F_{2\alpha}$	16-20 weeks	Constriction	–	Constriction
15-methyl $PGF_{2\alpha}$	Carboprost	Prostin 15/M	13-20 weeks	–	–	–
PGE_1	Alprotadil	Prostin VR	–	Dilation	–	–
PGI_2	Epoprostanol	Flolan	–	–	Inhibition aggregation	Dilation

Adverse effects of Prostaglandin Analogs :

Acid inhibition by available prostaglandin analogs is moderate. Comparative studies are few but there are no analogues where it is clearly established that clinically useful doses are more effective than cimetidine. All available analogues caused diarrhoea to varying degree. There are also chances that the motility of the pregnant human uterus be increased to induce abortion.

Dinoprostone :

It is marketed in the form of vaginal suppositories containing 20 mg of PGE_2. It is used to induce abortion and to treat benign hydatidiform mole. Carboprost tromethamine is a solution containing 0.25 mg of carboprost (15-methyl $PGF_{2\alpha}$) per ml. It may be used intramuscularly to induce abortion or to treat postpartum haemorrhage owing to uterine atony.

SAR-studies of Prostaglandins

(1) Expansion or contraction of the cyclo-pentane ring or its replacement by heteroaromatic rings results in decrease in the activity of the E_2 and F_2 series.

(2) Replacement of hydroxyl group in the ring gives more stable analogs. For example, thia-PGI_2 (I) possesses platelet aggregation-inhibiting activity with vasodilatory effect. Similarly the aromatic pyridazo derivative (II) is an excellent vasodilator.

(3) Modification of the carboxylic acid side-chain has also been reported. For example, the phenoxy derivative (III) is about 10 times more active than PGE as an inhibitor of platelet aggregation while the sulfonamide derivative (IV) is 15-30 times more active than PGE_2 as an anti-fertility agent and possesses less side-effects.

(4) The 7-oxo and 7-thia analogs were found to show an antagonistic activity on isolated smooth-muscles.

(5) Incorporation of a methyl group in the lower side-chain leads to an increase in uterotonic activity. For example, carboprost and compound (V) are used to induce abortions while nileprost (VI) is an experimental antiulcer agent. The former probably inhibit the dehydrase enzyme that inactivates prostaglandins by removing the 15-hydroxyl group.

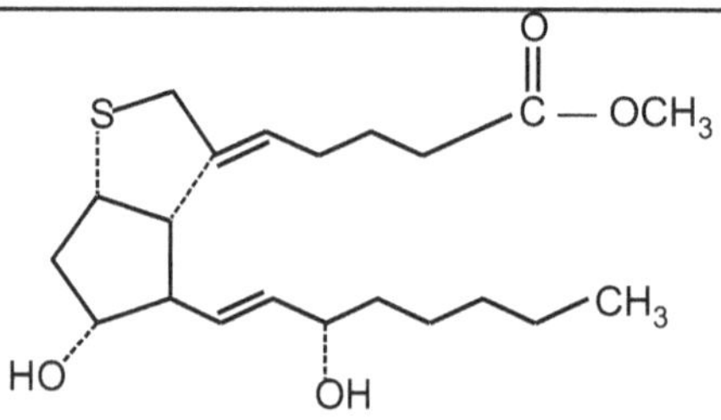

C — OCH3
S
CH3
HO
OH

(I)

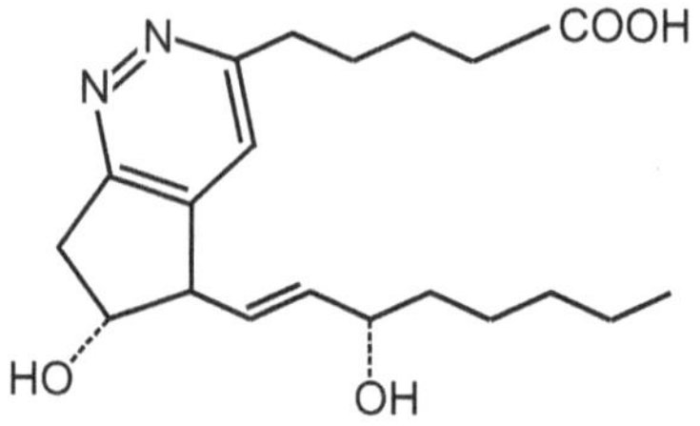

N
N
COOH
HO
OH

(II)

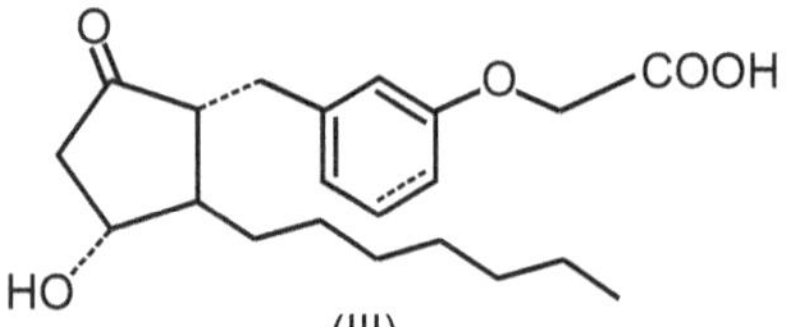

O
COOH
HO

(III)

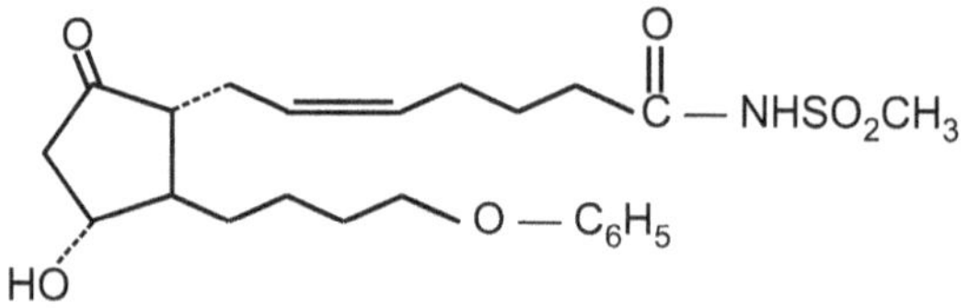

O
C — NHSO2CH3
O — C6H5
HO

(IV)

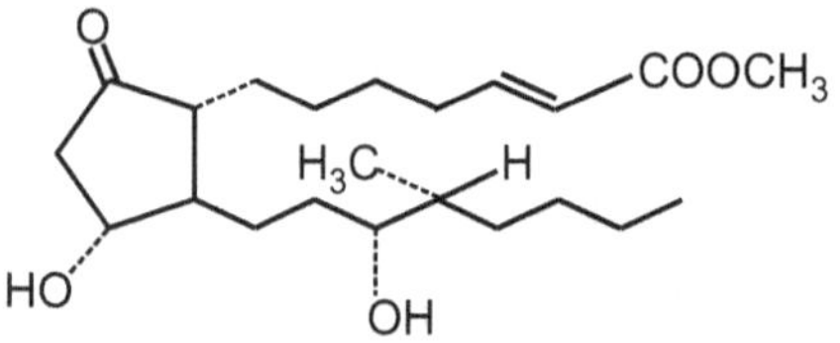

O
COOCH3
H3C
H
HO
OH

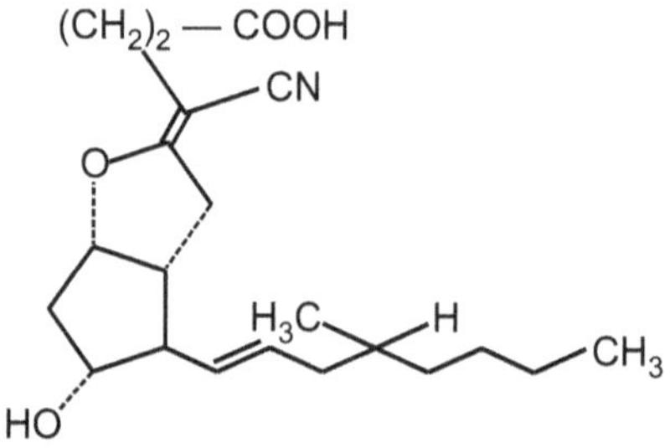

(CH2)2 — COOH
CN
O
H3C
H
CH3
HO

(V) (VI)

Synthesis

(I) Prolidine :

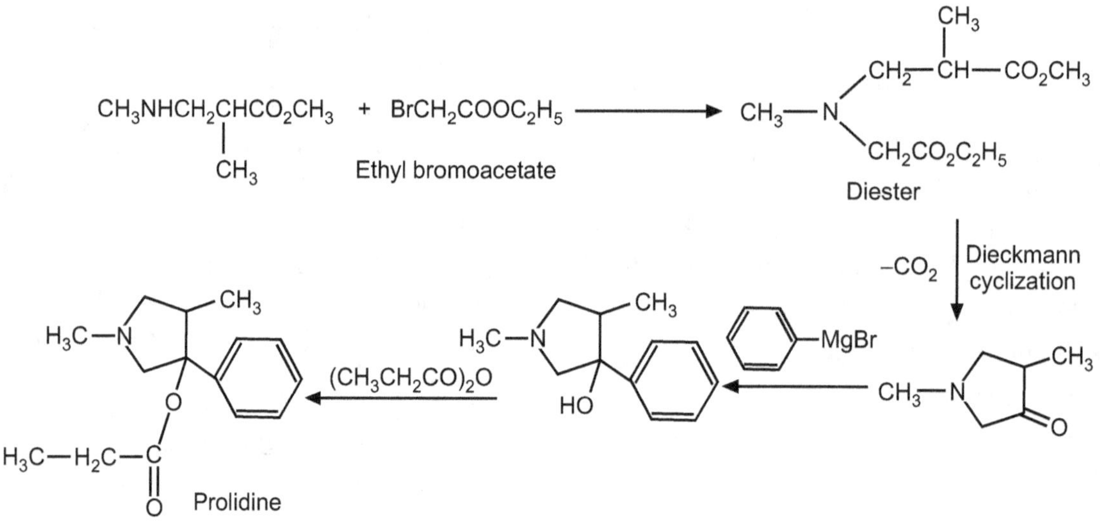

CH3NHCH2CHCO2CH3
CH3
+ BrCH2COOC2H5
Ethyl bromoacetate
CH3
CH2—CH—CO2CH3
CH3—N
CH2CO2C2H5
Diester
–CO2
Dieckmann cyclization
CH3—N
CH3
O
MgBr
H3C—N
CH3
HO
(CH3CH2CO)2O
H3C—N
CH3
O
H3C—H2C—C
O
Prolidine

(II) Ranitidine :

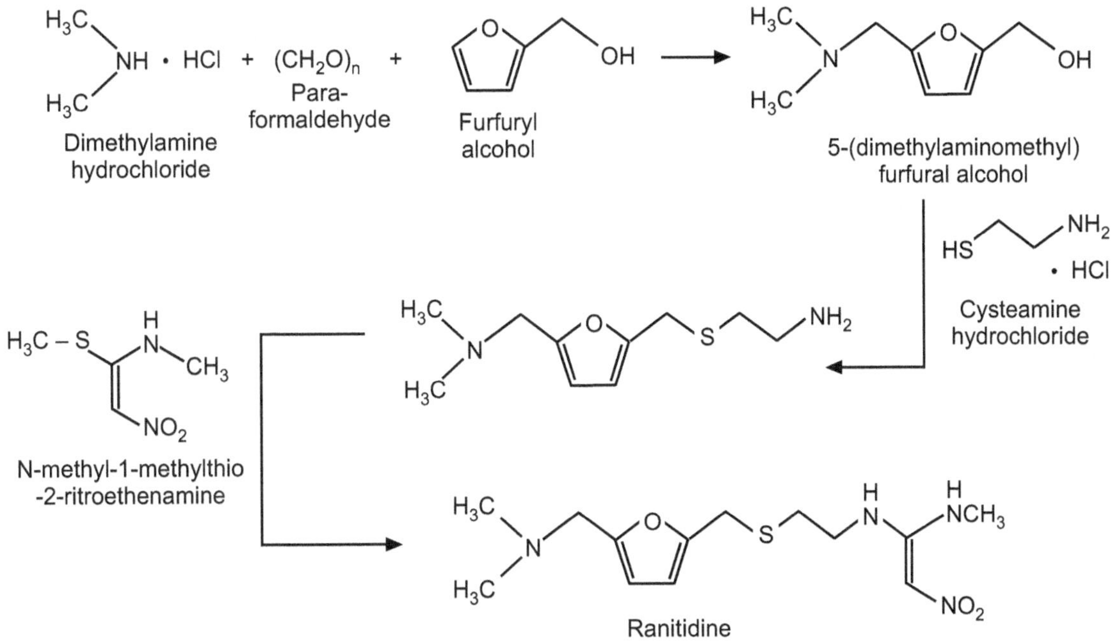

Dimethylamine hydrochloride + Para-formaldehyde + Furfuryl alcohol → 5-(dimethylaminomethyl) furfural alcohol

Cysteamine hydrochloride

N-methyl-1-methylthio-2-ritroethenamine

Ranitidine

(III) Diphenhydramine :

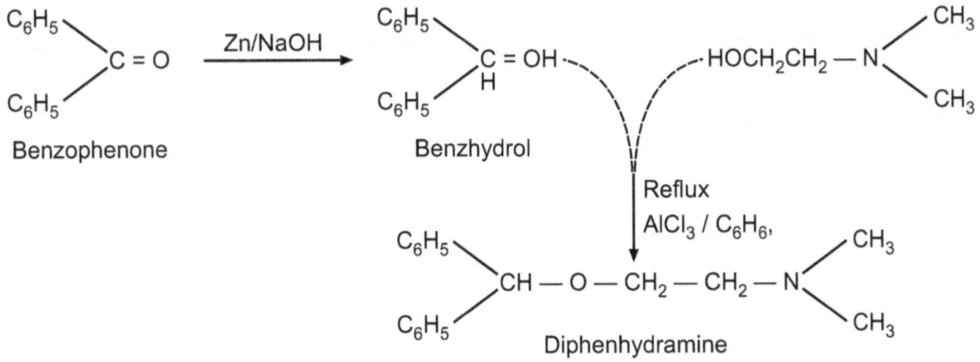

Benzophenone $\xrightarrow{Zn/NaOH}$ Benzhydrol · · · · HOCH$_2$CH$_2$—N(CH$_3$)(CH$_3$)

Reflux
AlCl$_3$ / C$_6$H$_6$,

C$_6$H$_5$—CH—O—CH$_2$—CH$_2$—N(CH$_3$)(CH$_3$)
Diphenhydramine

(IV) Chlorpheniramine :

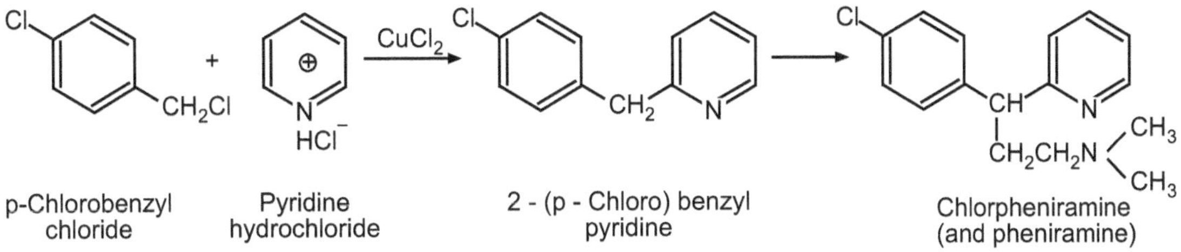

p-Chlorobenzyl chloride + Pyridine hydrochloride $\xrightarrow{CuCl_2}$ 2-(p-Chloro)benzyl pyridine → Chlorpheniramine (and pheniramine)

(V) Cetrizine :

$Cl(CH_2)_2OCH_2CN$

K_2CO_3; xylene

$CH_2CH_2OCH_2CN$

1. KOH/C_2H_5OH
2. HCl

• 2HCl

Cetrizine

$CH_2CH_2OCH_2COOH$

(VI) Promethazine :

(i)

Sulfur

Diphenyl amine   Phenothiazine

(ii)

$N(CH_3)_2$

+ Cl

CH_3

$NaNH_2$

Phenothiazine   1-chloro-2-dimethylamino propane

$CH_2 — CH — N(CH_3)_2$

CH_3

Promethazine

4

DRUGS ACTING ON RESPIRATORY TRACT

4.1 INTRODUCTION

Lung may be considered as a mass of thin wet epithelium (the alveolar capillary membrane) which allows oxygen (O_2) to diffuse rapidly from the air into a network of capillaries in close contact with the terminal respiratory units of the lungs. At the same time, carbon-dioxide from these capillaries diffuses rapidly into the air. The function of the lungs is gas exchange which is the transfer of oxygen from the atmosphere to the tissues and the elimination of carbon dioxide from the tissues to the atmosphere.

The membrane with a surface area of approximately 60 m^2, is arranged as clusters of small air sacs (alveoli) and extends from the alveoli into the alveolar ducts. Several of these ducts unite to form a respiratory bronchiole (0.025 cm in diameter). This pattern of progressive union of smaller air passages forming a large air passage is repeated sequentially until the lobar bronchi (0.1 cm diameter) are formed. These unite to form the right and left primary bronchi which emerge from the root of each lung (hilus) to join to form the trachea.

Nutrient blood flow for the walls of the bronchi and other tissues is supplied by the left and right pulmonary arteries which branch into a network of capillaries to accompany the airways to the terminal respiratory units and then extend to pleura. These capillaries surround the alveoli and through their intimate contact with the terminal respiratory units of the lungs are involved in exchange of oxygen and carbon dioxide. Blood from the bronchial capillaries drains mainly into the pulmonary veins which progressively unite and pass through the substance of the lung to exit at the hilus. In addition, the lungs are supplied with an abundant network of lymphatic vessels which drain into the lymph nodes at the roots of the lungs.

Throughout each lung, a network of elastic and collagenous fibrous tissue forms a matrix surrounding the capillaries and alveoli. The fibrous connective tissue prevents over-expansion of the alveoli. The lungs fill but move freely within the thoracic cage. The sealed cavity formed due to the presence of thoracic cage is known as pleura cavity. It is lined with a lubricated membrane, the 'parietal pluera'. Lungs are also covered with a similar membrane, the visceral pleura so that they slide freely inside the pleural cavity and enlarge when the cavity enlarges.

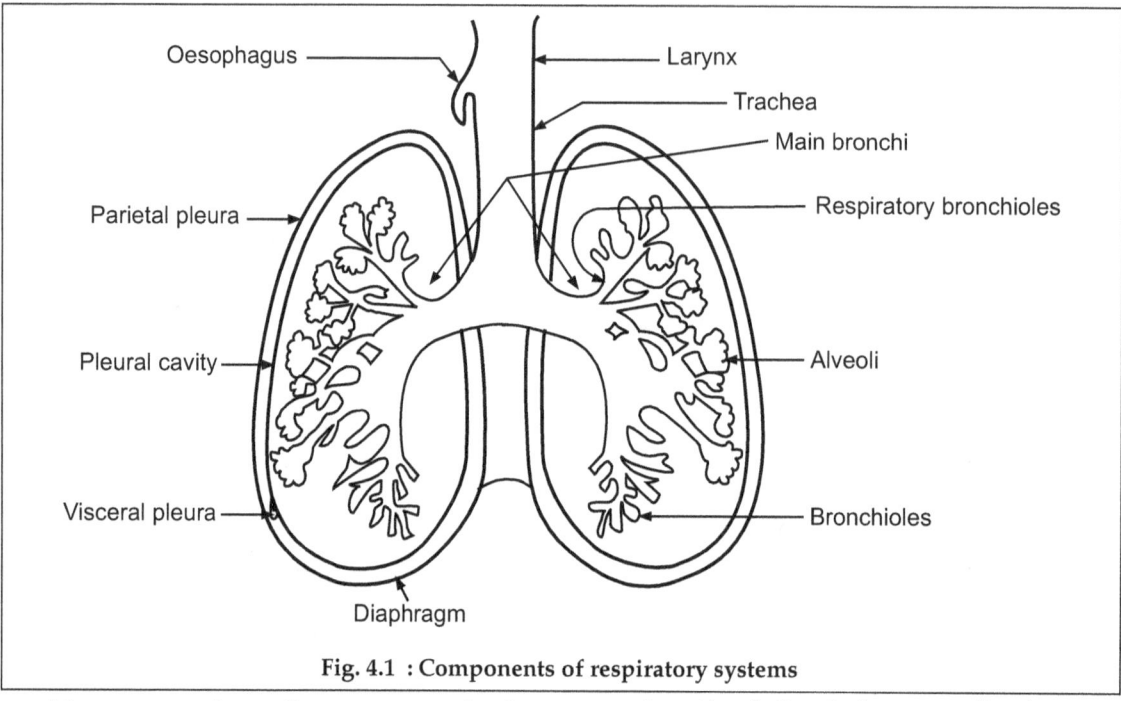

Fig. 4.1 : Components of respiratory systems

Mucous-secreting cells are present in the epithelium of the trachea, bronchi and bronchioles along with tall columnar cells. About 100 ml clear mucous is produced per day in the bronchial tree. This mucous is important to trap the dust particles in the air, which is then swept away from the lungs by constant beating of the cilia. Some fine dust particles that escape this trapping process and reach to the level of alveoli, are engulfed by phagocytic cells which move through the tissues.

Breathing movements are controlled and co-ordinated involuntarily by the respiratory center in the medulla oblongata via the lower motor neurones to the inspiratory and expiratory muscles. However, considerable voluntary control may be superimposed. Chemoreceptors are present in the carotid artery and the aorta. They are sensitive to decreased oxygen and excess carbon dioxide in the blood. These receptors are linked to the medullary respiratory centers and chemo-

receptor stimulation induces a reflex increase in the rate and depth of breathing.

Trachea contains bands of smooth muscles and the walls of the smaller respiratory passages contain a layer of smooth muscles beneath the mucosa. These smooth muscles contain both sympathetic β_2-adrenoceptors and parasympathetic (cholinergic) receptors.

4.2 SYMPTOMS OF RESPIRATORY DISEASE

(a) Sputum :

It is coughed up when normal mucociliary clearance mechanisms are overloaded by excessive mucous production. Daily volumes greater than 50 ml may be coughed up in conditions such as chronic bronchitis and cystic fibrosis.

(b) Cough :

It is a part of natural defence mechanism for clearing air passages of foreign materials and excess mucous. It is frequently attributed to upper respiratory tract diseases like commom cold or pharyngitis. Possibly the upper respiratory tract infection causes inflammation of the posterior wall of pharynx rendering it hypersensitive to the normal discharge of nasal secretions. Hence, complete supression of coughing is not beneficial although drugs may be useful to suppress the intensity and frequency of coughing in many cases where the cough is unproductive and annoying. Causes of cough include infections, tumors, inhaled foreign bodies and bronchial asthma. While bronchodilators and expectorants are effective, the prophylactic use of cromoglycate or an inhalation steroid is usually more appropriate.

(c) Breathlessness :

It is an unpleasant awareness about the sensation of breathing.

(d) Wheeze :

When the intra-thoracic airways are already narrowed, further reduction in airway calibre during expiration results in airway closure. This sensation of limited air flow is known as a 'wheeze'. It is often present in the patients with airways obstruction due to asthma or chronic bronchitis. Wheezing is the sound produced by air moving through the narrowed airways.

(e) Chest Pain :

Pleural pain may arise due to infection, inflammation or malignant involvement of the parietal pleura. Chest wall pain due to rib fractures causes local pain and tenderness.

4.3 UPPER RESPIRATORY TRACT DISEASES

These diseases include rhinitis, common cold, pharyngitis (sore throat), laryngitis, croup (acute laryngotracheobronchitis), bacterial tracheitis, supraglottitis and sinusitis.

(a) Rhinitis :

It may be infectious or non-infectious. The non-infectious rhinitis may be allergic or non-allergic. The infectious form is of short duration and the nasal exudate is often yellow-green. Rhinitis causes itching, sneezing, rhinorrhoea, congestion, nasal obstruction, headache, fever and pains. Antihistamines effectively alleviate rhinorrhea, sneezing and itching while decongestants reduce nasal congestion. Allergic rhinitis is often associated with allergic conjunctivitis and itching of the ears and throat. Complications of chronic rhinitis may include recurrent respiratory tract infections, secretory otitis media, sinusitis and nasal polyps.

A decongestant spray will relieve nasal congestion and obstruction while anticholinergic agents (e.g. ipratropium) may reduce rhinorrhea. In the treatment of allergic rhinitis, H_1-antagonists are usually drugs of first choice. Currently used antihistaminic agents for this purpose include promethazine, azatadine, astemizol, ioratadine and terfenadine. Cromoglycate and corticosteriod sprays would be useful prophylactically in the treatment of rhinitis.

(b) Common Cold :

It is characterized by increased nasal discharge and reddened nose. Other important symptoms that may be associated with common cold include chills, fever, headache, malaise, sneezing, sore throat, nasal congestion, rhinorrhea, non-productive cough, conjunctivitis and feeling of fullness in ears or paranasal sinuses. Pharyngeal, nasal or tympanic erythema may or may not appear. Rhinoviruses are the prominent cause of common cold in most of the cases. However, para-influenza viruses, respiratory syncytial viruses, enteroviruses, coxsackie viruses and coronaviruses are also reported to act as pathogens in this disease. Nasal discharge may initially be clear and watery and turns to be tenacious and purulent later on.

In the treatment of common cold, decongestants and antihistaminic agents are the drugs of choice. These drugs also prevent the development of rhinorrhea associated with nasal capillary permeability. Non-productive cough may disturb the sleep of the patient. Hence, antitussive agent (e.g. codeine, dextromethorphan) may be given along with an expectorant (to decrease sputum viscosity). Aspirin or paracetamol may also be given to treat minor pain or fever that may accompany a cold. Linus Pauling suggested that ascorbic acid in large doses (1-5 g/day) may be effective in the treatment of colds.

(c) Pharyngitis (sore throat) :

It is an acute inflammatory syndrome characterized by soreness, hoarseness, scratchiness, malaise, fever and lymphadenopathy. In some cases pharyngeal or tonsillar exudates and pharyngeal erythema appear.

Pharyngitis may be caused due to viruses or bacterial pathogens. Rhinoviruses, adenoviruses and herpes simplex virus are most implicated virus organisms. While streptococcus pyogenes cause streptococcal pharyngitis which is characterized by pharyngeal and tonsillar exudates, uvular edema, leukocytosis, cervical lymph adenopathy and acute glomerulonephritis. Sometimes a mild to moderate pharyngitis may appear as a symptom of common cold, influenza, infectious mononucleosis and gonorrheal infection.

In the treatment of pharyngitis, penicillin V or erythromycin may be used orally for 10 days or a single injection of benzathine penicillin G may be given intramuscularly. Besides this several mouth washes of antiseptic agents (e.g. benzyl alcohol, phenolic salts) are taken to assure killing of pathogens.

(d) Laryngitis :

It is an acute inflammatory process of larynx characterised by soreness, cough, hoarseness, dysphagia and loss of voice. In some cases, erythematous and edematous laryngeal mucosa and superficial ulceration may also be seen. Viruses commomly implicated in this disease include rhinoviruses, adenoviruses and influenza viruses. While Streptococcus pyogenes and B. catarrhalis are the common bacterial causes of laryngitis, in few cases, the underlying cause may be syphilitic, tubercular, herpetic or fungal in origin.

Antibiotics like erythromycin, amoxicillin, cephalosporins may be used when bacterial pathogen is involved. Some symptomatic relief may be seen if patient inhales humidified air. Voice rest is advocated till hoarseness subsides.

(e) Croup (acute laryngotracheobronchitis) :

In this disease, a characteristic non-productive cough and dyspnea is seen due to an infectious state of the subglottic area, mostly in children having age between 3 months to 3 years. Other symptoms include sore throat, rhinorrhea, hoarseness, fever, hypoxemia and inflammation and airway obstruction at subglottic level. Viral pathogens implicated in this disease include rhinoviruses, enteroviruses, adenoviruses, parainfluenza virus type 1 and parainfluenza virus type 3. Bacteria (e.g. Mycoplasma pneumoniae) is also reported to cause this disease.

Cold air is effective in decreasing upper airway resistance while oxygen therapy is important for the treatment of hypoxia.

(f) Bacterial Tracheitis :

It is similar to croup but is mainly of bacterial origin. It is commonly seen in older children and is characterized by dyspnea, high fever, purulent sputum and acutely inflammed subglottic area. Endotracheal intubation or tracheotomy is required if severe airway obstruction appears. It is mainly caused by *S. aureus*, *H. influenzae* type B or group A β-*hemolytic streptococci*.

(g) Supraglottitis (epiglottitis) :

It is a bacterial infection of epiglottis, aryepiglottic folds and arytenoids. Children between ages of 1 to 6 years are usually more susceptible. Symptoms include dysphagia, respiratory distress, stridor, tachycardia, fever, cervical lymphadenopathy, edema and inflammation of epiglottis and aryepiglottic folds and narrowing of supraglottic area. Bacterial pathogens involved include H. influenzae type B, streptococci, staphylococci and H. parainfluenzae.

Drugs effective in the treatment of supra-glottitis include ampicillin, chloramphenicol, cefuroxime, cefotaxime and ceftazidime. Patient may get benefited by taking humidified oxygen.

(h) Sinusitis :

The paranasal sinuses consists of four paired structures - the maxillary, ethmoidal, sphenoidal and frontal sinuses. Sinusitis results due to inflammation of one or more of these structures. It commonly affects adults. The disease is characterized by fever, headache, facial pain, purulent nasal discharge, nasal airway obstruction, excessive tearing, decreased olfactory sensation, edema of eyelids, fetid breath and dental infection. In some cases complications may arise due to the appearance of bacterial meningitis and subdural abscesses. In acute sinusitis a purulent post-nasal discharge will cause a productive cough.

The common pathogens suspected include rhinoviruses, adenoviruses, influenza virus, parainfluenza virus, S. aureus, S. pyogenes, S. pneumoniae, H. influenzae and B. catarrhalis.

Sinusitis can be treated with antibiotics including ampicillin, amoxicillin, erythromycin, cefaclor, sulfisoxazole and amoxicillin-clavulanic acid combination. For better relief antihistaminics and decongestants may be applied topically or may be taken orally.

4.4 LOWER RESPIRATORY TRACT DISEASES

Blood circulation, inhalation of aerosolized bacteria and habit of inspiration through oropharyngeal tract are the prominent sources through which bacteria may reach to the terminal alveoli.

In normal person, efficient natural defence mechanisms are in operation to supply a sterile airflow to the resipratory tract. These mechanisms are usually mechanical, secretory and phagocytic in nature. Nose acts as an air conditioner for the airflows causing warming, humidifying and filtering inspired air. Bacteria present in this airflow can be removed by filtration and humidification of upper airways. Similarly, the mucous secretions and ciliated respiratory epithelium efficiently trap bacteria that reach to the terminal bronchioles.

While at the level of lower respiratory tract, cellular immune system (alveolar macrophages and T lymphocytes) and humoral responses (immunoglobulins, complement and B lymphocytes) plays an important role to destroy bacteria. In addition, polymorphonuclear neutrophils are also found to be involved in phagocytizing bacteria.

Lower respiratory diseases mainly include pneumonia and asthma.

(a) Pneumonia :

It is an acute inflammation of pulmonary tissues induced by either bacteria, viruses, fungi, Legionella species and Pneumocystis carinii especially in immunodeficient patients. The major symptoms of the disease include nausea, vomiting, malaise, sore throat, sudden chills, dyspnea, fever, chest pain, productive cough, tachycardia, weakness, leukopenia, pleuritic chest pain and acute inflammation of pulmonary tissues.

The common bacterial pathogens suspected in this disease include *S. aureas, S. pneumoniae, H. influenzae*, Mycoplasma pneumoniae and gram negative pathogens.

(i) Pneumococcal pneumonia :

It is caused by *Streptococcus pneumoniae*. It can be treated with either giving 600,000 units of procaine penicillin G intramuscularly per 12 hours or penicillin V orally 250 mg 4 times a day. In penicillin-sensitive patients erythromycin may be given orally 500 mg 4 times a day.

Attempts to develop immunization techniques are being done. A polyvalent pneumococcal vaccine composed of 23 types of purified, capsular polysaccharide antigens of *S. pneumoniae* was found to be effective in preventing pneumococcal pneumoniae.

(ii) Hemophilus influenzae pneumonia :

It is caused by an aerobic gram-negative rod, H. influenzae. Drugs of choice in the treatment of this type of pneumoniae include ampicillin (1 to 2 g every 4-6 hours intravenously), chloramphenicol, cefuroxime, cefamandole, ceftazidime, cefotaxime, ceftriaxone and clavulanic acid amoxicillin combination .

(iii) Legionnaire's disease :

It is an acute bacterial bronchopneumonial disease caused by gram negative bacilli, Legionella pneumophilia. It is transmitted to the patient via airborne inhalation. Major symptoms include nausea, vomiting, diarrhoea, high fever, malaise, chills, myalgias, headache, confusion, disorientation and non-productive cough. The disease can be treated by giving erythromycin initially 4 gm per day intravenously followed by an oral dose of 2 gm per day for 3 weeks.

(iv) Mycoplasma pneumonia :

This disease is transmitted either by close contact or by inhalation of aerosolized organisms. It is reported mainly in children and young adults between the ages of 5 to 35 years. Beside the usual symptoms, some signs of upper respiratory dysfunctioning (e.g. sore throat, rhinorrhea, earache, pharyngitis, bronchitis) may also appear. Erythromycin and tetracyclines (500 mg four times a day for 14 days) are the drugs of choice.

(v) Staphylococcal pneumonia :

In this disease *Staphylococcus aureus* is a causative organism. Usually this disease appears as a complication of a viral infection. Drugs of choice in the treatment of this disease include methicillin, naficillin, oxacillin, cloxacillin, dicloxacillin (all are β-lactamase resistant penicillins), cefazolin and vancomycin. Therapy should be continued for at least 4-6 weeks.

(b) Asthma :

The word asthma is derived from a Greek word meaning difficulty in breathing. It is mainly caused by narrowing of airways or bronchial obstruction. It is hence characterized by dyspnea (pain on breathing), dry nocturnal cough, chest tightness, allergy, sputum production, wheezing and narrowing of airways. In asthma, airways are inflamed and edematous, the lumen is filled with sticky mucous and the airway epithelium is damaged. There is widespread mucous plugging of the airways and such plugs, made up of yellow, viscid mucous and desquamated epithelial cells which can be coughed up during acute attacks often producing marked relief of symptoms. The copious mucous in asthma is abnormally sticky and also has an inhibitory action on the cilia in the airways. Both these factors predispose to mucous retention and plugging. The mucosal oedema induced by the inflammatory changes causes narrowing of the lumen which is not reversed by bronchodilators. If remained untreated, the bronchial mucous glands may enlarge and basement membrane and bronchial smooth muscles may become thickened leading to permanent airflow limitation. There is also increased airway smooth muscle contraction in asthma which is normally rapidly reversible with bronchodilators.

The narrowing or bronchial obstruction may be brought about by :

(i) Excessive secretion of thick, tenacious mucous and its retention in the walls of airways,

(ii) Contraction of bronchial smooth muscles that surrounds the airways,

(iii) Edema of bronchial mucosa, and

(iv) Thickening of the bronchial wall.

The essential feature that distinguishes asthma from chronic bronchitis or emphysema is the reversibility of obstruction.

Asthmatics have an exaggerated response both to allergic and to irritant stimuli resulting into bronchoconstriction. Other inducers of bronchoconstriction include viral infections, animal danders, exercise and emotional disturbances. Allergy-induced asthma is known as 'extrinsic asthma' while asthma having no definite immunological basis is called as 'intrinsic asthma'.

In asthmatic attack an antigen may induce the formation of cytotrophic antibodies of IgE type. The antigen-antibody interaction sensitizes the mast cell. This results in the release of potent mediators like histamine, slow-releasing substance of anaphylaxis (SRS-A), prostaglandins, eosinophil chemotactic factor and other bioactive amines from mast cells and basophils in the lungs.

These mediators can initiate vagally mediated reflex bronchoconstriction. Edema may be produced in the small, non-muscle containing airways through the activation of prostaglandin thromboxane system.

Because of the potent contractile action in airways, TXA_2 may be considered as a mediator of brochoconstriction in asthma. Bronchoconstriction may also be brought about by exercise, cold air, upper respiratory infection, irritant gases, dust, cigarette smoke, allergens (grass pollen, house dust, mites etc.), emotional disturbances and drugs (like aspirin, cholinergic agonists, beta adrenergic blocking agents). In children and young adults, asthma is the only common cause of recurrent breathlessness, cough or wheeze although it is still often labelled as wheezy bronchitis and treated in appropriately with antibiotics only. Increasing severity at night is common with nocturnal coughing and early morning wakening.

Mild asthma is treated with inhaled sympathomimetics. Moderately severe asthma is treated with inhaled sympathomimetics and long acting theophylline preparation. Severe asthma is treated with combination therapy using inhaled sympathomimetics, long acting theophylline preparation and corticosteroids.

4.5 DRUG TREATMENT OF ASTHMA

Drug therapy for asthma should follow a rational sequence depending on its severity and response to the therapy. Most commonly used drugs in the treatment of asthma are presented in table 4.1. Asthma is known in terms of reversible airflow obstruction but the muscle contraction is the result and not the cause of the underlying inflammation. Such bronchial hyper-reactivity is a key feature of asthma and relates closely to its severity.

Table 4.1 : Clinically used antiasthmatic agents

		Drugs	Route of administration	Plasma half-life (hr)	Protein bound (%)	Adult dose
(A)		**Bronchodilators**				
	(i)	β-adrenergic agents				
		Albuterol	oral	2.7 - 5.0	–	2 - 8 mg
		Ephedrine	oral	–	–	25-50 mg
		Epinephrine	s.c.	–	–	0.2 - 0.5 ml
		Isoproterenol	inhalation	–	–	2.5 mg
		Metaproterenol	oral	–	–	10 - 20 mg
		Terbutaline	oral	16 - 19	25	2.5 - 5.0 mg
	(ii)	Phosphodiesterase inhibitors				
		Aminophylline	i.v.	5 - 8	–	5.6 mg/kg
		Theophylline	oral	9 - 11	56 - 60	65-500 mg
(B)		**Anticholinergic agents**				
		Atropine	oral	2.5	–	200 - 400 µg
		Ipratropium	inhalation	1.5 - 4.0	–	80 µg
(C)		**Corticosteroids**				
		Prednisone	oral	3.5 - 4.0	75 - 77	5 - 10 mg
		Prednisolone	oral	2.2 - 2.7	90 - 95	5 - 20 mg
		Methylprednisolone	oral	12 - 36	50	5 - 10 mg
		Hydrocortisone	i.v.	1.5	90	2-4 mg/kg/day
		Beclomethasone	inhalation	–	–	Two puffs (42 µg per puff)
		Triamcinolone	inhalation	2 - 5	85	5-10 puffs/day
(D)		**Inhibitors of mediator release**				
		Cromolyn sodium	inhalation	1.2	–	20 mg

During an asthma attack, the tissue of the airway inner wall is inflamed and the mucous is thick and sticky. Continuing production of mediators and messenger substances of inflammation such as histamine and leukotrienes keeps the process going. Recognition of the inflammatory component of asthma has led to more use of glucocorticoid steroids as anti-inflammatory agents. Medicinal chemists are perfecting even newer drugs against mediators of inflammation like leukotrienes, thromboxanes, and phospho-diesterases III and IV. In seeking the cause of asthma and its increasing frequency, there are various factors to be evaluated. These include heredity, infection, allergy, indoor and outdoor pollution, and social, economic, and psychological factors.

Asthmatic symptoms may be partly an imbalance between the bronchoconstrictive action of the cholinergic nervous system and the bronchodilatory effect of the β-adrenergic system.

One anticholinergic agent is ipratropium bromide, a derivative of atropine that lacks many of atropine's unpleasant side effects. The patient inhales an aqueous solution of the drug by mouth out of an aerosol or can spray pump.

Drugs that act on the β-adrenergic system target β-receptors. The β-receptors in lung tissue are of the β$_2$-type, different from β$_1$-receptors in heart tissue. Medicinal chemists have progressed over the years in the discovery of β$_2$-selective agonists. The action of β-agonists stimulate adenylate cyclase, which converts adenosine triphosphate to cyclic adenosine monophosphate (cAMP), a second messenger substance that mediates bronchodilation.

Several β$_2$-adrenergic drugs are approved in the U.S. : albuterol, bitolterol, pirbuterol, salmeterol and terbutaline. These are inhaled as powders or aerosols of solution, or taken internally as tablets or syrups.

Corticosteroids used as anti-inflammatory agents include beclomethasone dipropionate, buclesonide, flunisolide, fluticasone propionate, prednisolone, prednisone and triamcinolone acetonide. These are formulated as inhalers, tablets or syrups. Ciclesonide is a glucocorticoid used to treat obstructive airway diseases. It is inhaled as a prodrug activated by cleavage by esterases in bronchial epithelial cells.

Cromolyn and nedocromil have chromone (benzopyranone) units in their structures. Neither drug has bronchodilating activity and patients use them for prophylaxis to prevent attacks. Cromolyn is though to act by stabilizing mast cells and preventing mast

cells, from secreting from their internal granules such mediators of inflammation as histamine and leukotrienes when allergens bind to IgE molecules on mast cell surfaces.

The therapeutic dose for theophylline is very close to the toxic dose. Side-effects are diarrhoea, headache, insomnia, nausea and vomiting. An overdose can lead to seizures, brain damage, and death. For these reasons, some doctors tend to shy away from theophylline.

Newer drug blocks leukotriene receptors are given below :

Zafirlukast
(It blocks leukotriene synthesis.)

Zileuton

Zileuton is an orally active inhibitor of 5-lipooxygenase and thus inhibits leukotrienes. It is used in maintenance treatment of asthama.

Seratrodast

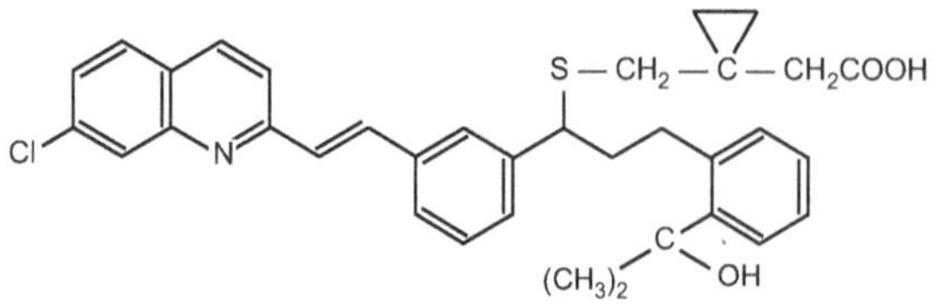

Montelukast

Some physicians favour theophylline to supplement β_2-adrenergic agents and steroids. There is renewed interest in theophylline because of indications that it modifies the immune response, relieves inflammation, and protects airways from antigens in ways that seem to go beyond any activity as a phosphodiesterase inhibitor. Theophylline-ephedrine combinations are available as tablets and syrups.

Salmeterol and formoterol last about 12 hours as compared to four to five hours for the shorter-acting types of albuterol, bitolterol, pirbuterol, or terbutaline.

Short-acting β-agonists :

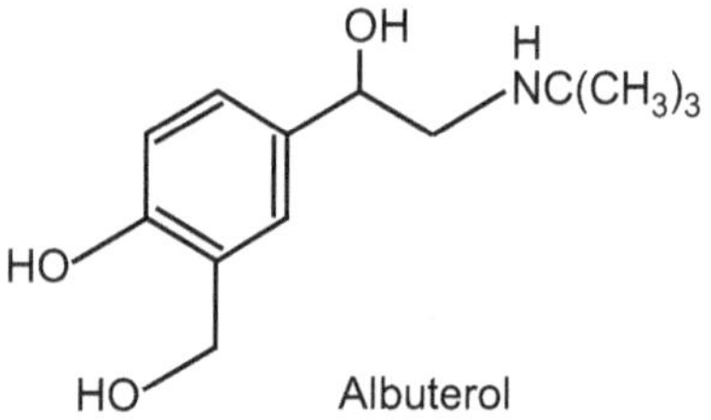

Albuterol

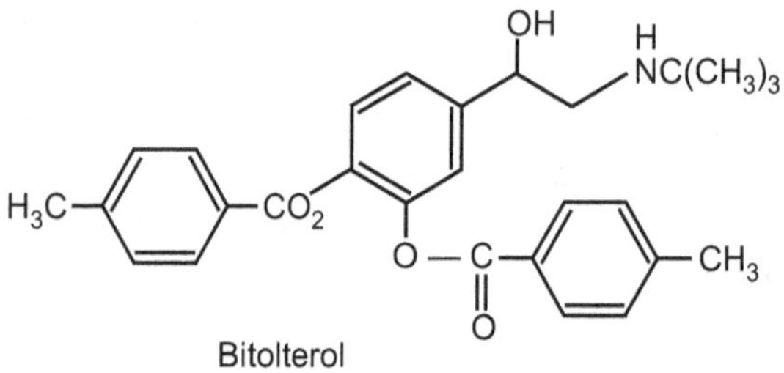

Bitolterol

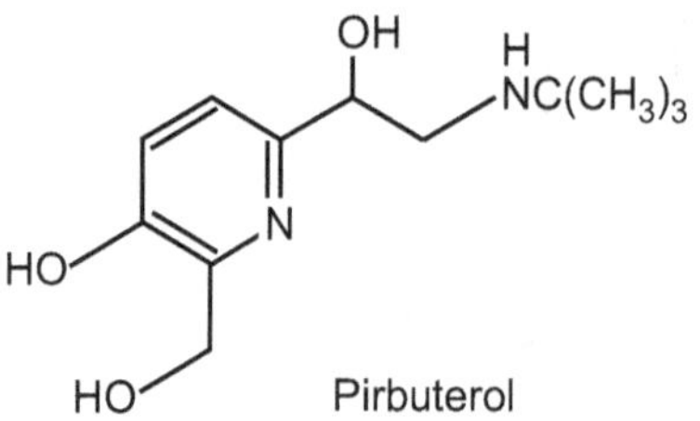

Pirbuterol

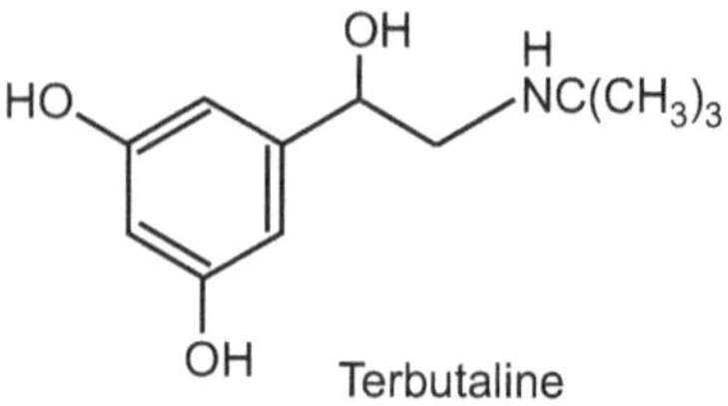

Terbutaline

......now joined by longer-acting ones :

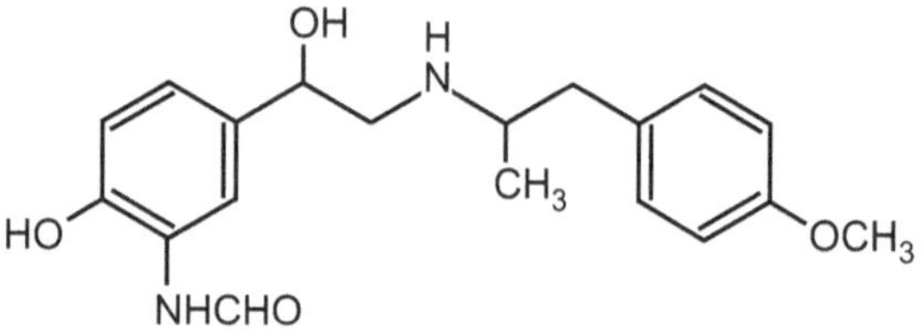

Formoterol

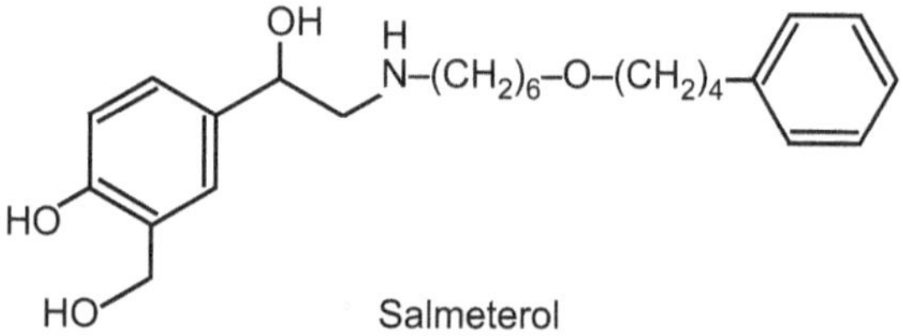

Salmeterol

4.6 DRUGS COMMONLY USED IN THE TREATMENT OF RESPIRATORY TRACT DISEASES

(a) Antihistaminic Agents :

Antihistaminic agents are usually drugs of first choice in the treatment of allergic rhinitis and common cold. They can however be used only for symptomatic benefit. Examples include promethazine, azatadine, astemizol, ketotifen, ioratadine and terfenadine. They mainly act by antagonising histamine action on bronchial smooth muscle and mucous secretion. They are used to inhibit histamine-induced bronchoconstriction and hyper-secretion of mucous. They are usually given with decongestants where because of their sedative effect they may offset CNS-stimulating effect of decongestants. Main adverse effects include sedation, dry mouth, tachycardia, mucosal drying, decreased gastrointestinal motility and urinary retention.

Terfenadine is a butyrophenone derivative having antihistaminic activity without sedative action. It is used in the treatment of seasonal and perennial allergic rhinitis. Adult oral dose is 60 mg every 8-12 hours.

(b) Anticholinergic Agents :

Some degree of airway tone is modulated by cholinergic innervation. Acetylcholine and its analogs facilitate the formation of cyclic-GMP which brings about both, bronchoconstriction and release of bioactive substances by sensitizing mast cells. This is known as 'cholinergic mediated reflex bronchospasm'. Hence, anticholinergic agents (e.g. atropine and ipratropium bromide) can be used in the treatment of asthama.

Though effective in the treatment of asthma, atropine is inconvenient because of its intolerable side-effects. Ipratropium is a derivative of N-isopropylnoratropine. It acts by causing bronchodilation. It also reduces bronchial secretions and cholinergic bronchial spasms. Ipratropium nasal spray is very useful for the treatment of rhinorrhea. When used by inhalation, minor fraction gets systemically absorbed which is eliminated in the urine in the form of inactive metabolites. It has a plasma half-life of 1.5-4.0 hours.

Adverse effects include nausea, dry mouth, blurred vision, slurred speech, skin rash, fever, dizziness, drowsiness, headache, confusion and hallucinations.

It is used to relieve chronic airways obstruction, particularly in chronic bronchitis.

Tiotropium bromide : It is a long acting anticholinergic bronchodilator used in the management of chronic obstructive pulmonary diseases like chronic bronchitis and emphysema.

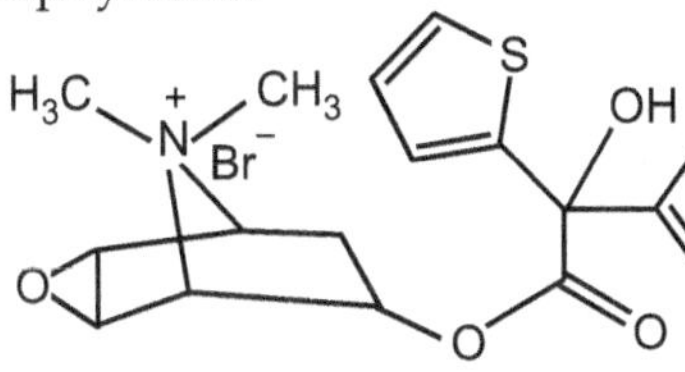

Other clinically used anticholinergic agents for this purpose include isopropamide and methscopolamine. They may be used in combination with decongestants. They decrease nasal, salivary and bronchial secretions and would be beneficial in case of profuse watery nasal discharge. Thus, anticholinergics and antihistaminergic drugs may be used as drying agents to control allergic upper airway symptoms.

(c) Soothing Agents (demulcents) :

These are bland, mucilaginous or oily agents used to sooth irritated or inflamed tissues when cough stems from irritated pharyngeal mucosa. Examples of soothing agents include alcohols, propylene glycol, compound tincture of benzoin, linseed, elm bark, guaifenesin etc. They are usually given in the form of cough drops to treat minor irritation for shorter duration. They are devoid of adverse effects.

(d) Expectorants :

Cough is an important mechanism for expectorating bronchial secretions. Expectorants are the drugs that facilitate the expectoration of bronchial secretions by decreasing viscosity of sputum. Clinically, used agents from this category include ammonium chloride, potassium iodide, syrup of ipecac, terpin hydrate, guaifenesin, potassium guaiacolsulfonate and acetyl-cysteine.

Guaifenesin is an expectorant used to relieve cough secretion due to colds, influenza or minor upper respiratory tract infections. It acts by virtue of its local pharyngeal effects. It is usually used along with a mucolytic agent to liquify or to loosen the mucous or phlegm present in the lungs. Adverse effects include nausea, vomiting, diarrhoea, stomach pain and drowsiness. Adult oral dose is 200-400 mg after every 4 hours a day.

Acetylcysteine (N-acetyl-L-cysteine) is a sulfur containing amino acid used as a mucolytic agent in the form of 10-20% sterile solution. It lowers the viscosity of purulent and non-purulent pulmonary secretion by breaking the disulfide linkages in pulmonary mucus secretion. The mucolytic effect is maximum between pH 7-9. It may be used either by inhalation or may be applied directly to the site.

(e) Decongestants :

These are the agents used to cause a relief or reduction of accumulated fluid because of excessive nasal secretions in the glands of nasal and paranasal area. Besides inflammatory and allergic response, nasal obstruction is also caused by excessive nasal secretions. Vasoconstriction of nasal capillary bed is brought about by activation of local α-adrenergic receptors. Vasoconstriction of engorged nasal mucosa allows the inhibition of vascular leakage, drainage of sinuses and clearing of airways. This results in reduction in nasal secretory rate. Hence, α-adrenergic agonists may be used locally or systemically to exert decongestant action. However when used orally, these drugs may cause urinary retention (by stimulating urinary sphincter) and hypertension. Similarly anticholinergic agents may be used as decongestant because of their antisecretory effect on the glands of nasal and paranasal area.

Locally used decongesants include ephedrine (1% aqueous solution), phenylephrine (solutions of 0.125 – 1.0%), oxymetazoline (as a 0.05% solution), naphazoline (0.05% solution), tetrahydrozoline (0.05-0.1% solution) and xylometazoline (0.05-1% solution). All these are sympathomimetic agents that produce α-adrenergic stimulation at low concentration when applied locally. However, their duration of action is shorter than that of systemic decongestants. Phenylephrine is the most favoured local decongestant because of high potency, minimal systemic effects and lack of CNS-depressant action. It is also used as a systemic decongestant.

The clinically used examples of systemic decongestants include phenylephrine, phenylpropanolamine, ephedrine and pseudoephedrine. However, these drugs have a stimulant effect on CNS and heart because of their activity on β-adrenergic receptors. Main adverse effects include hallucinations, restlessness, tachycardia, nausea, vomiting, anorexia and hypertension. Phenylephrine is usually given in combination with chlorpheniramine (antihistaminic agent) or with phenylpropanolamine. While *l*-ephedrine is an orally effective, longer acting bronchodilator having pronounced CNS effects. It is used in bronchospasm, in Strokes-Adams syndrome, as a nasal decongestant, as a sympathomimetic mydriatic and in certain allergic disorders.

(f) Topical Antiallergic Agents :

The nasal obstruction may also be produced by local allergic reactions mediated by immunoglobulin E. Hence, glucocorticoids and disodium cromoglycate may be used in the form of aerosol spray and drops to suppress the nasal allergic reactions. Glucocorticoids used for this purpose include :

-- dexamethasone phosphate 0.2 mg 2-3 times a day.

-- beclomethasone dipropionate 42 µg in each nostril 2-4 times a day, and

-- flunisolide 1-2 sprays of 0.25% solution 2-3 times a day.

(g) Central Antitussive Agents :

These are the drugs that relieve cough by acting through central mechanisms. They act by inhibiting afferent nervous input in lungs as well as by a central mechanism. They are usually used along with antihistaminics, decongestants or expectorants to relieve cough.

This class is further subdivided into :

(i) Opiate antitussive agents :

Examples include codeine, hydrocodone, noscapine and dextromethorphan. They owe their activity to their ability to decrease the sensitivity of brain chemoreceptors to carbon dioxide. They have less addiction liability in comparison to morphine. Adverse effects asssociated with their use include nausea, constipation, dizziness, palpitation, drowsiness, dryness of throat and tightness of chest.

Codeine is an orally active antitussive agent having relatively weak analgesic potential. While dextromethorphan lacks analgesic and addictive properties. It produces less constipation than codeine. It may be used alone or in combination with antihistaminic agent for cough suppression. It is the most appropriate antitussive recommonded for pediatric use. Adult oral dose is 15-30 mg, 3-4 times a day.

(ii) Non-opiate antitussive agents :

Examples include benzonatate, and diphenhydramine. They lack respiratory depressant, euphoriant and addictive potential of opiates. Adverse effects associated with these agents include nausea, constipation, headache, vertigo, drowsiness, nasal congestion and hypersensitivity reactions. Benzonatate is a long chain polyglycol derivative chemically related to tetracaine. It can be administered by almost all routes. Diphenhydramine is an antihistaminic agent having weak central antitussive activity.

(h) Topical Anaesthetic Agents :

These agents are employed to control minor throat irritation and cough during instrumentation of airways, as in bronchoscopy, Lidocaine 0.5-4.0% in solution or in the form of jelly and dyclonine 0.5-1.0% in solution form are employed for this purpose. Benzonatate is an example of orally active local anaesthetic agent.

(i) Bronchodilators :

These agents are used to reduce difficulty in breathing by improving the ventilation. The airway obstruction is reduced by relieving bronchospasms. The main categories of bronchodilatory agents include xanthine analogus, β_2-adrenergic agonists and prostacyclin analogs.

(1) Xanthine analogous :

The bronchial smooth muscle relaxation is brought about by c-AMP, an intracellular cyclic nucleotide which prevents the release of SRS-A (slow releasing substance of anaphylaxis) and histamine, the known mediators of bronchoconstriction during IgE-mediated allergic reactions.

c-AMP also has direct relaxant effect on bronchial smooth muscle which is mediated by its ability to decrease the concentration of Ca^{++} ions in the muscles. Phosphodiesterase enzymes cause inactivation of c-AMP. Xanthine analogs relax bronchial smooth muscles by competitively inhibiting the enzyme, phosphodiesterase. Clinically used bronchodilators from this category include theophylline and aminophylline.

Piclamilast : It is selective PDE 4 inhibitor. Inhibition of PDE 4 blocks hydrolysis of c-AMP thereby increasing levels of c-AMP within cells. c-AMP suppresses the activity of immune and inflammatory cascade. Piclamilast is a second generation compound that exihibits structural functionalities of PDE4 inhibitors cilomilast and roflumilast. It may be used to treat chronic obstructive pulmonary disease, bronchopulmonary dysplasia and asthma.

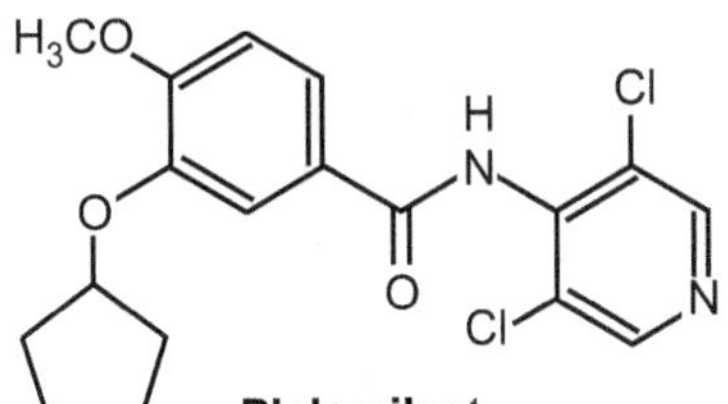

Piclamilast 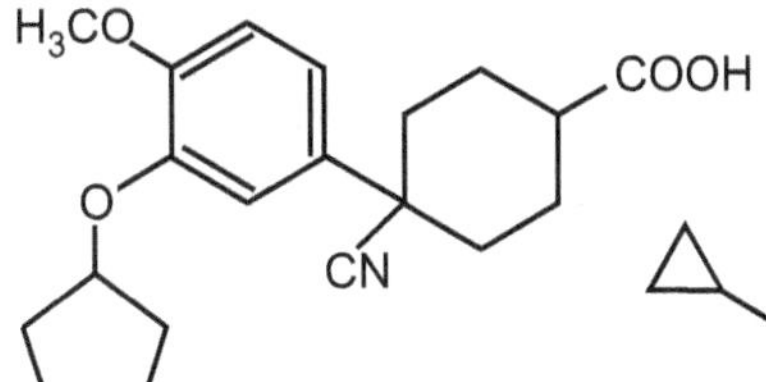   Cilomilast 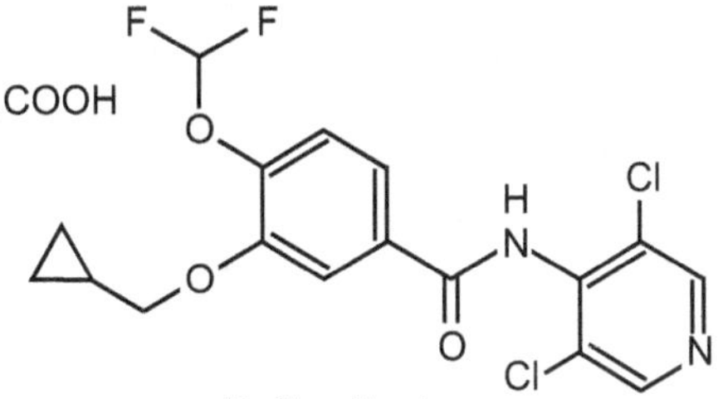   Roflumilast

Table 4.2 : Central antitussive agents

Name	Route	Plasma half-life (hr)	Adult oral dose per day
Codeine	Oral	2.5 - 3.0	10-30 mg 3-4 times
hydrocodone	Oral	3.8	5-10 mg 3-4 times
Noscapine	Oral	–	15-30 mg 3-4 times
Dextromethorphan	Oral	–	15-30 mg 3-4 times
Benzonatate	Oral	–	100-200 mg 3-4 times
Diphenhydramine	Oral	4.0	25-50 mg 3-4 times

Other mechanisms proposed to explain bronchodilatory effect of xanthines include antagonism of adenosine and increased sympathetic activity. They improve pulmonary function in a dose-dependent manner. They are also used to relieve dyspnea which is associated with pulmonary edema that develops from congestive heart failure.

Aminophylline is a soluble theophylline salt prepared by complexation between theophylline and ethylenediamine. The latter compound is pharmacologically inert but helps to increase the amount of theophylline in the solution. It is mainly used in the management of asthma, chronic obstructive pulmonary disease and reversible bronchospasm associated with emphysema. It is administered by slow i.v. infusion in a dose of 5.6 mg/kg body weight. Theophylline may be used orally in a dose of 65-500 mg per day. Other theophylline salts include oxtriphylline, theophylline sodium glycinate and theophylline monohydrate. These salts of theophylline have a better absorption pattern than theophylline when given orally.

(2) β_2-adrenergic agonists :

Relaxation of bronchial smooth muscles (β_2), increase in the heart rate, force of contraction (β_1) and CNS-stimulation are some important effects mediated by activation of β-adrenergic receptors. All these effects are brought about by increased concentration of c-AMP through drug induced activation of adenylate cyclase. Hence, anxiety, tremors (arised by a direct stimulation of β_2-adrenoceptors persent in the skeletal muscle), tachycardia, hypertension, increased cardiac output and decrease in systemic vascular resistance are the common effects seen with the therapy of sympathomimetic bronchodilators. Upon continuous use of these agents, tolerance and/or desensitization of some β-adrenoceptors can be demonstrated. Most of these effects are due to unwanted activation of cardiac β_1-adrenoceptors. Hence, these effects can be minimised by the use of selective β_2-adrenergic agonists. Clinically, used examples of this category include epinephrine (s.c.), isoetharine, isoproterenol and metaproterenol (inhalation). All these are non-selective β-adrenergic agonists. While the tertiary butyl derivatives of epinephrine like, terbutaline, albuterol and bitolterol have higher affinity for β_2-adrenoceptors and may be given orally for prolonged bronchodilatory effects.

For the rapid relief of an acute attack, epinephrine (s.c.) and terbutaline (s.c.) are the drugs of choice. For the mild attack of asthma, beneficial effects are seen by the administration of isoproterenol isoetharine or through inhalation. Terbutaline or albuterol are preferred when chronic administration is desired.

Table 4.3 : Bronchodilatory adrenergic agonists

	Name	Route	Plasma half-life (hr)	Adult dose
1.	Epinephrine	s.c.	–	0.2 - 0.5 ml
2.	Metaproterenol	Oral	–	10-20 mg
3.	Albuterol	Oral	2.5 - 5.0	2-8 mg
4.	Ephedrine	Oral	–	25-50 mg
5.	Isoproterenol	inhalation	–	2.5 mg
6.	Terbutaline	Oral	16-19	2.5-5.0 mg

Epinephrine is used exclusively to manage acute episodes of bronchospasm. Epinephrine and isoproterenol are rapidly metabolised in the intestine and liver. Hence, they can not be used orally. Isoproterenol is administered almost exclusively by inhalation, from a metered dose inhaler or from nebulizer, while terbutaline is effective by inhalation, oral and parenteral routes.

It is used in the treatment of exercise-induced bronchospasm and in the management of acute bronchospasm in stable asthmatic patients.

(3) Prostaglandin analogous :

Prostaglandins were reported to be present in lungs and bronchial tissues. Out of these, prostacyclin has been shown to have marked bronchodilating action. However, it is rapidly destroyed and irritating when inhaled. Hence, its synthetic analogs have been prepared. It is an unstable natural anticoagulant produced from the metabolism of prostaglandin H_2 by prostacyclin synthetase enzyme in the vascular endothelium.

It is the most potent inhibitor of platelet aggregation and has a plasma half-life of 3 minutes. It inhibits histamine and gastric acid secretion. It further metabolizes to 6-keto prostaglandin. Its various synthetic analogs are being evaluated for bronchodilatory.

(j) Glucocorticoids :

Control of airway inflammation prevents bronchospasm. Inhaled topical corticosteriods and less potently, sodium cromoglycate suppress the inflammation. These agents are used in the treatment of asthama because of their antiallergic activity. They reduce inflammation and potentiate the action of β-adrenergic agonists.

Glucocorticoids and hydration would be necessary for the total relief of airway obstruction. Clinically used agents from this category include prednisone, prednisolone, methylprednisolone, hydro-cortisone, dexamethasone, beclomethasone, triamcinolone acetonide and flunisolide. They are all favoured because of their short duration of action.

They are usually indicated only for short term treatment because of their adverse effects. Appearance of adverse effects is dependent upon age, dose and duration of treatment. The major adverse effects of corticosteriod therapy include cataracts, peptic ulcer, diabetes, Cushing's syndrome, adrenal atrophy, osteoporosis, and increased susceptibility to fungal infection.

For example, upon chronic inhalation therapy with beclomethasone, there occurs increased chances of development of oropharyngeal fungal infection with Monilia fungus.

Table 4.4 : Antiasthmatic glucocorticoids

	Name	Route	Adult oral dose per day
1.	Beclomethasone dipropionate	inhalation	42 µg
2.	Triamcinolone acetonide	inhalation	42-80 µg
3.	Prednisone/prednisolone	oral	5-10 mg
4.	Methylprednisolone	oral	5-10 mg
5.	Hydrocortisone	i. v.	2-4 mg/kg body weight

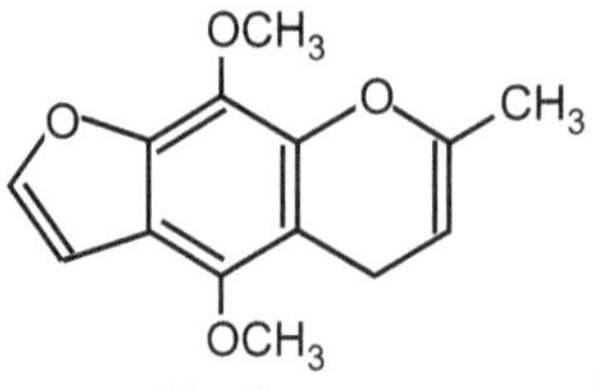

Khellin

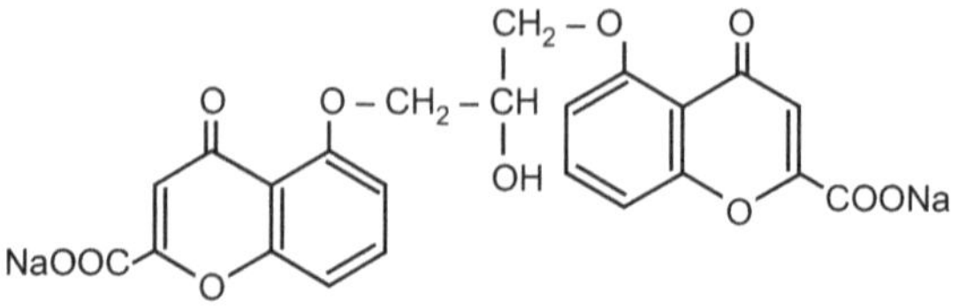

Cromolyn sodium

The intensity and frequency of all the above adverse effects remain insignificantly low if the therapy is less than one month of duration. To minimize the risk of adverse effects they may be used either in alternate day therapy or as aerosol to avoid the appearance of systemic effects. However to control the severe asthmatic attack, methyl prednisolone may be given intravenously 125 mg every 6 hours.

(k) Inhibitors of Release of Allergy-Mediators :

During allergic asthama, sensitization of mast cells occur through IgE allergic reaction. Degranulation of mast cells results in the release of the mediators (i.e. histamine, SRS-A, eosinophil chemotatic factor, etc.) that induce severe bronchial constriction. Cromolyn sodium or disodium cromoglycate, derivative of Khellin a vasodilatory benzopyrone isolated from the umbelliferous plant Ammi visnaga, is the example of drugs that inhibit the release of mediators by stabilizing the mast cells.

They do not have direct bronchodilatory effect. However they prevent broncho-constriction if given prior to the asthmatic attack. Since, they are not antagonists of the mediators, they cannot prevent or reverse the bronchoconstriction once produced by the mediators.

Cromolyn sodium is an orally ineffective derivative of Khellin, benzopyrone of plant origin. It has antihistaminic activity. It inhibits antigenically induced tissue release of histamine and leukotrienes. When used by inhalation, about 10% dose is systemically absorbed. This results from both pulmonary and GIT - absorption. It has a plasma half - life of 80 minutes. It is excreted almost in unchanged form in the faeces. It is marketed in the form of an aqueous solution (4%) for nasal and ophthalmic use. It is used prophylactically in the treatment of allergic rhinitis, atopic diseases of eye, giant papillary conjuctivitis and bronchial asthma. Adult inhalation dose is 20 mg four times a day.

Ketotifen is yet another inhibitor of the release of mediators. It is an orally active, less effective antihistaminic agent used for long-term prophylaxis of bronchial asthma. Chemically, it is a benzocyclohepta thiophene derivative. However, it must be administered at least for 6-12 weeks before any beneficial effect is seen.

Synthesis

Guaifensin:

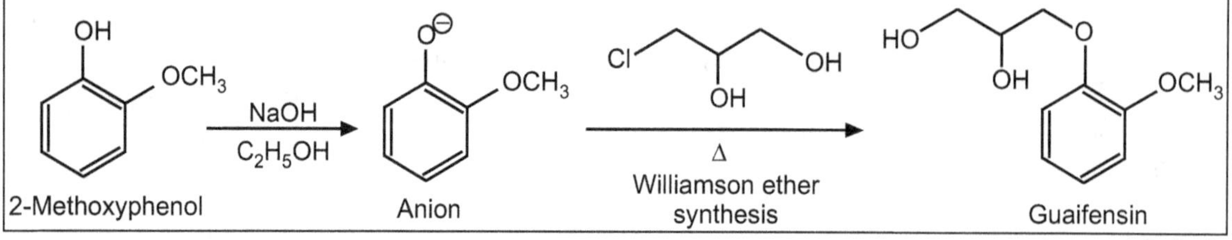

| 2-Methoxyphenol | Anion | Williamson ether synthesis | Guaifensin |

❖ ❖ ❖

5

DRUGS ACTING ON GIT

5.1 INTRODUCTION

Gastrointestinal tract is one of the vital organs present in the body. It possesses a battery of hormones and secretions which control and carry out the processing to get the food in easily absorbable form. This is affected by the enzymatic breakdown of complex food molecules into monosaccharides, amino acids and glycerides. Dysfunctioning of any one of the GIT compartments may lead to human illness and discomfort. Most of the orally active drugs generally choose the signals of nausea and/or vomiting to inaugurate their side-effect session. Diarrhoea or constipation may sometimes mark their appearance. To be on the safer side, it is therefore needed to understand better the pharmacology of drugs acting on gastrointestinal tract. Drugs acting on GIT may be broadly divided into gastric antacids, antiemetics, spasmolytic agents, laxatives-purgatives, antidiarrhoeals and anthelmintics.

5.2 GASTRIC ANTACIDS

As the name indicates, these agents are used to neutralize the excess of gastric acid secretion. In digestion of food, the important constituents of gastric juice are pepsin (a proteolytic enzyme) and hydrochloric acid. Pepsin is produced from pepsinogens which are located in mucous neck cells of oxyntic gland area, mucous neck cells of pyloric gland and in Brunner's gland. It has molecular weight of 35,000 and is most active at pH 2.0. Hydrochloric acid is secreted by the oxyntic (or parietal) cells of the stomach. This secretion is under the control of acetylcholine, histamine and gastrin. Gastrin, a heptadecapeptide was first reported in 1905 by Edkins. It contains seventeen amino acids out of which, only four at the acid end are concerned with its role in the stimulation of acid secretion. It is released from antrum of stomach while secretin and pancreozymin are released from duodenal wall in response to a fall in pH and stimulate the secretion of pancreatic juices. Pentagastrin, one of the gastrin analogs, is a powerful stimulant of acid secretion. All the three bases i.e., histamine, acetylcholine and gastrin, through an interlinked mechanism control the turnover of gastric acid. Gastric antacids neutralise excess gastric acid secretion by mechanism which propagates through

(i) non-receptor mediated events or

(ii) receptor mediated events.

Examples include H_2 - receptor blocking agents like cemetidine, ranitidine etc.

Gastric acid has an important role in :

(a) formation of proteolytic enzyme, pepsin from an inactive precursor, pepsinogen. Gastric acid also provides lower pH to make the pepsin activated, and

(b) inducing the release of secretin.

Gastric acid secretion is governed by histamine receptors, muscarinic receptors and gastrin receptors. Histamine, acetylcholine and gastrin promote the secretion of gastric acid by activating these respective receptor sites. Histamine is released by mast cells located in the lamina propria, acetylcholine is released by postganglionic vagal neurons and gastrin is released from the G cells located in the gastric mucosal antrum.

H^+ - K^+ - ATPase pump is involved in the secretion of gastric acid. It is located in the apical membrane of the parietal cell. The release of gastric acid (i.e., intracellular hydrogen ions) occurs through this pump by one to one exchange with luminal potassium ions. It is an energy dependent process. Cyclic AMP and calcium ions stimulate this proton pump resulting into the secretion of gastric acid, while prostaglandins, somatostatin, calcitonin, glucagon, dopamine and vasoactive intestinal peptide inhibit gastric acid secretion. Usually the basal acid secretion is high in the night hours with the low levels of acid secretion occurring during the daytime.

Mucous is the thick, viscous, physiological barrier which protects the gastric mucosa from the attack of pepsin and gastric acid. It is secreted from the surface epithelium columnar cells and the mucous neck cells of the cardiac, oxyntic and pyloric gland areas. It is secreted alongwith an alkaline fluid. It consists of glycoproteins and mucopolysaccharides. It increases the life span of gastric epithelial cells by providing a tenacious, slimy and alkaline coat over the inner surface of gastric mucosa.

One of the serious complications of hyper-acidity is peptic ulcer which results due to the digestive action of pepsin and hydrochloric acid on the inner wall of stomach and duodenum. This results due to the failure of protective mechanisms of mucosa to prevent the autodigestion process. The feeling of gastric irritation is further potentiated due to increased spasms of GIT. The goals in peptic ulcer treatment are to reduce pain, accelerate healing rate, prevent complications and prevent ulcer recurrence. Peptic ulcer consists of a group of ulcerative disorders affecting the upper gastrointestinal tract. It is thought to occur from an imbalance between the effects of destructive factors (acid, pepsin, bile salts) and protective factor (mucous, bicarbonate, blood flow, epithelial cell regeneration and prostaglandin synthesis). Depending upon their location, ulcers can be classified as :

(i) *Esophageal ulcers :* They affect esopha-gus.

(ii) *Gastric ulcers :* They affect gastric mucosa.

(iii) *Duodenal ulcers :* They affect duodenum, and

(iv) *Stress-induced* or *drug-induced ulcers.*

When an ulcer is formed, the gastric acid present in the stomach causes pain and spasm. This in turn, inhibits healing process. The severity of hyperacidity ranges from gastritis (mucosal inflammation) to peptic ulcer. Most peptic ulcers are chronic in nature and visit the patient in the periodic fashion. Recurrence is associated with the development of complications, such as bleeding, perforation, penetration and obstruction. Depending upon the severity and location of an ulcer, one can start the treatment. An ideal treatment of peptic ulcer usually should cause :

(i) relaxation of the GIT smooth muscles (i.e., spasmolytic action). It is brought about by anticholinergic agents. However, they are now replaced by more potent and specific antisecretory agents which have fewer side-effects, and

(ii) reduction in the gastric acid secretion rate (i.e., antacids and H_2 - blockers).

If drug treatment fails to achieve satisfactory results, bed rest and surgery may be needed to manage this chronic, relapsing condition. People with hyperacidity should avoid taking alcohol, coffee and cigarette smoking (stimulants of acid secretion) and mucosa irritating diet.

5.3 TREATMENT OF GASTRIC HYPERACIDITY

The stomach pH ranges from pH 1 when empty to 7 when food is present. In normal adult, about 22 mEq of acid is secreted per hour by about 1 billion parietal cells present in the gastric mucosa. In duodenal and gastric ulcers, the amount of acid secreted per hour reaches to 42 mEq and 18 mEq respectively. Emotional status of the person, smoking, alcohol and spicy food are known to be predisposing factors in peptic ulcer disease. To avoid this, mixture of antacids are often used. Antacids are weak bases and they raise the gastric pH above 4 (certain antacids like sodium bicarbonate may even elevate the pH to 7). It reduces the proteolytic action of pepsin. Antacids also help to reduce spasms and cause symptomatic relief to pain. Absorption of antacids may disturb the acid-

base balance of the body and cause alkalosis and local effects like, constipation or diarrhoea. Because the actual mechanism for relieving pain is not known, the evaluation of antacids is done quantitatively in terms of their Acid-Neutralising Capacity (ANC value).

Gastric antacids are classified mainly into :

(a) Systemic Antacids (alkalotic agents) :

They get easily absorbed into systemic circulation and therefore are capable of changing pH of the blood. They may cause systemic alkalosis. Such alkalosis is enhanced by chloride loss (vomiting, gastric suction or diarrhoea) and by Na^+ - ion absorption. Examples of antacids belonging to the category include sodium bicarbonate and sodium citrate. Side-effects of these agents include nausea, vomiting, diarrhoea, abdominal pain, irritability, headache, insomnia, myalgia and tetany.

(i) Sodium bicarbonate (baking soda) :

It is a popular and widely used antacid. Due to its high water solubility, it neutralises gastric acid very quickly. Thus, it has a rapid onset but relatively very short duration of action. The pH may be significantly increased upto 7.

It is given orally. Major fraction appears in the urine while small amounts are decomposed to release carbon dioxide which is exhaled through the lungs.

$$NaHCO_3 + HCl \rightarrow NaCl + H_2O + CO_2 \uparrow$$

The carbon-di-oxide evolved during the reaction can cause belching and flatulence alongwith carminative action. In many antacid preparations, sodium bicarbonate is one of the ingredients. It is used in the dose of 1 - 5 gm to give rapid relief from heartburn and dyspepsia. In general, the carbonate and bicarbonate antacids are preferably used when short-term antacid treatment is required. Adverse effects include nausea, vomiting, anorexia, stomach cramps, headache, frequent urination, weakness, nervousness, muscle cramps and irregular heartbeats. It is mainly used to treat metabolic acidosis (i.e., excessively high concentration of the acid in the urine like, cysteine in cystinuria or uric acid in hyperuricemia) due to a variety of conditions, including renal disease, diabetes, shock, dehydration or cardiac arrest. A 0.05 N solution may be used for continuous nasogastric irritation. Similarly a 5.0% solution is recommended for the treatment of dehydration.

(b) Non-systemic Antacids (local antacids) :

They are insoluble in water and are poorly absorbed due to their cationic nature. Since, they do not have direct effect upon the acid-base equilibrium of the blood, systemic alkalosis does not result. Examples include aluminium hydroxide gel, magnesium trisilicate etc.

Systemic antacids are used to combat acidosis while local antacids are used in the treatment of peptic ulcer and hyperacidity. Most of the marketed antacid preparations contain aluminium and magnesium hydroxides. However, due to the toxicity reactions of sodium and calcium ions, their salts are not used for this purpose.

(i) Compounds of aluminium :

These include aluminium hydroxide, aluminium oxide hydrate, aluminium carbonate, dihydroxy aluminium aminoacetate, dihydroxy aluminium sodium carbonate and aluminium phosphate. All these aluminium compounds are used as antacids. These preparations possess both, the neutralising activity and protective activity on the tender mucosal surface of the stomach and duodenum. They are used in the form of colloidal, viscous suspension and are found to possess a steady and prolonged action. The antacid activity is due to the liberation of aluminium cations. They also possess adsorbent activity for various gases and toxins. Independent of their buffering effect on gastric pH, they may also inhibit pepsin activity. These preparations impede peristalsis and tend to induce constipation. But this drawback can be overcome by their combination with magnesium salts. For example, aluminium hydroxide is marketed mostly in combination with magnesium hydroxide. In prolonged use, aluminium salts produce phosphate deficiency. This is due to the reaction of aluminium chloride and dietary phosphate in the stomach to form insoluble aluminium phosphate. Due to the increased fecal phosphate excretion, additional dietary supplements of phosphate are to be given.

The commercially available aluminium hydroxide gel is generally a mixture of the hydroxide, the hydrated oxide and a small amount of the basic carbonate. Various other preparations include aluminium phosphate gel, aluminium carbonate, aluminium glycinate (i.e., dihydroxy-aluminium aminoacetate) and dihydroxy aluminium sodium carbonate.

In pharmacopoeia, aluminium hydroxide gel is described under suspension and anhydrous forms. In both dosage forms, aluminium hydroxide gel is popularly used. A loss of antacid property of the gels during the aging process is reported. Hence, the gel preparations are needed to be stabilised.

(ii) Magnesium containing antacids :

A large number of official antacid preparations contain magnesium in the form of magnesium oxide (MgO) light magnesium carbonate ($3\ MgCO_3;\ Mg\ (OH)_2;\ 3H_2O$), heavy magnesium carbonate, magnesium hydroxide, magnesium phosphate and magnesium trisilicate. Due to their insoluble nature, these compounds do not cause systemic alkalosis. Their antacid mechanism does not involve the liberation of CO_2 gas. The anion portion of magnesium salts seems to be important for their antacid property. They all function in the same manner, with magnesium trisilicate being the only exception.

$$MgO + 2\ HCl \rightarrow MgCl_2 + H_2O$$

The newly formed magnesium chloride undergoes further reaction with the bicarbonate (of the pancreatic juice) in the intestinal juice to form magnesium carbonate. The antacid action of magnesium trisilicate is slow, prolonged and powerful.

$$2\ MgO\ .\ 3\ SiO_2\ .\ XH_2O + 4\ HCl$$

$$\rightarrow 2\ MgCl_2 + 3\ SiO_2 + (X + 2)\ H_2O$$

The neutralising reaction yields hydrated silicon oxide which serves as an adsorbent and provides the protective coating over the mucosal layer and thus protects it from further attack of acid and pepsin. It may also absorb the pepsin. Thus, the activity of trisilicate may be considered as a protective and as an adsorbent. This group of antacids is found to possess purgative action due to magnesium chloride and magnesium carbonate (formed in the GIT). For this reason, they are generally used with such antacids (e.g., aluminium or calcium salts) which cause constipation. For example, Gelusil is a preparation containing aluminium hydroxide gel and magnesium trisilicate combination. Similarly, Magaldrate is a chemical combination of aluminium hydroxide and magnesium hydroxide.

In patients with impaired renal function, magnesium ion retention may lead to magnesium poisoning. Hence magnesium salts are contraindicated in such patients.

(iii) Calcium antacids :

This category includes calcium carbonate and calcium hydroxide. They have quick onset of action. They raise gastric pH to nearly 7 and do not cause systemic alkalosis. Chalk is a natural calcium carbonate. It interacts with gastric acid in the stomach as per the following equation :

$$CaCO_3 + 2HCl \rightarrow CaCl_2 + CO_2 + H_2O$$
$$\downarrow$$
$$HCO_3 \text{ present in intestine}$$
$$\downarrow$$
$$CaCO_3$$

The carbonate present in the intestine leads to constipation similar to aluminium antacids. But unlike aluminium salts, their action is dependent upon their basic properties rather than on any amphoteric effect. To counteract constipating effect due to calcium, most of the calcium carbonate preparations are given in combination with magnesium antacids. Calcium antacids are contra-indicated in patients having impaired renal function because they may increase the serum calcium level during prolonged use. The release of carbondi-oxide in acid neutralization reaction adds to discomfort in some patients. Combination preparations of aluminium hydroxide gel, magnesium antacid and calcium carbonate are also available.

(iv) Bismuth containing compounds :

These agents are commonly used for the treatment of mild diarrhoea. Bismuth carbonate and subnitrate also possess antacid property. This property is due to their ability to cover the gastrointestinal mucosa with a dry, inert and protective coating. Tripotassium dicitrato bismuthate is one of the agents from this category which is used in the treatment of ulcer. Along with the protective activity this compound has antipepsin and spasmolytic activities. It actually promotes the healing of ulcers and also prevents their recurrence.

(v) Milk :

It is regarded as a weak antacid having an additional protective action. Recently antacid formulations have come up with dried milk plus calcium carbonate and magnesium salts. The prolonged administration of such antacid formulations lead to the milk-alkali syndrome. This syndrome is characterized by hypercalcemia, hypoparathyroidism, acute alkalosis and renal damage. Usually, the syndrome disappears as one discontinues the treatment.

Besides their use in peptic ulcer treatment, antacids may also be used in the treatment of Mendelson's syndrome, reflux esophagitis, dyspepsia, heartburn in pregnancy and in some cases of non-specific constipation or diarrhoea.

5.4 H_2-RECEPTOR ANTAGONISTS

Histamine is a powerful stimulant of hydrochloric acid secretion in gastric mucosa. In larger doses, histamine also augments the secretion of pepsin. These actions of histamine are mediated via H_2-receptors.

Hence, H_2 - receptor antagonists are also termed as antisecretory drugs. In 1972, Black et al first described selective H_2-receptor blockade for acid secretion. With the successful introduction of cimetidine in 1977, other analogs like ranitidine, famotidine and nizatidine are now available for the treatment of peptic ulcer.

Famotidine and nizatidine consist of a thiazole ring. In addition, nizatidine has the same ring side-chain of ranitidine. All these agents act as reversible, dose-dependent competitive antagonists at H_2-receptor site resulting in inhibition of gastric acid secretion. They do not reduce gastric secretion of pepsin or pancreatic secretion of bicarbonate or enzymes. Famotidine has a potency 50 - 80 times more than that of cimetidine and 9 - 15 times more than that of ranitidine, while nizatidine is 6 - 10 times more potent than cimetidine.

Famotidine currently is indicated for the treatment of active duodenal ulcer and active benign gastric ulcer and for the treatment of pathological hypersecretory conditions (e.g., Zollinger - Ellison syndrome, multiple endocrine adenomas etc.)

Nizatidine is indicated for the treatment of active duodenal ulcer and maintenance therapy for duodenal ulcer patients. Both, famotidine and nizatidine may also be used in the treatment of gastroesophageal reflux disease, systemic mastocytosis and in the prophylaxis of stress ulceration.

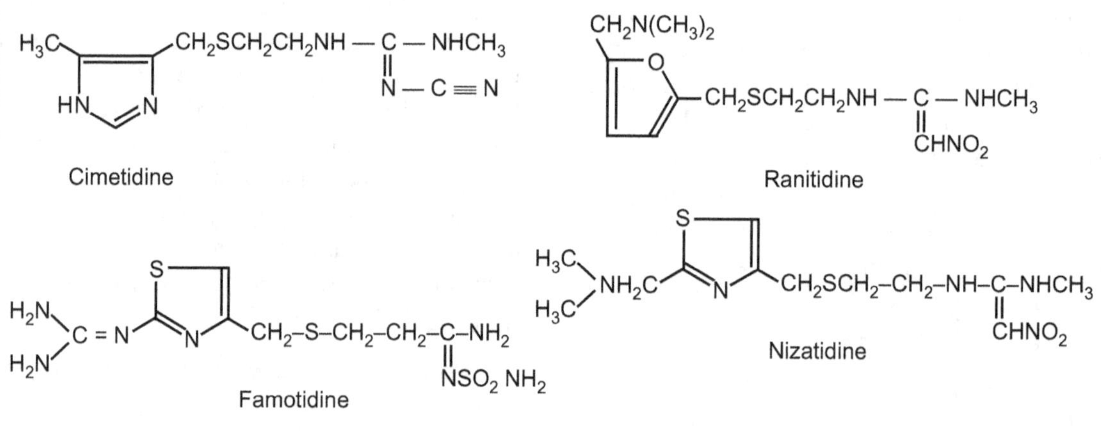

Fig. 5.1 : Some clinically used H_2-receptor antagonists

5.5 ANTIMUSCARINIC AGENTS

Pirenzepine :

It is an antimuscarinic agent having structural similarity with tricyclic antidepressant agents. However, it lacks antidepressant activity because of its poor penetration ability in the CNS. It selectively inhibits cholinergic receptors present in the gastrointestinal tract due to its greater affinity for the muscarinic receptors located in the gastric mucosa.

Adverse effects are few and include dry mouth, blurred vision, constipation and urinary retention. It is used orally to heal gastric and duodenal ulcers in the dose of 100 - 150 mg per day.

Trimebutine :

It is an antimuscarinic agent used to treat irritable bowel syndrome.

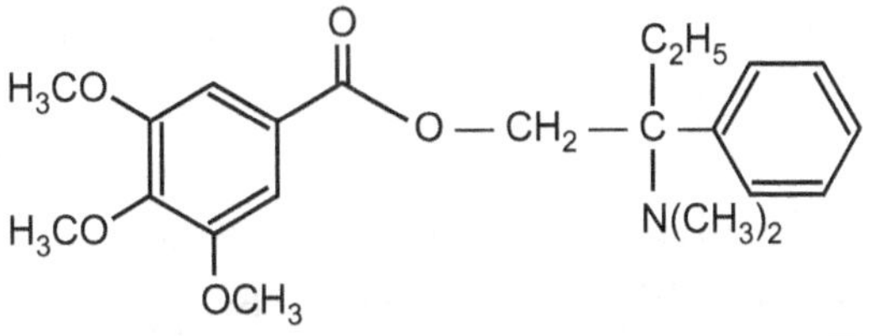

5.6 TRICYCLIC ANTIDEPRESSANTS

These agents possess anticholinergic activity. The reduction in the gastric acid secretion is also brought about by their antagonistic action on both, H_1 and H_2-receptors. Doxepin and trimipramine are undergoing clinical investigations for their utility in the treatment of gastric and duodenal ulcers.

Adverse effects include drowsiness and anticholinergic features. These agents may be used in patients unresponsive to conventional drug regimens.

5.7 H^+-K^+-ATPase INHIBITORS

Omeprazole :

It is an orally effective benzimidazole derivative. It reversibly inhibits H^+ - K^+ - ATPase pump system in the parietal cell membranes resulting into decrease in the gastric acid secretion. It blocks the terminal phase of acid production by binding to an enzyme, hydrogen / potassium adenosine triphosphatase that is needed for extrusion of hydrogen ions into the gastric lumen. Suppression of gastric acid with omeprazole is long-lasting and may persist for three days or longer. Adverse effects include nausea, diarrhoea and insomnia. It promotes rapid healing of peptic ulcers. It is used in the treatment of peptic and duodenal ulcers. In large oral dose, it is effective to control severe gastric acid hypersecretion seen in Zollinger - Ellison syndrome. Adult oral dose is 30 - 80 mg per day prior to breakfast.

5.8 PROSTAGLANDINS

These are naturally occurring substances that mediate almost every biological function in the body. Chemically they are 20 - carbon oxygenated fatty acid derivatives of prostanoic acid. Prostaglandins inhibit gastric acid secretion stimulated by feeding, histamine or gastrin. Reduction in gastric acid secretion results in reductions in the gastric volume of secretions, acidity and pepsin content.

Prostaglandins, especially of the E class (e.g. 15, 15 - dimethyl PGE_2 and 16, 16 - dimethyl PGE_2) possess antisecretory and cytoprotective (i.e., mucosal protective action) effects in the gastrointestinal tract. They appear to protect the mucosal layers by stimulating gastric mucous secretion and gastric and duodenal bicarbonate production. They reduce acid back diffusion. They also allow substantial movement of water and electrolytes in the intestinal lumen.

Misoprostol, a synthetic prostaglandin has been clinically used for the prevention of gastric ulcers caused by prolonged use of non-steroidal anti-inflammatory agents. Other synthetic prostaglandins which are under clinical trials include abraprostil, enprostil, riboprostil and trimoprostil.

5.9 MISCELLANEOUS AGENTS

(a) Carbenoxolone :

It is an orally well absorbed oleandane derivative of glycyrrhizinic acid which is a constituent of licorice. Due to its ability to stimulate the production of 11-hydroxy corti-costeroids, it possesses anti-inflammatory activity.

It is orally absorbed rapidly when pH is 2 or less. More than 99.9% of absorbed dose is bound to the plasma-proteins. Small amount undergoes metabolism to yield inactive glucuronide and sulphuric acid conjugates which are excreted in the bile. Minor amounts also appear in the urine.

It is used as an antiulcer agent to promote healing of gastric and duodenal ulcers. Its activity is due to its protective antipepsin and mucous secretion promoting properties. It also increases the volume of mucous secreted and increases its effectiveness. It reduces acid back diffusion and possibly augments secretin release.

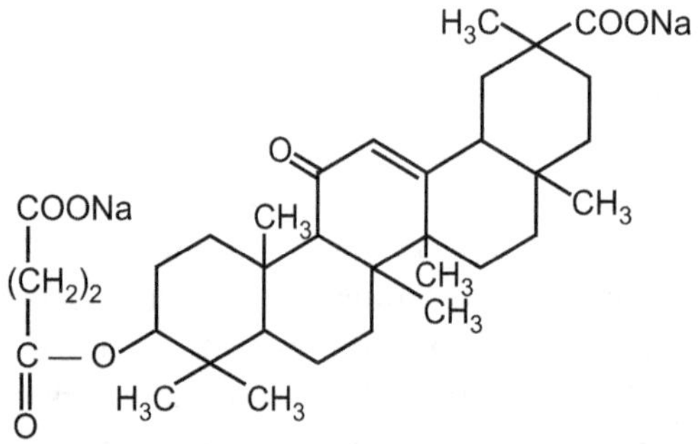

Carbenoxolone sodium

Adverse effects include alkalosis, oedema and hypokalemia, all are due to the mineralo-corticoidal nature of the drug. It is contra-indicated in cardiac failure and hypertensive patients. Adult oral dose is 100 mg two to three times a day for 4 - 8 weeks.

(b) Deglycyrrhizinated licorice :

It contains about 1-3% glycyrrhizinic acid. It possesses weak antispasmodic activity. It minimally depresses gastric acid secretion and does not affect mucous secretion.

(c) Metoclopramide :

Basically, this drug is a good antiemetic because of its dopaminergic blocking action. It does not affect the secretion of either gastric acid or pepsin.

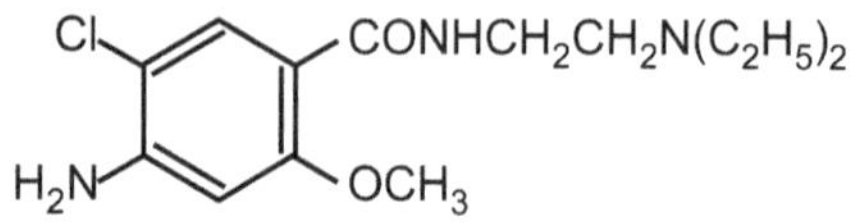

Metoclopramide

It promotes gastric emptying and relieves flatulence, dyspepsia and heart-burn. Due to its indirect actions on peristalsis and ability to abolish the enterogastric reflux of bile, it is of value in the treatment of gastric ulcer.

Adverse effects include nausea, bowel disturbances, headache, facial grimacing, fatigue, drowsiness, lassitude, insomnia, restlessness, involuntary movement, dizziness and extrapyramidal effects.

It is used in the treatment of gastric and peptic ulcer. It is also employed in the management of reflux esophagitis and the control of gastroparesis in diabetes.

Adult oral dose is 10 mg about 30 minutes before each meal and at the bedtime.

(d) Sucralfate :

It is a complex of sulfated sucrose and polyaluminium hydroxide. It acts as a gastric mucosa protectant by adhering strongly to epithelial cells. It forms a protective barrier on the ulcer and prevents gastric acid, pepsin and bile salts from aggravating the ulceratic lesions. It also adsorbs pepsin, trypsin and bile acids. However, it does not have acid neutralising capacity.

About 3 - 5% dose is orally absorbed, rest of the fraction appears unchanged in the faeces. Systemically absorbed drug appears in the urine in the form of sulfate disaccharide. Adverse effects include dry mouth, stomach discomfort, constipation, nausea, vomiting, xerostomia, dizziness and elevated plasma aluminium concentration. It is used to promote healing rate in duodenal and gastric ulcers. It is more effective in duodenal than in gastric ulcers. Antacids should not be taken for 30 minutes prior and after the dose of sucralfate.

Adult oral dose is 1 gm about one hour before meal and at bed time.

(e) Gefarnate :

It is a synthetic terpene that contains a number of isoprene units. Originally, it was extracted from the white-headed cabbage. It has antipepsin activity. It is used in the treatment of gastric ulcer in the dose of 200 - 400 mg every 8 hours. However, it is not effective in the treatment of duodenal ulcer.

Maintenance Therapy :

Maintenance therapy is indicated in patients having a history of frequent relapses of hyperacidity. It reduces the rate of ulcer recurrences as long as the therapy is continued. It consists of continuous low-dose treatment with one of the H_2 - receptor antagonists cimetidine - 400 mg, famotidine - 20 mg or nizatidine -150 mg at bed time. Other miscellaneous drugs include urogastrone and sulglycotide. Urogastrone is a 52 amino acid polypeptide isolated from human urine. It is found to depress gastric acid secretion after parenteral administration, while sulglycotide is isolated from porcine duodenal mucosa. It was found to reduce peptic activity.

5.10 ULCERATIVE COLITIS

It is an inflammatory bowel disease characterized by inflammation of the mucosal layer of the colon and rectum.

(a) Sulfasalazine :

It is the drug of choice for the treatment of mild to moderate disease condition. It is a poor orally absorbed sulfonamide that does not have antibacterial activity. It splits into the gut to sulfapyridine and 5 - aminosalicylate moieties. The former is absorbed systemically and appears in the urine while the latter is excreted in the faeces and hence it is effective in inflammatory bowel disease. Adverse effects appear to be related to sulfapyridine while the therapeutic effects are related to 5-aminosalicylate.

Adverse effects include nausea, vomiting, anorexia, gastric distress, pancreatitis, headache, fever, arthralgia, malaise, dyspepsia, anemia, agranulocytosis and thrombocytopenia.

Adult oral dose is 4 - 12 gm in 4 - 8 divided doses per day. The effect is then maintained by a dose of 500 mg four times a day.

(b) Mesalamine :

It contains only 5-aminosalicylate. It is available in the form of oral preparations and as enemas. It acts locally on the lumen of the intestine and is thought to decrease inflammation in patients with ulcerative colitis by interference with arachidonic acid metabolism, resulting in a decreased production of leukotrienes.

Mesalamine enema is indicated for the treatment of mild to moderate distal ulcerative colitis, including ulcerative proctosigmoiditis and ulcerative proctitis.

Adverse effects include anal irritation, headache and loss of hair. It is contraindicated in patients allergic to salicylates. It is available as a rectally administered suspension enema formulation which should be shaken prior to use. The usual dose is 60 ml enema once a day at bed time to improve retention for mild to moderate ulcerative colitis.

Table 5.1 : Some clinically useful antispasmodic agents

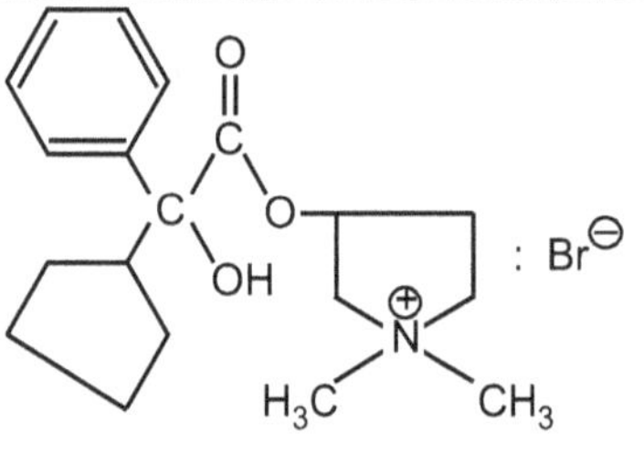

Glycopyrrolate

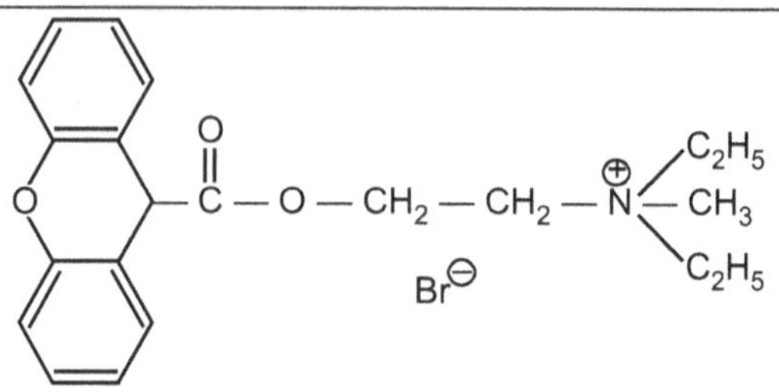

Methantheline bromide

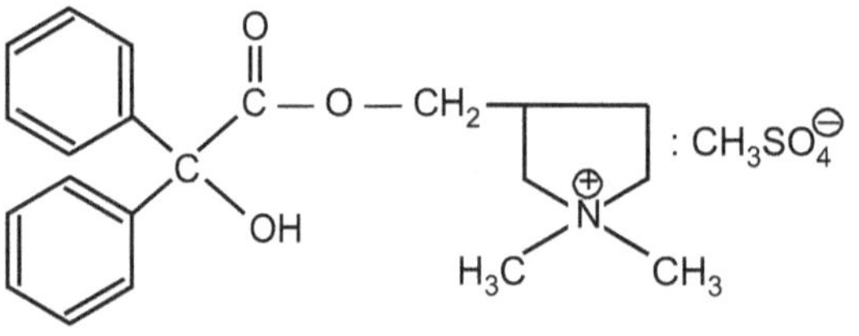

Poldine methylsulfate

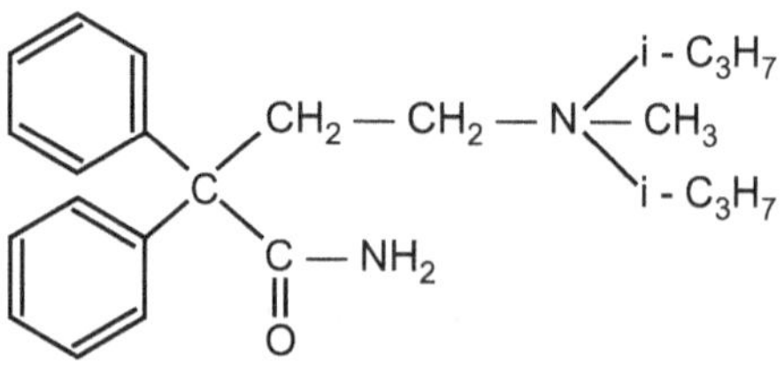

Isopropamide

5.11 ANTISPASMODICS

(Spasmolytic agents)

These are the agents that have an ability to relax smooth muscles of gastrointestinal tract. On the chemical basis, antispasmodic agents can be classified as :

(i)　Atropine and its synthetic analogs
(ii)　Synthetic aminoalcohol esters
(iii)　Aminoalcohol ethers
(iv)　Aminoalcohols
(v)　Aminoamides, and
(vi)　Papaverine and its synthetic analogs

Out of these, class (i) to (v) act by anticholinergic mechanism while class (vi) does not act by interfering with cholinergic nerve transmission. Anticholinergic compounds have some structural similarity with acetylcholine and contain some additional substituents that enhance their binding with cholinergic receptors. The acetyl-choline molecule does not cover all the area of receptor. The area of a receptor which is not covered by acetylcholine molecule appears to be chiefly hydrophobic in nature. Hence, hydrophobic substituents increase the affinity of the antagonist for the receptor surface. The large hydrophobic group may not only increase the affinity of the blocking agent but through an 'umbrella effect' may also block the access of acetylcholine to the receptor site.

Papaverine and its analogs do not produce antispasmodic effect by interferring with cholinergic nerve transmission. It is believed to inhibit phosphodiesterase activity and adenosine uptake into the muscle cells. Since, cholinergic nerve stimulation increases peristaltic movements of GIT (spasmodic), adrenergic nerve stimulation will produce antispasmodic effect through the stimulation of β-adrenergic receptor. Cyclic-AMP is the active factor which is a product of the response of β - adrenergic receptors. Papaverine and its analogs are inhibitors of phosphodiesterase, an enzyme that degrades cyclic - AMP.

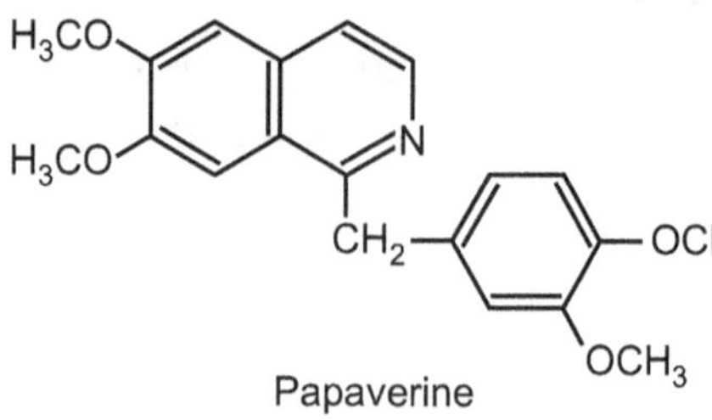

Papaverine

5.12 EMETICS AND ANTIEMETICS

Nausea and vomiting are the most usual side-effects of many drugs. When a toxic or irritant substance is ingested, the body will try to expel it out and vomiting results. In sick condition, vomiting or nausea may often occur as a symptom of the disease.

Nausea, an unpleasant sensation is generally associated with vomiting. Severe nausea may sometimes occur in the absence of vomiting and severe vomiting can occur without the nauseating feeling. Vomiting (emesis) is a complex physiological process. Emetic centers present in the lateral reticular formation of medulla oblongata, regulate the process. These centers may get stimulated due to mechanical, chemical or peripheral stimuli. Sometimes, certain drugs may also activate these centers which results in vomiting. The chemoreceptor trigger zone (CTZ) plays an important role in stimulating the emetic process. It contains dopaminergic receptors. Since it lies outside the blood-brain barrier, it can be easily activated by the attack of drugs. Certain drugs (e.g. apomorphine) activate CTZ and lead to vomiting. While some drugs depress the CTZ activity (e.g., chlorpromazine) and lead to antiemetic activity. In the medulla other important controlling centers of autonomic, cardiovascular and respiratory systems are also located in the viscinity of emetic centers. Hence, vomiting is usually preceeded by the signs of autonomic stimulation, sweating, salivation, pallor, bradycardia and other cardiovascular effects. Psychological factors plays an important role in both, the emesis and antiemetic processes.

5.12.1 Emetics

These drugs constitute a valuable part of treatment in poisoning cases. They are sometimes also used in low doses in cough preparations to stimulate flow or respiratory tract secretions. These drugs act either by local irritation (reflux) mechanisms or directly on the chemoreceptor trigger zone (i.e., central mechanism).

(a) Reflux or Local Emetics :

These drugs cause vomiting by stimulating both, the vagus and the sympathetic nerve endings in the stomach and refluxly stimulate the emetic centers present in the medulla. The commonly used examples of this class include sodium chloride, mustard, copper sulphate, zinc sulphate, ammonium bicarbonate and ipecacuanha. In case, if vomiting is not induced by copper sulphate, its absorption into the circulation may lead to serious toxic effect. Ipecacuanha tincture, in larger doses, has a strong emetic action and is very safe in use. It is prepared from the dried roots of Cephaelis ipecacuanha. It contains emetine, an alkaloid as an active constituent. It acts directly on CTZ as well as indirectly by irritating stomach. Action is enhanced if 200 - 300 ml water is ingested immediately after the administration of the syrup.

Adverse effects include stomach cramps, headache, itching, muscle stiffness, weakness, faintness, mild drowsiness, sweating and hypotension. It should not be given to semi-conscious or unconscious patients because of the risk of passing the vomitted material into the lungs.

Syrup of ipecacuanha is used to induce vomiting in the cases of drug overdoses or poisoning due to other chemicals. Adult oral dose is 15 - 30 ml of syrup of Ipecac.

(b) Central Emetics :

These drugs activate the chemoreceptor trigger zone in medulla which then sends impulses to the vomiting centre itself. Examples include apomorphine, cardiac glycosides, morphine, veratrum alkaloids, nicotine, lobeline etc. Apomorphine is a morphine analog. It is a very short-acting central and peripheral dopaminergic agonist obtained by exposure of morphine to strong mineral acids. It is devoid of analgesic activity and exerts emetic effect by stimulating chemoreceptor zone in the brain stem which is connected with the vomiting centre. Like other opioids, it may cause respiratory depression alongwith circulatory collapse, if it is given in higher doses. Adverse effects include depression, euphoria, restlessness and tremors.

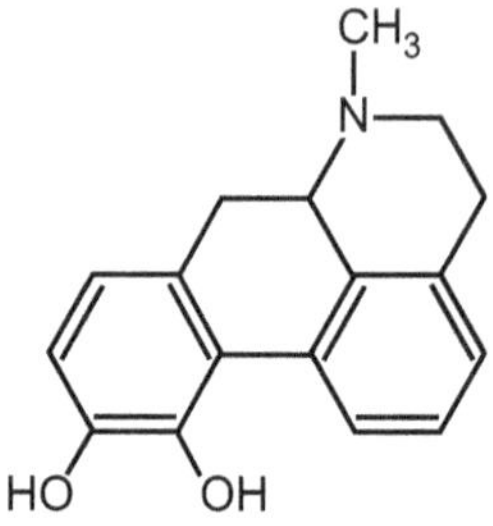

Apomorphine

It is used in the management of poisoning due to oral ingestion of poisons or drug overdoses. When given subcutaneously or by intramuscularly in dosage upto 8 mg, it leads to vomiting within few minutes. Due to its short duration of action and adverse effects, it is not preferred in the treatment of Parkinson's disease.

5.12.2 Antiemetics

These drugs are used to reduce or to prevent vomiting in conditions where it is common or may be expected. Vomiting occurs as :

(1) undesired side-effect of many drugs,

(2) in motion sickness or other diseases conditions, and

(3) in pregnancy.

Most of the antiemetic agents possess atleast some degree of central depressant action. Many anticholinergics and antihistaminergic agents possess antiemetic property. The vomiting in pregnancy does not need the drug treatment, atleast for first trimester. Thereafter, apparently safer drugs are to be used to avoid the possibility of teratogenic effects of the drugs. The commonly used drugs in such cases are phenothiazines (e.g., chlorpromazine, prochlorperazine and promazine). Pyridoxine, one of B-complex

vitamins, is also used in various combinations. Drowsiness, dry mouth and related side-effects are due to the anticholinergic and antihistaminic nature of these drugs.

Classification of Antiemetics :

These agents are classified on the basis of their mechanism of action.

(i) CNS depressants :

These agents depress the vomiting centres present in the medulla by non-specific mechanism. Examples include barbiturates, bromides, chloral hydrate etc.

(ii) Anticholinergic agents :

These drugs relax the spasm of gastrointestinal muscles. They also act centrally to give antiemetic effects by inhibiting the cholinergic transmission. Examples include atropine and hyoscine. Side-effects associated with the use of these agents include dry mouth, blurred vision and giddiness which are mainly due to anticholinergic activity.

(iii) Antihistaminic agents :

Histamine causes the contractions of smooth muscles of GIT. It also acts as a central neurotransmitter. Thus antihistaminics act by both, relaxing the smooth muscles and also act centrally to depress vomiting centres. Examples include dimenhydrinate, buclizine, cyclizine, meclozine and promethazine. The selective activity of these drugs contributes further to their antiemetic activity. Some of these agents also possess anticholinergic action.

All agents from this class are H_1-receptor blockers. Dimenhydrinate is a combination of diphenhydramine and 8 - chlorotheophylline in equal molar proportions. It retains significant antimuscarinic and sedation properties. Adult oral dose is about 25 - 50 mg per day.

(iv) Drugs forming a protective covering over the gastric mucosa :

Examples include bismuth compounds, kaolin, etc. It has only a prophylactic use.

(v) Miscellaneous agents :

Diazepam and diphenidol are vestibular depressants and can be used in the treatment of physiologically induced vomiting. Other miscellaneous agents include ipecacuanha preparation, pyridoxine, calomel and menthol.

(vi) Newer antiemetic agents :

(a) Trimethobenzamide :

It is an orally active non-phenothiazine antiemetic agent. Inactive metabolites appear in the urine alongwith 30 - 50% dose in unchanged form.

Adverse effects include diarrhoea, headache, blurred vision, skin rash, drowsiness, dizziness, convulsions, disorientation, coma, muscle cramps, jaundice and hypotension. Trimethobenzamide suppositories contain benzocaine which may produce hypersensitivity reactions. Adult oral dose is 250 mg three to four times a day.

(b) Metoclopramide :

Basically, it is an antiemetic agent but it can also be used in the treatment of peptic ulcer. It is a cholinergic agonist which also has dopaminergic blocking action. It is used as an antiemetic agent in cancer chemotherapy (initially 2 mg/kg dose). It acts centrally to depress vomiting centres and also promotes emptying of the stomach.

Since, metoclopramide also antagonises $5-HT_3$ receptor, similar antagonists like granisetron and ondansetron were developed as antiemetic drugs.

(c) Diphenidol :

It is used as antiemetic agent. Adverse effects include nausea, indigestion, headache, nervousness, drowsiness and hypotension. In sensitive patients, anticholinergic symptoms may develop.

(d) Benzaquinamide :

It is a short acting drug used to prevent postoperative vomiting.

(e) Tetrahydrocannabinol (l - Δ^9 – THC) :

It is a psychoactive substance isolated from the flowering heads of hemp plant, Cannabis sativa. Though it is orally absorbed, it undergoes an extensive first pass metabolism. It has a biphasic plasma half-life. Initial half-life is 10 - 20 minutes while terminal half-life is 30 hours. Principal metabolites include 11 - hydroxy - Δ^9 - THC (active) and 11 - nor - Δ^9 THC - 9 - carboxylic acid (inactive). They are excreted in urine as well as in faeces.

Table 5.2 : Some clinically used antiemetic agents

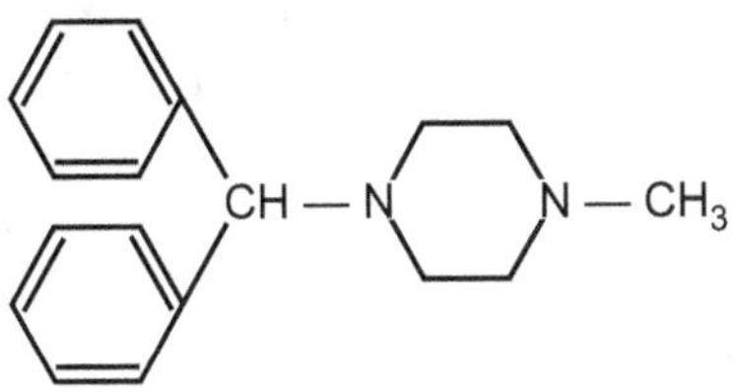

Cyclizine

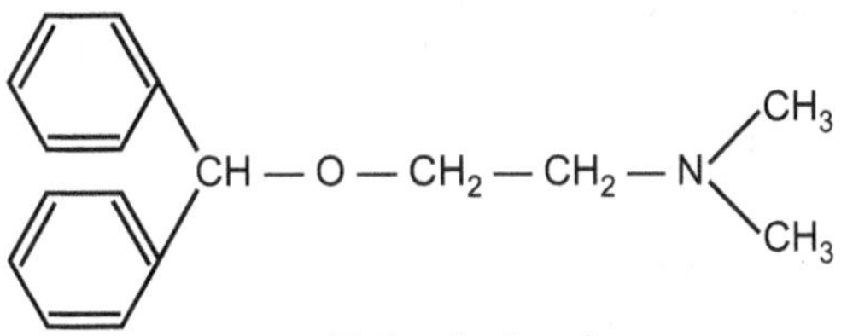

Diphenhydramine

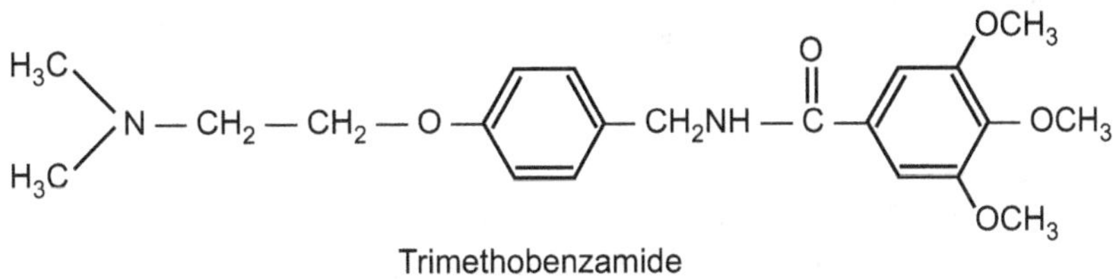

Trimethobenzamide

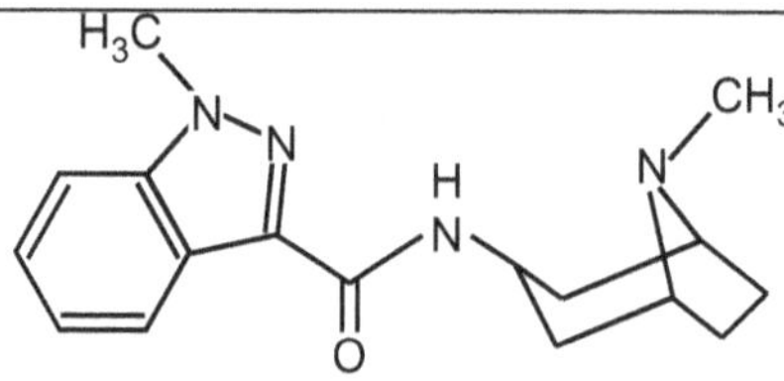

Granisetron

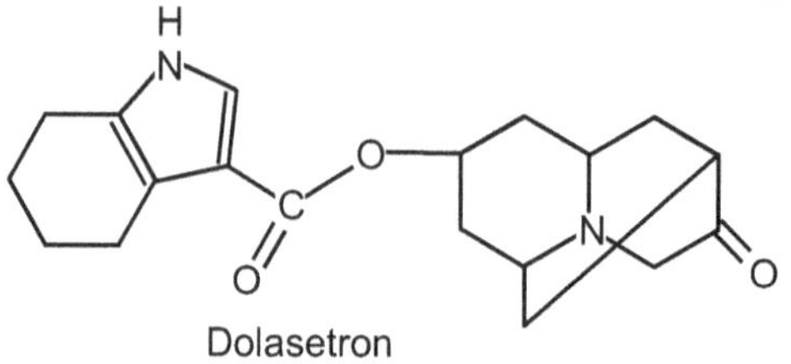

Dolasetron

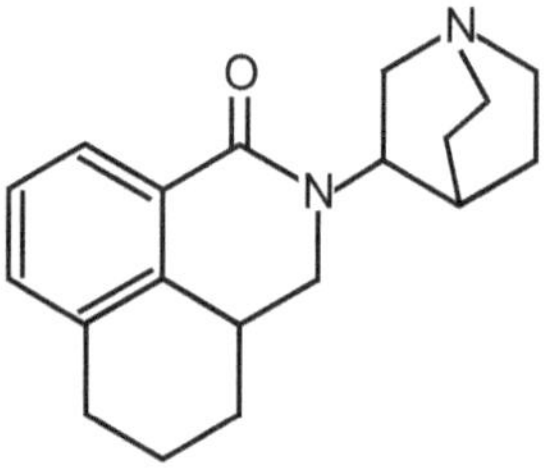

Palonosetron

Ondansetron : It is 5HT$_3$-receptor antagonist, used as an antiemetic following chemotherapy. It has no effect on vomiting caused by motion sickness.

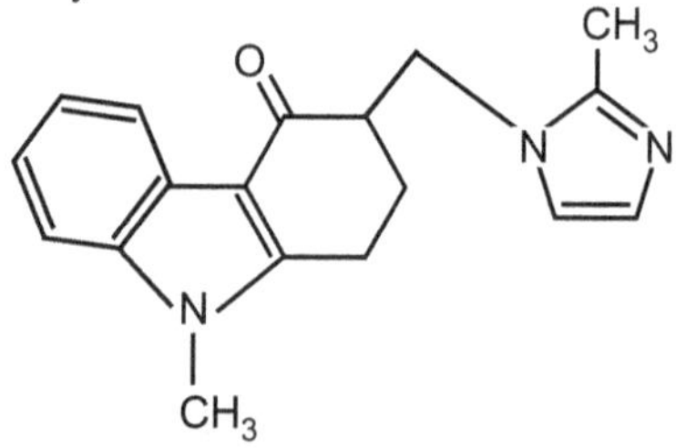

Ondansetron

Adverse effects include dry mouth, dizziness, somnolence, confusion, hallucination, dysphoria, euphoria, depersonalization, conjunctivitis, hypotension, tachycardia, tolerance and addiction.

It is used as an antiemetic agent to control nausea and vomiting induced by cancer chemotherapeutic agents. It may be given orally or by smoke.

5.13 LAXATIVES AND PURGATIVES

Constipation and illness have historically been associated with each other. Constipation is the infrequent or delayed evacuation of the faeces. It is a battle between the bowl and bowel. Regularity of the bowel movement is necessary to avoid a vague feeling of discomfort. Constipation is different from dyschesia (i.e., difficulty in a defaecation).

In a normal adult, approximately 9 litres of fluid and partly undigested food reach the cecum per day : Fecal fluid content of 200 - 300 ml usually results in some softening of stool. Large amounts of fluids can be retained in large intestine due to the hydrophilic properties of laxative. This increased pressure then facilitates the process of defecation. Fecal fluid values greater than 300 ml usually result in diarrhoea.

Cathartic (Greek term, katharsis = purification) is the general term used to describe all such agents which promote the passage of faeces. This category includes aperient, laxative, purgative and drastic agents all of which have intensity of cathartic action in increasing order. Drastic agents include colocynth, croton oil, jalap and podophyllum. Since, they have potent cathartic action, they may induce severe mucosal irritation and gastroenteritis. Laxatives are the drugs which stimulate peristalsis, promote evacuation through the powerful contractions of the bowel. Defecation results due to powerful peristalsis. Fluid and electrolyte changes develop in both, the large and small intestine with laxative use.

Classification of Laxatives :

These agents can be classified on the basis of their mode of action as follows :

(i) Stimulant or irritant laxatives :

These agents irritate the intestinal mucosa. This results into quick response to the distention. They also lead to the accumulation of fluids in the colon resulting into an increased pressure and stool softening effects. Examples include anthraquinone derivatives, castor oil, diphenylmethane derivatives (phenol phthalein and bisacodyl) and bile acids.

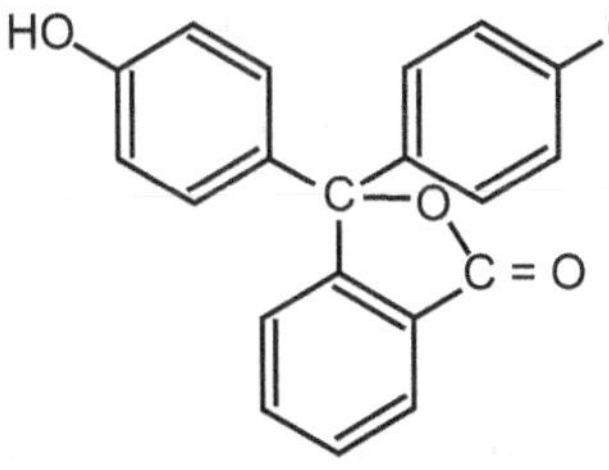

Phenolphthalein

All the above agents produce laxative effect by stimulating peristalsis by irritation. They induce a reflux increase in the gut motility. They are inactive if given parenterally. Castor oil contains the tri-glyceride of ricinoleic acid which undergoes enzymatic hydrolysis in body to give glycerol and ricinoleate. The laxative action of castor oil is mainly due to ricinoleate. In addition, it has an emollient activity. It is obtained from the plant, Ricinus communis. Adult oral dose is 15 - 30 ml per day.

Senna, rhubarb, aloe and cascara are the main sources of anthraquinone glycosides. These plants contain various oxymethyl quinones present, partly in free form and partly as inactive glycosides. These glycosides are released in the intestinal lumen under the influence of microbial flora. Emodin (trioxymethyl anthraquinone) and chrysophanic acid (dioxymethyl anthraquinone) are the active laxative constituents of anthraquinone glycosides. Emodin increases the retention of water and sodium ions in the lumen by inhibiting Na^+ - K^+ - ATPase pump present in the lumen mucosa. Danthron is a synthetic derivative of anthraquinone glycoside. Anthraquinone glycosides can be obtained from :

(i) dried leaves of Cassia acutifolia and Cassia angustifolia (Senna leaves),

(ii) dried roots and rhyzomes of Rheum officinale (Rhubarb),

(iii) bark of Rhamnus purshiana (Cascara sagrada), and

(iv) juice of Aloe perryi (Aloe).

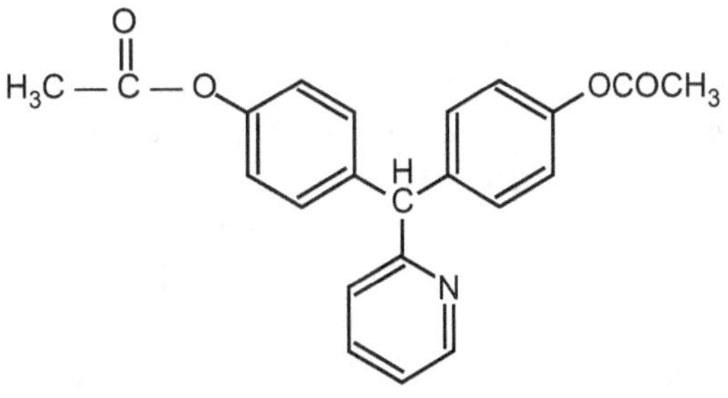

Bisacodyl

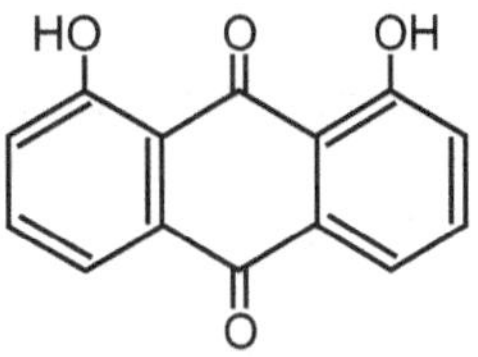

Danthron
(1, 8-dihydroxyanthraquinone)

Tegaserod : It is 5HT$_4$ – against used for the management of irritable bowel syndrome and constipation. It acts as a motility stimulant.

Adverse effects of stimulant laxatives include excessive purgative action. Sometimes larger doses of these agents may produce nephritis. They should not be used in pregnancy.

(ii) Bulk-forming laxatives :

If the diet contains a bulk of non-absorbable residue, this part, by filling the intestine, exerts the pressure on the bowel wall. This pressure serves as a stimulus for normal defecation. Since, part of their activity can be attributed to their ability to absorb water (i.e., a hydrogel), patients should drink adequate amount of water to avoid dehydration. Examples of this category include methylcellulose, isapghula, agar, banana and psyllium seeds.

They act as the mechanical laxatives and are used when the faeces are dry and hard. Most of them are marketed in the form of granules which absorb water and swell up into the thick mucilage that is not digested but excreted unchanged. They indirectly stimulate peristalsis by their water content and their content of undigestible matter. The hydrogel which is formed, facilitates defaecation by lubrication of fecal mass because of its emolient property.

Bran is yet another example of bulk-forming laxatives. It comprises all undigestible fibre material derived from either fruits and vegetables or from cereals. It mainly contains carbohydrates in the form of cellulose, lignin and pectin. It is usually used in the treatment of diverticulitis.

(iii) Emollient laxatives (lubricants) :

These agents are also called as stool softners. They act simply by lubricating intestinal mucosa. Softening of stool is assisted by reducing intestinal electrolyte and fluid transport. Examples include olive oil, glycerine, liquid paraffin etc.

Liquid paraffin is a mixture of liquid hydrocarbons, used as an emollient to lubricate and soften the fecal matter in constipation. It is available as oil or as a white emulsion. When given orally, it is not absorbed. Its continued use is contraindicated. It is a thick clear mineral oil which passes into the intenstine in undigested form, softens the bowel contents, lubricates the intestinal channel resulting in smooth, painless movements. It is usually prescribed in the form of emulsion to which agar or phenol-phthalein is sometimes added. Dose ranges from 8 ml to 30 ml.

Docusate sodium

Docusate sodium (dioctyl sodium sulpho-succinate) is yet another example of this category. It is an anionic type of surfactant having a wide variety of emulsifying, wetting and dispersing applications.

It is used as a fecal softner due to its emulsifying action. It increases the secretion of water and electrolytes into intestinal lumen. It apparently hydrates and softens the stool. It is incorporated into retention enemas. Because of detergent nature, it allows water to penetrate and soften the hard fecal matter. It is available in the form of docusate sodium, docusate calcium and docusate potassium. Adult oral dose is 50-300 mg per day while adult rectal dose is 50-100 mg as 0.10% solution. The polymers of polyoxyethylene and polyoxypropylene also possess the detergent properties and may find use as emollient laxatives.

(iv) Saline laxatives (osmotic laxatives) :

They are salts of poorly absorbable anions and sometimes cations. Here the word, "saline" indicates certain compounds of sodium and magnesium. This class includes water soluble inorganic salts that contain multivalent cations or anions. Because of their ionic nature, these ions are slowly or incompletely absorbed from intestine. Consequently, water is retained in the intestinal lumen through osmotic effect exerted by these non-absorbed ions. Osmotic pressure depends upon molecular weight of the drug and concentration of such unabsorbed ions. The resulting semifluid fecal matter exerts a pressure on the luminal wall. Peristalsis is induced by the activation of stretch receptor present in the GIT mucosa resulting into a laxative effect. Magnesium salts, in addition stimulate the secretion of cholecystokinin-pancreozymin, a hormone that stimulates the fluid secretion and motility and reduces absorption of sodium chloride. More commonly used saline purgatives include :

(a) Magnesium salts : e.g., magnesium sulphate and milk of magnesia (magnesium hydroxide).

(b) Sodium or potassium salts : e.g., tartarate, sulphate, phosphate and biphosphate.

(c) Potassium-sodium tartarate (Rochelle salt) and

(d) Lactulose.

Magnesium sulphate (epsom salt) is the most powerful saline laxative since both ions are least absorbed. It is used as a cathartic to provide complete evacuation of small and large intestine in patients with chronic liver disease. Adult oral dose is 5 - 20 gm per day in divided doses. In patients with renal dysfunctioning, higher blood concentrations of magnesium are reported to occur due to inadequate removal of magnesium ions from blood. This may lead to CNS - depression or coma. Hence, its use is contraindicated in patients with renal dysfunctioning.

Lactulose is a semisynthetic disaccharide sugar. About 2 - 3% dose is orally absorbed. The unabsorbed dose is metabolized by intestinal bacterial (Lactobacilli, Bacteroides species, *E. coli* and Clostridia species) to lactic, acetic and formic acids and carbon di-oxide. These low molecular weight acids initiate an osmotic drive. Systemically absorbed portion appears in urine in unchanged form. Each 15 ml contains 10 gm of lactulose and minor amounts of other sugars like galactose and lactose. It is used orally (7 - 10 gm) alongwith sufficient water to treat constipation.

Adverse effects of saline laxatives include anorexia, headache, hypogastric pain, bloating, flatulence, dehydration, weakness, myalgias, depression, and disturbance in water-electrolyte balance. Chronic treatment with saline laxatives may cause damage to colonic mucosa resulting into proctocolitis. In certain cases, systemic toxicity is reported to occur. Adequate fluid intake should be maintained to avoid dehydration due to hypertonic solution of the saline laxatives.

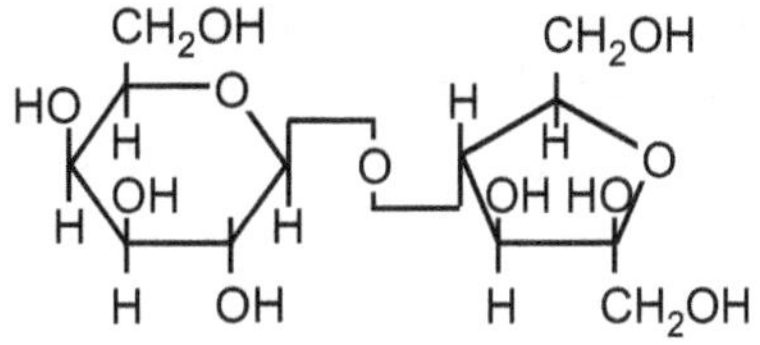

Lactulose

(v) Enemas :

These are the detergent containing preparations which are introduced through the rectum. Soapy water, saline, olive oil, cotton seed oil, glycerine, sodium phosphate or sodium biphosphate are the common ingredients of enema preparations. Hypertonic saline solution offers certain advantages over the detergent substances. They soften faeces and produce laxation either by fragmentation, liquefaction or lubrication. They increase the muscle tone of colon and rectum. Phosphate enemas lower the serum calcium level by inducing considerable loss of calcium.

(vi) Sulfur :

Chemically, sulfur is very active element. It is therapeutically employed both internally as well as topically. Topically, it acts as fungicide, parasiticide and keratolytic agent. If used internally, it exhibits a mild cathartic action which is due to its reduction to the sulphide anion in the intestine. This sulphide anion (S^-) neutralizes excess gastric acid to give hydrogen sulphide which is a mild intestinal irritant.

$$S + 2H_3O^+ \rightarrow H_2S + 2H_2O$$

(vii) Calomel :

Chemically, it is mercurous chloride. Its cathartic action is due to the strong intestinal irritant property of mercuric cation (i.e., mercury albuminate) formed in the small intestine. The possibility of mercury poisoning has posed limitations on its use.

5.14 ANTIDIARRHOEALS

Diarrhoea means loose bowel movements resulting into the frequent passage of watery, uniformed stools with or without mucous and blood. This condition may arise due to the change in the nature of diet and routine or sometimes due to bacterial infection. The former type of diarrhoea is the mild form while the infective diarrhoea is more powerful and persistant. Organism escapes from gastric acid and other digestive processes and reaches the bowel. Its metabolic products irritate the nerve ending of intestinal wall leading to severe diarrhoea. In this condition, to compensate the loss of body fluids, a mixture of salt (sodium chloride or sodium bicarbonate) and water is to be given frequently). The simple type of diarrhoea may be controlled just by using intestinal adsorbents while infected diarrhoea needs the use of intestinal antiseptics.

(i) Adsorbents :

These substances have the power of adsorbing gases, bacteria or toxins without undergoing any chemical reaction. In addition to adsorbent action, they also possess the protective property. They form a coating over the intestinal mucosa to reduce its irritation. Examples include :

(a) Kaolin :

It is a hydrated aluminium silicate used internally and externally in the form of very fine powder for its adsorbent properties. It adsorbs irritant toxins and bacterial toxins, reduces mucous secretion and binds water. It also provides a sort of protective coating over the inflamed mucosal walls. It is often used alongwith pectin (kaopectate is a mixture of 20% kaolin, pectin and hydrated aluminium silicate) for the symptomatic treatment of chronic diarrhoea. Adult oral dose is 45-90 ml after each loose bowel movement. Kaolin and morphine mixture is useful in the treatment of mild diarrhoea. Because of its constipatory effect, morphine increases effectiveness of this preparation.

(b) Calcium carbonate (chalk) :

Its properties are quite similar to those of kaolin. Chalk and opium mixture is also available. It also helps to release flatulence and distension.

(c) Magnesium trisilicate and aluminium hydroxide :

They have adsorbent property which is beneficial in the treatment of acidity and diarrhoea. They are also used in the treatment of flatulence and distension.

(d) Pectin :

It is a purified carbohydrate product obtained from an acid extraction of the rind of citrus fruits or from apple pomace. It is mainly made up of polygalacturonic acid with some of the methylated hydroxyl functional groups.

It is used along with kaolin as an adsorbent and demulcent in the treatment of diarrhoea. Each 30 ml of this preparation contains 5.85 g of kaolin and 130 mg of pectin. Activated charcoal and bentonite are also used in the treatment of mild diarrhoea.

(e) Bismuth subsalicylate :

Because of adsorbent property, it binds with intestinal toxins and provides protective coating to mucosal surfaces. Its administration leads to formation of grey-black discoloration of stools.

(f) Polycarbophil and various psyllium seed derivatives :

It binds with water and bile salts. It is used to control diarrhoea that is associated with passing of excessively watery stools.

(ii) Diphenoxylate Hydrochloride :

It is a weak meperidine congener lacking analgesic activity. It has the plasma half-life of 2.5 hours. Upon metabolism, diphenoxylic acid (active metabolite) and hydroxy-diphenoxylic acid are excreted in the faeces.

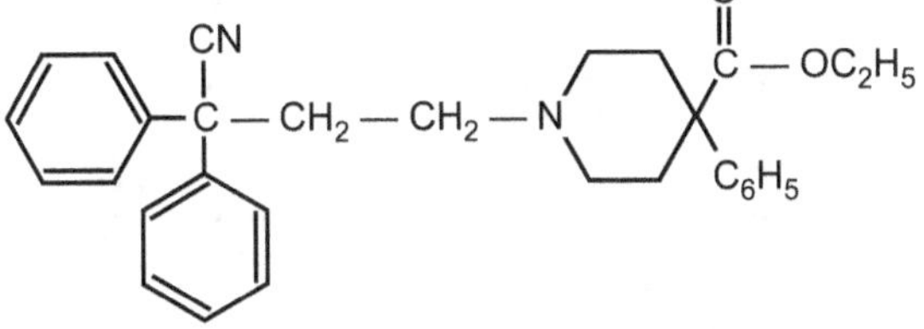

Diphenoxylate

Adverse effects include nausea, vomiting, abdominal discomfort, miosis, blurred vision, dry mouth, flushing, sedation and tachycardia. It is contraindicated in children under 2 years and in patients with obstructive jaundice.

Because of its constipating effect, it is used for the symptomatic relief of diarrhoea in patients with mild chronic inflammatory bowel disease and for infectious gastroenteritis. Atropine is added in subtherapeutic dose because of its spasmolytic activity. In lomotil, a mixture of diphenoxylate and atropine is present. Adult parenteral dose is 20 mg per day.

(iii) Loperamide :

It is a synthetic meperidine congener devoid of sedative or respiratory depressant actions. It is orally used as an antidiarrhoeal agent. About 97% administered dose is bound to the plasma-proteins. It has a plasma half-life of 7 - 14 hours.

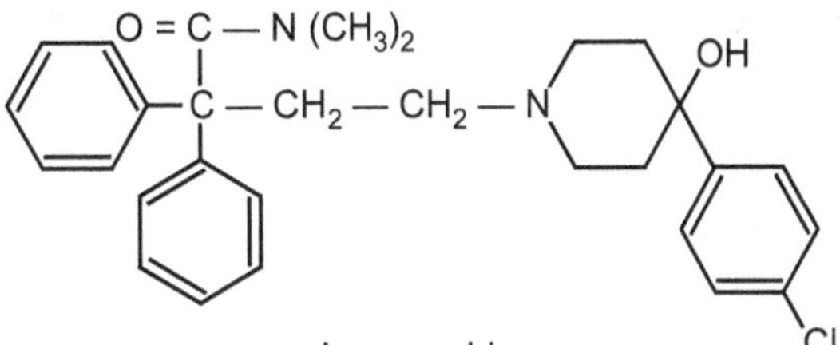

Loperamide

Major portion of administered dose appears unchanged in the faeces. Inactive metabolites are excreted in the urine alongwith 10% dose in unchanged form.

Loperamide exerts spasmolytic effect on GIT muscles by depressing slow cholinergic phase and rapid prostaglandin mediated phase of smooth muscle contraction. It may act on intestinal nerve endings or ganglia.

Adverse effects include nausea, vomiting, anorexia, skin rashes, crampy abdominal pain, dry mouth and drowsiness. It is used in the symptomatic treatment of both acute non-specific diarrhoea and chronic diarrhoea. Adult oral dose is 4 - 8 mg per day.

(iv) Intestinal Antiseptics :

These agents are used to treat severe diarrhoeal forms which are due to microbial infection. They mainly comprise of certain members of the sulphonamides and antibiotics that are poorly absorbable in GIT and thus reach in high concentration to the small and large bowel. Examples include sulphasalazine, sulphaguanidine, phthalyl sulphathiazol, succinyl sulphathiazole, etc.

Various combinations of sulphonamides and antibiotics alongwith kaolin are available either in the form of cream or suspension. Streptomycin, neomycin, chloramphenicol, tetracyclines, nystatin are the examples of such antibiotics used for this purpose.

A reduction in fecal volume contributes to the effectiveness of any antidiarrhoeal preparation. This is achieved by inclusion of a strong water absorbing agent (e.g. methyl cellulose) in the formulation.

5.15 PROKINETICS

These agents enhance the gastrointestinal motility and relieve nausea, vomitting, abdominal discomfort, bloating, constipation, heart burn, etc. They are used in the treatment of gastritis, acid reflux, functional dyspepsia, gastroparesis and irritable bowel syndrome.

Various mechanisms by which this prokinetic effect can be achieved, are as follows :

(i) **5-HT$_4$-receptor agonists** induce enhanced gastrointestinal motility. e.g. mosapride, prucalopride, etc. Most of them are benzamide derivatives.

(ii) Higher acetylcholine concentration is achieved either by **stimulating M$_1$ receptors** or by **inhibiting acetylcholinesterase enzymes**. Higher ACh levels increase gastro intestinal peristalsis, accelerate gastric emptying and improve gastro-duodenal co-ordination e.g., itopride.

(iii) Drugs like mitemcinal and erythromycin are **motilin receptor agonists** resulting in enhanced gastrointestinal motility. Mitemcinal is a motilin agonist derived from the macrolide antibiotic, erythromycin. It increases gastric motility and is devoid of antibiotic properties of erythromycin. It relieves the symptoms of reflux by speeding the clearance of acid from the oesophagus and stomach.

(iv) **Probiotics** have been found effective in the treatment of constipation.

e.g., (a) Lactobacillus reuteri ..... in infants,

(b) Lactobacillus casei and Bifidobacterium brevi ...... in children, and

(c) Lactobacillus plantarum....in adults.

(v) **Dopamine D$_2$ receptor antagonists :** Dopamine D$_2$ receptor is the main receptor for all antipsychotic agents. It is a G protein-coupled receptor that inhibits adenylyl cyclase activity. Hence, its antagonists will elevate adenylyl cyclase activity and will enhance gastrointestinal motility.

e.g. metoclopramide, domperidone, levosulpiride.

5-HT Receptor Subtypes :

Serotonin (5-hydroxytryptamine, 5-HT) produces its effects through a variety of membrane bound receptors. These are a group of G-protein coupled receptors. Out of these only 5-HT$_3$ receptor is ligand gated ion channel. They are the targets of many antidepressants, antipsychotics, anorectics, antimigraine, hallucinogens, antiemetics and gastroprokinetic agents. The seven general serotonin receptor families include a total of 14 known serotonin receptors.

Table 5.2 : 5-HT receptor subtypes

Sr. No.	Family	Type	Mechanism	Response
01	5-HT$_1$ 5-HT$_5$	Gi/Go – Protein coupled	$\downarrow$ Cellular levels of c-AMP	Inhibitory
02	5-HT$_2$	Protein coupled	$\uparrow$ IP$_3$	Excitatory
03	5-HT$_4$ 5-HT$_6$ 5-HT$_7$	G$_S$ protein coupled	$\uparrow$ Cellular levels of c-AMP	Excitatory
04	5-HT$_3$	Ligand gated Na$^+$ and K$^+$ ion channel	Depolarizing plasma membrane	Excitatory

Multiple human 5-HT$_4$ receptor isoforms have been described. The expression of 5-HT$_{4D}$ receptor isoform appears to be restricted to gut whereas other isoforms are expressed in cardiac atria and brain. In addition to adenylyl cyclase stimulation, direct coupling to potassium channels and voltage sensitive calcium channels have been proposed as postreceptor events.

The 5-HT$_4$ receptors plays a significant role in increasing GIT motility. The 5-HT$_4$ receptor activation triggers acetylcholine release and contracts the oesophagus and colon. In addition, 5-HT$_4$ receptor also mediates secretory responses to serotonin in intestinal mucosa. Selective 5-HT$_4$ receptor ligands thus have a role as gastroprokinetic agents. Besides this, they have therapeutic utility in cardiac arrhythmia, neurodegenerotive disease and urinary incontinence.

Cisapride (benzamide derivatives) was marketed as a gastro-prokinetic. It was withdrawn from the market due to its cardiovascular side-effects.

Table 5.3 : Prokinetics

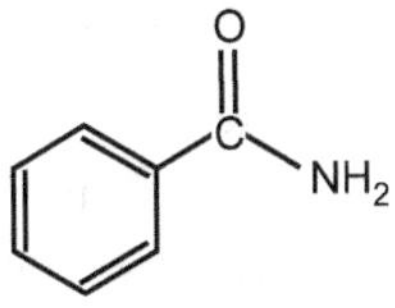

Benzamide

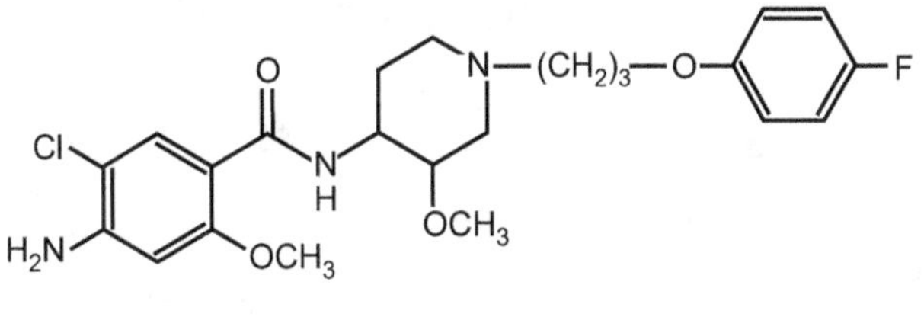

Cisapride
(5-HT$_4$ agonist)

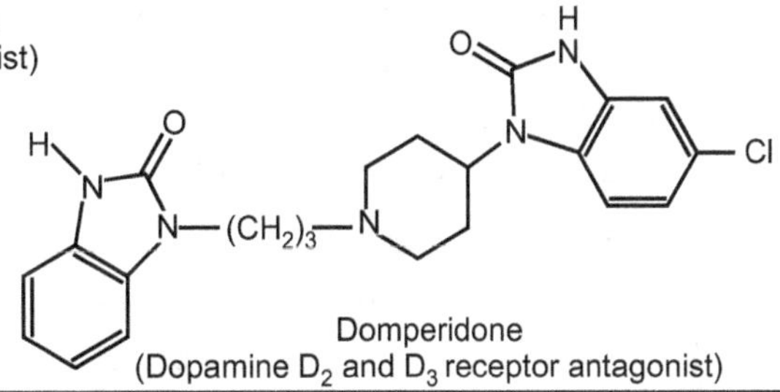

Domperidone
(Dopamine D$_2$ and D$_3$ receptor antagonist)

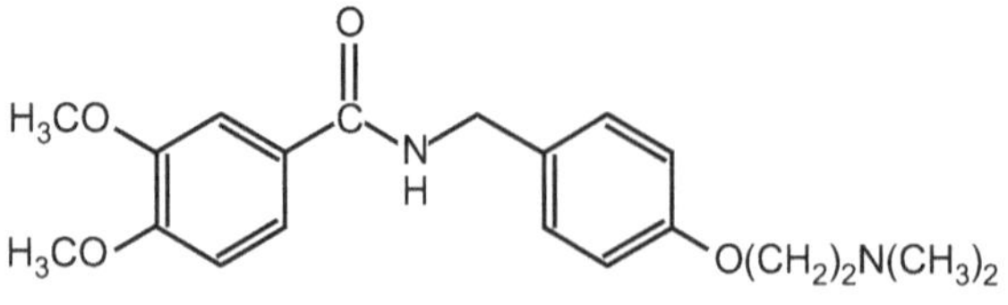

Itopride
(Inhibitor of dopamine D_2
receptor and acetylcholinesterase enzyme)

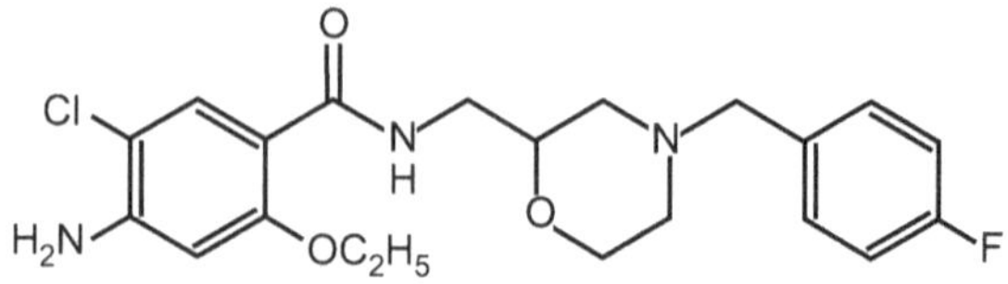

Mosapride
(5-HT$_4$ agonist)

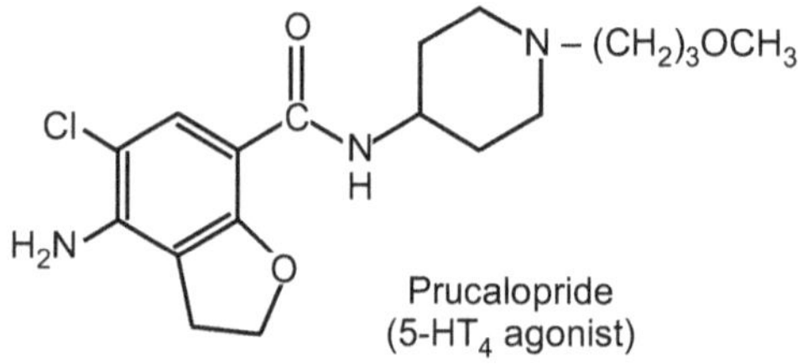

Prucalopride
(5-HT$_4$ agonist)

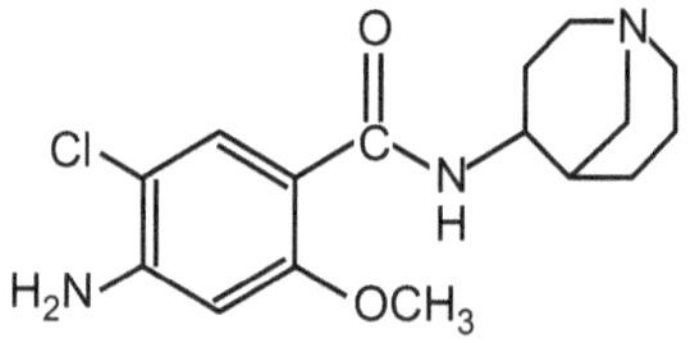

Renzapride
(5-HT$_4$ agonist)

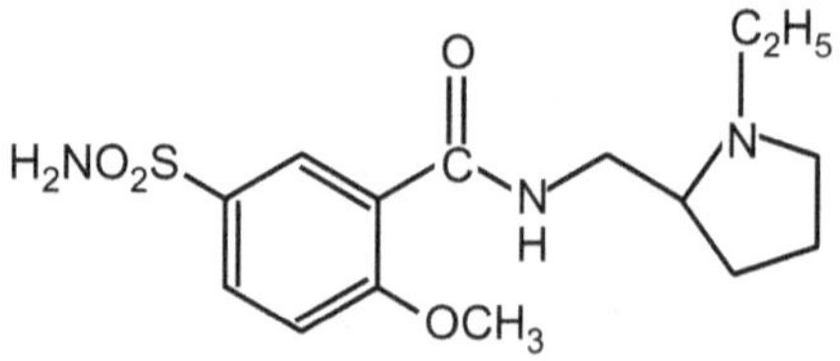

Levosulpiride
(Dopamine D_2 receptor
antagonist)

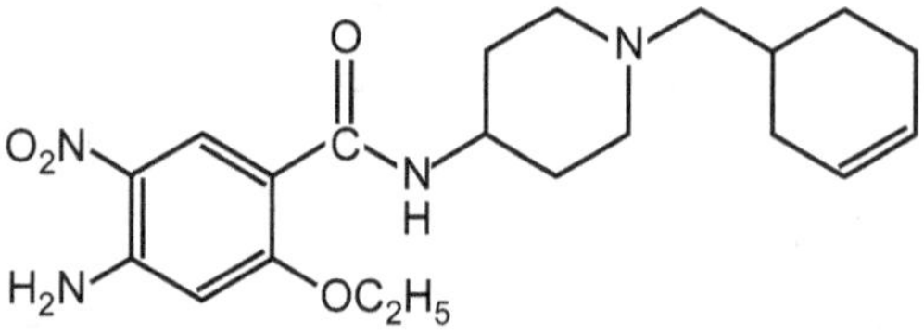

Cintapride
(5HT$_4$- agonist)

5.16 SIALAGOGUES

Salivary secretion contains amylases (ptyalin) which initiates the process of digestion of food. Similarly salivary secretion has a mouth clearing function. Drying of mouth is due to cessation of saliva secretion and indicates body's low water content.

Vasodilation and secretion are two associated phenomena occurring in salivary glands. These are under the influence of both, sympathetic and parasympathetic nervous systems. Vasodilation is under the control of parasympathetic nerves which when stimulated leads to the release of kallikrein (a proteolytic enzyme). The latter liberates the vasodilatory polypeptides (plasma kinins) from the plasma. Same channel operates in several other glands. Sialagogues are the drugs which increase the saliva secretion. These include,

(a) **Cholinergic drugs :** e.g. pilocarpine, physostigmine.

(b) **Adrenergic drugs :** e.g., ephedrine.

(c) **Bitters :** These are the substances which by virtue of their taste, stimulate reflexly efferent nerves supplied to the taste buds. They stimulate indirectly the appetite. To be effective, they are to be taken half-an-hour before the meals. Examples include strychnine, quinine, tincture of cinchona and nux vomica.

5.17 ANTISIALAGOGUES

These are the drugs which induce a reduction in the salivary secretions. These include,

Anticholinergic agents :

This class comprises of atropine sulphate. It is an alkaloid obtained from the plant, Atropa belladona. It is used as a preanaesthetic medication to inhibit salivary and bronchial secretions. Scopolamine is also a belladona alkaloid obtained from the shrub, Hyoscyamus niger and Scopolia carniolica. It may be used as a preanaesthetic agent due to its antisialagogue and antiarrhythmic properties. Glycopyrrolate is a long-acting synthetic quaternary amine having antimuscarinic actions. It may also be used as antisialogogue.

5.18 APPETITE AFFECTING DRUGS

(a) **Appetite stimulants :**

These include alkaloids having bitter taste. They stimulate appetite mainly by reflex vagal stimulation. They include strychnine, nux vomica and alcoholic beverages.

(b) **Anorexiants :**

These agents depress the appetite. They may be used as an adjunct in the management of obesity. They act mainly through the following mechanisms :

(i) by increasing the levels of plasma free fatty acids resulting in depression of appetite centres in lateral hypothalamus,

(ii) by inhibiting impulses reaching the appetite centers, or

(iii) by stimulating satiety center present in the medial hypothalamus.

Examples include :

(i) **Diethylpropion hydrochloride :**

It is a sympathomimetic agent having properties similar to amphetamine. Adverse effects include nausea, diarrhoea, constipation, dry mouth, mydriasis, restlessness, insomnia, tremors, increased blood pressure and tachycardia.

It is used as an anorexiant in the management of obesity.

(ii) **Fenfluramine hydrochloride :**

Chemically, it is a trifluoromethyl derivative of amphetamine and is a sympathomimetic appetite suppressant agent. It has a plasma half-life of 13 - 30 hours. Inactive metabolites are excreted in the urine alongwith 10 - 20% unchanged drug. Adverse effects include vomiting, diarrhoea, abdominal pain, dry mouth, alopecia, impotence and pulmonary hypertension.

It is used as a weight-reducing agent in obesity. Adult oral dose is 20 - 40 mg three times a day. Treatment may be continued upto 3 months and then the therapy can be gradually terminated.

(iii) **Phendimetrazine tartrate :**

It is an orally active sympathomimetic agent having appetite suppressant activity. Upon hepatic inactivation, metabolites are excreted in the urine. Adult oral dose is 85 mg two to three times a day.

5.19 CARMINATIVES

These agents are mild mucosal irritants. They relieve gastric distension (e.g. flatulence, colic pain etc.) by expelling the gas from the gastro-intestinal tract. In addition to this, they also propagate the feeling of warmth in the stomach. Examples include sodium bicarbonate, tincture of ginger, dill water, soda water, oil of peppermint, aniseed, camphor, glycyrrhiza, cardamom and cinnamon.

Peppermint oil is a volatile oil obtained from the steam distillation of fresh aerial parts of Mentha piperita. It relaxes the colonic smooth muscles. Hence, it is beneficial in the irritable bowel syndrome. It is a weak antispasmodic.

Simethicone (Dimethylpolysiloxane) :

It is a surface active agent used as an antiflatulent usually in combination with antacids, antispasmodics, sedative or digestants. It is not absorbed orally and appears totally unchanged in the faeces. It does not exhibit any noticeable adverse effect.

It is used in the control of flatulence, gastric bloating and postoperative gaseous distension. It diminishes gastro-oesophageal reflux and exhibits despectic symptoms. It may also be used in the radiography of the bowel to reduce gas shadows and to improve visualization.

Adult oral dose is 40 - 80 mg after each meal and at bed time.

5.20 DIGESTANTS

Gastrointestinal tract is one of the vital organs of the body. It possesses a battery of hormones and secretions which controls and carry out the processing to get the food in easily absorbable form. In digestion of food, the important constituents of gastric juice are pepsin and hydrochloric acid. Digestants are the substances which are used to compensate the deficiency of normal components of gastrointestinal secretion. They include,

(i) Betaine hydrochloride :

It is a digestive preparation containing the equivalent amount 1.0 ml of dilute hydrochloric acid, 32.4 mg pepsin and 110 mg of methyl cellulose. It induces a slow release of hydrochloric acid alongwith the release of gastric acid that occurs during digestion.

(ii) Pepsin :

It is a proteolytic enzyme which is an important constituent of gastric juice. The marketed preparation contains pepsin powder obtained from the oxyntic cells of the fresh stomach of the hog.

(iii) Dehydrocholic acid and sodium dehydrocholate :

It is a semisynthetic cholate and is used as safe and effective oral laxative agent. It decreases the excretion of bilirubin and enhances the secretion of bile of low specific gravity (i.e., hydrocholeretic effect). Its administration may help to increase the absorption of fat and fat-soluble vitamins in conditions of partial biliary obstructive disease. Choline dehydrogen citrate may be effective as a lipotropic agent in patients with hepatic cirrhosis. Adult oral dose is 250-500 mg three times a day preferably after meals.

(iv) Pancreatic extract :

It includes pancreatin and pancrelipase. Pancreatin is a cream coloured, amorphous powder obtained from fresh pancreas of hog or ox. It contains amylase, lipase and trypsin. While pancrelipase is obtained from porcine pancreas.

These enzymes may be used to treat conditions where pancreatic enzymes are either absent or deficient (e.g., chronic pancreatitis, pancreatectomy, cystic fibrosis, mucoviscidosis, gastrointestinal bypass surgery, ductal obstruction from neoplasm or steatorrhea). In postgastrectomy syndrome, these enzymes cause a reduction in steatorrhea and improve the nutritional state of a patient. Pancreatic extracts should be given with food, milk or alkali in an attempt to buffer the gastric contents. This is necessary to prevent inactivation of pancreatic enzymes.

(v) Chenodiol (chenodeoxycholic acid) :

It is the human bile acid mainly present in the form of glycine and taurine conjugates. When bile becomes supersaturated with cholesterol, it induces formation of cholesterol gall-stones. Chenodiol is used to decrease the cholesterol content of bile so that formation of cholesterolic gall-stones is inhibited. It acts by:

(a) reducing the rate of bile salt synthesis in the liver,

(b) inhibiting cholesterol absorption from intestine, and

(c) blocking HMG - Co reductase and cholesterol 7α - hydroxylase enzymes which play an important role in cholesterol synthesis.

Chenodiol is used to dissolve cholesterol gall-stones only in those patients in whom gall bladder function is in order and where gallstones do not exceed 2 cm in diameter. Usual adult dose is 14 - 16 mg /kg /day for 6 - 24 months.

5.21 IRRITABLE BOWEL SYNDROME (IBS)

It is a chronic gastrointestinal and functional colon (i.e. large intestine) disorder first described in 1820. It is associated with changes in the pattern of bowel movements with abdominal pain. It is thus a mix of belly discomfort, indigestion, or pain with either diarrhea or constipation. A lot of gas or bloating may be seen. It affects 10 – 25% of world population. The IBS affected population has women : men = 3 : 1.

IBS may be categorised into four types. These include

(i)   IBS with constipation (IBS – C)

(ii) IBS with diarrhea (IBS – D)

(iii) IBS with alternative constipation/ diarrhea or mix pattern (IBS – M), and

(iv) IBS without constipation and diarrhea, i.e. unsubtyped pattern (IBS – U)

Causes of IBS :

(i)   **Visceral hypersensitivity :** In certain cases, the colon gets hypersensitive, overacting to even mild stimulation.

(ii) **Hormonal factors :** The balance between serotonin and gastrin that control nerve signals between the brain and digestive tract, is disturbed.

(iii) **Small Intestine Bacterial Overgrowth (SIBO) :** Certain bacteria in the bowel may lead to IBS. SIBO may lead to bloating, abdominal pain, diarrhea or constipation.

(iv) **Food allergies or intolerance**

(v) **Psychological factors :** Emotional stress and life sytle.

Treatment :

It does not have a permanent cure. It can be managed with a combination of dietary modification, lifestyle changes, medicines and probiotics. Soluble fibre supplementaiton (e.g., psyllium/ispagula husk) is effective. Drinking more water at regular intervals and going for smaller meals instead of big meals may reduce the symptoms of the disease. Increasing dietary fibre is sensible advice. The drug treatment may include :

(i)   Antispasmodics : e.g. mebeverine, dicyclomine

(ii)   Antidiarrheals : e.g. imodium, loperamide

(iii) Laxatives : Milk of magnesia, lubiprostone

(iv) Bulking agents : e.g. psyllium

(v)   Antidepressants : e.g. imipramine, amitriptyline

(vi) Antibloating agents : e.g., peppermint oil, rifaximin

(vii) Serotonin agonists : Tegaserod

(viii) Serotonin antagonists : Alosetron (selective 5-HT$_3$ antagonist) and cilansetron (selective 5-HT$_3$ antagonist)

(ix) Probiotics : e.g. Lactobacillus plantarum, Bifidobacteria infantis, Saccharomyces boulardii.

(x) Miscellaneous drugs : These drugs include magnesium aluminium silicates and alverine citrate.

Table 5.4 : Inflammatory bowel disease (IBD) Vs Irritable bowel syndrome (IBS)

Sr. No.	Name	Symptoms
01	IBD	People with IBD may display IBS – like symptoms, Inflammatory disease (identifiable cause)
		IBS symptoms + eye discomfort, extreme fatigue, joint pain, rectal bleeding. Examples include ulcerative colitis, Crohn disease. It is a group of inflammatory condition of the colon and small intestine.
02	IBS	People with IBS will never develop IBD, non-inflammatory functional disorder (lacks identifiable cause)
		Symptons are abdominal pain, cramps, constipation, diarrhea.

Synthesis

Omeprazole :

4-Nitro-2,3,5-trimethyl pyridine-N-oxide

Benzimidazole

(O) Oxidation

Omeprazole

❖ ❖ ❖

INDEX